Pippa Roscoe lives in Norfolk, near her family, and makes daily promises to herself that this is the day she'll leave the computer to take a long walk in the countryside. She can't remember a time when she wasn't dreaming about handsome heroes and innocent heroines. Totally her mother's fault, of course—she gave Pippa her first romance to read at the age of seven! She is inconceivably happy that she gets to share those daydreams with you. Follow her on Twitter @PippaRoscoe.

Lorraine Hall is a part-time hermit and full-time writer. She was born with an old soul and her head in the clouds—which, it turns out, is the perfect combination for spending her days creating thunderous alpha heroes and the fierce, determined heroines who win their hearts. She lives in a potentially haunted house with her soulmate and a rumbustious band of hermits in training. When she's not writing romance, she's reading it.

EXPECTING HER ENEMY'S HEIR

PIPPA ROSCOE

HIRED FOR HIS ROYAL REVENGE

LORRAINE HALL

MILLS & BOON

First published in Great Britain 2023
by Mills & Boon, an imprint of HarperCollins*Publishers* Ltd,
1 London Bridge Street, London, SE1 9GF

www.harpercollins.co.uk

HarperCollins*Publishers*, Macken House, 39/40 Mayor Street Upper, Dublin 1, D01 C9W8, Ireland

Expecting Her Enemy's Heir © 2023 Pippa Roscoe

Hired for His Royal Revenge © 2023 Lorraine Hall

ISBN: 978-0-263-30675-0

04/23

This book is produced from independently certified FSC™ paper to ensure responsible forest management.
For more information visit: www.harpercollins.co.uk/green.

Printed and Bound in the UK using 100% Renewable Electricity at CPI Group (UK) Ltd, Croydon, CR0 4YY

EXPECTING HER ENEMY'S HEIR

PIPPA ROSCOE

MILLS & BOON

For Michelle,
who knew exactly what I meant when I said,
'And he kept the land because...'
Working with people who understand you is a dream,
but being friends with them is a gift.
Loves ya!

CHAPTER ONE

TODAY WAS THE DAY.

Amelia Seymore peered through the window at the dark grey clouds on the horizon, while early morning joggers and cyclists risked life and limb in the narrow juncture between the bus and the pavement. The start, stop of the number 176 as it crawled north across the bridge was making her nauseous, but it was the smell of damp wool and deodorant that forced her from the bus a stop early, gasping for fresh air. Or at least as fresh as you got in Central London during peak commuter hours. Amelia shook her head trying to regain the focus and sense of stability she had a reputation for. Maybe she was coming down with something.

Get yourself together, she ordered herself firmly. Nothing could distract her or knock her off course. Today had been ten years in the making, but it wasn't the long hours, sleepless nights or the punishingly hard work that steeled her. It was the memory of her father's face the last time they had spoken. The look in his eyes as he had turned away from her, his shaking hand reaching for the bottle of whisky on his desk. *That* was the reason she and her sister, Issy, were doing this. That was why she *had* to succeed today.

Scanning the four-lane road, and too impatient to wait

at the lights, Amelia skipped behind a cyclist and in front of a police car. Waving an awkward 'oops' at the cops, she arrived in front of a building considered to be the brightest addition to the crown jewels of the London skyline. While the Shard glittered like a diamond and the Gherkin shone emerald green, the imposing rose-hued building that housed Rossi Industries had been affectionately nicknamed The Ruby and was considered the perfect edifice for the two devastatingly handsome property tycoons who owned it.

Amelia craned her neck to look up at the impressive head office of the international conglomerate that inspired both awe and anger in her. Every single day for the last two years she had made this same walk, knowing that she was entering the lair of the two men that had destroyed her family. And every single day she had promised herself and her sister that they would have their revenge.

Vengeance hadn't come naturally to Amelia. And it certainly hadn't been immediate. She and her sister had been fifteen and thirteen, respectively, when they had first seen Alessandro and Gianni Rossi. Not that they'd known who they were back then. No, they had simply been two young men who had interrupted a Sunday roast to speak with their father. And in one conversation, the Rossi cousins had stolen their father's company out from under him and decimated everything that she and her sister had ever known.

Cold fury tripped down her spine as she retrieved the ID swipe card that proclaimed her Project Manager for Rossi Industries and entered the building. Amelia smiled at the security guard in spite of the memories that held her stomach in a vice, passing through the barriers to the bank of lifts that would take her to the sixty-fourth floor.

As she waited in the deserted lobby for the lift to arrive, she counted down the floors as if it were a ticking bomb the Rossis had no idea of and she *relished* that today would be the day their world shattered, just as hers and Issy's had. And then it wouldn't matter if she had nearly thrown it all away in one night, just over a month ago...

We shouldn't be doing this.

Amelia clenched her teeth, trying to ignore the way the rough, gravelly voice rubbed against her skin even now and once again desire wrapped around a part of her she'd never known she had. A desire that hit her like a tsunami, drawing her beneath the surface and snaring her in the undertow.

I... I want to.

With those three words she had betrayed her family, her sister, *herself.*

No!

She wouldn't let that one night, that one *mistake*, ruin everything she and Issy had worked so hard for. Yes, she had spent one illicit night with her boss—her enemy— Alessandro Rossi. But it didn't change anything. She just had to ignore the cascade of erotic memories that haunted her. Because no matter what had happened six weeks ago in Hong Kong, it in no way justified or excused what Alessandro and Gianni had done ten years ago to her family. And because of that, today was the day that the Rossi cousins would fall.

Alessandro looked out of the floor-to-ceiling window of his penthouse office to see London stretched out below him like a supplicant. Power. It ran through his veins, not just because of his immeasurable wealth, or the considerable achievements he and his cousin had accomplished in the years since they claimed control of their first business. It might have once belonged to another, but it had flourished into an empire under the Rossi name. No, the power came from the knowledge that the first meeting of his very busy day would green light a deal that promised to send shock waves through the business world.

The Rossi name was already renowned, but this deal would see it written in the history books. In years to come, there might even be two young upstarts who would read of the Rossi name and success and think—*that's what I want to be.*

Alessandro caught the grim smile on the face of his reflection and nodded. How would his father feel when he saw it? When he heard that Alessandro and Gianni had achieved success beyond his wildest dreams...but not under the name of the men who had fathered them. *No.* The first chance he and Gianni got, they legally changed their names, desperate to erase the stain of their fathers in a way that they would feel to the core of their blackened souls. They had chosen Rossi to honour their *nonna*— the only member of their family who had truly shown them kindness.

My blood runs in your veins, boy. And it will run in your children's and your children's children's.

But his father's warning was irrelevant. The blood line would end with him. He would make sure of it.

Not that Alessandro indulged in self-sabotage. Rossi Industries was his life, consuming all his time and energy. Where his father sought to destroy and strangle the last breath from the vineyards he overworked, or the wife he had constantly abused, Alessandro was determined to leave the world better than it had been; *that* was his legacy.

His watch beeped with a fifteen-minute alert for the morning's meeting. It really was bad timing that it coincided with Gianni's one and utterly immoveable holiday of the year. But, he reminded himself, the Aurora deal had been vetted by his cousin, everyone on the board, by his most trusted advisors, and the project manager he trusted far more quickly than was deserved after just two years of service.

Amelia Seymore.

Alessandro straightened the knot in his tie, checking the button behind it, but in his mind he was undoing the button and yanking the tie from his neck as he watched that same woman looking at him, breathless want filling her words.

I... I want you.

Are you sure, Amelia? Because—

Just tonight. Just now. But we will never speak of it. Ever.

He'd been so desperate for another taste of her lips he'd have agreed to anything. *Cristo*, if she'd known how much power she'd wielded in that moment, she could have had him on his knees begging to give her everything he owned. Embarrassment crept up his neck in angry red patches.

He flexed his hand, the memory of her naked thigh beneath his palm taunting him, leading him deeper into the one night—the *only* night—he'd crossed a line both professionally and personally. A line that was as much a taboo as it was utterly wrong. Shame, thick, heavy and ugly, crawled across his skin. He wasn't *that man*—he didn't sleep with his staff. Only apparently he was.

We will never speak of it.

A knock cut through the memory of Amelia's edict and he returned to the seat behind his desk, hiding the near constant state of arousal he'd been in since he and Amelia Seymore had returned from the successful deal in Hong Kong six weeks ago.

'Come.'

His secretary entered the room two strides and stopped, having learned quickly that he liked his space.

'There are no changes to the schedule for today. Asimov has checked into his hotel and he and his people will be here for the eleven a.m. briefing. Lunch is booked at Alain Ducasse at The Dorchester and Gianni called to say, "Don't mess it up."'

'He said "mess"?' Alessandro queried.

'I'm paraphrasing.'

Alessandro held back the smirk at what his cousin would have really said. Raised as close as brothers, their knowledge of each other's thoughts was only one of the reasons for their immense success.

'And the nine a.m. meeting?' he asked his secretary.

'The room is set up, the audio and visuals have been tested by IT, Ms Seymore is already in the room and has given me a spare presentation pack for you to view now, if you'd like.'

'That won't be necessary.'

And it really wouldn't. If Amelia Seymore said that she'd do something, she did it. She assessed projects, met with clients, ran projections, assessed workflows and got it done. She was nearly as exacting as himself. Which was why he'd entrusted the Aurora project to her.

Not because they had shared one utterly incendiary and completely forbidden night together, but because she was excellent at her job, always early, always correct and always had the right answer. She could have been made purposefully for him.

'Sir?'

If only she didn't distract him in ways that no other person had ever done.

'Repeat the question?' he forced himself to ask, as distasteful as he found it.

'Would you like your coffee in here, or down at the meeting?'

'Here.' Clearly, he needed to gather himself.

As members of her team filtered into the glass-walled meeting room, Amelia lined up the presentation packs with the notebooks and pens she'd asked Housekeeping to provide. Alessandro was particular, he liked things neat and exact.

And he'd liked the way she'd sounded when—

Red slashes heated her cheeks and a light sweat broke out across her shoulders. She slammed the door shut on her memories, trying to ground herself in the moment. Stepping back from the large boardroom table, she caught sight of the sketch of the building that might have changed the face of inner-city apartment living across the world, had the Rossi cousins not built their empire on the back of her father's broken soul. Really, Alessandro and Gianni had brought this on themselves.

For ten years *this* was what she and Issy had planned for. The stars had aligned in a way that had seemed almost preordained. After two years of project after project, Amelia's position within RI was unquestionable. And because of that, the most important project the Rossis had ever undertaken was in her hands, just as Gianni's annual holiday broached the horizon. Everyone knew that together Alessandro and Gianni were undefeatable. But separated? It was the only time there was a chink in their legendary armour. A chink that Amelia and her sister would use to bring them to their knees.

Issy had spent years turning herself into the perfect distraction for the legendary playboy with his own hashtag #TheHotRossi. Yesterday, an Issy styled perfectly to Gianni's tastes had flown to the Caribbean with the sole purpose of luring him onto a boat and keeping him away from Alessandro while the final decision on Aurora deal was made. And with Gianni safely out of contact, Amelia could now commit the greatest act of industrial sabotage ever recorded, ensuring that the Rossis' world was left as obliterated as hers and her sister's had been.

We're doing the right thing, aren't we?

The question Issy had asked before she left for the airport yesterday had poked and prodded at Amelia's conscience. Not because Amelia didn't absolutely know that they were doing the right thing, because she *did*. But in order to set their plan in motion, she had been forced to lie to her sister. Something she'd never thought she'd ever do.

Years before, when they had first started their quest for vengeance, they had made a pact. *No revenge without proof of corruption.* From even the beginning they had refused to become the very monsters they hunted. And, of course, Amelia had agreed. Because there *would* be a paper trail. There *would* be evidence of countless corrupt deals and ruined businesses Alessandro and Gianni had left in their wake on their journey to becoming a globally recognised name in property development. But

in two years she'd found...*nothing*. Nothing other than
what had been done to their father.

Panic had begun to nip at her heels. What if she could
never give Issy the justice she'd promised her? What if
everything they'd sacrificed to achieve their revenge
was for nothing? While normal teenage girls had been
going to parties and clubs, Issy and Amelia Seymore had
planned and plotted. Amelia had forced herself through
every business course and language module possible to
make herself the perfect future employee for Rossi Industries. And her sister? Issy had trawled through the
online world, researching every inch of their enemies'
lives. No corporate press release, business deal, tweet or
social media post was left unseen. They had spent *years*
on their mission, forsaking so much of their teenage and
young adult years.

But then had come the business trip to Hong Kong;
her third major project with Rossi Industries and one she
and her team had invested months of work on. Alessandro wasn't supposed to have flown out for the meeting
himself. It was highly unusual, but she hadn't let it put
her off her stride. She'd nailed the presentation, and the
strong relationship she'd built with the client had earned
them not only the commission but a personal invitation
for her and Alessandro to dine with Kai Choi. It would
have been a grave insult to refuse, so while her team
members had returned to London, she and Alessandro
had remained in Hong Kong.

Even now she was shocked by how thrilled she'd been
to land the deal. Amelia's job was supposed to be a ruse.
A means to an end. But instead, the dizzying excitement
she'd felt had been reflected in the eyes of the very man
whose opinion should matter least. Eyes that had turned

excitement into heat after holding her gaze for just a little too long. Her heart jerked in her chest, as if it were
tied to the memory of the moment that the line between
them had been shattered.

A shattering that had forced her to do something she
had never intended. She couldn't wait to find proof any
more. The guilt, tension, the *desire* she still felt for a man
who had destroyed her family was pulling her apart from
the inside, spinning her further away from the control
that she was known for. Amelia's plans were beginning
to unravel, her command of the situation slipping from
her fingers like sand.

So, she had done the unthinkable.

Amelia had told her sister that she'd found proof of
their corruption and, in doing so, set in motion the take-
down of the Rossi cousins. It was a lie that would take
Issy's trust—the beautiful, delicate but utterly unbreak-
able thing that it was—and break it. Amelia had betrayed
the one person who had been her constant companion
since the death of their father and the emotional and physical retreat of their mother. Issy, who was bright and
lovely and always, unfailingly, *good*. Just the thought of
it chipped away at the crack that had formed in her heart,
even as she told herself that she had done it for the right
reason. The Rossis *needed* punishing.

Thomas Seymore had died by their hands as surely as
if they'd killed him themselves. The demons sent by Alessandro and Gianni had haunted their father until he had
finally drunk himself into an early grave—never recov-
ering from the damage done to his reputation or status.
And their mother? She had never been the same. Leaving their friends, their school, their social circle, losing
her husband, declaring bankruptcy had broken some-

thing in the once vibrant Jane Seymore and no matter what Amelia and Issy had done, their mother had never come back to them.

'I hope Gianni comes back soon. I hate meetings when it's just Alessandro.'

'He's such a ballbreaker.'

'At least by the end of this meeting we'll know which company the project will partner with. The back and forth has been going on for months.'

For the first time that morning, the erratic beat of Amelia's heart settled because this was it. At the end of this meeting, she would guide Rossi Industries to partner with the wrong company and seal their fate. She would deliver Issy the revenge that Amelia had promised her ten years before and finally, *finally*, they would be done with this; she would walk away and never look back.

The room went quiet and she looked up to see Alessandro take his seat at the head of the table. When everyone was sitting up, backs straight, silent and waiting, he nodded for Amelia to begin what would be the last deal Rossi Industries ever undertook.

Today was the day.

Alessandro turned a page on the printout Amelia had provided the team. She was articulate and concise—nothing was wasted. Even the image she presented was considered; elegant but subtle, nothing intrusive, almost nothing memorable. He imagined she'd rehearsed the presentation over and over again. He would have, in her position. She stood to the left of the large screen displaying the two companies vying for partnership on this once-in-a-lifetime opportunity, the gentle glow of the screen making her nothing more than a silhouette.

Just as she had been against the gauzy curtain of the hotel room in Hong Kong when he'd reached for the tie holding her wrap dress together and pulled. The dress had sighed open to reveal perfection. The black-lace-underwear-embellished skin that drew his hand like a magnet. The slide of his palm over the smooth planes set off a wave of restlessness that crested over her body, her breasts heaving with each inhalation and when he reached for her, his own body trembled.

'And this is the problem we have,' Amelia claimed to the room, bringing him back to the present with a start he managed to disguise by reaching for his coffee, when caffeine was patently the last thing he needed.

He tuned out her words, remembering the first time he'd encountered her. His attention had snagged on her name, linking her to a moment in time that Alessandro refused to dwell on. Her file had revealed an impressive academic record, a notable drive, and enthusiastic references. She had interviewed well and he was sure that she would excel in her role, just like all of RI's other employees. And it should have ended there. But...

She had ignored him.

And that was unusual. It wasn't arrogance talking, but experience. Over the years, Alessandro had attracted as much attention as his charming playboy cousin, Gianni. He simply chose not to indulge. Alessandro had no desire to entertain anyone with expectations of a *more* he had absolutely no interest in pursuing. Which had earned him the nickname 'The Monk'. Despite this, it hadn't escaped Alessandro's notice that the looks he owed to an impressive combination of genes attracted a certain amount of attention, wanted or not. Yet, Amelia Seymore had treated him with the same cool impartiality as she did every other colleague in the building. It might not have made her close friends with her colleagues, but her talent and efficiency were undeniable, and she impressed her managers and team alike.

Her hair—rich admittedly, with reds and chestnuts and hints of golds—was always up, efficient in a bun, or plait, or some kind of twist that Alessandro was sure defied the laws of gravity. He shouldn't know that when it was down, it reached just below her shoulder blades, curled with the curve of her breast and curtained over nipples that were a fascinating shade of pink.

Her features were small, equally proportioned to ensure that nothing stood out, except that they *all* stood out. Lips of the palest pink that were neither lush, nor dramatically shaped into a bow, but that had explored his body with a ravenous fascination that had driven him to the edge of his control. The arch of a mahogany eyebrow framed her face in perfect symmetry with the line of a jaw that had fitted perfectly in the palm of his hand, concealing a pulse point behind her ear that flushed when she became aroused.

An arousal that when he had lain between her thighs, her body trembling beneath his touch, the wet heat welcoming him, calling to him, enticing him to taste, to tease, to—

Cristo.

He cleared his throat and the entire boardroom looked up at him. Amelia pinned him with a gaze that showed nothing but professionalism—and yet he still felt her censure. A flick of his hand and she continued.

'It is clear that this decision is one of utmost importance and will shape the face of not only the project, but the future of this company.'

He needed better control over himself. Control that Amelia seemed to have mastered.

She had been true to her word. Absolutely nothing had changed. It was almost as if it had never happened. Which was absolutely for the best, he assured himself. Once this meeting was done, and the choice of partnership had been decided, he would have nothing further to do with Amelia Seymore other than as a name on paperwork pertaining to the project. There would be no need for any kind of interaction other than that, which, Alessandro decided firmly, was most definitely a good thing.

As Amelia began wrapping up the presentation, a sense of eager expectation filled the room. Her team wanted to get this decision made and move on, but they had no idea of the true consequences that would follow which company was chosen.

Everything about the presentation had been created to seem as if she was offering them a choice between Chapel Developments and Firstview Ltd. If Rossi Industries partnered with Chapel Developments, then it would be the most successful partnership in the property development world working on a venture that was as daring as it was creatively ingenious. But if they chose to partner with Firstview Ltd, then every hope and dream in this room would turn into a nightmare. Firstview didn't have the infrastructure or the financial backing to support the project to fruition. Of course, Amelia had worked incredibly hard to ensure that wasn't evident in the least, but a partnership would be the ruin of them all.

She looked at Alessandro's leadership team—she could see it in their eyes. Respect, understanding, eagerness and more than just a little avarice. This deal could make them billionaires in their own right. And it turned her stomach. Greed, the same greed that had destroyed her family. The nausea hit her hard again, throwing her momentarily. As if needing to see the one person her vengeance hung on, she looked up to find Alessandro's gaze firmly on hers. Waves of unnatural fire arced across her body, short-circuiting her brain for just a nanosecond— and she remembered. Remembered the crushing endlessness of the orgasm he had given her, flooding her body with a rush she'd never experienced, one that had threatened to undo everything she'd known, everything she'd sacrificed. And in the crushing aftermath of that wave, she found her voice.

'My suggestion is that Firstview is the only possible way forward to achieve the desired outcome.'

And with that one sentence, she started the process of destroying one of the biggest property companies in the world—ensuring that finally, ten years after Alessandro and Gianni had taken everything from Amelia and her sister, they would know how it felt for their world to crumble.

CHAPTER TWO

SOMETHING WAS WRONG, but Alessandro couldn't put his finger on what. The feeling had started around the time that Amelia wrapped up her presentation that morning, successfully getting one hundred per cent agreement on her partnership proposal for the Aurora project.

He checked his watch. The day had all but disappeared. If he left now, he might be able to make it back in time to hit the gym, grab dinner and check over the Aurora contracts for whatever it was his subconscious was snagging on. In the ten years since he and Gianni had taken the Englishman's business and turned it into an empire, Alessandro had learned to trust his gut. And his gut was telling him that something was wrong.

Alessandro was tempted to call Gianni. He'd messaged him earlier about the decision to move ahead with Firstview Ltd, but his cousin's yearly holiday was sacrosanct and Alessandro disliked the idea of disrupting it. Outside the twelve days Gianni spent each year in the Caribbean, he worked as if the Devil himself held the reins and he deserved the break. Alessandro switched off his computer, grabbed his jacket, turned off the lights in his office and made his way towards the elevator that ran through the centre of the building.

Designed by Rob Weller, the Rossis' preferred architect, the atrium that extended through the entire building was a marvel. Built five years ago, Rossi Industries rented out the lower floors to various businesses, a newspaper and a TV studio. But the upper levels were used solely by RI and had been created with meticulous eye for detail and consideration for the needs and well-being of his staff.

The dynamic open-plan design made the most of the natural light brought into the building through lightly tinted windows. Rose on the outside but not on the inside, the light worked with the white accents to create a bright, easy space in which to be. Social spaces were balanced with work areas, with healthcare facilities, staff restaurant, a gym, and a landscaped terrace and café on the wraparound balcony. The roof garden was accessible by only his and Gianni's offices on the penthouse floor, but was often used as a space for company events.

Alessandro was proud of what they had achieved. Pleased to know that Rossi Industries was a company that looked after its staff, never wanting them to push themselves to the brink, always knowing that the health of his staff was first and foremost to him.

I don't care how tired you are. There is more work to be done.

Refusing to shy away from the vicious childhood memory of his father's demands, Alessandro embraced it. Happy to know that he had walked away from his childhood refusing to be cowed by the mean-spirited, violent man. Everything he'd done was to ensure that he was nothing like Saverio Vizzini.

When the lift arrived, he faced the 'back', which displayed all the floors and staff areas of Rossi Industries. With the evening pouring into the building, the few lights bouncing off glass meeting rooms and breakout areas sparkled like stars in the night sky. Housekeeping staff would turn off any forgotten lights but one in particular caught his eye, and he'd pressed the corresponding floor's button before he knew it.

For one brief moment he wavered. Told himself not to get out of the lift. To continue on to the parking level and leave. He wondered, later, what might have happened if he had. Whether things would have been different and whether he'd have wanted them to be. In the end it didn't much matter. Things had been set in motion long before that day, and Alessandro doubted that he'd have managed to escape them.

They'd done it. Amelia had sent Issy a message to let her know that Rossi Industries had taken the bait, that Alessandro's and Gianni's destruction was all but assured. Not that the end of Alessandro and Gianni would be immediate. No, her plan of vengeance hadn't been as simple as a swift, painless death.

Just like what had happened to her father, to her mother and the lives she and her sister had known, the destruction of Rossi Industries would take months, perhaps even as long as a year if Firstview managed to hide their ineptitude better than she thought they might. But Amelia would be long gone by then. She would be offered 'a job that she couldn't refuse' and she would leave, without even seeing out her notice. There was, of course, no dream job. Amelia Seymore would simply disappear into thin air.

All she needed to do now was wait out the next few days while the contracts with Firstview Ltd were signed,

then Issy could leave Gianni in the Caribbean and return
to the UK and the sisters could celebrate.

But Amelia didn't feel like celebrating. Instead she was
effectively emptying her desk. Not so that anyone would
notice, because she'd need to continue to work here for
the next few days, she rationalised. But when the time
came, it would probably be best if she was able to make
a quick exit. A *very* quick exit.

He would be so angry.

It didn't matter, she told herself firmly, resenting the
way that even a small part of her worried about Alessandro. Guilt throbbed in her heart, knowing that her immediate concern should be her sister, not a man who had
caused such irreparable damage to her family.

She had just switched her computer off when the hairs
on the back of her neck lifted and her heart beat a little
too late and a little too hard. *He* was there. She didn't have
to turn around to look. She *knew* it. Unbidden, his words
from that night ran through her mind like raindrops.

*If this is only for one night, then I would give you ev-
erything you could ever want for. You only need to ask.
So ask me,* cara. *Ask, and I will make it so.*

She'd asked for things she'd never even dreamed of in
a moment of unbridled desperate desire and he'd done
them and more.

'Amelia?'

She couldn't face him, not yet. Not when she had to
bite her lip to stop herself from crying out in need, in
want. Instead, she did the only thing she was capable of
and nodded. Inexplicably, her eyes felt damp.

Was she crying? For *him* or for herself?

Enough!

She pasted a bright smile on her face and turned to meet him.

'Mr Rossi. What can I do for you?'

Something flashed in his eyes, hot, angry even, but it was gone in less than one of her frantic heartbeats. She thought she saw him look to her neck—where he had pressed open-mouthed kisses before drowning her in a pleasure she never knew existed, before he had taken possession of her body and—

'What are you still doing here?' Alessandro asked.

'Just finishing a few things. I was just…leaving,' she said, realising that he was too. Now she was going to be stuck in a lift with him for the entire journey down to the ground floor. 'You?' she asked, inanely because… well. What really was there to say to a man she had slept with and was on the brink of completely and utterly destroying?

'On my way out,' he replied, his features almost too guarded, as if he knew exactly how silly this conversation was.

Neither of them moved. Instead, the silence spun a cocoon around them, the air thickened by heated looks and unsteady breaths. Her desire pawed at her when she noticed his hand flex by his thigh. A hand that had caressed her skin, had delved between her legs, had pulled her harder and deeper against his open mouth.

Could he hear the thud of her heart? The way that her breath caught in her throat? His gaze flickered between her lips and her eyes before he turned away, her heart aching and angry and wanting and she didn't know any more. If only he weren't so *handsome*.

His body was angled proprietorially towards her and she felt crowded even though there were nearly two feet between them. The powerful cords of his neck stood out as he reached up to fuss with his tie knot, the deep tan of his skin rich and evocative next to the starched white origami-like fold of his collar. A stubble Amelia was half convinced that he hated was already visible across his jawline and neck, and she was haunted by the memory of how it had felt beneath her fingertips, how it had sounded as she'd explored every single inch of him that night.

The broad shoulders she'd gripped, the lush thick raven-dark hair she'd fisted in her hands as he'd thrust into her. Amelia hated to think that she had been brought so low by good looks, but what else could it have been? The man had utterly destroyed her family and she had all but begged him to ruin her too as she had gripped the edge of the table in his hotel suite. She'd spread her legs wider, to make room for him between them, her body welcoming the hard angles of his hips. The brush of his arousal at her core had sent a gasp through her body...

Amelia slammed the door shut on a memory she should have buried so deep she could never find it again. The only way she'd survived the last six weeks was knowing that they'd never speak of what had happened in Hong Kong. Keeping it tucked away behind a pane of impenetrable glass was the only thing that had kept her sane.

'Shall we?' she asked, assuming the emotionally indifferent tone she had worn for two years, as if she didn't feel torn apart by the weight of desire and the need for a vengeance that had begun to taste bitter in the last few months.

Amelia's breezy tone ate at Alessandro. There he was feeling as if his life had been upended by this innocuous English girl, and she was utterly unaffected by the most sensuous night of his life. Perhaps somewhere in the recent years of his *'Monkdom'*, he had developed perversions. The thought horrified him so much that for a shocking moment, he stilled, causing a flash of concern to pass across Amelia's features.

'Are you—?'

He turned on his heel and stalked back towards the lifts. He should never have stopped on her floor. Once again he wrestled with that sense of frustrated desire and shame. Resisting the urge to pull at his collar, he reminded himself that he had taken advantage of a junior member of staff and he deserved every ounce of inner turmoil that he was currently struggling with.

Crossing the floor, he recognised that it had been rude to cut her off mid-sentence but had he not, he might have—*God forbid*—actually answered her question and admitted that no, he wasn't okay in the slightest and was, in fact, being driven out of his mind with a need for her that felt unnatural.

'Maybe I should take the stairs,' he said as they reached the lift, realising that he probably shouldn't be taking the lift with her.

A slight frown across her brow appeared to question the sense in walking down *sixty-four* flights of stairs. And now he couldn't ignore the fact that he'd just volunteered to do precisely that in order to avoid spending the minute and a half journey with her in the lift.

She blinked at him, shutters over an unfathomable gaze, and turned to face the elevator doors. 'If you like,' she said.

Her response had him grinding his teeth and he was about to leave when the lift arrived, the doors sliding open, and now there was no escape. Leaving would be the height of stupidity, showing the exact extent of how much her presence affected him *beyond* what he had already revealed.

He gestured for her to enter before him and he caught her glancing at his hand before she stepped into the lift. As she turned to look out into the centre of the building he saw the delicate blush at the pulse point behind her ear, his gaze snagging on the way her shirt had come open beneath the pull of the strap of her bag on her shoulder.

Heat crawled across his shoulders, making Alessandro want to yank at the collar of his shirt. She wasn't as unaffected as she appeared and just the thought of that enflamed *everything*. This time, instead of staying in the lift he should damn well get out. Alessandro closed his eyes but instead of blessed darkness he saw her straddled across his lap, taking him deep within her, riding a sensuous wave that consumed them both. The doors closed behind him and the lurch in his gut had nothing to do with the gentle descent.

'Congratulations,' he forced out through numb lips.

For a moment, he thought he saw guilt flash in the golden green depths of eyes that he had once, inconceivably, thought unnoteworthy. But he must have been projecting, because the guilt was his burden to bear.

'Thank you,' Amelia said before biting her lip and turning her attention back to the floors flying past the glass windows.

'Are you celebrating?' he asked.

Minchione! Clearly, she didn't want to speak to him and no wonder. The burning shame of self-loathing now heated his internal body temperature rather than arousal and he was unusually thankful for it.

'No, my sister is…'

Amelia swallowed her words, wishing she could have bitten off her own tongue. 'Away,' she concluded, aware that Alessandro was waiting for her to finish her sentence. Oh, God, this was her punishment. To be stuck in a small enclosed space with the man she'd just ruined—the man that, in spite of everything, she still wanted with a desperation that left her breathless.

Enemy, enemy, enemy!

'What was that?' Alessandro asked, bending slightly as if to listen more closely.

Instinctively she jerked away from him and instantly regretted it. From the tic in his jaw, Alessandro hadn't missed it. His hands fisted by his thighs and oh, God, what was wrong with her? Why was that so sexy?

She had become a stranger to herself in the last six weeks. Ever since she had secured the deal in Hong Kong, something had changed. Because how could she recognise the woman who would sleep with the man that destroyed her family? How could she have betrayed everything she and her sister had worked towards? How could she have weighed one night of pleasure with a childhood of misery and chosen *him*?

Once again a wetness pressed against the backs of her eyes. Not here. And not now! She just needed to get out of this lift and away from Alessandro Rossi. She could have her breakdown when she was home.

Count to ten, darling, and it will be fine.

But the words she'd whispered to her sister through their teenage years didn't work this time. It wouldn't be fine. Issy was off in the Caribbean somewhere, having kidnapped Gianni Rossi, and she was lusting after a man who was the Devil incarnate.

She hadn't expected it to feel like this. Wasn't she supposed to feel victorious? Wasn't it supposed to be amazing, this feeling? Vengeance almost guaranteed, it should have been the crowning achievement of all she'd ever wanted. But she didn't. Instead she felt...*guilty*. She felt sick. And shivery. And no, she hadn't come down with a cold. But...something was *wrong*.

'If this is...' he said, and trailed off, awkwardness looking strange on Alessandro's handsome features. She'd never seen him like this. In the boardroom he was powerful, determined...confidence didn't even factor, it was something beyond that. A supreme self-belief. And the night they'd shared in Hong Kong? A shiver ran the length of her spine. He'd unlocked fantasies that night she'd never even known she'd had. 'If you want to speak to HR... I think we should speak to HR.'

Her head snapped up out of the desire-dazed fog. She almost laughed. She *wanted* to, absurdly. In three days' time, their one night in Hong Kong would be the least of his problems. She would be gone and Alessandro Rossi would never see her again, no matter how hard he might look.

'I don't know what you think we would need to speak to HR about,' she said, purposefully keeping her face blank.

He frowned, his eyes, usually so clear, clouded and confused, she almost didn't like to see it.

'Hong Kong,' he said, as if trying to find a tether to hold onto in the conversation that was clearly difficult.

'Hong Kong was a roaring success. We finalised the deal with Kai Choi, went for dinner with him and his team to celebrate, and then I returned to my hotel room and you returned to yours. I'm not exactly sure why we would need to share that with HR.'

'So, nothing happened?'

'Nothing happened.' It couldn't have. Because she couldn't have been that person. Shame and guilt—and the traces of a desire so heavy it still ran in her veins— made her just a little dizzy.

Alessandro nearly reached out a hand to Amelia as she swayed a little. But she flickered an angry gaze at where his hand twitched and he stopped himself just in time.

Because, of course, grabbing her right now, putting his hands on her was an excellent *idea.*

Alessandro was really beginning to dislike his inner voice, though he could hardly argue with being called a fool. He opened his mouth to object to Amelia's statement. Because there was something inherently wrong about her denying that night had happened. Denying that what they'd shared had happened. Because it had.

Unlike Gianni, Alessandro stayed out of the limelight. His photograph was never in the newspapers, his name only appearing in print if linked to his cousin. He was not instantly recognisable to the person on the street, and were they ever asked if they knew of him, their answer would be 'Alessandro who?' His privacy was a closely guarded thing, so Alessandro could perhaps forgive Amelia for thinking that he did this kind of thing all the time. Not with staff—no, she had at least, thankfully, acknowledged that it was unusual for both of them.

But beyond that, the last time he had shared a bed with someone had been... He tried to think back. Years? Certainly more than two. He was incredibly discerning in his choice of partners, in what attracted him, which was why he had been so shocked to find that Amelia, the perfect employee, who on the surface could have defined English 'plainness', had grabbed his attention and yanked on it, leading him into a night that had proved as unforgettable as it was indescribable.

So he was about to reply, to refute her statement, to tell her that he knew it wasn't just him affected by that night, that he wanted more, to tell her all of the most asinine things that it had never once occurred to him to say to another human being before now, when the doors to the lift opened and Amelia practically ran out into the foyer.

'Amelia,' he called after her as she hurried towards the exit, no longer caring who saw or heard him.

'See you tomorrow, Mr Rossi,' she called over her shoulder without looking back.

He stood, in the centre of the atrium, watching her leave through the main entrance to The Ruby and thought, *yes*. He *would* see her tomorrow. And this time, he'd not let her run away, because he hadn't missed the way that her breath had caught, that her pulse had flickered, and her skin had crested pink with desire. It wasn't just him in this madness. It couldn't be.

He was brought back to earth by a ringtone reserved exclusively for his cousin and could only imagine what Gianni would say when he confessed his sin of sleeping with a junior member of staff. Their lawyers would have a field day.

'Gianni, how—?'

'Andro, listen, I don't have much time.'

'Okay, but what's the—?'

'Amelia Seymore,' Gianni interrupted. 'She's Thomas Seymore's daughter.'

'What?' Alessandro demanded. 'I can't hear you properly.' He *couldn't* have heard Gianni properly. It was just the crackle on the line.

'Listen to me, Amelia Seymore is a traitor. She's been…spy this whole time. She's…with her sister to destroy us.'

'Amelia Seymore?' Alessandro repeated like an idiot, the line was so bad, but he knew if he wanted to he could read between the crackle.

'Yes! Seymore. The…project is compromised.'

'Which project?' he demanded, but he realised Gianni hadn't heard his question.

'And listen, she claims to have found some kind of proof of corruption against us.'

'Corruption? What corruption?' The line was getting even worse. Frustration and incredulity were vying to escape the tight fist he had on his emotions.

'I don't know, but…the messages I read, Amelia… found evidence of corruption… I'm in the Caribbean with her sister. I'll…and stop her communicating with anyone and causing any more damage. Can you deal with Amelia? This needs to be nipped in the bud and damage limitation undertaken immediately.'

'Consider it done,' Alessandro growled darkly.

'I maybe out of reach for a while, but I'll try and get a message to you when I know what's going on.'

'Likewise. Speak soon, cousin.'

When Alessandro ended the call, his jaw was clenched so tight it had started to ache. He was *still* standing in the centre of the atrium, *still* looking at where he had last seen Amelia.

She was Thomas Seymore's daughter, come to destroy them?

He scoffed, surely not. Amelia? Capable of sabotage? No. The thought was so strong that he gestured with his hand, cutting through the empty air. But then a montage

flickered through his mind. Amelia hesitant, guilty, conflicted, angry...

My sister is away...

And suddenly it all started to make sense. Fury found
its way into his veins and travelled throughout his body in
a single pump of his heart. *Cristo*, he could have laughed
at himself. He'd been so stupid. Taken in by the oldest of
ruses. He shook his head in disgust. And he'd more than
simply let her. He'd asked her for it, *begged* her to let him
sign his own ruination. But it wasn't just his own—it was
his cousin's, it was his company, his staff...

No!

Gianni had warned him in time. Alessandro still had
a chance to turn things around. He spun on his heel and,
instead of going home to his apartment, he went back
up to his office and started to plan. Thomas Seymore's
daughters had no idea what they had started and he and
Gianni would make damn sure they would live to regret
the day they messed with the Rossi cousins.

CHAPTER THREE

HANDS BRACED AGAINST the sink, Amelia stared at herself in the mirror the next morning. Accusations and sleeplessness had drawn dark slashes beneath her eyes and she looked unnaturally pale, even considering the harsh bathroom lighting.

You can do this, she told herself sternly. *It's two measly days. Alessandro will be in meetings for most, if not all, of that time.* All she had to do was play nice with her team for two days. All she had to do was smile.

All she had to do was let go of the sink.

She released the death grip she'd had on the porcelain and with one last glare at herself in the mirror, she grabbed her jacket and bag and let herself out of the small flat she shared with her sister in Brockley. The broken lift and the unusual heatwave made the stairwell unbearable and she emerged onto the pavement already hot, sweaty and out of sorts. That was why she came to a stop and simply stared at the sight that met her, genuinely unsure whether it was real or not.

Alessandro was leaning against a sleek black vehicle that to call a car would probably be some kind of insult. Hands fisted deep in his pockets and eyes hidden behind aviator sunglasses that screamed money, he exuded a lazy sexuality that should have come with a health warning.

But there was also something else. Something that put her senses on alert.

It was a slow roll of emotion, building to a crescendo as sharp as any sudden fright and she had to press her hand over her heart to keep it in place. She forced herself to take a deep breath, wishing it were still because of the fright, but honestly, the sight of Alessandro made her sex *ache*. A pulse flared across her body, a chain reaction that touched from sense to sense until her whole body practically trembled with want.

'You scared me,' she accused, trying to catch her breath as she searched for a reason why Alessandro Rossi would be waiting on a South London street, for *her*.

Could he know?

No, she dismissed. There was absolutely no way that he could have discovered Firstview's inadequacies already, especially as it had taken her months.

'My sincere apologies, Ms Seymore. I'm afraid we are quite short on time.'

'Time? For what?' Amelia asked, closing the distance between them. There was an unusual tension in the way Alessandro held himself. Dark glasses might have hidden eyes from her, but she sensed that she was under the very intense microscope of his focus.

'We've just received news of an important business proposal and with the Aurora project all wrapped up, you're the only project lead that I can spare.'

Only Alessandro would wrap up one deal the night before and start a new one before coffee the next morning. 'My team needs briefing and there are a few things...' She might not understand what was going on, but, whatever it was, she knew she couldn't spend any more time with him in such close proximity. 'Is there not someone else who could—?'

'I'm afraid not. You are the only person it can be.'

'But—'

'Ms Seymore, is there a problem?' His words were like a leash, yanking her back into place.

'No. Of course not,' she replied as she stepped forward to meet him beside the car. And he still didn't move. Now that she was this close, she could see that he hadn't shaved and the stubble from last night was now a dark swathe across his jaw. A muscle flexed at the hollow just beneath the dark line and she felt the tension thicken between them, building until finally he stepped aside to open the door, gesturing for her to get in.

'Where are we going?' she asked as the car pulled into the road, attracting more than a few stares from neighbours who were understandably shocked to see such an expensive car in the area.

'Not too far.'

He passed her a file, explaining that it was a brief he needed her to read ahead of the meeting. Frowning, she scanned the opening documents outlining a prospective client they were considering. There were nearly fifty pages here and an anxious heat crawled across her shoulders.

Amelia was finding it hard to focus, not just from the motion of the car and trying to read, but the awareness of Alessandro himself. Arm propped up against the window, chin rested in his palm, his gaze glued on some invisible point in the distance.

Concentrate. It was just one meeting and then she'd be back with her team and done for the day before she knew it.

Only, rather than turning off the South Circular into London, they continued to head out east.

'It's a very important deal, Amelia. I'd really like to get it right,' he warned, as if noticing that she was distracted.

'Of course.'

She turned back to the pages and lost herself in what could be an exciting new deal for Rossi Industries. Scanning the projections, the highly sought-after location of the land for sale and the cultural interest in the surrounding area, she could see how it would come together. It would be incredible. Partnering with Chalendar Enterprises was clever and would save Rossi Industries time overall, the two businesses having worked together before.

And even though Amelia wouldn't be there to see it happen, she was already identifying which team members would be best, what areas might be problematic and how to navigate them. In her absence they would probably give the project to Brent Bennet, but he often made mistakes on the contracts. She should give Legal a heads up...only she wouldn't. Because she would be long gone by the time that happened. The car slowed to a stop and she looked out of the window to see tarmac.

'Alessandro, where is this meeting?'

Alessandro said nothing, opening the door of the car and getting out onto the runway of a private airfield just outside London. He said nothing because a worryingly large part of him wanted to shout and rage and yell. But now wasn't the time for that. There was too much at stake.

He held the door to the car open for her and hated the way that, no matter how the shocking discovery of her true identity had blown his world apart, his body hadn't got the memo, and the soft scent of jasmine that rose from her skin as she passed in front of him hardened his arousal as much as his anger.

The betrayal of it. Of her. He would deal with that later, but for now his one focus, his only goal, was to find out what she had done and stop it before the rot could take hold. His plan was simple—isolate, interrogate and eliminate.

No one other than her father, Thomas Seymore, had managed to pull the wool over their eyes so successfully. Alessandro choked back a bitter laugh. He and Gianni had, naively, believed that they had learned their lesson that one and only time. Clearly, they were mistaken.

And to think she had the gall not to even change her surname. It had been staring him in the face the whole time and what had he done? Smiled at her, thanked her, and asked her for more.

'Sir?'

'*Sì?*' he snapped and Lucinda, a member of his air crew who had been with RI for nearly six years, flinched a little. 'My apologies. Truly, Lucinda,' he said, warning himself to keep his cool.

His emotions swung like a giant pendulum, back and forth between the weight of the past and the future of his company.

He watched Amelia settle into a large cream leather seat, fasten the safety belt and look out of the window. She seemed a little disconcerted but he knew, now, just how good an actress she really was.

'Coffee, Mr Rossi?'

'*Grazie mille*, Lucinda,' he replied sincerely, taking the espresso over to a seat on the opposite side of the cabin.

He just needed to get to Villa Vittoria. It might have been a refuge for him and Gianni for the past ten years, but there was also a deep irony in taking Amelia Seymore back to the scene of the crime. He refused to think of it as kidnap, even though his conscience contorted itself in order not to do so. He was simply taking her to a place where he intended to cut her off from any possible forms of communication until he could identify just how badly she had sabotaged his company and the hundreds of thousands of people he employed globally. It was the only solution he had been able to come up with in the twelve hours since he had received the call from Gianni.

When they were safely at the villa, all hell could break loose. He just had to get her there first without her realising what was happening. It was why he'd given her the file, to distract her and keep her from asking too many questions.

'How long has Lexicon been looking to develop the land?' Amelia asked, flicking back and forth between a few pages. Unease gripped his stomach, empty aside from the coffee he'd all but inhaled. He'd not had long to put together the fake file—in half an hour he'd brought together a mishmash of four old, and failed, pitches. But he could play this game better than anyone, he thought, subtly rolling his shoulders. The Seymore sisters had messed with the wrong billionaires.

'A while,' he replied, knowing that she had been seeking a specific answer. A perverse part of him delighted in withholding it, wanting to needle, to irritate, to annoy. It was a small petty victory, but he could not lose sight of the greater picture. Because so much more than his ego depended on him rooting out the damage she had done and putting an end to it immediately.

'We will soon be taking off, so if your safety belts are fastened?' Lucinda asked, smiling when they had both nodded to affirm that they were. 'Lovely. Flight time should be just under two hours—winds are in our favour and the journey should be smooth sailing.'

With that she retreated before Amelia could get a word out of the partly opened mouth. That delectable, betraying mouth.

I think we should speak to HR.

He couldn't believe the words he'd uttered. Lust-ridden fool. Perhaps that had been her plan after all. To seduce him and—no. Her refusal to speak to HR, her insistence that they never speak of it, her behaviour since Hong Kong, it didn't make sense if that was her plan.

That he had been foolish enough to open the door to any kind of impropriety in the first place was his very own cross to bear. Self-disgust and acceptance—they burned with enough heat to bring pinpricks of sweat to the back of his neck. Alessandro would take whatever punishment he deserved for his transgression. But the sisters' text messages had claimed to have identified proof of corruption.

Impossibile.

Even the word 'corruption' left a bitter taste in his mouth. It was an outrage that this younger Seymore was trying to claim that against them. The audacity of it was simply incomprehensible and while he could concede that there was a certain ingenuity to their plan of attack, it was this—this supposed evidence of corruption—that betrayed the sheer magnitude of their stupidity.

It was simple. Once he had the information he needed, he would ensure that neither he nor his cousin would hear the name Seymore ever again.

* * *

Amelia was feeling really quite uncomfortable by the time they disembarked the plane and got into the limousine waiting for them. She had enough sense to know that any more questions would be met with either silence or derision, which had kept her pretty much quiet no matter how strange the situation was becoming. She pressed a hand to her stomach, and although she desperately wanted to turn up the air conditioning in the back section of the sleek vehicle, the thought of attracting Alessandro's attention was worse.

Italy. They were in Italy.

And even though they had left London comparatively early, the travel and time difference meant that it was now midday and Amelia was hot. Everything felt a little damp and stifling. The air between them was thick and heavy, and she had to work hard to calm her breathing.

She had never got over the way that the Rossis travelled continents as if by the click of their fingers. When she'd interviewed for her position, Amelia had known international travel would be expected, which was why she'd not been able to lie about her name. A copy of her passport was held on file by Rossi Industries and she was expected to carry proof of identification with her at all times.

But as she gazed out of the window, trying to ease the roil in her stomach, the sight of cypress trees in the distance struck her with such a wave of familiarity. The sound of little girls laughing and the scent of sunscreen rose up around her. A warm dry heat hit her skin, turning it rosy in her mind, and the taste of lemon sorbet made her mouth water.

Amelia hadn't been back to Italy since her and Issy's lives had changed for ever. But for just a moment, Amelia wanted to bask in her memories. Her parents enjoying a lazy afternoon beside an azure blue pool in a sprawling villa on the far edges of Capri. Her father's cream linen shorts and brown sandals displaying pale English skin and the mosquito bites their mother used to tease him about. Jane Seymore's smile when she looked at her husband as they had lunch looking out across a stunning sea punctuated by jagged rocky outcrops. Issy's terrible aim as she threw beach balls at her while she was trying—and failing—to get a tan.

She had forgotten it. The last family holiday they'd had before the Rossis had ripped apart everything they'd known, and her heart filled with an old ache she hadn't allowed herself to feel since she and Issy had chosen vengeance.

She felt, rather than saw, Alessandro's attention fix on her. The touch of it so different from the heated *yearning* from the past few weeks that it brought her out of her memories. Now it felt cool and tasted like anger and Amelia began to fear that just maybe he *had* discovered who she was.

Italy, Lexicon, the deal. It could almost have been purpose built for her. She spoke fluent Italian—one of the three languages she had studied in order to embellish her résumé for Rossi Industries. The land—it was similar to a deal RI had rejected about two months before she'd interviewed for her position—a deal Issy had researched to help Amelia with her interview. The sudden change in Alessandro's temperament—she'd seen him under huge amounts of pressure before, right down to the last beats on several billion-dollar deals, and he'd never been *cold*. Clipped, harsh, demanding and exacting to the point of brutal? Absolutely. But there was a heat, drive, a momentum that swept you up and made you want to meet those standards, made you want to be with him in that success. It was…attractive, *alluring*.

Stop!

There was no way that Alessandro could have discovered anything wrong with the deal and she had covered her tracks too well in the company to have been identified as Thomas's daughter. But, oh, God, what if something had happened to Issy? What if Gianni had—?

Her swift gasp of shock drew not just Alessandro's focus, but his gaze.

'Ms Seymore, is something wrong?'

His words, full of grit and gravel, shifted her pulse into a higher gear.

'No, Mr Rossi,' she replied through bloodless lips. She had to know. Picking up the file beside her, she scanned the documents and looked at the memo date from Lexicon to Rossi Industries. Second of June. She managed to stop her hands fisting before the crumpled paper could betray her discovery. It would be highly unlikely to near inconceivable for anyone in Italy to have sent a work memo on *Festa Della Republica*. Italy's Republic Day was a fiercely celebrated bank holiday on which *no one*—bar first responders—worked.

'You put the documents together yourself?'

He nodded, his gaze inscrutable.

Oh, God. He knew who she was.

Amelia Seymore was in serious trouble. And if she was, so was her sister.

* * *

Alessandro knew there was a risk that something in the documents could tip Amelia off, but with such little time he'd had no choice. And now, as the limousine made the last twists and turns towards the only place in the world he could have brought her, did it really matter if she knew that she had been found out? Because that had been the only conclusion to draw from the shocked gasp she'd tried to hide.

And in interesting contrast to that momentary betrayal of emotions, the woman beside him seemed unduly calm. He could almost be impressed by her. *Almost*. He looked out of the window before he did something stupid like look at her again.

The opening move of the game had been made. He had brought her into his domain and if she hadn't already, then soon she would realise the reality of her situation. That she was completely and utterly at his mercy.

The thought detonated such a riot of emotions, it infuriated him that Amelia Seymore could be so…*calm*.

The electronic gates at Villa Vittoria parted smoothly and the driver took the fork in the road that would lead to Alessandro's half of the dramatic oval-shaped compound. The other would have taken them to Gianni's half of the unique estate. With near enough two hundred and fifty acres across the entire property the estate was worth more than ten million euros. But it was what lay at the heart of the compound that made it priceless to Alessandro and Gianni.

As the car took the road that swept alongside a large area of land that looked to the world like a pretty wildflower meadow, it was so much more to Alessandro. To him and Gianni, it was what could have utterly broken them, but instead it had become the thing that defined them.

Poppies, cornflowers, daisies and violets covered the stretch of land that Alessandro and Gianni had bought after years of secretly saving every single penny they could. Scrimping and sacrifice had garnered enough money to make the initial purchase, and a savage loan with near-insurmountable interest rates from a highly unscrupulous money lender was to cover the build that would have been their first property.

Would have. Had it not been for Thomas Seymore.

Thomas Seymore had seen Alessandro and Gianni, two eighteen-year-olds with hope in their eyes and barely enough money in their pockets, and considered them easy targets for his villainy. He had been wrong to underestimate them. And he had paid the price.

And now, it seemed, he had to teach the daughter exactly the same lesson.

So be it.

The car pulled up alongside his half of the estate that bracketed one side of the land that had been sold to them illegally. Oh, they could have tried to sell it on, offloading it onto another poor unsuspecting bastard, perhaps even pay off a surveyor as Seymore had, to ensure that the buyer didn't discover until it was too late that the land was unfit for development. But instead, they'd kept it. As a reminder, not to ever forget the sting of that betrayal, a reminder of just how far they had come. Slowly, but surely, they had bought the land surrounding the little parcel Seymore had sold them and they had eventually turned it into Villa Vittoria, their home and their refuge.

Beside him, Amelia opened the door of the limousine and stepped out, her gaze scanning the impressive vista before her with something like awe. He exited the vehicle and, with a knock on the roof, the driver departed, leaving just the two of them standing on the sandy driveway facing off against each other.

'Why am I here?' Amelia demanded, only a slight tremble in her voice.

'To face the consequences of your actions, *cara*,' he growled in warning.

'Funny.' The word sliced out through tightly clenched teeth. The paleness of her skin serving to highlight the slashes of anger painting her cheeks red. 'I was about to say the same to you.'

CHAPTER FOUR

DESPITE HER FIERY RESPONSE, the sun heated Amelia's skin to the point of discomfort and her mouth was dryer than a desert. During Issy's online investigations, she had found mention of the estate that the Rossi cousins shared, but there were no photographs or plans anywhere online. From the scarce descriptions her sister had been able to cobble together though, it could only be where Amelia was now.

Alessandro had discovered who she was and brought her onto his territory—a move calculated to cause her the maximum amount of disturbance. He clearly thought she was at his mercy. But he had also, clearly, underestimated her.

This was her mess and she had to fix it. Her first priority was to make sure that her sister was okay. The last message she'd had from Issy was a picture she'd sent yesterday of her in a luxurious room on the yacht she'd obtained to lure Gianni Rossi away from contact. Everything in her wanted to grab her phone and call Issy immediately. But she had to play this carefully. Once she knew that her sister was okay, Amelia would identify exactly what it was that he knew, what he *thought* he knew, and what damage she could still do. She just needed to get him talking.

And the best way to do that? Make him think he was the one in control.

She looked around. In the distance she caught sight of a wall that ran the length of the estate from what she could tell. On the far side of the large wildflower meadow was a villa—similar in design to the buildings behind her, but with slight differences. She narrowed her gaze, recognising Gianni's flair for the dramatic in contrast to the starker, more serious lines of property that suited Alessandro's personality. But she was surprised that he had chosen to bring her to such a private place—his *home*.

She shaded her gaze from the midday sun and craned her neck to look up at Alessandro, who had, once again, chosen to hide behind his sunglasses. *Coward.* He gestured behind her to a small stone pathway leading away from the main building. Fighting him on such a small thing would be foolish. She was going to have to be very careful and very clever.

They turned their back on the drive and skirted the edge of the main building. Large trees provided blessed relief from the Italian sun and in the near distance she spied what could only be their destination—a low-slung building beside an azure-blue pool. Floor-to-ceiling gently tinted windows wrapped around the structure, making it one of the most lavish pool houses she'd ever seen.

Only the best for the Rossis, her sister's voice reminded her.

From here Amelia could just make out a large open-plan kitchenette and lounge to one side and a glass-fronted shower with a half-wall that presumably hid a toilet. Her eyes returned to the shower, where butter-coloured marble stood stark against powerful lines of dark granite. It suited Alessandro to perfection. She could just imagine him hauling himself from the pool, stripping out of his costume and prowling straight into the shower and—

'Is there a problem?' Alessandro asked with faux civility.

She had stopped walking. At some point in the midst of her daydream she had actually stopped walking. She *had* to get better control over herself.

'You mean aside from the fact that you have, to all intents and purposes, kidnapped me and I am now trapped in a foreign country with no money or clothes?'

He notched his head to one side. 'You have your phone?'

'Yes, of course I...'

He held out his hand.

'No. Absolutely not,' she said, punctuating it with a shake of her head.

'No one will help you, *cara*. You are mine until I find out exactly what you've done and how you can fix it, before I remove you from my and my cousin's lives for good.'

'I still think I'll be keeping hold of it,' she said as she pushed past him and continued towards the pool house, hastily pressing the call button for her sister. In her peripheral vision she saw him take out his phone and press a button. Instantly the signal bars on her phone disappeared. What the—?

He had a signal jammer?

'You actually blocked the phone signal?' she demanded.

'Of course. You are a threat and you need to be contained.' Despite his words, his tone was painfully civilised and that, Amelia knew, was when Alessandro was at his most dangerous.

Panic nipped at her pulse, but she ignored it as they reached the pool house, the glass door frame sliding back as if ready for their arrival.

'Would you like some lunch? I had my staff prepare something,' he said as he walked towards the clean, simply designed kitchen.

If he had staff, then…

'*Before* I gave them all the rest of the week off,' he added, as if reading her mind.

A week? Just how long did he plan on keeping her here?

'Oh, I get a meal before you start the interrogation, then?' she threw at him.

'If you like,' he said with a shrug as if he cared little if she ate or starved to death.

She picked at her thumbnail, struggling to play it cool while her mind conjured all manner of scenarios Issy might be going through. She couldn't take it any more. Concern for Issy eclipsed everything.

'I'll not say another word until I know if my sister is okay.'

Alessandro bit back a curse. She was a traitor. A spy. She had done who knew what damage to his company and yet still every single inch of her shone with defiance, the burning heat in her eyes curling around him like a flame. Taunting him. Daring him.

And for the first time in his life, he was at risk of losing his legendary cool. He'd kept himself in check ever since his father had first used his fists on him, determined never ever to become anything like the monster who had provided half of his DNA.

He turned away from her before he did something he'd regret—something that had none of the violence of his father and all of the passion of a lust-filled youth. What kind of spell had she cast upon him? He placed the plates his staff had put together on the table and retrieved a bottle of wine from the fridge. At her raised eyebrow, he simply stared at her.

'I'm less concerned about your sister, and more worried about what she is doing to my cousin.'

Amelia opened her mouth as if to say something but snapped it shut. She was apparently planning to stick to her word not to say anything until she heard from her sister.

Amelia and Isabelle—sisters and daughters of Thomas Seymore. He searched Amelia's face for signs of the tall, thin British man who had sold them a worthless plot of land all those years ago. He couldn't quite see it. Where her father had been lean and long, his features sharp and harsh, Amelia was petite, softer, *sweeter*. Looks that were clearly deceiving.

He frowned. Perhaps he should have kept an eye on the Seymore family. But he'd thought the business done with the moment he and Gianni visited the old man to let him know that his company was not his own any more. After that, Alessandro had cared only about the harsh lesson they'd learned at the hands of a selfish, corrupt, rich Englishman.

He took out his phone and pressed the button to lift the signal blocker. The technology had been installed as part of the electronic security system designed by Thiakos Securities, one of the best in the business.

'Call her,' he said, with a careless shrug.

Before he'd finished speaking Amelia had her phone pressed to her ear.

Alessandro poured himself a glass of wine as she turned her back on him.

It was no great loss to let her speak to her sister—if anything it would hopefully loosen her tongue enough to talk. *Then* he would uncover just what it was she had sabotaged. Of course, the most logical target would have been the Aurora project. But it could have been anything she'd worked on in the last two years. And that was a lot of projects. Because she'd been so *good* at her job.

He watched a drip of condensation glide from the lip of the water jug and down over the shoulder and remembered chasing a bead of her sweat with his tongue, her cries in his ears and her skin hot and flushed beneath him. It had fallen into the wide valley between her breasts but he'd became distracted by a taut rosy nipple. He'd palmed both breasts as he thrust deeper into her, licking up the salt from her skin and—

The slam of her phone against the table yanked his attention back to the present, his gaze clashing with her mute anger. He pulled at the collar of his shirt and rolled his shoulders.

'No answer?'

She simply glared at him and, for the first time since Gianni had called him the night before, he almost laughed. Here they were, dealing with the highest stakes possible, and she was playing a child's game of silence.

Sighing in frustration, he dialled Gianni's number and listened as a recorded message informed him that the number he was trying to reach was unavailable. Irritation mixed with a touch of concern, he called again even knowing it wouldn't produce a different outcome. Frowning, he tried to reach the captain of Gianni's yacht.

A brief conversation revealed that Gianni and Amelia's sister had just been let off the ship.

'Satisfied?' he asked, hanging up the phone, knowing Amelia had followed the conversation in Italian.

The swift, single shake of her head was expected. If he were in her shoes, he doubted he would have been either. He brought up the search engine on his mobile and searched for #TheHotRossi. The hashtag the press had given Gianni usually made him smile, but not today.

Choosing the images tab, he scrolled through pictures of his sharp-cheekboned, chiselled-jawed cousin and found what he was looking for. A model with her thumbs hooked—supposedly seductively—in the waistband of her bikini had failed to realise that the photographer's gaze had shifted over her shoulder to the couple at the end of a jetty. Gianni's yacht was backing away from St Lovells, the small Caribbean private island owned by Alessandro's cousin, but it was the couple that drew the eye. Long blonde hair had been caught by the wind, a face similar to Amelia's, but different too, staring up at Gianni with so much intensity the photograph felt intrusive.

Unsure what to make of it, he nevertheless slid the phone back across the table to Amelia.

'It was time-stamped less than an hour ago.'

Amelia scrutinised the picture. 'I want to talk to her.'

'I'm sure you do. I've a few things I'd like to say to her myself.'

'You will stay away from her, you beast.'

Alessandro laughed. 'Beast?' he demanded, but it was

his eyes that taunted her, reminding her that it wasn't what she'd called him in Hong Kong.

Amelia looked away, needing to hide her illogical reaction. This constant push and pull between them was making her nauseous. Wasn't it why she'd been forced to lie to her sister and tell Issy that she had proof of their corruption? She'd just wanted it all over. The vengeance, the lies, the pretence. Fighting Alessandro, fighting herself. It had been so exhausting and so *hard*.

'You needn't worry about your sister. Gianni is, despite popular opinion, a gentleman.'

'Yes,' she said. 'By all accounts, he's most definitely the nicer of the two of you.'

Alessandro glared at her from across the table. She'd meant what she said though. From all of Issy's research it was clear that, where Alessandro ran cold, Gianni ran a passionate hot, full of charm hc used as indiscriminately as he did freely. And a huge part of all of Amelia's plans had been to ensure that her sister would be safe no matter what.

It had always been Alessandro that was the wild card.

She poured herself a glass of water, hastily making and discarding various plans and options. She didn't feel physically threatened in the slightest and she didn't think for one minute that Alessandro would lay a finger on her.

But he had. In Hong Kong. There, he'd touched, teased, delved with those fingers, bringing her to orgasm again and again and—

She thumped the empty glass of water she'd consumed in one go down on the table. Alessandro watched her with steady eyes as she refilled it, not caring that she looked rattled, she was thirsty and she would drink all the water she needed.

She squared her shoulders, placed her hands in her lap and composed herself. She'd always known that discovery was a possibility. She'd rehearsed this moment over and over in her mind—what she'd say, how she'd answer whatever questions she could imagine him asking. In some ways it was a relief to finally be here and get it over with. 'Interrogate away, Mr Rossi,' she said with a dismissive sweep of her hand.

'What did you do?' His words were clipped, his tone uncompromising.

'You might have to be a little more specific than that, Mr Rossi,' she said, leaning back in her chair, unconsciously trying to put just a little more distance between them. As if he'd noticed, he leaned forward, erasing her momentary reprieve.

'You have done something to damage Rossi Industries.'

She held his gaze, trying to ignore the muscle flaring at his jaw like a warning beacon.

'Well?'

'I believe that was a statement, not a question,' she replied. The flash of anger, a gold lightning strike, was expected but the rumbling thunder of disdain cut her to the quick. Gritting her teeth, she stared at a point just below his chin. The tie of his knot was slightly skewed, as if he'd pulled at it and then tried to twist it back into place.

'According to your sister, you claim to have found proof of corruption.'

Her adrenaline spiked, sending a scattering of stings to nerve endings all over her body.

'But as we both know that is simply neither true nor possible, so there is only one logical conclusion. You have lied; to your sister—maybe even to yourself. An act that is desperate and dangerous and I don't like either of those things. So I ask again, *Amelia*. What. Did. You. Do?'

Stubborn and mutinous, Amelia refused to answer his question. Refused to meet his eye. Refused to engage. But she couldn't deny that everything he said was true. She had lied to her sister, to herself. She *was* desperate and it *had* been dangerous. But if she told him now then it would all have been for nothing.

'You are playing a very dangerous game.'

And finally, she couldn't hold it back any more. 'With rules *you* wrote, ten years ago,' she accused, the words dripping with bitterness and resentment.

'Frankly, Ms Seymore, I don't care. I don't care what you think happened ten years ago, what you think your father did or did not deserve, or what happened to him or you after that.'

Outrage lashed at her soul, in a silent cry of pure injustice. It howled and raged in her chest, wanting out, wanting to cause as much hurt as had been done to her and her sister.

'What I care about is the nearly hundred thousand employees in Rossi Industries and the countless associated businesses that would be negatively impacted by your temper tantrum.'

She gasped. 'Temper—'

'And honestly? It is inconceivable that you and your sister are playing a petty game of revenge for a man who was more corrupt than anyone I know. And given the number of billionaires, businessmen and politicians, that's really saying something.'

He was breathing hard, but not as hard as Amelia. The blood had drained from her face, leaving her worryingly pale, but the sheer force of his anger was still riding him hard. So he missed the genuine disbelief and confusion shadowing her gaze before it was shuttered.

No, all he saw was misplaced outrage and indignation. How dared she? The little fool had put so much at risk he was incandescent with anger.

'You can spare me your lies, Alessandro, there's no gallery here to play to.'

'Lies? *You* talk to *me* of lies?' he accused as he saw his barb hitting home.

'I did what I had to,' Amelia replied, unable this time to meet his gaze.

'With no thought to the consequence of your actions?'

'Why should I have? What more can you do to me? You've already taken *everything*.'

Refusing to let her words needle into his conscience, he pressed on.

'Amelia—I wasn't speaking of you. The consequences of any kind of sabotage will put hundreds if not thousands of jobs on the line, the ramifications for their families could be devastating. Didn't you think of them?'

'No!' she cried, the first real sense of emotion breaking through the façade that she had held in place for two years. 'No. I didn't. I was thinking of my father, who you *broke*. I was thinking of the way he lost not only his business, but his house and his friends and his social standing. It destroyed him.'

He hardened himself against the emotion bringing tears to her eyes that she was too proud to shed. Her loyalty, passion, her love for her father might have been alien emotions to him, but even he would have to have been a rock not to be moved by her. He looked away, out to the edge of the pool and beyond to the piece of land that Thomas Seymore had sold them.

Land that was so unstable it would never have supported the foundations needed for any kind of housing or development. Thomas Seymore's deception had set them back years and thousands of euros and had been a both brutal and harsh lesson. They had nearly broken themselves, working every single hour they could to buy, fix and flip a much cheaper property nearly a hundred miles away from where he now sat with Amelia. He and Gianni had clawed their way, property by property, deal by deal to the point where they had been able to finally mount a hostile takeover of Seymore's own business.

'I remember it, you know. The day you came to our house.'

Alessandro turned his gaze back to Amelia. But there was no indignation in her tone this time, it wasn't strong with conviction. It was the voice of a daughter who had heard things said about her father that she shouldn't have.

'I remember what you said to him.'

The single thread of shame woven into that whole encounter began to unravel deep within him. Alessandro hadn't taken pleasure from that day—in fact it had been precisely that point that had brought him back from the edge of a cliff he'd been far too close to. In that moment, he'd never been more like his own father and Alessandro had sworn never to be that man again.

'Don't,' he said, before she could repeat the words he and his cousin had said that day.

The look she gave him shamed him anew.

'You might not have made him drink, but you put the bottle in his hand. You might not have put him in the ground, but you dug that hole, Alessandro. You and Gianni.'

Angry at the truth of her words, at the events that he had unknowingly started, Alessandro lashed out.

'Amelia, you might be a lot of things, but you're not stupid. Didn't you ever wonder why it was so easy for two twenty-year-olds to take over your father's business? Did you ever think that we shouldn't have been able to do it?'

'Why should I?' she demanded with the blind loyalty of a child. 'He was my father!'

Perhaps it was the differences in their upbringing. Perhaps he might have been the same had he had a father with even an ounce of love in him. But he hadn't, so he couldn't conceive of her naivety. He shook his head, intensely disliking that he was going to have to destroy Thomas Seymore all over again.

'You might not have the proof of *our* corruption,' he said to her, pushing back to stand. 'But you should know that I kept everything about our dealings with your father.'

He walked over to the corner of the living room and retrieved an old faded brown folder from a side cabinet. He returned and placed it in front of her on the table.

She looked up at him, her eyes betraying the first glimpse of doubt he'd seen in her. His conscience told him not to do this. But it was already done.

'Proof of corruption indeed,' he said, looking out to the wildflower meadow. 'How fitting.'

And he left, knowing that she would read the contents of that folder. She wouldn't be able not to. As the sun began to fall, he paced around the large swimming pool, his gaze returning far too often to the female form bent over the table, turning page after page. With her experience at his company, he knew she would easily interpret the sale documents, evaluations, the different surveys. He'd even left the paperwork for the loan in there—he didn't care if she read that. He had no shame about how desperate they had been to agree to the punishing repayment rate, nor how hard they'd worked to pay it back, seeing it only as proof of how far they had come. Their plans, their hopes and dreams...*everything* was in that folder.

He heard the scrape of her chair against the floor and turned. She pinned him with such a look his heart lurched. Or at least he thought it had. Then, as the papers in Amelia's hands scattered, he realised it was her—and he was running before she hit the floor.

CHAPTER FIVE

HER HEART HURT. That was the first thing she noticed. Not the dull pain in her head that kept her eyes closed, or the hot agony in her shoulder that forced her onto her side. It was the ache radiating out from her heart and soul, confusing her momentarily until she remembered.

She turned to bury her face in a pillow so plush and silky soft she wanted to climb into it. A breath left her lips in a shudder and she curled in on herself like a child. But that only made her think of her father. The father she had looked up to, even as he sank deeper and deeper and further and further into a bottle. Even as he ignored his daughters' pleas and his wife's desperation—a wife who would then choose to follow him into a drug-induced oblivion after his death.

In the aftermath of their neglect, Amelia had stepped in to pick up the pieces. To make sure that Issy had a meal to eat after school, did her homework on time. That clothes were washed and bills were paid. She'd had to wrestle money for food from their mother before she could spend it on whatever drug she could find to fill the hole left by her husband's death. And in those horrible early years it had only been the idea of retribution against the Rossis that had kept her and Issy going. It had been her suggestion—their plan of vengeance—and they had clung to it like a lifeline. But she couldn't hide from the truth any more. Page after page in that horrible file had peeled back the scales from her eyes and she had seen. Seen more than she'd ever wanted to.

It had *never* crossed her mind that her father had been corrupt. Never. By the time Thomas Seymore lost his company she had been only fifteen years old. She'd been to his office only twice, his talk of work so boring when her life was full of the exclusive private school she and Issy had attended, piano lessons, ballet, the occasional horse-riding lesson. Until it had been snatched away from her, she had lived a life of blissful ignorance, never truly understanding the depth of her privilege. And when it had been snatched away? She'd known exactly who had been responsible. The two men who had visited with her father that Sunday afternoon.

Just like every week, Issy had prepared the vegetables while she'd made the Yorkshire pudding. The small glass of wine they'd been allowed with the meal had tasted rich and decadent and naughty. And when it had been interrupted, Amelia and Issy had listened at the doorway to their father's office, giggling at the handsome Italian men meeting so importantly with their father. Until the conversation had become harsh and angry.

You are done, old man. Finished. You will never work in this industry again. And if you even think to try, we will make sure that you will regret it.

Everything you thought you had—it's ours now and there is not a thing you can do about it. Any pathetic attempt to crawl back into this industry will be met with swift and significant reprisal. Know that and choose not to test us.

When they had left, Thomas Seymore had looked up

to find the eyes of his wife and children on him, having heard the entire exchange. For a man whose pride and standing was everything, the two youths Alessandro and Gianni had been had struck their mark.

Only now, lying there cocooned in luxury once again, the words took on a different meaning—and rather than sheer hatred towards Alessandro and Gianni, Amelia now tossed and turned in the wake their accusations and taunts left behind them. Instead of arrogance and venomous poison, she heard the quake of injustice. Her father had conned them into buying land he knew they'd never be able to build on. He'd not simply seen them as soft targets, he'd purposefully set out to bribe an official to make it happen. How many other times had he done something like that? How many other people had he scammed and conned?

And... *Oh, God. Firstview. The Aurora project. Issy!*

A sob rose to her lips and she tried to cover her mouth with her hand.

'Amelia...'

Her sob turned into a cry of alarm. She hadn't realised she wasn't alone and the thought that Alessandro had witnessed her pain made her feel vulnerable and exposed in a way she'd never experienced before.

'I'm sorry... It's okay, *you're* okay,' Alessandro said, his tone unusually gentle and careful.

She inhaled a shaky breath and turned to find him sitting in a chair in the corner of a room she didn't recognise. He looked...terrible. His shirt was undone at the collar, sleeves rolled back and there wasn't an inch of clothing that wasn't creased or crumpled in some way. The stubble she remembered had morphed into something much more substantial—the beard lending him even more of a forbidding appearance.

'Where am I?' she asked, trying to sit up. Hand out in a gesture for her to stop, he took a breath—nearly as shaken as her own.

'In my home.'

'Not the pool house?'

He shook his head once.

Taking a quick assessment, she realised she was no longer in the business suit she'd worn before. She shot him a look full of accusation and the hand he'd held out shot up in surrender.

'Not me,' he said simply.

'Then who?' she growled.

'My doctor.'

She frowned. She remembered standing from the table, the shock loosening her fingers on the file, the paper dropping and a look of alarm so stark in his eyes that she felt genuinely scared but she didn't know what for and then...

'I fainted,' she remembered. 'You called a doctor?'

'Of course,' he replied, outraged by her surprise—as if she'd accused him of breaking the Geneva Convention. She swallowed, her throat painfully dry. Alessandro must have noticed as he stood from the chair and brought her a glass of water. She had to crane her neck to look up at him, and he stared at a spot beside her on the bed as if not wanting to make eye contact. 'Can you...?'

She nodded, levering herself up against the headboard. She took the glass from his hands, careful not to make contact. She didn't know if that might send her back into a faint.

A knock on the door drew her attention to a little old man with deeply tanned skin and a shock of white hair.

'Ahh, you are awake. Marvellous,' he pronounced, as if she knew exactly who he was and why he would think it was marvellous. 'Alessandro, if you would?' The old man gestured for him to leave and Amelia held her breath. This was her chance! She needed to get out of here.

Once Alessandro left, she took a breath and turned to the old man. 'I've been kidnapped. I'm being held against my will,' she whispered urgently.

'I know, dear,' he said, sitting on the bed beside her, picking up her hand and patting it gently. 'Alessandro explained everything.'

'Wait, what?' she asked, confused by a response that was entirely the opposite of what she'd been expecting.

'He really is quite lovely, when you get to know him.'

'Alessandro? Lovely?' she asked, truly bewildered.

'Yes, well. You know, aside from...*that*,' the old man said, apparently reluctant to use the word kidnap. 'Now. I need to talk to you about some tests we would like to run to find out why you might have fainted.'

Alessandro sat in the early morning sun, with his head in his hands and his mind completely blank. Instead of the dawn chorus of birds, or the chatter of cicadas, a high-pitched buzz rang in his ears. He'd been awake for nearly forty-eight hours now, having only really caught the odd hour or so the night before as he sat vigil by Amelia's beside. He hadn't reached her in time. She'd hit the floor with an alarming thud, the sound of which would haunt him for the rest of his life.

He'd called Dr Moretti before moving her and only when the man had agreed to come straight away had he allowed himself to breathe. He'd picked her up and carried her straight to this room. Moretti had arrived in under twenty minutes—but the damage had been done.

Alessandro had been plunged right back into a nightmare from his childhood and the horror of waiting for the doctor to come for his mother, lying bruised, bloodied and broken on her bed. His father's gaze had been full of anger, resentment and indignation, but the whites of his eyes had held only fear. Fear that he'd finally gone too far.

A cold sweat and tremors had racked his body so much so that Moretti had tried to assess him first, but Alessandro had thrown him off in favour of Amelia. Only when the man had started making his assessment had Alessandro begun to calm down.

For a while at least.

Because then had come the questions—about her medical history, any allergies, intolerances, how long since she'd last eaten, was she on any medication. Thankfully he had access to her medical file on his work computer and he'd shared it with Moretti. Having read it, the doctor had declared that, as there was no immediate life-threatening urgency, any further diagnosis could wait until she woke.

Alessandro had been tempted to argue but his mouth had been quicker than his brain. 'What tests?'

'Oh, the usual. FBC, LFT, U and E, glucose, HCG.'

The first he'd recognised from reruns of medical dramas he'd catch late night on TV when he couldn't sleep. But HCG?

'Yes. HCG levels will let us know if she's pregnant,' Moretti had blithely declared.

And that was when Alessandro's mind had gone blank

and the doctor had put two and two together much quicker than he and Amelia might have.

It wasn't possible. They had used protection. Every. Single. Time.

Because Alessandro would never have taken such a risk. Never. Alessandro had made a promise to his father—his direct bloodline would end with him. And he'd meant it. He had absolutely no intention of forcing such a heritage on any other poor bastard. What Gianni chose to do was on him. But Alessandro? No, he had been clear about this since the very night that Amelia's collapse had reminded him of; he would never have a child.

He scoffed, laughing bitterly at himself. He'd always thought of it as his decision, as if his will alone were enough to make it so. Now he could see that the sheer arrogance of such a thought was shockingly naïve and ignorant. Because if she *was* pregnant, if there *was* a baby, Alessandro knew that whatever happened from here on out was up to her.

A woman who had hidden her true identity, snuck into Rossi Industries like a spy, determined to prove them corrupt, and, when that hadn't happened, had sabotaged them. And from the little he did know about Amelia? She was excellent. Quick, intelligent, focused, determined. Without a shadow of a doubt, if she had intended destruction, it was assured. And he still had absolutely no clue what she'd done. He had a team of people searching through everything she'd touched, but that could take too long.

He shook his head. Was that really important? They needed to deal with one thing at a time. And first—

Dr Moretti came out into the small courtyard, eyes

bright as always. 'It is a beautiful day,' he announced unnecessarily.

Alessandro resisted the urge to growl. The old man had always been kind. Had always been there when his mother or Gianni's mother had needed him, the mean, vicious streak shared by the two Vizzini brothers. An image formed in his mind of the two bitter old men, slowly drinking their vineyard into insignificance. The pure glee in his father's eyes that his direct bloodline might continue made his throat thick with acrid bile.

'*Come sta?*'

'Tired, thirsty, a little confused, but she's better than you from the look of things,' the doctor replied in quick-fire Italian. 'She's asking for you.'

Alessandro swallowed. His heart began to race, his pulse pounding in his ears.

'Take a breath, Alessandro, or *you'll* faint this time.'

He nodded and drew quick and deep, holding it there for a few seconds before controlling the release. And then readied himself for whatever was to come. Even if that meant he was tied for the rest of his life to a woman he could never trust and who could probably never trust him.

Amelia shook her head back and forth. This couldn't be happening.

'I'm on the pill,' she said, looking up at the doctor.

'And I used a condom,' Alessandro said, also staring at the poor man as if delivering the news of Amelia's pregnancy made it his fault.

'I had a period,' Amelia said, her lips numb with shock. 'I didn't… Oh, God, I've been taking the pill all this time…' The sudden and shocking fear that she might have somehow already hurt the little bundle of cells trying desperately to grow into a tiny human was horrible.

'Please...' Dr Moretti said in a way that clearly requested some calm from the other two adults in the room. 'Firstly, there is no evidence to suggest that continuing to take the hormonal contraception harms a pregnancy. Secondly, no contraception is one hundred per cent assured. It seems this is an instance of...' He looked between Amelia and Alessandro as if trying to gauge the appropriate word, and decided it didn't need clarifying. 'It is possible that, for some women, periods continue throughout the entire pregnancy. You will want to monitor this with your own doctor when you get home.'

Home. A flat she shared with her sister. A sister still hell-bent on vengeance against her baby's father and his cousin. Oh, God, Rossi Industries. Firstview. She pressed her fingers to her mouth, trying to keep the swell of nausea down. It was all too much.

'Water biscuits. My wife swore by them through all four of her pregnancies.'

She glanced up at the doctor and then to Alessandro, who looked as pale and shocked as she felt.

Moretti, realising that there was clearly much to be discussed, announced that he would let himself out and left the two of them alone in a room that suddenly felt stifling. She needed air. She decided that she wanted to get up at exactly the time that Alessandro collapsed back into the chair she had woken to find him in that morning, only a few hours ago when the world had been completely different.

When she wasn't carrying her enemy's baby. Only, wasn't *she* the enemy?

She bit back a groan. It was all so confusing. She lifted

the sheet back and swung her legs out, her feet hitting the cold floor with a slap, yanking Alessandro's attention back to her. Or more specifically her legs. Slashes of red appeared across cheekbones that could cut glass, and she looked away, clenching her teeth against the shocking wave of responding arousal she felt at the sheer *heat* in his eyes.

She might have been able to blame a lot of what had happened in the past six weeks on the hormones, she now realised, but not what had initially driven her into the arms of this enigmatic, powerful and, most definitely, dangerous Italian.

By the time she looked back up, Alessandro had found something intensely interesting out of the window to look at.

'Where are you going?' he asked, his voice thick and rough.

'I'd like some air,' she replied, fighting another wave of nausea that had more to do with guilt than her pregnancy.

The large Alessandro-sized T-shirt hung from her small frame, beneath which was—thankfully—her underwear. The hemline hit her high on her thigh but she decided that modesty and propriety were the least of her and Alessandro's problems.

She stood, testing her strength, and was happy to find that she wasn't as weak as she'd feared. She got to the door of the room, the burning touch of Alessandro's gaze on her the entire time, and realised she didn't know where to go.

'A little help?' she asked, ruefully.

A hand appeared at her elbow and she jerked away from it. 'Not that kind of help. How do I get out of here?' She stood aside to let him pass and lead the way. Beams of sunlight flooded the hallway and she realised she didn't know what time it was.

'How long was I out?'

'The entire night,' Alessandro replied.

She frowned. 'And you?'

'I stayed with you.'

Instinctively she reached out to take his wrist, pulling him round and dropping his hand the moment he looked at where they touched—as if he wasn't sure whether to push her away or hold on.

'Have you slept at all in the last two days?'

He laughed, a single punch of bitterness and incredulity. 'That matters to you?'

Yes, it did, she was surprised to find. Without the line her vendetta had drawn between them, the feelings she'd tried to deny were creeping in. But, clearly, he wouldn't have believed her if she'd admitted as much. Instead, she bit her lip to prevent any further stupidity from escaping and when he turned back to lead her out of the house, she followed in silence.

Step by step, very quickly, Amelia was realising just how dire her situation truly was. As someone whose job was to make assessments, identify problems and present solutions in order to achieve the greatest success, she was under no illusions about her current predicament.

She had nothing—no savings, no inheritance, no security. After their father had passed, they had finally been able to declare bankruptcy, Thomas Seymore's pride refusing to countenance such a necessary but drastic move while alive. Nine years on, Amelia lived in a one-bedroom flat with her sister in South East London. The majority of her—admittedly impressive—salary from Rossi Industries went to pay for her mother's stay at the rehab centre in South America from her very first pay cheque. What wasn't eaten up by rent had gone into the props Issy had needed to grab the attention of the notoriously extravagant Gianni Rossi. Issy had contributed what she could from her salary as an auxiliary nurse at the children's hospital, when she wasn't spending hours online hunting down every single little bit of information she could get on the Rossi cousins. *Everything* the two girls had done had been streamlined to ensure that as much time and finances as possible could be poured into a vendetta she had instigated. And it had all been for nothing.

Because Alessandro and Gianni had done nothing wrong. There had never been any corruption on their parts. They were completely innocent and she had sabotaged the business owned by the soon-to-be father of her child.

As Alessandro opened a door, she rushed out into the courtyard taking huge gulps of much-needed fresh air. Because if their unborn child were going to have any hopes at a better life than either of its parents, then she would need Alessandro Rossi's help. And she had absolutely no idea if he would give it to her.

Alessandro watched Amelia, hands braced against her thighs, bent at the waist, taking giant breaths of the cool morning air. Gone was the perfectly poised controlled employee who had impressed, not just her manager, his board, but himself with her quick, smart, intelligent and controlled approach to the projects. Gone, too, was the passionate, sensual woman with a desire that eclipsed common sense in a way that was only matched by his own.

But all he could think, all he could hear in his head

on a loop, was *you're pregnant*. He felt strangely numb, recognising dimly that the shock of it had robbed him of any sense. He was going to be a father.

But the images that word threw at him were not the kind of loving, doting parent that inspired the kind of loyalty that had driven Amelia to attempt revenge. They were the kind that brought him out in a cold sweat.

He hated that in front of him was a woman in quite obvious emotional turmoil and all he could feel was panic. He looked away as Amelia pulled herself up straight and felt her gaze on him, even though he wished for the world to be anywhere but here in that moment.

'I can't…imagine what you must think of me.'

'I'm trying very hard not to form an opinion right now, because I don't have all the facts and I don't like jumping to conclusions,' he announced while his molars groaned under the intense pressure of his tightened jaw. It wasn't a lie; he was very close to an edge she had driven him to.

'This… I…' She shook her head, words coming hard for both of them, clearly. She took a deep breath, as if she knew that this was important. To him, to her, he didn't know any more, but he couldn't help but admire the strength she drew on to stand before him under the weight of his scrutiny—a scrutiny that had buckled many a lesser person.

'This wasn't part of the plan. Sleeping with you, or the baby.'

His heart pounded in his chest. Her declaration tapped into a question he'd struggled with from the very first moment Gianni had called him. Did he believe her? He studied her, head held high, back straight, shoulders drawn down. She looked like a soldier facing a firing squad, who had spoken her final words. She met and held his gaze, the pale green orbs so open it was as if she'd flung back the shutters and was asking him to look deep within her. Instead, he looked away and missed the slash of hurt that nearly rocked her on her feet.

'It's yours.'

Cristo. That he hadn't even considered any other possibility showed just how powerful a spell she had cast on him. He nodded to convey his understanding but still couldn't look at her. He went to pull at his collar, to relieve the tightness around his throat, only to find that it was already open. Intensely disliking that she might have caught the sign of his discomfort, he moved his hand to the back of his neck, his fingers brushing against the cold sweat that was gathering there with alarming frequency whenever Amelia was near.

Think it through. Be rational, he ordered himself. He had used a condom and even if she had lied about being on contraception, the chances were slim that pregnancy could have been a secured outcome. And after two years at his company, he might not know her—the *real* her— but she couldn't hide the way she thought. He'd seen it in the choices she made, how she approached and assessed a project, the solutions she offered to problems. And at the very least he knew that she would never have created a plan around a possible pregnancy resulting from one single night with him, that couldn't have been guaranteed in itself.

'So Hong Kong was...' he asked, wanting to know.

She shook her head and looked away, a blush rising to her cheeks and the gentle shrug of her shoulder, the fine bones there marked by his oversized T-shirt. It appeared she was as unable to explain that night as he was.

When she looked back at him, she was squinting up

at him, the early morning Tuscan sun turning her brown hair into burnished gold, her pale skin into a sunburst as if even the morning were conspiring against him.

'What now?' she asked.

That was a very good question.

CHAPTER SIX

AMELIA FOUND THE KITCHEN. It was bigger than her flat in Brockley and it made her heart thud. The countertops looked like—and most probably were—marble. She and Issy had money growing up. *Before.* But nothing like this. This was…unfathomable.

She ran her fingers across the cool slabs of white, shot through with grey. It would have looked clinical had it not been for the deep brown wooden floorboards and the copper fixtures. There was a large twenty-seater table between the counter and the floor-to-ceiling windows that wrapped around the entire ground floor of the villa's main building. Having worked out the coffee machine and made herself a decaffeinated espresso, she had been too uncomfortable to sit at the table. The thought of Alessandro sitting here to eat, all by himself, it just… it had made her heart ache in a way she tried to ignore.

He had retired to finally get some sleep, but the warning he'd left her with still sounded in her ears.

Do not think of trying to leave, Amelia.

Oh, she wanted to. She wanted to run. Wished she could click her fingers and be back in Brockley with her sister. Which had just made her worry about Issy. What was she doing now? Was she with Gianni? Was she okay?

Feeling a little unbalanced, she made her way to the sunken seating area facing a fireplace—the mixture of modern and new creating a sense of old comfort that was so lovely she couldn't help but sink into the lush leather. Leaning back, she felt something poke into her hip. Turning, she saw her handbag, and inside she found her phone.

It had signal! Alessandro must have forgotten to turn the signal jammer back on. Without thinking, her fingers had hit call on Issy's number. And then she hung up before it could connect.

What would she tell her sister about her pregnancy? How would she explain herself? How could she ever apologise enough for lying to her and setting them on a path of revenge that was so wholly misdirected?

The questions piled up one after the other, making her head swim. It was her fault they were in this mess, but she couldn't afford to wallow in self-pity. She needed to know if Issy was okay, so she hit the call button again. Her heart dropped when an automated response told her the phone was not in use. Unease swept through her, but she reminded herself that Alessandro and Gianni were not the monsters they had thought they were. And while Issy was impulsive and chaotic in the most adorable way, there was only so much trouble she could get herself into.

No. At this point, Amelia really needed to think about the trouble *she* was in. But trouble felt like the wrong word. Because she couldn't use that word and think of the child growing within her.

It had surprised her, really. It had been like the swell of a wave, starting slowly at first but growing larger and larger until it became an unstoppable feeling, gathering momentum and washing aside everything in its path. This immoveable force had whispered into her heart and soul and she had felt utterly and irrevocably changed by it.

She wanted this baby.

It was a knowing, settling deep into her very being— standing out in stark contrast to Alessandro's feelings.

Because she hadn't missed the way he had looked at her. Hadn't missed the accusation in his gaze, or the sense of something deeper, swelling beneath it all like a monster from the deep. He didn't want this, but for some reason she was sure that it had nothing to do with her attempts to sabotage Rossi Industries. And an ache began to form in her chest. She rubbed at her sternum, wondering whether the decaf coffee was to blame, but really she knew. She knew that it was because of what she had seen in Alessandro's gaze. Fear and alarm.

And on some level, she could understand. A child was a huge responsibility. One that would not only change her life but connect her to Alessandro for ever. It would be all consuming with, or without, his help and it would change the very essence of who she was.

But it could also be a beautiful thing, her heart whispered. One she wanted so much she could scarcely bear to hope for it. A child that she would love and never reject, never subjugate to her own needs. A child that would have so much more of a chance than she and Issy ever had.

Guilt swirled heavily in her stomach. Issy had lost so much, sacrificed so much for a vendetta that she had instigated. Had her mother known? That their father had been corrupt? That he had sold land knowing it wasn't fit for development? That he had conned people—people who had put everything they had into their plans? People like Alessandro and Gianni. So much had been lost to her father's greed. Who would she and Issy have become had they not spent ten years on this path of vengeance? Where would they be now?

Free.

The thought came unbidden to her mind and for such a soft word it hit her with the force of a truck, rocking her to her core.

Standing in the doorway, he saw her sway. The phone he'd seen her use to make a call—probably to her sister—hung listlessly from her fingers. He fought against every instinct he had to go to her. Earlier that morning, he might have. But he'd managed at least four hours' sleep and now he was thinking more clearly.

This woman had committed an act of sabotage against his business. Her motivation mattered little. She had done something to Rossi Industries and before he could even think about her pregnancy, he needed to know what she'd done. Only once that was resolved, could they talk about...

His gaze landed on her stomach, knowing that there would not be any signs of the baby she carried for at least another three months. Instead of letting his thoughts linger there, he took in the rest of her. She was dressed in the clothes he'd put out for her before he'd retreated to his room. Despite the way she had rolled the waistband of the trousers, they still hung a little low on her hips.

He probably could have raided Gianni's compound, fairly sure that there would be some women's clothing left behind by one of his lovers, but the thought of dressing Amelia in another woman's clothes made him faintly nauseous. Instead, he'd found a shirt from years ago, before he'd filled out into the broad shoulders he was now used to. Still large on her, she'd twisted the edges of the shirt into a knot and somehow looked carelessly fashionable. *Desirable.*

No. In his mind a hand slashed through his thoughts, sending them scattering. Enough. Ever since the phone call from Gianni, he had been on the back foot. With so much at stake, he needed to take control of the situation.

'Amelia,' he said, calling her attention to him. When she came out of her thoughts, her gaze cleared enough to look at where he was gesturing to the table. She returned her phone to her bag and left it on the sofa, slowly making her way to a table she eyed with discomfort.

'Would you prefer to talk elsewhere?' he asked, not out of consideration for her feelings, he told himself, but more for curiosity.

'What, for Interrogation Take Two?' she asked, a forced lightness to her tone attempting to take the sting out of her words as she sat on the opposite side of the table. He eyed her coffee cup with a suspicion that must have been obvious because she defensively explained that it was decaf.

He sat down and rolled his shoulders, trying not to pull at the collar of the shirt he had dressed in. Earlier it had made him feel in control, but now that Amelia was dressed more casually, it felt almost puritanical and obvious. As if he were trying too hard to maintain a boundary between them that had already been obliterated.

'Obviously the...' baby '...*pregnancy* changes a lot. But I need to know what you did,' he said.

Her eyes flared, guilty slashes painting the paleness of her cheeks a glowing red, and his stomach dropped.

'It's the Aurora project,' she confessed. 'I'm sorry, if I'd known—'

'Just that? Or are there any other projects that are at risk?' he interrupted, his thoughts scrambling to damage limitation. The instinct to call his CFO was riding him hard, but he didn't know if there was more.

'No. Just Aurora.'

He nodded once. 'Is it salvageable?' he asked, a buzz ringing in his ears. It had been a project he'd spent years on. One that would be visible from his father and uncle's vineyard, it was meant to be not only Rossi Industries' crowning glory, but the final twist of the knife in his father and uncle's back.

She bit her lip. Neither lush nor pouty, her mouth shouldn't have been cause for any kind of fascination— but still he noticed the way the top lip line was more straight than curved, the bottom lip marginally fuller than its partner, exposed by the straight white teeth pinning and blooming the soft pink flesh—

Dio mio, he needed to get a grip.

'Have the contracts been signed?' she asked, shoving him back into the conversation at hand.

Before he'd caught the few hours of sleep he'd needed, he'd managed to get a message out to his staff to stop any paperwork going through at all on any project. It had caused absolute chaos, but clearly it had been worth it.

'Have they?' she asked in the face of his silence.

He was tempted to let her stew, but that seemed almost petty now.

'No.'

She breathed a huge sigh of relief, her head falling into her hands, before she swept the hair back from her face and he caught a glimpse of the woman he had worked beside for two years.

She nodded as if to herself. 'It's Firstview. They don't have the capability to see the project through.'

'We would have picked that up,' he said, dismissing her statement.

'I made sure you didn't.'

He scoffed.

She raised an eyebrow and he got worried.

'How?' he demanded.

'They hid it well enough, but I knew what to look for and I erased or covered the things they hadn't managed to hide.'

'You falsified documents?'

'Yes.'

He shook his head in disbelief. They would never have found it. She could have got away with it, and the damage to the Aurora project—the knock-on effect for not only that project's contracts, but their finance repayments, the partnerships, their reputation—it could have bankrupted them. He struggled to fight back the wave of poisonous anger.

'Does anyone else in the company know? Do you have anyone else in the company working with you?'

'No and no,' she replied clearly and without hesitation.

'You did all this on your own?'

'Mostly,' she admitted with some reluctance.

'Your sister,' he realised. 'And what does she have to do with it?'

'She was to distract Gianni and keep him away until the Aurora project contracts are signed. We knew that were the two of you together it was likely you'd uncover something to bring our plan crashing down.' Amelia looked away, unable to meet his gaze.

'Issy doesn't know,' she confessed, guilt and shame eating at her. 'Anything she does…it's…she's innocent.'

Alessandro looked down on her, disgust pouring from him, and it was nothing she didn't deserve.

'Why?'

Amelia could have pretended to misunderstand his question. Remind him she was getting vengeance for her father, but that wasn't what he was asking. Alessandro valued loyalty above all else, it was clear from his work ethics and his relationship with Gianni. She had shamed herself by lying to her sister and involving her in the first place and Alessandro wanted to know why.

A jagged breath tore through her lungs. Could she admit to him that *he* was the reason? That ever since whatever madness had taken over them in Hong Kong, she'd not been able to sleep without dreaming of him? That she'd walk through The Ruby in London, her skin a hair's breadth from fire every single day because she might round a corner and see him? That her heart was constantly running too fast or too slow, depending on whether she had a meeting with him? That after ten years of wanting his destruction, all she wanted was his touch?

She was about to answer but he cut her off with a huff of bitterness. 'Would it even matter if you did answer? I have no idea which Amelia I'd get.'

A frown cracked through the mask she was trying to hastily adopt but his quick gaze snagged on it.

'The perfect employee? The traitor?' he clarified unnecessarily.

But he was wrong. Issy was the one who had adopted a persona, who had made herself into exactly what Gianni liked—half starving herself into a smaller physique, wearing heels for his desired height, dying her hair to his preferred blonde. But Amelia? She had been herself. She hadn't had to change at all because she'd enjoyed her work. Deep down, she could admit to herself that she'd even been thrilled by it. The cut and thrust of it. The success of projects was *her* success. The pleasure she took from impressing the powerful figures in Rossi Industries. No. Deep down, one of the most painful regrets would be that she would actually miss it when she was no longer there.

'The seducer?' Alessandro's question burst through her thoughts.

'No.' The denial rose to her lips before she could call it back. She deserved his scepticism, but their child deserved more. Their baby that was little more than a few cells held together by hope and possibility. A hope that seemed to pour from her soul in an endless stream. 'No,' she repeated, this time with more strength and meeting the storm in his eyes. 'I told you before, that was nothing to do with the plan.'

'And you expect me to believe that?' he all but spat.

'Frankly, I don't expect you to believe anything that comes out of my mouth ever again,' she admitted and seemed to have shocked him. 'But you have a situation that only *I* can resolve.'

Alessandro went deadly still, his eyes going from stormy to horrified before passing to shock, sending her headlong into an ocean of emotion that she hadn't expected.

'No!' she exclaimed, her hands flying to her abdomen as if to physically protect their child. 'No,' she said, pushing away from the table, the chair screeching against the floor painfully. She walked along the window line to the far end of the table, looking out at the meadow. She knew that there were many options out there and that this wasn't a decision that should be made lightly. But she also knew the truth of her heart, so she turned back to Alessandro and said, 'I'm sorry if I hadn't made that clear but I'm keeping the baby. Whether you're a part of their life or not, I am having this baby.'

He stared at her, his gaze again unfathomable, his silence absolute. It was as if he were giving her all the rope he could in the hope that she might somehow hang herself with it.

'I meant Aurora. I can save Aurora. I *want* to. Please let me help?'

Instead of relief she saw disbelief and it angered her, even though she knew it was deserved.

'I think I'll handle it from here on out,' he replied, his words dripping with disdain.

'Well, good luck with that,' she replied, sarcastically.

'What's that supposed to mean?' he demanded, leaning back into his chair, even though instinctively she knew that he wanted to close the distance, to crowd her, dominate, and Amelia bit back a curse. Why did that set her pulse racing? Why did that determined look flare between her legs and make her ache with want?

She blinked and the moment was gone. While her heart rate settled to something as close to normal as possible, she gathered herself to answer his question.

'You've only two options now. You give up the project or find another partner. Chapel Developments won't touch you—their CEO doesn't like to be considered second best. And yes, you could have another team at RI look through the project to see if they can find an alternative, but you don't have time. The quotes, the projections, the contracts are all time sensitive. With the cost of materials changing near daily, you've got a month, at most, and that's being generous. And you have no one that could vet an alternative partner and do the ground-work to build a relationship that could support the part-nership in that time.'

'No one other than you,' he said, zeroing in on her point.

'I know this project inside out. I know the players… and I know the substitutes.'

'You have someone in mind.'

'I do.'

'Who?'

She stared at him as he waited for an answer. This was her only bargaining chip. This was her only chance to make a deal that would force him to listen to what she had to say. To what she *needed* to say. This was the one and only time she would get to set the tone for her future, for their child's future, and if she got it wrong, it would be disastrous for them all.

Dio, she was good. Glorious even. She had been made for the cut and thrust of the boardroom, of his world. Her mind was sharp, her intellect quick, and her confidence? He might not be quite sure about who she was half the time but no, that wasn't fake at all. He was turned on. Not by her body, but by *her* and he hated it. Hated how dangerous and traitorous this woman truly was.

'I will tell you, but I want something in exchange.'

He shouldn't have been surprised, but he was still somehow insulted and disappointed at the same time.

'How much?' He pushed the words through teeth he'd ground together.

She blinked as if shocked by his words and he begrudgingly had to admit, she was a very good actress. But she was an actress that was also going to be the mother of his child. The reminder cut through him like a knife.

'How much what?' she asked through pale lips.

'Money? How much money do you want?'

The shutters came down and for a moment he thought that he might have it wrong. She turned around and looked out at the meadow her father had sold him all those years ago. She probably didn't even know that it was that particular plot of land and perversely he wanted to keep that from her.

She looked away, her words spoken to him over her shoulder. 'I don't want money. I wanted a…détente.'

'You want to make peace, while holding back the fix to a problem *you* created?' he demanded, wondering at the brass balls on the woman he'd got pregnant.

'I wanted for us to try to start again without all this,' she said, weaving a hand back and forth between them before shrugging her slender shoulders. 'I wanted us to be able to have a conversation about what we're going to do about our child, without wanting to tear each other raw.' There was a helplessness in her eyes that he couldn't deny—fake or not, and he was leaning towards the latter. 'I wanted us to find a way forward that wasn't destroyed by the past, but I can see now that's impossible.'

Her breath caught, the old linen shirt she wore stretched across her chest, and he dragged his eyes away before he could be distracted by her again.

Our child.

Alessandro had done everything he could to honour the promise he'd made his father—he'd been so determined that his direct bloodline would end with him, that he'd never—not even once—allowed for any other possibility. He'd been happy with that. Welcomed it even.

But his child was growing within Amelia Seymore. A real child and deep within him something turned—years and years of determination and belief were twisting and morphing beneath the weight of something else. His child was here and no matter how he'd thought he'd feel in that moment, and he was feeling a lot, it *wasn't* horror. It *wasn't* anger, or disappointment. As scary as it was, it felt something like hope. The hope that maybe he could do better, be better, than his own father. That he could provide his child with more than he'd ever had, with a better life than he'd ever imagined for himself. And now that determination to end his bloodline seemed petty in comparison to the feeling of protectiveness pouring through him with the power of a tsunami.

He looked back to where Amelia stood, shoulders slumped in defeat, breath almost painfully slow in comparison to what it had been only moments ago.

'You want peace? You want to start again?'

Amelia turned, her eyes filled with such hope—hope that was worryingly close to the way she had looked up at him that night in Hong Kong, as if she were half afraid that he'd say no to their one night and half afraid that he'd say yes. Just as it had that night, her gaze had cleared and a truth had come pouring into her gaze.

'Yes.'

Could he do it? Start afresh with her?

He *had* to. She was carrying his child. Their child. And no, he would never trust her. That bond had been broken irrevocably. But that didn't mean they couldn't at the least be cordial. Whatever happened, he would ensure that his child grew up in a world nothing like his own childhood. He would do whatever it took.

'Who?' he demanded, forcing to push through the exchange, because his first goal was to make sure that Rossi Industries didn't fall because the mother of his child had sabotaged it.

'I don't think you're going to like it.'

'There's a lot that I don't like at the moment. This will be the least of it, I'd imagine.'

She had the grace to look away.

'Who?' he demanded again.

'Sofia Obeid.'

He pinched the bridge of his nose. 'Amelia,' he said, not knowing whether he was cursing her or begging her.

'I know what you think of her,' she said, her hands gesturing for patience or peace, he wasn't sure which. 'But hers is the only company with the capital to help see Aurora to fruition within the timeline and without incurring incredibly painful financial penalties.'

He glared up at her, frustration and intense irritation coursing through him. Sofia Obeid had a reputation for being incredibly difficult and impossible to work with. Not that RI would know as she had refused to take a meeting or even a phone call from the Rossi cousins before now.

'What makes you think you can get a meeting with her?'

'Because I can,' she replied simply.

He scowled as he took in the way the sun streamed in the window and slipped through the linen shirt to outline the subtle curves of the woman not only carrying his child, but who had clearly been sent to test him to his very limits.

'Please. I want a chance to fix this, but I also want a chance to start again,' she said, courage and something like hope shining in her eyes. 'A chance for our child to have more than we did.'

And he was helpless to refuse. 'Okay. But before we do anything, we need to get you some clothes of your own.'

CHAPTER SEVEN

ALESSANDRO WOULD USUALLY have driven himself, but he needed all his wits around him with Amelia present, so had reached out to the driver he kept on staff. In the distance he could see their destination, the city of Orvieto, sitting on a large stretch of rock rising dramatically and almost vertically from the surrounding landscape.

While they were out, his staff would air the main part of the house and fill the kitchen with whatever they might need for the next week and disappear as if they'd never been there. No matter what she said about wanting to rectify her sabotage, Alessandro wanted to keep the people Amelia interacted with to a minimum. He still couldn't be sure that she was telling him the truth.

Liar.

He refused to acknowledge his conscience's taunt. He disliked that her desire to make amends had softened his response to her, but her solution? He pressed a closed fist lightly against his mouth. Sofia Obeid. Of all the people that Amelia could have offered up as a new partner on the Aurora project, why did it have to be the one woman who had refused until now to give them even the time of day? Alessandro and Gianni had considered and discarded her before the start of the project because of that. Amelia wasn't wrong—she was their best option, and if

Amelia could get Obeid to sit down with them then who was he to argue?

Alessandro wanted to speak to Gianni. But he'd tried his mobile again last night and couldn't get through. Deep down, Alessandro knew that he could have tried to reach him on St Lovells, Gianni's private island, but what would he have said? That he'd not only opened them up to sabotage, but he'd managed to get their enemy pregnant? He didn't need to speak to Gianni about the project because he knew what his cousin would say. *Do what you need to do. And get it done.* Alessandro didn't need Gianni's permission—he needed absolution.

Amelia sat in the car beside him, picking at the bed of her thumbnail, and he wanted nothing more than to slap her hands apart and tell her to stop. Because the sign of deep worry made him feel like a monster. Because…his mother had used to do the same exact thing, each night while she waited for his father to come in from the vineyards. But he was nothing like his father and she was nothing like his mother. Amelia Seymore was hardly an innocent in all this.

Her mobile phone beeped and he resisted the urge to try and check the screen in case it was a message from her sister. Instead he looked out of the window as they drew closer to the city famous for the defensive walls built from the same rock on which it sat, the stunningly beautiful duomo with its striking white and green façade, and some reasonably decent wine. Certainly, better than anything his father and uncle had produced on their vineyards.

I don't care if your fingers are bleeding or your back hurts. You will not stop until these grapes are harvested, do you hear me, boy?

'Alessandro? Did you hear me?' Amelia's soft voice punctuated the hold his memory had on him and he turned to look at her. A shadow passed across her face before she turned back to her phone. 'Sofia has agreed to meet. But the window is tight. She says she is considering a similar proposition—'

Alessandro scoffed. 'Doubtful. There is nothing remotely similar out there to Aurora.'

Amelia nodded in agreement. 'She's willing to meet us in Marrakesh tomorrow, but she has warned us not to get our hopes up.'

'Playing hard to get?'

'Most definitely. She's interested but cautious. Historically her company has partnered with those with a longer track record than RI.'

'What makes you think this will work?' he asked, genuinely curious.

'Because she will respect who you are and what you have done,' she replied.

'Why? You didn't?' he said, his tone darker than he'd intended. He hated losing his legendary control around her. Her compliment—intended or not—had grated, but not as much as the way she simply took his harsh retort as her due. Feeling disconcertingly mean, he was about to apologise when their driver pulled to a stop at the pedestrian area within Orvieto's walls.

Instinctively after exiting the car, he came around the vehicle to open the door for Amelia. She was back in the clothes she'd travelled to Italy in and, despite the slight creases, she looked composed and collected. The way she had looked to him for the two years before Hong Kong. Because after? After Hong Kong, all he'd seen was lust and want and need.

Shaking off the thought, he saw her eyes soften as she looked into the old town in Orvieto.

'What?' he asked, curious to see the city through her eyes.

She gazed up at him, the answer on the tip of her tongue, but looked away as she answered him in a small voice. 'We talked about coming here—my family—when I was younger.'

He tried to temper the anger that rose in him at the mention of her family—of her father. What was it about this woman that pushed buttons that had lain dormant for years? She cleared her throat as if aware of the impact of her words and slowly made her way towards the open square in the heart of Orvieto. He watched her go, letting her rebuild her armour piece by piece—because he *wasn't* a monster.

Catching up with her a few moments later, he gestured with his head towards the shopping district where Gucci sat next to Ferragamo, Dolce and Gabbana rubbed shoulders with Tom Ford.

Her steps slowed, pulling his attention back to her.

'Something wrong?' he asked, his patience wearing thin.

'I can't… These shops…' She stared at them with an expression that somehow merged shame and embarrassment. 'I can't afford them,' she concluded on a whisper.

Fury etched his body into hard lines. He closed the distance between them in a stride, letting loose only a fraction of the anger that was almost constantly simmering beneath the surface whenever she was near.

'What game are you playing now?' he demanded.

Confusion blew her eyes wide open. 'I don't know what you mean—'

Outrage poured through him. He'd given her the dé-
tente she'd asked for, he was trusting her with so damn
much and she was *still* trying to pull the wool over
his eyes. 'I know exactly how much I pay my staff, so
don't try the "poor me" pity act,' he forced out through
clenched teeth.

Amelia took a step back from the overpowering wave
of his frustration. Nostrils flaring and breathing hard,
Alessandro looked pushed beyond an edge she'd never
even seen him close to and that she had done this to such
a powerful man filled her with shame, but also with an
anger to match his own.

So instead of backing down, she stepped forward,
stealing back some of that righteous indignation that had
fuelled her for years.

'Yes, you pay your staff very well, Alessandro, but how
many of your staff have student loans to pay off?' She
jabbed an angry finger at him that he stared at in outrage.
'How many of your staff have to pay not only for their
own needs but those of their sisters?' She stepped into
him again, losing some of the control that restraint had
given her. 'How many of your staff have to pay for their
mother's rehab facility in South America? How many of
your staff had to be a parent to their own mother and father when they were just fifteen years old?'

The shock in his gaze cut through her fury and she realised what she'd just revealed. She pulled back her hand,
covering her mouth and shaking, and turned away. She
heard the approach of two tourists so she crossed the
cobbled street to lose herself in a shop window displaying an inconceivable amount of fridge magnets.

She forced herself to calm down—it wasn't just her

any more that she had to think of. But the venom in his tone—the anger. They would *never* get past it. How on earth was she supposed to raise a child with a man who hated her?

How do you even know he wants to?

'I didn't…' His voice behind her was thick and rough, like the crunch of gravel. He cleared his throat. 'I didn't know.'

'Isn't that the point?' she asked, feeling helpless. 'I believe you said that you didn't want to know or care.'

He had the good grace to look about as shamed as she'd seen him—which extended to the clench of a jaw she wanted to soothe, and the fisting of his palms she wanted to release. Seeing him anything other than determined and powerful felt wrong somehow, as if she'd caught a glimpse of a vulnerability that few saw.

He took a breath—for patience or strength, she couldn't tell—and it emerged from his lips on a sigh that she felt gently against the nape of her neck.

'Are you hungry?' he asked, his tone an awkward shade of gentle.

She nodded and let him guide her away from the shop window, down the cobbled street, and towards a little café with seats overlooking the city walls and down into the stunning patchwork quilt of fields interspersed by the tall, thin cypress trees that made it look so different from England.

She ignored the exchange of Italian between Alessandro and the manager, who seemed desperately eager to find them only the best table in the café. She ignored it because she was numb.

Because she realised what she had been doing—that she had been trying to distract herself from the fact that she was having a baby with a man who hated her. That she was about to have a child that would look to her to show them how to be, how to behave, how to see the world and how to love. And she didn't want that child raised in anger or arguments. She didn't want that child raised in struggle, or instability, as she and Issy had been.

Alessandro appeared at her side, and she let him guide her by the arm to the small, white-cloth-covered table. She took a seat as the waiter poured ice-cold water into their glasses and disappeared. Not once had Alessandro looked at her since they arrived.

'We can't keep at each other like this.'

'No, we can't,' he agreed.

Amelia looked at her hands, at the bitten skin around her thumb, knowing that it was a sign of distress and worry. Their baby deserved more than this. She wanted Alessandro to understand her. She needed him to know where she came from and what had pushed her to do what she had done. Only then might they have a chance to move on from the hurts of the past.

'I... After my father lost the business,' she explained, 'he wouldn't work for anyone else. He was a proud man, but no longer had the capital or will to start over. Whatever income he had went into pretending that we hadn't lost everything, for a while at least. My parents spent more money in those first months than I think they had when they'd had the financial security to do so.'

'That is unforgivable.'

She might deep down agree, but there was still a large part of her that wanted to defend her parents, wanted—needed—to see them as the victims. Because if they hadn't been, then how could they have allowed what happened next?

'It wasn't long before we were forced to sell the house. To downsize. We moved to a different area in London, to a different school where Issy and I didn't fit in. Without his money and largess, the people Dad had thought of as friends soon lost interest. Mum became bitter and Dad became mean. His drinking got out of hand and the physical and financial toll was irreparable.

'I tried to keep the worst of it from Issy, but by that point she was old enough to see what was going on. It's a miracle that she didn't veer off the rails and rebel.'

Alessandro was beginning to suspect it was less to do with miracles and more to do with Amelia and the strength she had to keep what was left of her family together. 'And your mother?' he couldn't help but ask.

For the first time since he'd known her Amelia actually looked defeated. 'She never recovered. She loved him so much, but she had also loved that lifestyle and without either she just gave up. She started leaning on anything that would help her escape the reality of her new life.'

Her words shattered something old and brittle deep within him, resonating with the exact frequency he had felt himself. He knew what it was like to be let down by not just one but two parents and while he would never, *ever*, blame his mother, nor would he forgive her her betrayal. Because if she had kept her word, then the world would be a very different place right now. He opened his mouth to say something, to try and reassure Amelia as he'd never been quite able to reassure himself, but she continued.

'It was…difficult, trying to make sure Issy and I had what we needed. But we made it happen.'

Amelia left a lot unsaid, but he could imagine her

struggle had been incredibly hard, fighting her mother at every turn. He could see how she had become the head of the family and how, just in the way she described it, she had done so without question or complaint. Perhaps it hadn't even occurred to her that she shouldn't have had to. And against his will he felt guilt. Guilt over his involvement that had left two children so vulnerable.

'And we had you.'

Her words surprised him.

'You and Gianni became a focus for us. Became something that drew us together and drove us forward. Our need to avenge our father gave us strength even in the darkest of times. While our mother wallowed, we used our thirst for revenge to get us up in the morning and keep us going. And while I am truly sorry for what I have done to Rossi Industries, I…we…needed it.'

In her eyes, he saw only truth and he couldn't stop the understanding blooming in his chest. He knew how strong that drive and purpose could be, the power it could provide, but he still struggled with what could have happened to Rossi Industries and the thousands of people employed there.

'Is that why you thought we were corrupt?' he asked.

She bit her lip before answering. 'I needed you to be. Because I needed to blame someone—anyone—that wasn't the two people who were supposed to be…my parents, my guides, my role models.'

Once again, her words and his childhood began to fold together and he wasn't sure how to feel about it. He sighed and gave up the urge to fight the sympathetic feelings trying to emerge.

'I understand. If I'd had someone to blame for my parents' misdeeds, I would have,' he admitted. Something flared in her gaze. Surprise, shock...that indefinable thing that had sparked one night in Hong Kong and had yet to blow out.

Connection.

Alessandro batted the errant thought away, instead focusing on the fact that she had given him something, and he felt the unaccountable need to meet her in kind. But could he do it? Gianni was the only other person on the planet who knew where they came from, the rest of the world believing that the Rossi cousins were placed on this earth as fully formed, financially powerful property gods.

'This wasn't supposed to happen,' he admitted, opening his hand to the skies.

'You and me, or me and...'

'Both?' he admitted, even as a fist twisted his gut and something close to pain roared in his body to take the words back, as if it were sacrilege to say such a thing to the woman carrying his child. He could see that his words had struck her just as hard and hastened to explain, even when speaking of his childhood was the last thing he'd ever willingly talk about.

'My father was...*is*...he *still* is...a despicable man. He is mean, violent, prejudiced, ignorant and vile in the worst ways. And he doesn't have an alcohol addiction to excuse it.' His voice was rough, scratched out from hatred and hurt. 'Gianni and I grew up on a vineyard in Umbria. I am assuming you know this?'

Amelia nodded. 'You and Gianni have never tried to hide your beginnings. And even if you had, Issy would have found it.'

'I'm beginning to think we might have employed the wrong Seymore,' he said, genuinely impressed by the accurate and detailed research Isabelle Seymore had seemed to gather. He was momentarily distracted by the slight curve of Amelia's lip, her pride in her sister something he respected and understood.

'No, we're not ashamed of our humble beginnings, but we don't like to think on it much. It wasn't a nice place to grow up for either Gianni or myself. We certainly don't talk about it.'

'Then why are you talking about it now?'

'Because you need to understand where I'm coming from as much as I needed to understand you.'

She nodded, slowly, that connection again becoming stronger between them.

'Vizzini Vineyards produces a really quite disappointing Sangiovese. My father and his brother have neither the patience nor the interest to produce anything but. The ground is hard and barely fertile, and my father and uncle too stubborn, too mean and too lazy to do anything about it.

'But every day they go out there and ravage the land and vines as if they might actually one day produce something that would be half decent and make them rich beyond their wildest dreams.

'It will never happen,' Alessandro stated adamantly. 'But that didn't stop them from forcing Gianni and me to work ourselves to the bone.' He huffed out a bitter laugh. 'You want to know why we're so successful? Yes, we're hungry for it, yes, we're determined, but what puts us above everyone else? We were born breaking ourselves; it's in our blood, not by nature, but by nurture. Our only saving grace was our *nonna*. She was the only person that could still the hand of my father and his brother. She was devastated by her sons' abuse and helped us as much as she could, protecting our mothers and us. It is why we chose her maiden name as our surname.'

* * *

His eyes softened, making him look so utterly different from the man that ruled boardrooms with an unquestionable authority and conviction, that seared ineptitude away with a single look. This was a youth who had loved and hurt, who was soft and warm. Gianni and Alessandro could have easily each taken their own mother's maiden name. But they had chosen someone who had loved and tried to protect them, they had chosen something that bonded them together as a family, perhaps even closer than brothers, despite only being cousins.

But then his face darkened, as if a cloud had covered the sun.

'She passed when Gianni and I were eight years old.'

His loss was so palpable that Amelia wanted to reach for him, but he had waded too far into the waters of his memories.

'After that, there was nothing holding my father and uncle back. They treated us little better than slaves, working the fields and the machinery during the day, and being their punching bags at night.'

'What about your mother? Gianni's mother?' she asked, unconsciously echoing his earlier question to her.

Alessandro looked away. 'Mine was unable to help,' he said, the simple words concealing so, so very much. 'And Gianni's story is his own.' He shook off her question and turned back to the table.

'My father used to say, "The Vizzini name is all that matters." He was obsessed with it. Every single day, he would say, "It will live on for generations to come." And I promised him, the day that I left, that the Vizzini name, the blood in his veins…it would end with me. It is—*was*—the only vengeance I could take against him.'

He said it looking deep into her eyes, opening himself to her so that she would understand, that she would know the truth—the depth of his promise. And she did. She knew the power of such a promise. Her heart ached for the boy he had been but it also ached for the child they had made together and the future that she had barely hoped for that was beginning to disappear like sand on the wind.

'But now that promise doesn't matter,' he dismissed. Eyes that had been so expressive moments before, so free with their emotions, shuttered, the barrier falling between them with shocking speed and ferocity. 'The child will never even hear of the Vizzini name if I have my way.' There was a determination that she had never seen from Alessandro darkening his words to a level that sounded almost threatening, but not. Amelia realised that it was more like an oath or a promise.

'I need you to hear this and know this.' He pinned her with a steady gaze that she couldn't look away from. 'Our child will not want for anything. *Everything* I have is theirs. I don't know what the future holds for us, but no matter what—our child will be protected from anything it is in my power to protect them from.'

Amelia's heart pounded in her chest. The vehemence in his words, his promise, wrapped tightly around her, but rather than suffocating, it was comforting. A fear that she hadn't realised she'd had eased. Yes, she'd known that she could find a way to provide for herself and her child alone if she'd needed to. Issy would have helped without question. But Issy—bright, beautiful Issy—deserved more, she deserved not to be held back by family vendettas or obligations.

But what did his promise mean for her? Did he want to raise their child together? Did he want more? The thought of sharing a family with Alessandro, of sharing that responsibility, of working together to care for their child without fighting, bickering or mistrust... That was something that lived in a fantasy tied deeply to one night in Hong Kong that she couldn't yet bring herself to name.

She knew Alessandro was still angry, and he clearly didn't trust her, both of which he had a right to. But Alessandro was also a man who loved his grandmother, who was loyal to his cousin beyond all else. She knew and appreciated the tenets he lived by. She knew *him*. He was a good man.

That was why she'd been forced to lie to Issy, who would never have embarked on their plan unless Amelia had promised her proof of that corruption. Because Amelia had known, even then, that there was no proof. That this strong, powerful, proud and determined Italian would never have done such a thing. So she had launched them into their vendetta in a bid to be free of a man she was hopelessly and irrevocably falling for. She bit her teeth together to force back her feelings again.

Because wanting a man who would protect her the way he had promised to protect their child—the way no one had ever promised to protect *her*—was a hope too far. Willing back the wet heat pressing against her eyes, she could at least hope for something smaller. If she could help him save the Aurora deal, she could hope for a place to start at least.

CHAPTER EIGHT

As THE PLANE banked into a hard turn, steeply angling the private jet, Alessandro felt his stomach drop. He looked across the cabin to where Amelia accepted a glass of orange juice from the air steward with a smile that did things to him. He'd checked with Dr Moretti three times that it was safe for Amelia to fly at this stage of her pregnancy. The concern he felt for her, the *possessiveness*, had shocked him. For years he'd been determined to ensure that his father's blood ended with him.

But now? Now that Amelia was carrying his child, when his mind wandered it went to a place where there was a dark-haired child wrapped safely in their mother's arms, where there was an uncle who looked like Gianni who would spoil that child rotten, where there was a bond between him and a woman he had never imagined for himself that looked very much like Amelia Seymore.

But when he opened his eyes, there was a company he needed to save from damage done by that very same woman. He had meant what he said to Amelia the day before. That he would give their child whatever they needed, but...

I want a chance.

He cast another gaze to where Amelia sat poring over documents at the table. He'd spent half the night reading the same material the Aurora team had sent over while they'd been in Orvieto. They had returned to Villa Vittoria after a shopping trip that had been less than easy. Apparently offering to pay for it hadn't made things better, only worse. The only thing that had forced her through the doors of the clothing store where Amelia had bought everything she needed was the prospect of meeting with Sofia Obeid in three-day-old clothes.

They had been nearly done when the shop assistant guided Amelia to the lingerie section.

Monk indeed.

Lace, straps, belts, hooks, bows, ribbons, ties... *Cavolo*. It wasn't as if his fevered imagination needed any more to think about. There hadn't been a single night since Hong Kong when he hadn't woken up in a cold sweat relieving none of the fire of want and need in his body. And last night had been the worst yet. As if the knowledge that she was carrying his child had suddenly made everything so much more intense.

He looked out of the window cutting off any curiosity as to what she was wearing under the cream silk shirt that should be conservatively respectable had he not seen the lithe body beneath it. *Cristo*, what madness was this? And why—all of a sudden—was he fascinated by little buttons? A row of them at each wrist and another row at the nape of her neck leading all the way down the back of her top to where it tucked into a pair of wide, high-waisted navy trousers.

Sophisticated. Attractive.

They made her look confident. He hadn't realised how much he'd missed seeing her like that, until that very moment. That he was making her less somehow stirred his

conscience and reminded him of things he never wanted
to think on.

He cleared his throat. 'Talk me through the meeting.'

He knew the plan but he needed something to focus
on that wasn't Amelia, their child and their future. Especially when all it made him do was think about his past.

A villa had been booked at the hotel where Obeid
had suggested they meet. Harrak Marrakech was a four-
teenth-century palace set amongst twenty-eight acres of
orchards that opened out towards a view of the snow-
capped Atlas Mountains. Comprised of deluxe villas,
each with private pools, gardens, a private chef and personal staff on hand twenty-four hours a day, it was a very
impressive hotel, even to Alessandro who, amongst the
sprawling property empire, owned several of his own
with Gianni.

While the car took them from the airport to the hotel,
Amelia talked him through the changes she'd made to the
pitch document in order to cater specifically for Obeid.
He agreed with most of the changes, made a few tweaks,
and left her to make the required amendments, trying to
ignore the fact that this was beginning to feel very much
like the trip to Hong Kong.

'She will expect you to do the talking, and she may be
offended that Gianni isn't there with you, at the meeting,'
Amelia warned as she got out of the car and waited for
him to join her. His gaze caught on features he'd once
thought plain, which he now knew beneath their subtlety
to be exquisite.

He nodded in response to Amelia's statement, knowing that the world was used to the Rossi cousins being
two halves of the same whole. Dammit, *he* was used to
it. But he had to keep a lid on the irritation lashing at

him, needling him, if he had a hope to claw any success back on this project.

He looked up at the building that had quaintly been called a villa and even though he had some of the most impressive buildings in the world under his company name, *this* was incredible.

'Is…is this okay? Sofia would expect you to stay in the most expensive accommodation. Anything less would be either insult or—'

'Weakness,' Alessandro concluded, agreeing with her choice of villa.

A uniformed staff member opened the door to their villa and beckoned them in. A second staff member waited in the marble hallway with two trays, one with glasses of champagne, cool, refreshing orange juice, or water, and the other with dainty pastries, bright with sprinklings of either paprika or pistachio, salty or sweet.

He thanked the staff, listening with one ear as their private concierge informed them of the suite's amenities, while the majority of his attention was spent taking in what could only be described as paradise. He felt Amelia's wary gaze on him like a tentative caress, and in a blinding moment of clarity he realised, that was it. *That* was what was irritating him so much.

There had been no hesitation in Hong Kong, there had been no timidity, nothing held back at all. She had met him touch for touch, taste for taste, thrust for—

'That will be all,' he said, cutting off the staff midsentence, knowing that he sounded insufferably rude, but he was being driven to distraction from wanting something that he couldn't allow himself to have. Before he could do any further damage, he turned on his heel and disappeared into his room.

* * *

Amelia looked out at the incredible view of the Atlas Mountains, more perfect than any picture. In the garden, a long narrow pool led towards an ornamental arch to reveal the majestic snow-capped peaks in the distance. This was a luxury like she had never known or seen before.

The villa alone had more rooms, bathrooms, and living areas than she could conceive of and that didn't take into consideration the subterranean pool and steam room. She looked over her shoulder at the dark wood table polished so that it was almost a mirror, sprawled with paperwork, charts, workflows, and research on Sofia Obeid. But what she really saw was the heated look in Alessandro's eyes after he dismissed the staff.

She had seen the face of the man she had spent a night with in Hong Kong. The man who had broken through every single barrier she had wedged between them, the man who made her want to give everything up for just one of his touches, one of his kisses.

She laughed quietly at herself. Back in Italy she had thought she only wanted, and had only negotiated for, a fresh start. But she couldn't afford any more lies. Not to others, or herself. She wanted more. A yearning in her heart, so deep, that only peeling back the layers of her desire for vengeance had revealed it, exposing that raw need to the air.

She wanted *him*.

She wanted to feel alive in the same way that she had that night in Hong Kong. She wanted him to look at her the way that he had that night. Not with anger, or distrust, but something like wonder. As if he'd been as surprised as she, that it was happening, that it was possible to feel that way... It had created an addiction in her. It was the only way to explain it. This constant craving coursing through her veins, travelling throughout her entire body, enslaving it to a need that felt unquenchable.

Focus.

She had to focus. It was imperative that this meeting was successful, that the damage that hung above Rossi Industries like the sword of Damocles—a sword *she* had put there—was removed. Only then would she be able to meet Alessandro on a level playing field. But in some ways, she also wanted to delay that moment. Because she could feel it on the horizon; building between them, getting bigger and bigger and harder to ignore. A storm, a reckoning, that she both wanted and feared.

Alessandro appeared in the arched doorway on the opposite side of the exquisitely decorated living area. If he was trying to hide his thoughts, he'd failed because she could easily read the intensely erotic images in his mind. Goosebumps broke out across her skin. Every single line of his body was drawn with tension, and more. The more that called to that secret place within her. A place that he had imprinted himself on, making sure that she would never be able to think of another man in the same way.

Amelia clenched her hands, his gaze drawn to the movement, and as he took a step forward she instinctively took a step back—halting him mid-stride. He'd opened his mouth as if to speak, when the villa phone's ringtone sliced the air between them.

Blindly she reached for the handset built into the wall beside her and listened to the voice on the other end.

'Yes… Absolutely… We look forward to seeing you soon.'

She placed the handset into the cradle on the wall and

looked up to find Alessandro staring studiously out of the window.

'Sofia Obeid is on her way.'

He nodded without sparing her a glance.

Get your damn head on straight, right now, or you're going to lose everything you and Gianni have worked so damned hard for.

Amelia instructed the private staff to provide refreshments and drinks in the shaded courtyard in the villa's garden. Covered by a pergola dripping with extravagant fuchsia blossom and rich green leaves, the courtyard edged a pool that reflected the mountains in the distance. It should have been peaceful, serene even, but Alessandro was on edge—a feeling he disliked intensely. Inviting Sofia Obeid into the villa felt personal, invasive. Again, that protective instinct rose in him, surprising in its intensity, wanting to keep this place, and Amelia, to himself. And it shook him to his core.

Presently she was fussing over the table in a way that reminded him of the day she had helped to pitch for Firstview, the day she had tried to sabotage his company. And he was trusting her to save it? This could just as easily be another trap. He pushed the thought away, searching for a calm that was far from natural, but successful nevertheless.

He grounded himself in facts, in the presentation, in the confidence that it was a sterling project that would be more than just a roaring success. In the belief that Obeid would see this and partner with them—even if it was a partnership born from desperation rather than choice.

Amelia looked up as if she'd felt the change in him. Awareness flashed in her golden green gaze, before she looked away. They heard the knock on the door, the villa's staff greeting their visitor, and Alessandro turned to welcome what would either be their salvation or damnation.

Sofia Obeid was a very attractive woman. Six feet of sheer elegance and beauty did nothing to distract from the lethal intelligence in her sharp gaze. Despite her reputation for being impossible to work with, Alessandro could at least appreciate her exacting standards. And though there had been whispers of impropriety, Amelia had assured and reassured him that she had found not one single ounce of evidence pointing to the truth of it. And given how ruthlessly she had investigated him, Alessandro was almost sure that that was what they were—whispers.

'Ms Obeid. Thank you for meeting with us. I know that it was both short notice and inconvenient for you.'

Her eyes narrowed momentarily, as if she was surprised that he was so openly acknowledging his need for her visit.

She hates obsequiousness with a passion. Be simple, be honest, be direct, Amelia's coaching whispered into his mind.

Sofia nodded once, glanced at Amelia, who bowed her head in a way that surprised Alessandro, but seemed to satisfy Sofia.

'Would you care to sit?' he asked, gesturing to the table.

'Thank you,' Sofia replied in a precise English accent that spoke of her years of private schooling in Britain.

She sat in the middle seat, gesturing for him and Amelia to take the chairs either side of her.

'Where is the other one?' she asked when they were all seated at the table.

'The other—?'

'The *Hot* Rossi?'

Alessandro just about managed not to choke on the coffee he'd just taken a sip of. The unconcealed disdain of Sofia's tone making his cousin's moniker somehow amusing. He was about to come up with a lie, when a warning flashed in Amelia's gaze. A warning Sofia might or might not have seen.

'He is in the Caribbean.'

'You expect me to take this business deal seriously while one half of Rossi Industries suns himself and his ego on a beach, presumably—if reports are true—surrounded by as many women as he can get his hands on?'

'I do. My cousin might—' he saw the flash of scepticism in Sofia's gaze '—*does* have a reputation, but he works harder than anyone else I know. He earns his one holiday a year, each and every other day in the office. And as you—and the world—have noted, we are effectively one and the same. If I speak, it is for the both of us, unquestionably. And I promise you, if he could be here, he would. It is not a reflection on how much we value your time and input here.'

Sofia looked between Alessandro and Amelia, and it was only because a part of him was trained almost exclusively on Amelia at all times that he noticed an imperceptible nod from Amelia that seemed to give Sofia some kind of reassurance.

Warning bells sounded in his mind, loud and impossible to ignore. Something was going on. He didn't know what yet, and he couldn't work out why, but he didn't like it at all. So while he gave Sofia the pitch he knew by heart, his mind tried to calculate all possible angles that could be played here. But he kept running up against one.

Amelia. If anyone needed this deal to go ahead as

much as he did, it was her. He couldn't see what was in it for her to sabotage this.

'What happened to the original partner?'

'It was discovered that they didn't have the capability to see the project through,' he replied, holding Sofia's enigmatic gaze.

Obeid raised the wing of a midnight-black eyebrow in surprise. 'That is either incompetent or inept.'

Alessandro kept his mouth shut, refusing to dignify her statement with a response.

'I heard you were hours away from signing,' she pressed again.

'We were,' he admitted. 'But I'm not the only one at this table who has backed out of their obligations at the last minute,' he said, his tone cracked like a whip, lashing out at yet another betrayal.

Obeid simply held his gaze. A lesser person might have flinched. Instead, what he read in Sofia's blue-black eyes was only impatience. As if she'd been surprised it had taken them this long to get to this part of the conversation.

'Good. We are done playing polite, then?' she asked, her cut-glass tone unflinching.

In the corner of his eye, he saw that Amelia looked away from the table.

'I don't believe you would have ever approached me unless you had absolutely no other option.'

'This is true,' he replied, his tone level now that hostilities were almost open on the table. 'But that doesn't mean I don't have a choice.'

'Explain.'

His stomach ground down at the thought of it, but he knew that Gianni would agree with him. They had lived too long with someone else's foot on their necks to ever allow themselves, or Rossi Industries, to be in that same position again.

'My choice. Partner with you, or drop the project altogether.'

But they would lose millions, a voice screamed in Amelia's head. *Not to mention the damage done to their reputation.*

No, no, no, no, no. Her pulse fluttered at a frantic speed and she looked to Sofia, who was considering Alessandro's words.

'And the money you have already invested in the project? Not to mention the irrevocable damage to your illustrious reputation?'

'Are nothing in comparison to our integrity,' Alessandro replied resolutely. Something twisted in her heart. This was the Alessandro that she had been with in Hong Kong. Integrity, loyalty, pride. She'd been confused by it, torn between the belief that he was corrupt and the instinctive knowledge that he wasn't. Amelia drew in a shaky breath and held it, appreciating the significance his words would have for Sofia.

'I know something of that, Mr Rossi,' Sofia replied. 'Some reputations are earned, some are not. Some are fabricated by bitterness, jealousy and lies and some are simply misunderstandings. If you want to move ahead as partners, I would like that.' She caught a flash of surprise in the tightening across Alessandro's shoulders, but his face betrayed nothing. 'My assistant has sent Ms Seymore several direct references of previous partnerships who are happy to speak to you plainly and truthfully about their experience working with my company.'

Sofia rose from the table, and though Alessandro

rose to bid her farewell, he stayed at the table as Amelia walked her from the villa.

It was just the shade of the interior that broke a cool sweat between her shoulder blades, Amelia told herself. The meeting was a success, she had to hold onto that.

Sofia turned just before reaching the front door. 'He knows,' the other woman warned her.

Amelia nodded. 'I know,' she replied, heart see-sawing painfully. She'd known the risk before arranging the meeting. 'He's not stupid.'

Something close to sympathy shone in Sofia's gaze. 'This is a dangerous game, Lia. I hope you know what you're doing.'

Amelia nodded, the warning an echo of the one Alessandro had given her only days earlier. But neither had recognised that the game had already been played and lost, she and Alessandro just hadn't admitted it yet.

She closed the door behind a woman who had once been her closest school friend ten years ago, and turned to find Alessandro staring at her from the end of the hallway, anger, bitterness and something else in his gaze that was quickly eaten up by the darkness.

'You are right about one thing. I'm not stupid,' he said, before turning on his heel and disappearing. And her heart dropped.

Despite that, she raced after him, desperate to explain before any more damage could be done. She reached the courtyard to find him pacing back and forth, all of the emotions he'd kept contained during the meeting finally unleashed in movement that reminded her of a caged panther.

'Alessandro—'

'But I am though, aren't I?' he demanded, his nostrils flaring at deep, quick breaths heaving his chest.

'Are what?'

'A fool!' he roared. 'A fool you have played not once, but twice. *Cristo.*' He cradled his head in his hands. 'How could I have ever trusted you?'

His words stung like a whip against her back. 'You can't, and you won't. Which is why it didn't matter,' she said, the truth almost too painful to bare.

Her response jerked his head from his hands. 'It didn't matter?' he demanded.

'No. All that mattered was that the meeting was a success. Sofia is—*was*—an old friend. We lost touch after I was forced to change schools. When I realised I needed to fix the Firstview problem, I reached out to her. She's been mistreated badly by...well. That's her story to tell. Safe to say, her reputation is unjust. Her only condition to meeting with a rich, Italian business titan who would never have considered lowering himself to meet with an Arabic businesswoman with a bad reputation was that I keep my existing relationship with her a secret.'

Her words were like barbs and she could see that they had struck home. Amelia knew what it was like to have to prove herself in a male-dominated world, and she couldn't even begin to imagine how hard it must be for Sofia. The dark shadows in her old friend's eyes were enough broad strokes to suggest that her road had been a hard one. But Amelia wouldn't let Alessandro throw this deal away because he was too stubborn to see the wondrous possibility of its success.

'That is unfair,' he said of her last words.

'But true. You are not the only one who has something at stake with this deal. This will be the making of her company—a chance to rise above rumour and prejudice. You will get to move ahead and achieve the success you forecasted for this project.

'And what will you get?' he demanded, the expectation of her betrayal vibrant in his gaze.

She could lie to him, but Amelia was so tired, and, unable to fight it any more, she confessed the truth. 'More. I'd wanted more between us.'

CHAPTER NINE

MORE? HIS INTERNAL voice roared. *She wanted more?*

'By lying?' he demanded incredulously.

'You can't have it both ways, Alessandro,' she replied. 'I undid the damage that I had done with the Firstview deal. You didn't set rules as to how I did it.' She looked up at him, her eyes wide with stubborn-willed refusal to back down. 'And it wasn't a lie,' she ground out through clenched teeth.

She was a magnificent madness in his veins. They stood, toe to toe, breathing heavy and hard and hot and all he could think of was how much he wanted to take her mouth with his, to plunder the complex essence of Amelia Seymore.

'I have done all that I can do,' she said. 'The decision is now yours.'

For a moment, he wasn't sure whether she was talking about the deal or the unspoken thing that practically throbbed in the air between them. Anger, resentment, need and want thrashed in his chest, twisting and turning, desperate to get out.

As if she sensed it, her pupils flared beneath the heat of his attention, the flutter in her neck flickering in a way that made him want to see if he could feel it beneath the pad of his thumb. Feel that she was as affected as him, know the truth of it in her body—a body that couldn't lie or betray him.

He forced himself to turn away and missed the flash of hurt that throbbed in Amelia's eyes.

You can't, and you won't. Which is why it didn't matter.

Her words taunted him as he stalked from the villa. Because she was right. He couldn't trust her, wouldn't. He punched Gianni's number into his phone, unsurprised but annoyed when he was told that it was still out of reach.

At the very least, he should have felt satisfied. With Obeid the project could go ahead if he and Gianni wanted it to. He should have felt relief, he should have felt victorious. So why was guilt slashing wounds into his chest at the memory of Amelia's words, of her accusation that he'd never trust her?

Because you want to.

The startling realisation pulled him up short.

He wanted to believe her, just as he'd wanted to believe his mother when she'd promised she'd take them away from his father and uncle.

And he'd never wanted anything more in his entire life. His father and uncle had become so much worse after their mother passed away that they had driven Gianni's mother from the house leaving Gianni behind. Alessandro's mother was all they'd had left but when Saverio had come in from the fields there was only so much Alessandro had been able to do to distract his father from his anger towards his mother. His desperation had been almost suffocating as he'd pleaded with her to take them away after one particularly brutal night.

We'll leave. I'll come for you and we'll leave.

Gianni and he had stayed up all night, whispering reassurances and making plans through the minutes and hours, neither wanting to give up hope that Aurora Vizzini would come to take them away. Even as dawn had crested over the vineyards, and they'd rubbed sleep and sadness from their eyes, knowing that Alessandro's mother had lied, the worst of it had been the hope; the desperate hope he'd had, the need to believe his mother when she had said that she would take them away, that they would be safe.

Nothing was spoken about that night ever again, not with his mother and not with Gianni. And sometimes, in the dead of night, he drove himself to distraction wondering if his mother's promise had even happened.

But Amelia was different, an inner voice taunted him. Her first concern, when he'd brought her to Italy, was her sister. The protective instinct and determination in her so clear and obvious he almost couldn't believe it. Truth had been the only note he'd heard when she'd told him of her childhood. And he'd read between the lines to see deeper, to *know* that she would do anything to protect her family. That she had sacrificed for her family, for what she thought was right. And she'd done it again when she'd agreed to lie to him for Obeid, putting Rossi Industries above her own needs, above *him*. Because she had known what that concealment would do to him.

But that anger—that constant simmering presence beneath his surface whenever she was near—lashed out. So much his life had changed in the space of just days. Or, he wondered, had the change started all those weeks ago in Hong Kong? When success, respect and admiration had led them down a path he'd never thought he'd take? One wrong move had completely undone the entire chessboard of his life. A move he was fighting hard not to repeat.

I'd wanted more between us.

The decision is now yours.

His mind hurt from working out all the angles, exhausted from days of too little sleep and entirely too much adrenaline. It had weakened his resolve and all he wanted, all he needed, was a taste of her to quench the maddening thirst for her.

He looked up to find himself back at the villa, his steps unconsciously bringing him back to where he needed to be. He found Amelia pacing in the living area.

Worry had etched lines across her features, a few wisps of hair had loosened from where it had been pinned back, but shutters came down on her concern as she turned to stand tall and proud beneath the storm of his gaze, determined to meet him head-on. No. Amelia Seymore might have lost her battle, but she wouldn't let herself be cowed.

And he hated how much that turned him on. He'd thought he'd recognised it, the fight. He'd thought that was what fed the burning lava hot in his veins, he'd thought anger was what had locked his chest in a vice ever since he'd left her at the villa hours before. He'd thought fury was what had driven him here.

But he'd been wrong.

In that one moment, he realised that it wasn't she who had fooled him. No. He had fooled *himself.* Because the only thing that was riding him now, and riding him hard, was the sheer desperation to feel her touch, to taste her once again, to feel her wrapped around him as she screamed his name.

He closed the distance between them in two short strides, gathering her into his arms, and claimed her mouth with an undeniable and unyielding possession.

A gasp that sounded like surrender and felt like fire engulfed his soul. *Mine.* And in a single heartbeat, her name etched itself irrevocably deep within him.

Every single defence she'd thought she had against him crumbled the moment his lips met hers. A summer storm, fierce and furious, answering every single one of her unspoken prayers—and then as quickly as he had come for her, he tore his mouth from hers.

'*Cristo,*' he said, his forehead pressed against hers, his chest heaving with their shared breath. 'Please,' he all but begged, 'send me away. Tell me you don't want this.'

'I can't,' she replied, closing her eyes against the sheer intensity of all that she wanted and all that she feared she would never have. But she wouldn't, couldn't hide from this any more. Opening her eyes, she looked deep into his gaze, saw the storm that threatened on the horizon and faced it. 'Because I do want this.'

'Then we're both damned.'

He claimed her lips with such possession for a moment she lost herself. She was his creature—one of pure sensation, responding only to his touch, his taste. The tongue taking her mouth teased her heart, the hands pulling her to him left fingerprints on her soul. And for the briefest moments she surrendered to it, luxuriating in the shocking intensity of his desire, before her own became too much to ignore.

Leaning into his kiss, her hands flew to his chest, fingers fisting the superfine cotton of his shirt and pulling him into her, deepening a kiss she'd already opened herself up to. She felt as much as heard the growl build from Alessandro, raising the hairs at her nape not from fear of him, but fear that she might not be rid of this feeling, this sensual high that fizzed and popped and burst through her body. She wanted to call it madness, but beneath it, beneath the intoxicating fever of his touch, it was the sanest she'd felt since Hong Kong. Because while her heartbeat raged out of control, he soothed her soul.

'Amelia.' He said her name like a plea—as if he too had finally found that same sense of peace. But as he pulled away from her, she followed him, unwilling— unable—to break the connection. Her lips found his and he groaned into the kiss in a way that melted her body against him.

Rising to her tiptoes, she pressed herself to the length of his body, desperate to feel the steely outline of toned and taut male heat against her. Heat flashed over her from the evidence of his arousal, coalescing deep in her throbbing sex.

Despite the ferocity of his kiss, he was being gentle with her, his touches light, his hold careful and it only frustrated her, making her want more. Because she knew what it was like when Alessandro Rossi lost himself in his desire and that, *that*, was what had kept her heart racing when she'd known he was near, *that* was what had filled her dreams with such eroticism she'd ached when awake. *That* was what she wanted now.

Reluctantly she pulled back from the kiss, studying the scorching heat of his gaze—a heat wrapped in chains. He wanted this as much as she did but he was holding himself back. She could almost read the thoughts in his eyes, the warring conflict of should they, shouldn't they.

The words she'd said to Alessandro that night in Hong Kong rose to her lips, a symmetry and irony to it that made her heart hurt a little.

'Just tonight. Just now. But we will never speak of it. Ever.'

Before she'd even finished the sentence, Alessandro had closed the distance between them, crowding her body in the most delicious of ways.

'Amelia, what we do now, here? We *will* speak of it.' The authority in his tone sent shivers of arousal across her skin, tightening her nipples, throbbing between her legs. 'We will acknowledge it. It will not be ignored. Not again. Do you understand?'

The sting of his admonishment dissolved beneath a tide of need so acute, so powerful, she trembled. The pure possession in his gaze, his refusal to ignore this thing between them...it was everything she'd ever wanted.

'Do you want this?' he demanded, and she saw chains holding his desire back begin to snap beneath the heat of their mutual need. She knew what he was asking, knew that it was about more than this one moment, than this night...it was more than the question he'd asked only moments ago.

'Yes. I do,' she replied as he searched her gaze and she opened herself to him, hoping that he saw the truth of her words, of her heart. 'But I want *you*. Not some careful, half touch. So I'm asking, do *you* want this?'

Surprise flared in the rich depths of his gaze. As if he'd thought he'd hidden his feelings better. And she was relieved when he didn't simply dismiss her question, but considered it as seriously as she had. This was the line they would draw—before and after. She knew it as she knew her next breath. And it had to be crossed now or never.

'Yes, I do,' he replied, the last chain of his restraint breaking in his gaze.

Relief sagged through her, but she had no time to dwell on it because that touch that had been gentle was suddenly a brand against her skin. He gathered her in his arms, lifting her up against him. Instinctively she wrapped her legs around his hips so as not to fall—not that she would have. The moment she was in his arms she felt safer than she could ever remember.

He kissed her as he walked them from the living room, the erotic play of his tongue against hers a promise of what was to come when they reached their destination. The arm braced beneath her thighs a tease of where she wanted him to touch her. Her breath caught in her lungs as his other hand wrapped around her hair and gently angled her head back to give him access to her neck as he pressed open-mouthed kisses across her collarbone and down between the v of her breasts, through the oyster satin of her shirt.

Her taut nipples punched at the silk and he covered them with the damp heat of his mouth. Her head fell back on its own, pleasure bursting through her as he reached the bed and laid her gently down on it.

The afternoon had given way to dusk, and still the soft honeyed rays of the sun streamed through white linen curtains. It was the exact opposite to Hong Kong and Alessandro was glad. He refused to allow this moment to be shrouded in darkness or secrecy. He wanted the light, wanted reality; undeniable, unhidden reality.

He wanted to see every single inch of her as he brought her to climax, he wanted to feel it and know it was real. A blush rose to Amelia's cheeks in response to the thoughts she could read in his gaze, he realised. And he bared himself and his desires to her as he reached up to undo the buttons on his shirt one by one.

She bit her lips, watching his hands lower down his body, hungry and heavy. Without taking her eyes from him, she reached behind her to undo one of those tantalising little buttons and drew the shirt over her head. He had reached the last of his shirt buttons as she did so. They both discarded their tops at the same time, eyes for nothing but each other.

He stood, frozen still at the sight of her lace-covered breasts, and when she leaned back on her elbows, his arousal shoved painfully against his trousers. The look in her eyes was pure want. His mouth ran dry and, spellbound, he climbed onto the bed, unable to resist the lure of her.

Instinct took over, powerful and primal and intense. He gently tugged at her ankle, pulling her down the bed as he rose to meet her, covering her body with his, and the sigh he bit back turned into a groan of sheer desire. He slipped an arm beneath her, gathering her to him as he feasted on the smooth planes of her chest and the wide v between her perfect breasts. With one hand he pulled at the lace cup of her bra, exposing her nipple, taut and tempting. He took her breast into his mouth, gorging on pleasure and teasing cries of delight from Amelia.

Her hands flew to his head, fisting in his hair, pulling, pushing as if she wasn't sure whether she wanted more or less of the delicious torment. 'Alessandro…'

'Tell me what you want, *amato*,' he said, desperate to bring her pleasure. 'Tell me what you want and you shall have it.'

She arched, as he turned his attention to her other breast, tugging the lace down and feasting on her flesh.

There hadn't been so many words between them in Hong Kong. The shocking intensity of their passion like a sudden firestorm, burning to extremes before burning out. But here? Now? This would be different. This would be no quick thing, he silently promised them both.

'Your desires are safe with me,' he said, pulling back so that she could see the truth of his words. 'Your needs are safe with me. *You* are safe with me.'

The flare of her pupils reminded him of a solar eclipse. Desire blotting out rationality and restraint. 'Put your hands on me,' she said, her tone husky with arousal and need.

'As you wish.'

He found the fastening of her trousers, flicking the button and making quick work of the zip. She shivered as his palm slipped beneath the cotton fabric and caressed the curve of her backside. She cried out as his fingers delved beneath the lace of her panties into the delicate soft wet heat of her.

In a single breath he was more aroused than he'd ever been in his life, and even then, holding back from what he wanted was shockingly easy in order to give her more.

He wanted this, her pleasure. He wanted to see starbursts in her eyes, not confusion, doubt or worry. He wanted to see what he had seen in Hong Kong. Feel what he had felt there. A gasp fell from her lips and he wanted to taste it, taste the surrender to all that was passion and sensuality on her lips. His heart pounded against his ribcage as she shifted in his arms, her eyes becoming soft and unfocused as his fingers circled her clitoris, sweeping around the soft delicate flesh and returning again and again to a sensual torment that teased them both in equal measure.

He studied every part of her face, the way that she bit her lower lip trying and failing to contain her responses, responses that were like a drug to him. *He* did this to her, *he* gave her this. A flush stained her cheeks and crept up her neck, her eyes closed then opened, unseeing, lost in sensation and sensual frustration as her orgasm danced just out of her reach.

In seconds, he had pulled at her trousers, slipped them from beneath her and removed them from her legs. Carefully caressing his way back, his hand pressed her thighs apart gently and he lowered himself between her legs. The heat of her gaze on him seared his soul, and as he parted her to him he felt her flinch. 'You are safe with me,' he promised again, as he gave into his need for the most intimate of kisses.

Her learned her song then, the cadence of her pleasure—in the cries and moans and pleas that filled the air. His heartbeat pounded the rhythm, the sound of his blood roaring in his veins the base line, and above it all rose a melody so sweet he'd never tire of hearing it, and when her orgasm crested, the crescendo was so powerful, he felt changed by it.

He gentled her with soft touches and words as she came back down—as affected by her pleasure as she had been. But when her eyes found his, focused, intent and full of need for more, his body answered without a thought.

He kissed her with the desperation of a dying man, as if this were the last thing he would do with his life. His body, hot and feverish for her touch, relished the way her hands skated across his skin, fingers soothing and then gripping his shoulders, biceps, flanks—as if she wanted to explore every inch of him.

Alessandro pulled away reluctantly to remove his trousers, his gaze not leaving hers once. Automatically he reached for his wallet and withdrew a condom from it and stopped to look at it in his hands. His mind utterly blank because...because...she was already pregnant.

Never, not once in his entire life, had he had sex without protection. Never had he been skin to skin with anyone and, looking up, he saw the same thought reflected in Amelia's eyes.

The realisation of how important this moment was nudged its way through the haze of Amelia's climax. For a man who had sworn never to have children, she imagined the question about whether to use protection or not would be as alien to him as it was to her. But she was pregnant already and the desire to feel him—to be with him—without a barrier between them suddenly became more than just a want. It was a need that she couldn't explain. Carefully she reached out to take the condom from his fingers and placed it on the side table.

He looked at her, studying her intently, and she opened herself up to him—laying herself bare to his silent inquisition. She wanted this and she trusted him. And in that moment, she saw that trust reflected back at her.

The bonds holding Alessandro back shattered and her heart soared to see the ferocious desire riding her hard reflected in his gaze. He leaned across the bed and thrust her into a realm of infinite pleasure with his kiss, the press of his body against hers igniting a hunger she feared would never be sated.

She wrapped her arms around him and held on tight, half afraid that he'd leave, as if already she could feel him slipping through her fingers. But the thought disappeared as he bent his head to her chest and claimed her breast as if it were already his.

Pleasure arrowed through her to the heart of her sex and when his deft fingers gently pressed her legs apart and delved into that exact same place, she couldn't contain the cry of sheer want that left her lips.

He gently pushed her legs aside to make space for himself and she trembled when she felt the jut of his erection against her sex. Both Amelia's and Alessandro's eyes drifted shut from the shared pleasure of the moment, luxuriating in the sensations that were new to them both, until neither could resist the lure of what was to come.

Slowly, Alessandro pushed into her, her muscles tightening, flexing, drawing him further into her. Amelia tried to capture the feeling with words, but nothing stuck, flitting away on a tide of sheer sensation and connection. They were both trembling with the force of their pleasure, with the shock of it, the surprise. It twisted something deep in Amelia, turned it, opening it into something beautiful. He filled her so perfectly that she felt as if they had been made for each other, as if finally something was beginning to make sense for her and her journey.

And then, when she thought she couldn't take any more feeling, he began to withdraw and she cried out at the loss. A rueful smile pulled at Alessandro's lips and in Italian he rained down praises and promises as he pushed into her again, and again, and again. The erotically slow strokes he teased them with seemed endless to her, launching her into that strange infinite place, until it seemed even Alessandro Rossi couldn't take it any more.

As his movements became quicker, his thrusts more powerful, their connection became more tangible. Sweat beaded his brow, her neck, between her shoulder blades, and down his chest, the air became hot with cries and moans and pants and pleas.

Harder and harder and higher and higher he drove her to the pinnacle of her climax until finally, just when she thought she couldn't take any more, Alessandro thrust them over the edge into an abyss of nothing but sheer pleasure.

CHAPTER TEN

IT TOOK A while for Amelia to realise she wasn't asleep any more. Nestled into the curve of Alessandro's huge frame, with his arm clamped over her waist, it had felt like an impossible dream. In Hong Kong, she'd not allowed herself to sleep. She'd stolen from the hotel room while Alessandro had been in the bathroom, unable to face the consequences of her actions...until those consequences had come looking for her.

But here, there was no chance of her sneaking out of bed. Alessandro's arm was a weight holding her in place and he, apparently, slept like the dead. It was such a normal everyday thing to know about him that it made her smile, and burrow deeper into his embrace, close her eyes and fall back asleep.

When Amelia woke, she was alone. The heat, the safety, the promise of the night before—noticeably absent. Alessandro was in the bathroom and she wondered if she'd conjured the comparison with Hong Kong into reality. Should she leave? Should she stay? Would he emerge from the bathroom with a smile, a frown, or that purposefully blank look that meant he was waiting to take his lead from her?

This was the father of her child and she didn't know. Hurt swirled with guilt. It wasn't good enough. She had to do better, *they* had to do better. Now that her sabotage had been undone, she had to turn her attention to them. Because if she did want the security he offered and the relationship her child deserved, then she had to feel more than…than…discomfort and awkwardness. She looked at her ringless finger and wondered if perhaps it might for ever be bare now. A ring promising her to Alessandro far too much to ever dream of, let alone hope for.

I want a chance.

She knew that Alessandro would keep their agreement, but it was what she did with that chance that mattered now. For the sake of their child, they needed to get to know each other, outside the boardroom and the bedroom. She just had to figure out how.

She slipped from the silken sheets of his bed, returned to her room, and took a shower, thinking about how she could achieve what she wanted. She rolled her shoulders beneath the spray of the powerful jets and felt his palm trace the length of her spine. She soaped her skin and felt his open-mouthed kisses and the pleasant ache between her thighs from where she had gripped him, urged him, held him deep within her. But despite the pleasure he had given her last night, the satisfaction, her body craved him again. It was a drumbeat just beneath her skin, always, constant, somehow slipping into time with her pulse. Reluctantly she pulled her thoughts back to the idea beginning to form in her mind. It was a little…*simple* but she believed that it would be effective.

By the time Alessandro emerged from the hotel suite room Amelia had dismissed the staff to give them some privacy, and was waiting for him at the table. He was dressed as if ready for the office, as always, and still as desperately handsome as he had been the night before.

Any hope that their shared passion might have somehow taken the edge off her desire for him was dashed, instantly and irrevocably.

His gaze flickered from her to the table and confusion pulled at his brow. He was probably wondering why there were bits of torn paper in a glass jar. She nudged the steaming shot of espresso she had made him and steeled herself. She was about to explain when—

'I've offered Obeid the Aurora project and she has agreed.'

Amelia's mouth shut with a snap. It was as she'd expected, but she couldn't help but feel hurt at being excluded.

'The team in London will push on with it from here.'

She stiffened, realising the implications of his words. *What did you think would happen, Amelia? That he'd keep you on the project?*

'You will no longer—'

'I understand,' she interrupted him, curt in her desire to not hear him say it. For two years working for Alessandro had been a ruse. But it also hadn't been. She'd enjoyed the work she'd done there. She'd been good at it too. But right now? She had more important things to worry about.

He studied her acceptance with something like scepticism that only proved her point.

'Will you sit?' she asked, pushing aside the small bruise forming on her heart.

'We should be getting back to the jet.'

She clenched her teeth together, fighting the impulse to reveal just how affected she was by his dismissal. He might be the boss, but he seemed to have forgotten that she had never been a mere underling who jumped at his every whim. He caught her gaze, held it, testing the strength of her will and, clearly finding it unbending, he took the chair opposite her.

There was an air of impatience about him and it was this, this power struggle, this discord that they had to get over.

'I am pregnant,' she stated.

'*Sì?*' he replied, his confusion evident.

'The threat hanging over the Aurora project and Rossi Industries has been neutralised.'

Begrudgingly, it seemed, he acknowledged that statement with a curt nod. '*Sì.*'

'But you don't trust me. You want me. I know that,' she said, a blush rising to her cheeks as she maintained control of the conversation. 'But you don't, we don't… *know* each other.'

His gaze flickered to the jar on the table that contained lots of little folds of paper.

'Yet,' she hurried to clarify. 'We don't know each other yet.' Amelia took a breath. 'You've said that you will protect our child financially and, I'm sure, well beyond that. But our child will need more than just financial support and physical security.'

It was something that she had learned the moment that both those things had been ripped away from her and her sister. Using that memory to give her strength, she asked, 'What about their emotional needs? In those precious first few months and years, and then later on in life? And where will we live? Will we even live together?' she asked, seeing his eyes flare in response to her last question. 'I want…to do this *with* you. I don't want to tell you about my first scan after the fact, or first steps or first anything. I want you to be there with us, I want… I want to share it with you.'

And it wasn't just for her child, Amelia realised as her heart quivered in her chest, waiting for his response. For years she had taken the reins, looked after her sister, taken care of her mother, made the hard decisions and had the difficult arguments and still, despite that, she wanted to give him part of this and it terrified her. Because if she learned to rely on him, if she learned to lean on him and he walked away? It would break her heart permanently.

But she couldn't let fear deter her and she pressed on. 'I don't know how long Issy and Gianni will be away, but when my sister comes back, I want to share this news with the happiness that it deserves. I want to be able to tell her what my future and our child's future is going to look like in the next few months. There is nothing that can be done about the Aurora project now for at least another week. And I want… I'm *hoping* that you will give us that time for us to learn enough about each other to see if this might work? To see if we can be more. To see if…you can trust me.'

Alessandro couldn't pretend that he hadn't seen the sincerity and the need behind her questions. She had laid herself more open here than in what they had shared last night. And her hopes fed almost directly into his daydreams, fantasies that were becoming more like wishes with each moment he shared with her. Wishes that had gold bands and diamond rings that shocked as much as scared him.

But he couldn't pretend that he didn't feel a sense of panic, a sense of being rushed that made him anxious, as if his hand was being forced before he'd had time to think things through properly himself.

He thought about what she'd said about Gianni and her sister. The moment he'd finished his call with Sofia he'd sent word to St Lovells, ensuring that his cousin would at least know that the project had been saved and there was now no longer any threat to Rossi Industries. But hadn't he avoided speaking directly to Gianni because he had no idea how to explain to the man closer to him than any brother what was happening with Amelia?

No matter what he felt, though, the last thing he would allow was for his child to grow up amongst frigid cordiality or burning mistrust and resentment. He and Amelia *did* need to work together to find a way through it all for the sake of their child.

'What are you suggesting?' he asked, curious as to how what she was hoping for fitted into the folded pieces of paper in the jar.

'I have written out a number of things we can do together.'

Dios mio. 'Amelia. Is this the romantic version of team-building exercises?'

He instantly wished he could call the errant thought back, until Amelia's surprised laugh fell between them, lightening the mood and brightening her eyes in the most incredible way. 'It is the solution to a problem,' she forced out through her smile.

Reluctant to lose the moment, he eyed the folded paper suspiciously and continued to play the grouch. 'Fine, but if you expect me to fall back with my eyes closed and trust that you'll catch me—'

This time the laughter that erupted from Amelia was

fresh and wild like the flowers on the meadow between his and Gianni's estates.

'You'd crush me,' she replied, after successfully swallowing her laugh.

He couldn't help the responding pull at the corner of his lips, or the way that it captured Amelia's gaze.

'I would,' he agreed and, somehow, they were no longer talking about trust exercises. Shaking the erotic thoughts from his increasingly dirty mind, he took a sip of the espresso, only mildly cooler since it had been made. She knew how he liked his coffee. Black and scalding. He refused to acknowledge it, but it meant something to him. 'Okay,' he said, taking a deep breath. 'But,' he said, bargaining, 'I reserve the right to veto.'

She considered his offer. 'You can have *one*,' she countered.

He narrowed his eyes, assessing her as an opposing player in this game she had created.

'If I do this, then you will do the same ones that I pick,' he demanded.

This time she narrowed her eyes as—he imagined—she remembered whatever it was she had written on those little pieces of paper. He held his breath, despite believing that she wouldn't have asked him to do anything that she wouldn't do herself.

'Okay,' she agreed.

Something eased in his chest. 'Then let's play,' he said, reaching towards the jar.

Amelia's hand shot out to halt him, drawing his eyes to hers. He would feel the punch to his gut for days.

'It's not a game,' she said quietly.

He just about managed to stop the flinch that pulled at his body. She was right and he knew it. There needed to be trust. They needed to find some kind of accord, because he couldn't, wouldn't let his child grow up in an environment that remotely resembled the one he had been born into. He would make sure that their child had better.

'I know, Amelia,' he promised.

You are safe with me.

His words from last night echoed into his mind, his vow one that he had meant and one that he wouldn't break.

'So, I just...' He dipped his hand into the jar and riffled around inside as he'd seen children do at the local village fete his father and uncle had tried to sell their horrible wine at.

The thanks in her eyes was painful to bear—that it was for such a small thing. Had he really been acting like such a monster? Swallowing, he pulled out a tear of paper and unfolded it. There in looping handwriting that belonged to Amelia was not what he had expected to read. He had been prepared for a checklist—dinner out, a film maybe. Even an art gallery.

He should have known better.

'Are they all like this?'

She nodded, watching him carefully.

'And you will also do these?' he reminded her.

'I will do every one that you do,' she said.

He placed the piece of torn paper on the table, smoothing it flat with his fingers as if the sudden slap of pain raised by this simple request hadn't caught him by surprise.

Take me somewhere from your childhood.

He cleared his throat. *Cristo.*

'Veto,' he said, not caring what weakness it revealed in him. He would never take her anywhere near his childhood. She nodded, looking sad but not surprised. Instead, she passed him the jar. He pulled another tear of paper, trying hard not to tense up from fear of what this one might say, and opened it.

Show me something you're proud of.

And he soon realised just how clever she really was. There was no doubt that after even just a few of these that sense of connection he'd felt from the very first would be strengthened. At least, he could readily acknowledge, his child would have a mother who would fight for them and fight hard, no matter the cost.

'Okay,' he said, sliding back his chair. 'Let's go.'

Amelia was only a little surprised to be heading back to Italy. Part of her had imagined that they would be on their way to London, to The Ruby that was the heart of his and Gianni's company or any of the other incredible buildings Rossi Industries had developed across the globe. But instead, they touched down at the same private airfield they had left the day before, the relatively short flight time between Italy and Morocco still a wonder to her.

Alessandro had been tight-lipped from the moment that he unfolded the first piece of paper. She'd caught sight of the one he'd vetoed and, although she understood why, it had still hurt to be shut out from such a huge part of what made him *him*.

And she was *so* drawn to him, she forced herself to acknowledge now. Handsome, powerful, brooding, absolutely and unquestionably. But it was the flashes of fallibility that sank claws into her, the lightness that he kept well hidden beneath that serious exterior—the way that, despite all his authority and power, he could still get flustered by her, that he could still be amusingly petulant. Beneath all the layers of hurt and damage done by his parents and her father, she could see glimpses of the boy he might have been and she grieved the loss of that boy with such intensity it shocked her to the core.

Amelia could understand the damage, hurt and fear that had led Alessandro to make that promise years ago. But in denying himself a future family, someone to love and be loved by, he had shrunk the people around him to one or two and she wanted more—not for her child and herself, but *him*. She wanted more for Alessandro than what he had allowed himself.

Rather than the sleek black car she expected, a small Prussian blue old MG convertible two-seater sparkled in the sunlight on the runway. She frowned and cast her gaze back to the staff carrying their luggage.

'Don't worry, *tesoro*. Our belongings will be taken back to the villa. We're just taking a detour along the way.'

The term of endearment was almost carelessly thrown her way, as if it hadn't been one of the words he'd whispered over and over and over again to her last night as they'd made love. She wouldn't, couldn't regret it. It had been the most magical experience of her life so far, but she knew that it would make it so much more difficult if this plan—the plan for her child's future happiness—went awry.

He opened the door for her, his chivalry ingrained in a way that felt natural and touching.

'Where are we going?' she couldn't help but ask.

'You'll see. For now, just enjoy the ride,' he said, slipping his sunglasses on, putting the car into gear and letting the engine loose in a roar that sent vibrations through her body. She laughed and the smile across Alessandro's features took another bite out of her heart.

An hour later, they pulled up to a residential street on the outskirts of a small town. It was pretty, but she wasn't quite sure what made it so particular to the billionaire beside her. He parked in a bay and got out of the car and, leaning against the silken surface, looked at a building on the opposite side of the road. It was the Italian equivalent of a two-up, two-down, Amelia thought as she realised that this was what he wanted to show her. A family came out of the door, the parents too distracted by their children to notice them by the car. Risking a glance at Alessandro, she saw a small smile pull at the corner of his lips as if happy to see the rambunctious family spilling from the house.

'When we realised we couldn't build on the land your father sold us, we were in trouble.' He shook his head, and cleared his throat. He didn't need to explain—she'd seen the terrible terms of the loan he and Gianni had taken to buy the land from her father, she knew how urgent the repayment schedule had been.

'We had to do something else and quickly. Renovating and reselling was our best option, so we started with this one. This house. We worked day and night, just the two of us, grit, determination, and a hell of a lot of luck. So many things could have gone wrong. But we did it. Renovated, decorated, sold and bought. We did it over and over and over again, flipping houses until we had enough capital to pay back the loan and start developing our own property. But this? This was the first house. This was the one that started what would one day be Rossi Industries.

'It's humble and I'm okay with that. But what I'm really proud of? Was that we got back up. We didn't let it break us. We got back up and we kept going, kept moving forward.'

His gaze, hidden behind his sunglasses, would have been full of vehemence but she didn't need to see it to feel it. She knew that need. That driving force pushing you back up, pushing you on, unable to break no matter what was thrown at you. Because he'd had Gianni and she'd had Issy and another thread was woven in place, binding them together, even if it was against their own will.

'Your turn,' Alessandro said, twisting the conversation away from himself and his past.

Amelia glanced at the café at the end of the road and he levered himself away from the car, offering his arm in a gesture that was supposed to be ironic, but, when she slipped her hand through the crook of his arm, was anything but.

When they sat at a table on the pavement shown to them by a waiter who barely spared them a glance he smiled, realising that he missed this. The simplicity of having a coffee and not needing to rush because of a meeting, or decision or…

Amelia was looking at him. He felt her gaze like a touch, a caress. Softer than he probably deserved and hotter than he expected. But when he caught it, and held it, a blush rose to her cheeks and memories of the night before crashed through his mind.

The waiter slapped down a bottle of water and impatiently demanded their orders. Amelia hid the choke of a laugh behind her hand as Alessandro ordered them coffee and a selection of pastries, sure that Amelia would be hungry by now.

'That's funny to you? People being rude to me?' he asked, amused by her reaction.

'I just wondered what your staff would think to have seen that interaction.'

'Why?'

'Well, they are…in awe of you. I doubt they'd even believe their eyes.'

He frowned. 'I don't…am I…?' He rarely stuttered, but the thought that his staff might be in any way intimidated by him was terrible.

As if sensing his thoughts, she reached across the table, her small fine hands cool despite the heat. 'No. You are an excellent boss. You can just be a little *stern*.'

He nodded, acknowledging the truth of it. He knew that. Stern was probably a good description. And when the waiter returned with their drinks and the pastries, he felt the shift in mood, as if she was gearing herself up to meet her part of the task she had set them.

She retrieved her phone, unlocked the screen and swiped it a few times as if searching for something on it. Then she passed it across the table to him where he saw a picture of Amelia with her arm around a beaming brunette, younger than her, but the connection between them unmistakable. Isabelle Seymore was holding a giant ice-cream sundae, the sisters cheek to cheek, the pure joy emanating from them infectious.

'Your sister?'

'Yes,' she said, smiling with such affection it was a physical presence. 'Taken on her eighteenth birthday.'

He frowned, searching Isabelle's features for the differences time had wrought between then and the recent picture of her with Gianni.

'I thought she was blonde.'

'Gianni doesn't like brunettes,' Amelia explained.

It was true. Gianni's tastes ran to blonde, tall, easy and quick—to leave, that was. But instinctively he knew that none of those descriptions would fit Isabelle Seymore.

'This is what you're most proud of?' he asked, distracted as to what her meaning was. Getting her sister to lure his cousin into a trap? Their plans for vengeance?

'My *sister*.' Amelia stressed the words as if reading his thoughts. 'My sister is what I'm most proud of. We weren't always close, not when we were younger.' She smiled ruefully. 'I'd imagine from the outside looking in, we were just two more rich girls spoiled silly for their entire lives. We bickered over unimportant things as if it were the end of the world and took everything, especially each other, for granted. But after… There were so many ways in which Issy could have taken a different path. A darker path. She was younger than me when our father's business collapsed. And in the year that followed both he and our mother battled their own demons. Bit by bit Mum lost herself to addiction and Dad lost his health, as you know.

'But there are so many ways a young woman can hurt without parental stability, so many ways that hurt can be twisted and turned into dangerous things—dangerous self-beliefs… There were so many ways in which she could have fallen off the rails and she didn't.'

'You didn't let her,' he guessed correctly.

'A little. But that doesn't take into account the fact that she is who she is—and that is a genuinely good person. She is an auxiliary nurse on a children's hospital ward. She is *good* in a selfless way that I admire and had absolutely nothing to do with. *She* nurtured that goodness, protected it, not once letting our parents' selfishness darken or break that.'

Just the way she spoke of her sister made him want to meet her. Different from Amelia, because there was a thread of darkness to Amelia. No, not darkness. Just... experience. Acceptance that bad things happened in life, bad things she'd seen and felt. Different from his own, but still present, and fundamentally entwined with him and his.

Because—now that the anger and sense of betrayal over the Aurora deal was dissipating—he could see just how much Amelia had needed to take on at such a young age. To care for her sister, herself and even her mother, that would have been a heavy burden to bear alone, with no real help.

Our only real concern, he remembered one of the senior management members saying of Amelia, *is that her self-sufficiency could lead to an isolation amongst her team members.* At the time, Alessandro hadn't been overly concerned, sure that she was just focusing too much on her projects. But now he wanted to curse the parents who had forced their daughter to grow up far too soon.

He wondered what would have happened to Amelia and her sister if they hadn't been set on the path of revenge that had consumed ten years of their lives. What their lives would have looked like, who they would have been. And then, he couldn't help but wonder what would have happened if Gianni hadn't called him with the news, if he hadn't been warned about Amelia. Not with him, or Rossi Industries, but for the two sisters who would have reached their goal.

'What did you plan to do after?' he asked.

'After?'

'Yes, if you were successful. If you'd brought RI to its knees. What were you going to do after?'

For the first time since he'd known Amelia she looked—blank, desperately trying to hide something behind that nothing expression.

'I don't know,' she whispered, and his heart broke just a little for the girl she had once been.

CHAPTER ELEVEN

AMELIA HAD FELT unsettled ever since the conversation at the café with Alessandro. She couldn't quite put her finger on it, but she couldn't deny that she was feeling out of sorts. Standing in front of the mirror in Alessandro's beautiful en suite in Villa Vittoria, she took in the changes since the day Alessandro found her outside her flat in Brockley.

Despite the subtle sense of unease, her skin was now sun-kissed with a gentle golden glow. Freckles that had only ever shown themselves in Italy had been sprinkled across her forearms and her nose, warming the paler complexion she was used to. Her cheeks, ever so slightly rounder, had taken on an almost permanent blush thanks to the passion that she shared with Alessandro during heady nights she could barely credit were real.

The day after visiting the café, Alessandro had picked another piece of paper from the jar.

Tell me something about yourself that no one else knows.

He could have chosen to speak of so much but secretly she'd been just a little relieved when, instead of delving into the harder conversations available to them, he'd confided that he didn't like cartoons. Obviously, she'd thought he was absurd, but he'd seemed equally bemused when in return she'd shared that she didn't like sandwiches that were cut the wrong way. He'd stared at her for a moment and then made her two sandwiches so that she could illustrate the diagonal cut versus the half cut. He shook his head, threw his hands up in the air and stalked off muttering about silly English sandwiches.

The next morning, Amelia woke to find Alessandro waiting for her with a smile. He held out one of the paper tasks, looking strangely excited.

Take me somewhere you've always wanted to go.

And she'd buried her laughter beneath the sheets because he'd looked so much like an impatient child that she'd half expected to end up in Disneyland. Instead, as the view from the jet's window morphed from stretches of sea into stretches of desert, she realised that they were in Egypt to visit the Pyramids of Giza. None of the pictures she'd seen had done them justice. The sheer size and sense of history was breathtaking, even in spite of the large groups of tourists around them, chatting happily away and taking pictures.

Alessandro had asked if she wanted a private tour, and she'd declined because she liked the way he was when he was surrounded by people. As if he could relax and disappear in the crowds, rather than adopt that aura of power needed when he was the sole focus. It surprised her how easily he was able to give over that control and that attention and go with the flow of the loud tour guide, and throughout it all she felt his gaze on her almost as much as she saw it on the pyramids.

The following day while making her a decaffeinated coffee, Alessandro asked if there was somewhere she'd always wanted to go. Amelia looked up at him, nestling her cup in the palm of her hand.

'Could we go to Capri?' she asked, yearning in her heart making her pulse a little erratic.

'Of course. If you want, we can take a drive down the Amalfi coast and a boat to cross the gulf of Naples. Or we could take a helicopter if you like?'

She thought back to the last holiday her family had taken together, before her father had given up and before addiction took over her mother. They'd taken a hot, sweaty and *scary* drive down from Naples along the Amalfi coast—her mother hiding her eyes from the oncoming drivers, she and Issy squealing in delight at the twists and turns, too young to know better. It made her smile despite the ache in her heart. 'Boat, I think. I'd really like to take the boat.'

'Are you going to make me stand in line at the ferry terminal with the other tourists?' His demand was full of mock outrage and she was beginning to suspect that he secretly enjoyed being so anonymous.

'Actually, this time I think I'd like it to be just the two of us.'

In what felt like the blink of an eye, Alessandro had whisked them down to Positano and hired the most beautiful little speedboat she'd ever seen. It was like something from an old black and white film. Silken mahogany glowed beneath the Italian sun, perfectly offset by the deep racing green paint, the boat's sleek lines so smooth she wanted to run her hands across it.

Alessandro took the helm with attractive confidence and welcomed her aboard as if she were some grand duchess and he a lowly captain. The playfulness between them was addictive and her heart began to stretch towards the hope that it could always be like this between them.

She closed her eyes, letting the sun's rays warm her, and simply enjoyed the tang of salt in the air, the spray of the water, the rocking of the boat as Alessandro navigated around the deep swells caused by other seafaring craft.

But as they drew closer to the beautiful island, beloved by the rich and famous and lowly tourists alike, a sense of panic began to chip away at her pulse. The waves felt harsh as they jolted her and the grey craggy rocks beneath the lush greenery of the coastline felt threatening. The heat became uncomfortable and she began to feel breathless.

'*Tesoro*, are you okay?'

Usually, the endearment would have warmed her, but it barely even registered as she began to shake her head.

'Is it the baby? Is—?'

'No, it's not the baby. But…can we go back? Can we just…?' She gripped onto the seat beneath her, knuckles white, desperate to hold on while her world swayed in a way that went far beyond the sea.

Her obvious distress caused Alessandro serious concern and he quickly sped them away from the paths of the large tourist ferries and any other vessels, slowing only where it was safe, and he moored them just off a craggy coastal inlet. Turning off the engine, he sat and wordlessly pulled her into his lap, not stopping to question her need for him.

Amelia wrapped her hands around his neck and clung

to him as he swept circles on her back, trying to sooth the jagged breaths.

'*Cara...*'

She buried her head in his neck, scared to explain her feelings.

'Whatever it is, Amelia, it will be okay.'

You are safe with me.

Remembered words enticed her to speak, encouraged her to share the feelings so strong they had overwhelmed her.

'How could they?' she whispered. 'How could they have left us like that?' she asked him, even then knowing it was not his place to answer. 'I'm so...angry,' she said, realising the truth of the feeling thundering through her veins. 'I'm furious,' she cried, her hands fisting against the fact that the two people in the world who should have protected her and her sister had been so utterly selfish.

'We lost so much,' she said as the tears dampened Alessandro's linen shirt and her heart buckled beneath the onslaught of her feelings. 'Not money, or houses or friends. We lost *them*.' And for the first time she opened the door to the room where she had locked all that anger and all that resentment—not at having to look after and care for her sister, but resentment of her parents' utter neglect. And as her hurts poured out into the sea around them, Amelia let herself be comforted by the man who had, only days before, been her enemy.

Alessandro whispered to her in Italian; words of comfort to the incredible woman in his arms, until the storm of emotions that had gripped her had passed enough for him to talk to her about it. He knew that fury, he knew how hard it was to keep it controlled—he struggled with that himself. But Amelia, it seemed, had not realised what she had been fighting, her revenge plan keeping her and her sister from realising who had hurt them the most.

In that moment Alessandro wanted to destroy Thomas Seymore all over again. But if he had the chance to do so all over again, would he have? Knowing what it had done to Amelia and Isabelle? He could not take it back, and he could not apologise for it either. It had been a fundamental part of what had made him and Gianni who they were today and he was not, and would not be, ashamed of the men they had become. But that didn't mean he couldn't recognise the damage that had been done to Amelia and Isabelle Seymore's lives by his and Gianni's own need for revenge.

The sigh building deep in his chest was tired and heavy with thoughts of the past, clashing with the hopes he knew Amelia had for the future. A hope to do and be better. And he wanted it. He wanted it so damn much it terrified him. Because he'd had that same look, that same hope, once before and when that hope had been betrayed it had taken him decades to recover. He didn't think he'd survive it again. As if noticing the edge of darkness to his thoughts, Amelia stiffened in his embrace, until he forced the thought from his mind. Determined, instead, to soothe her hurts in this moment.

'Amelia,' he said, pulling back so that she could read the truth of his words. 'I really am truly sorry for what happened to your family. That was never an outcome we intended.'

She nodded her head, but he could still see the upset in her eyes. An almost violent urge to conquer any hurt she faced, any pain, and remove it from her path rocked him to his core. Despite the shocking power of that emotion, he gently swept back a sleek chestnut tendril of hair from her face. 'I'm sorry that you struggled and I'm sorry that you didn't have people there to look after you and take care of you when you needed it most. I'm sorry you had to do so much on your own.'

As he said the words, his own heart turned—like a sunflower following the sun—as if his words were trying to heal a hurt of his own, as if they were just as relevant to his childhood as hers. And this time when tears flowed freely down her cheeks, he knew that they were good tears, healing tears, necessary, so that she could be freer than she had been before. He placed a gentle kiss on a watery smile, and a little laugh escaped her.

'You can't kiss me now, I'm all…gross from crying.'

And Alessandro barked out a laugh. 'Amelia, *cara*, you are many things, but gross is not and never will be one of them.'

'I have a feeling,' she replied ruefully, 'that the next seven months might test that statement.'

For a moment they were caught up in a shared smile, his gaze dropping to her stomach where their child was slowly growing. Amelia, bottom lip pinned by a flash of white teeth, reached for his hand slowly—as if giving him enough time to back away. He felt hypnotised, unable to move—unsure whether he wanted this or not, scared in a way that he only vaguely remembered from a very long time ago. He let her take his hand and she placed it over her abdomen.

Surely, he wouldn't be able to feel the flare of her stomach this early on in the pregnancy, but he imagined that he did. Imagined that in there was the best part of both him and Amelia. They stayed like that for a while, lost in thoughts and hopes and dreams of a future they both wanted too much to say, until the blare of a passenger ferry startled them apart, and they turned to find tourists waving and yelling their greetings across the stretch of water.

Alessandro smiled, to cover the disquiet the moment had brought him, and said instead, 'Shall we go home?'

Amelia would remember the next few days with the hazy glow of summer and heat and a softness that she hadn't encountered before—from Alessandro or anyone other than her sister, for that matter. Alessandro could be funny, she discovered, enjoying the way that she could tease his ego without denting it or provoking a retaliation. He'd made her laugh as he'd answered another paper task to tell her something about Gianni that no one else knew.

She'd not been able to hold back the tears of laughter as Alessandro described in great detail, and a not inconsiderate delight, the time Gianni had tried to 'frost' the tips of his hair with bleach, only to have to shave his head and wait for his hair to grow back.

In exchange she'd told Alessandro about the time that Issy had fallen off her 'Gianni diet', ordered four pizzas, ice cream, garlic bread and sides, then got so scared about what her evil gym instructor would say the next day, she'd been too upset to eat it all, and she'd taken the entire lot downstairs to their neighbour.

Alessandro surprised her again with his impressive cooking and the fact that he was a secret foodie was almost one of her favourite things about him. From the incredible ingredients in the fully stocked fridge, Alessandro would create dinners at an almost gourmet level. After which, they continued to explore the passion they had discovered in Morocco. Amelia's nights were full of a heady sensuality that left her breathless and wanting in the daylight. Slowly they learned each other's pleasures, indulging in pleasing and receiving in ways that she could never have imagined.

But that, Amelia would later recognise, was the end of that brief momentary paradise they had together. Because the evening they returned from an idyllic day in Umbria, Alessandro received a message from work that had him locked in his office until long past midnight. And when he'd come to their shared bed that night, tiptoeing and trying to be so quiet, she let him think she was still asleep because she didn't have the courage to ask him about it.

The following morning, he was gone from the bed before she woke. But by the time she came down for breakfast, she was surprised to find him waiting for her. When he saw her, he put his phone away and offered her the decaffeinated coffee he had made for her and a slip of torn paper and it didn't matter what the paper said, just that he was still willing to do the silly tasks she had hoped would bring them together.

They were barely twenty minutes' drive away from the estate when he received another call and he cursed.

'You can put it on speaker if you like?' she offered, hoping that way he might be able to continue driving. And maybe, even, that she'd discover what was wrong and see if she could help.

'No, it's okay,' he replied, not meeting her gaze and signalling to pull over.

He got out of the car and took the call, pacing up and down the side of a dusty road. She tried to catch some of the conversation in between the roar from passing cars but it was useless. And she felt…frustrated and cut out. Even if it wasn't the Aurora project, she had worked with him for two years—she was good at her job. She could help if he would let her, but he wouldn't.

'I'm sorry, I have to go back,' he announced when he returned to the car.

The sudden engine ignition and the sweep of the U-turn prevented any further response from her. Only it turned out that Alessandro hadn't meant back to the villa, but back to London. Without her.

He returned that evening and Amelia clung harder to him that night than she had done before, as if sensing that he was slipping through her fingers, just as she had begun to realise that she loved him. It hadn't been quick, or sudden, it hadn't hit her like a punch, or stolen her breath. It had grown, piece by piece, as she'd uncovered little bits of him, like precious stones on a beach, hidden beneath sand and sea.

The loyalty he had to Gianni, the integrity he'd had with his business and his staff, the standard he held himself to, and the drive and determination to succeed. Those had all made him admirable in her mind even as she'd tried to sabotage him. And the physical connection they'd had? The strength of it had overpowered her own mind—her own determination to hate him, to make him pay for what had been done to her family. But his concern and care for her when she had collapsed, and then when she had emotionally broken on the way to Capri, made her feel as if she was seeing the *real* Alessandro Rossi. The way that he made her coffee, made her favourite dishes, those things had built in her heart. He had considered her in a way that no one had ever done before and it made her realise what she would lose if he walked away from her.

She worried about him when he went to London again the next day. The entire time he was away, her focus was on him and what he was doing, what was going wrong to take so much of his focus. And she could hear it, the whispered warning in the back of her mind. That he was cutting her out because he didn't trust her. That she was relying on him too much. That restless feeling creeping up on her grated on raw nerves and pacing inside the villa wasn't helping. Instead, she looked out across the pool and knew where she wanted to go.

As she entered the pretty wildflower meadow she was greeted by the red thumbprints of poppies bobbing and weaving across the tall grasses, reminding her of the finger paintings that her sister would bring back from the children's ward. Soft smudges of purples and cornflower blue, crested on the waves of gentle colours that called to her and softened her fears.

She lost track of time, just enjoying the simplicity of being here, until she found a rocky outcrop that nudged at her memory. It wasn't far from the section of land that belonged to Gianni, but she had known it would be there somehow and it unsettled her. She looked around, mentally drawing the boundaries of the land she had traversed, and her pulse began to thud heavily in her heart.

She knew this land.

She had seen it in drawings, and paperwork and a folder that had her father's name on it. And the realisation horrified her because finally she knew what it meant. Not just for the past, but for her future.

CHAPTER TWELVE

IT WAS LATER than Alessandro had hoped, but finally they were beginning to make headway on the problems that had stalled the Aurora project. Sofia Obeid had been impressive and as dedicated as he had been throughout the tense renegotiation with their contractors. Bitterly, he had to agree with Obeid; it would have been much quicker if they'd had Amelia on board, but he had dismissed the suggestion without excuse. Because how could he tell Sofia why he had cut Amelia out, when he couldn't even explain it to himself? Still. What was done was done and all he wanted to do was sink into a soft bed, and find that blessed oblivion only Amelia could offer him.

It was dusk by the time he returned to the villa, the sun reluctantly loosening its grip on the day. But Amelia wasn't in the house. He searched the rooms, not yet worried until she saw that the sliding door to the garden was open.

He marched towards the pool, concern sweeping through him like a wave, images of Amelia fainting again, of being in trouble and out of his reach, flung through his mind like sea spray. He gathered his speed and couldn't resist the urge to call out. Her name echoed in the vast area of the sprawling estate and something twisted in him at how lonely and desolate it sounded.

He rounded the corner to find her standing at the edge of the wildflower meadow, relief cutting through him to reveal a thread of heated anger, now that fear was edging from his system.

'Didn't you hear me calling?' he demanded as he reached closer to where she stood.

She turned to pin him with a gaze that nearly stopped him in his tracks.

Accusations, hurt and anger simmered there and he felt as if he had stepped back in time, as if they belonged on the face of a woman who wasn't yet carrying his child. He looked between her and the field and realised that she knew, that somehow she had figured it out.

'This is the land my father sold you.'

He wanted to curse. He wanted to deny it. He'd known that this moment would come and yet he'd prayed it wouldn't. Finally he nodded, watching her warily, as if suddenly she had become a great threat to him. And she was. In some ways that was exactly what she was. Ever since Hong Kong, she had changed him, had him thinking things, feeling things, remembering things—none were welcome and none were wanted. *Cristo*, he should have been able to resolve the issues they'd had on the Aurora project with the click of his fingers, but no, it had taken three days, because of her.

'You kept it.'

'Yes.'

'Well, let's face it. You did more than just keep it,' she said, her tone heavy with a cynicism he didn't recognise in her.

He frowned.

'Really?' she demanded. 'You aren't that clueless,

Alessandro. You are self-aware enough to know what you were doing.'

The taunt cut deep. 'Of course I knew what I was doing. Gianni and I made the decision the moment we could afford to,' he bit out. 'We built our homes around that one moment of betrayal so that we would never forget. *Never.* So that we would know the value of our hard work, and know that the only people we could trust was ourselves.'

She shook her head as if horrified by his words. 'This is more than my father,' she said, needling out the truth from him against his will. 'This is deeper than that.'

He reached for her instinctively—and she pulled away. He fisted the outstretched hand that dropped to his side.

'I need to know,' she said, her words barely audible in the gentle buzz and flutter of night-time wildlife. In the dusk he saw her place a hand over where their child grew within her and Alessandro knew she was right.

'To know what?'

'If you are capable of forgiveness. If there is even the slightest bit of hope for our future. You wake up every morning and look out at *this*,' she said, gesturing to the field behind her. 'You force yourself to hold onto that bitterness, to that symbol of betrayal. Is this how you feel about your mother?' she asked, her words hitting him like bullets in the chest, her eyes shining like diamonds in the darkness, her tears for him hurting more than he could possibly say.

'She betrayed us.' He slashed his hand through the air as if cutting off any more conversation. 'I know she tried the best she could,' he forced out, his heart and his hurt at war as it always had been. 'I know that she loves me—and Gianni too. And I love her too. So much that it hurts. But she still betrayed us.'

* * *

'Alessandro,' Amelia said, shaking her head helplessly, not knowing what to say. 'What happened to you was devastating. It was so wrong and I am truly sorry,' she said, hoping that he would hear the sincerity in her words. Her heart broke for him, for the child he had never been allowed to be. But that hurt made her even more sure that what she was doing was right. 'You have never forgiven her?' she dared to ask.

His silence was a knife to her heart. And now it was breaking for her, as the flame of hope she'd nurtured in his absence had just been snuffed out.

'Will you ever forgive *me*?' she asked, refusing to be cowed by the question. Her words rang into the night, clear and true. And she saw it—in his eyes—the past, his pain, his demons, all rising in the shadows around him.

'Amelia, you are pushing this too far too fast,' he warned her. And he was right, because she *was* pushing this too fast—even as she knew she shouldn't, but she couldn't stop herself from throwing them towards an impossible conclusion. Because if she didn't, she would only watch him walk away from her again and again and again. She was never going to be enough for him, just as she hadn't been enough for either of her parents.

'Does it matter?' she asked.

'Yes,' he said, sincerely. 'It does. I need time. Please...'

But she couldn't give him that, she thought, even as she knew she was wrong to refuse him it. The idea of watching another person in her life give up on her was too much. She had given her heart to him and he was already shutting her out because he didn't trust her. It rocked her to be standing here in the proof of how adamantly he clung to his betrayals.

'You won't forgive me, will you?' she said, her heart shattering beneath his gaze. 'It's why you kept the problems with Aurora from me, because you can't trust me.'

It was as if he'd been turned to stone, her statement proved truer for it. The only reason she knew he was still alive was the breath sawing in and out of his chest.

'Yet you trust me with your child?' she asked, half terrified, her breath caught in her lungs, because if he didn't—

'Yes.'

The word burst from his lips and she knew, instinctively, that he was telling the truth. She was thankful for it, but it wasn't enough.

'I need more than that, and our child does too.' She needed to know that their child would be raised in love and support without bitter undercurrents that dragged unformed hearts under.

He flinched. She barely caught it in the shadows of a night descending relentlessly, as if time was—and had always been—running out for them. And he simply stared at her while their lives began to come apart at the seams. Everything she'd hoped for, wished for in the sweetest of dreams, was falling away and he was doing nothing to stop it.

'Say something, damn you,' she hurled at him.

'There is nothing left to say.' His voice was raw as if he'd struggled to say even that.

'Yes, there is,' she said, her voice now shaking with a hurt and devastation that was only just beginning. 'You lied to me, Alessandro. You told me that you would keep me safe, you would protect me. You cling so tightly to others' betrayal, but it's you. *You* are the one who betrayed me, this time, Alessandro. *You* are guilty of that.'

And with that, she stalked past him and returned to the house, every step dimming the hope that he might stop her until it was snuffed out completely with the message that dinged her phone.

The jet is at your disposal.

Amelia hadn't been surprised to find a car waiting for her by the time she came downstairs with her clothes all packed in her suitcase. She'd been tempted to leave the things he had bought for her in Orvieto behind, but stubborn and stupid were close enough and it was possible she would need the clothes before long.

She knew that Alessandro would give her whatever she needed. He would never turn his back on her or their child. There would be painful, difficult, stilted conversations to come, but all she needed, right now, was time, space and...*her sister.*

She wanted to go home. But as the private jet swept in the arc that would bring them down to the English runway, she knew that the flat she shared with her sister just wasn't it. Home was where the heart was and she had just left that in Italy in the keeping of a man who was so determined to protect himself, he might never understand the value of what she'd given him.

She was holding herself together with numb fingers and desperation when she received a text message, and then another and then another. Hope turned to ash the moment she caught her sister's name on the phone's screen and she hated herself for being disappointed that it wasn't Alessandro.

Are you okay?

I'm back.

Where are you?

I don't know, her mind cried in reply. Amelia didn't have a plan for this. And for the first time in her life she wanted to give up, to curl up in a ball, to howl her pain as her mother had, to lose herself as her father had. But she couldn't. She had a little life to protect and, as much as her fragile heart was fractured and breaking, she needed to get up. She needed to make a plan. She needed to be the strong one.

Issy's name flashed up on the screen a second before her phone started to ring. Evidently her sister was too impatient to wait any longer.

'Issy?'

'Oh, my God, Amelia. Oh, thank God. Are you okay? Where are you?'

Amelia struggled to respond, wanting to tell her, wanting to give her answers to her questions, wanting to explain so much more, wanting to beg for forgiveness for lying to her about the evidence of corruption, for putting her in jeopardy with Gianni, for ruining her childhood on some naïve and mistaken path of vengeance. But instead, all she was capable of saying was her sister's name, before a sob took over and the tears came and they wouldn't stop.

In some distant part of her mind she knew she was on the verge of hysteria, that she needed to stop, pull herself together, but she just couldn't. It wasn't just Alessandro, it was her mother, her father, it was all of it and she couldn't keep it in any more. It was pouring out of her and nothing would make it stop.

Then she felt hands come around her. Small hands, but strong arms and she looked up to find Issy staring at her, tears in her own eyes, and concern stark across her features.

'Lia, please. You're okay. It's okay, I promise. It will all be okay,' her younger sister said, smoothing damp tendrils of hair away from her hot wet face.

Amelia didn't even think to ask how Issy had found her on a private jet on a runway in England. She didn't think to feel shame or embarrassment about what the staff had witnessed or where they were. She just let her sister envelop her, let herself sink into her sister's loving embrace and let that feeling heal and soothe just enough to get through the next minute and the minute after.

'I'm so sorry, Issy. I'm so, so sorry.'

'Shh. You have nothing to be sorry for. Nothing,' her sister said with such vehemence, it nearly made Amelia smile.

As her jagged breathing slowed and eased, she looked up and saw Issy for the first time. The Caribbean had glazed her skin golden, the blonde of her hair actually suiting her. 'Issy, you look beautiful.'

'Thank you,' she said, a simple shoulder shrug accepting the compliment without deflection or dismissal and it was lovely to see. 'You, however, Lia, look bloody awful.'

Amelia barked out a laugh and something eased in her chest. 'Oh, Issy. I've made such a mess of things,' she said, the sadness returning as swiftly as the flutter of a bird's wings.

'Whatever it is, we will fix it,' Issy replied confidently, and Amelia relished the feeling of being comforted, of being cared for. Issy turned to look behind her at the man standing at the top of the cabin.

Amelia's heart lurched, the height and breadth so similar to Alessandro it had fooled her for a moment. But then she saw all the ways in which Gianni Rossi was different from his cousin, one of them being the sheer love she saw when he looked at her sister.

Something unspoken passed between them and Issy turned back to her and asked, 'Can you come with us? I want to take you home.'

And even though the word jarred, even though Amelia was sure her sister didn't mean back to the one-bedroom flat in Brockley, even though she nodded and let herself be gently taken from the cabin of the private jet, she knew that wherever she was going it wasn't home, because Alessandro wouldn't be there.

For the next few weeks Alessandro stayed at Villa Vittoria, taking complete control of the Aurora project. He saw every email, every message, every report—it all went through him. And he knew that he was behaving like a tyrant, but somehow it had become imperative that nothing go wrong on this project. That nothing caught him by surprise again.

Gianni had tried to talk to him when he'd returned from the Caribbean, but for the first time in his life Alessandro didn't want to talk to his cousin. Just seeing the happiness Gianni had found with Isabelle Seymore, of all people, was unbearable and he *hated* that he felt that way. Never had he been jealous or resentful of the cousin who was more like a brother to him, but Gianni's joy came too soon after the sheer shock of Amelia's departure from his life.

You're hiding. I understand that. But it can only last so long.

But Gianni was wrong. Alessandro could make it last as long as he needed it to. Technology allowed him to stay in Tuscany and only fly out when necessary for meetings in both Europe and on the African continent should Sofia Obeid need it.

If she had noticed anything different about his exchanges, she had said nothing. Nor had she mentioned Amelia once. Which, instead of soothing his curiosity, only made it worse as he wondered if they were in communication, wondered if they spoke regularly, or at all.

He was not that surprised when he received the first message from Amelia informing him of her obstetrician's details. Of the first appointment. Of the results of the first scan. He hated himself for answering each message with one-word answers, but he wasn't capable of more. Because he would trail off into explanations, or justifications or demands that she return to him, or pleas that she let him return to her. And he wasn't ready for that. He knew that. *Recognised* that. Because she'd been right. He was still stuck in the past, its grip a vice around his heart and soul holding him in a place where he was not worthy of a future with Amelia and his child. Not yet.

He knew what it looked like from the outside…that he'd abandoned everything, including the mother of his unborn child, but he had never—*would* never do that. He had sent Amelia access to an account just for her that was separate from an account for their child. He had sent her the paperwork that showed he had no access to that account, would not be able to see any expenditures or receive notifications, knowing that it was the least he could do.

The only person he saw, aside from Gianni or Sofia in the occasional meeting he attended, was his mother. As the weeks turned into months, he began to travel to Milan almost once a week. The first time he'd visited it had been intensely painful. He had been full of resentment, anger and hurt. He hadn't expected much, he hadn't even really expected to talk, but his mother had appeared relieved, as if she'd been waiting for this day to come. That time they had simply, and very awkwardly, made polite conversation. Aurora Vizzini hadn't questioned him, asked him why he was there, or pushed him beyond what he was capable of, which was probably for the best. If she had, he might have left and not come back.

On the third visit they'd argued, impatience getting the better of him, hurt taking over, but as he'd left, she'd told him that she loved him. On the fifth visit he'd told her about Amelia and on the seventh he finally asked why they hadn't left that night. Why—when he and Gianni had needed to leave so badly—had she stayed?

Sitting in the chair, she couldn't meet his gaze. 'The shame and guilt that I couldn't be strong enough for you and Gianni…it will never leave. The horror that I allowed that man to inflict upon you…' She trailed off, shadows haunting her gaze.

And that was when his hurt and anger welled up to the surface, only to be swept back down in a whirlpool of guilt and anguish. 'But what about what he inflicted upon you? I couldn't stop it, Mamma,' he said, his voice quiet, but as rough as if he'd been howling his pain for years. Hot damp heat pressed against his eyes. 'I couldn't stop him, Mamma,' he repeated uselessly.

'You were a child, Alessandro, of course you couldn't stop it.'

'But I wasn't always—I grew, I was—'

'No, *mio bambino*, it was not for you to protect me. I was…glad when he realised that he could no longer… behave the way he had done.'

The anger and frustration that Alessandro had felt, once he had become bigger than his father and the physical threats had lessened but the manipulations and constant mental abuse had increased. And still he'd been powerless to do anything until they'd been old enough to escape, to get out, find jobs and work to support themselves—to support her.

'I couldn't get us out sooner,' he replied, the hot, furious energy leaving him utterly drained, as if he'd run a marathon.

'You got us out,' his mother stated, her eyes full of vehemence, determined that he would see how much that meant to her. *It is more than I did,* came the silent conclusion. 'I am so sorry for what I was unable to do as your mother.'

He shook off her apologies and she snatched up his hand, her skin silky soft and paper thin, her age startling to him as if only moments ago she'd been a young woman at the mercy of her husband.

'You need to hear it, know it and believe it. I am sorry that I could not protect you.'

'And I am sorry for exactly the same thing,' he replied, all that anger, all that hot rage melting away beneath the realisation that it was never about betrayal. It was never about being let down or lied to…it was about the helplessness that he'd felt as a child that had stifled and terrified him.

All these years he'd thought that he'd got up and got out, all these years he'd taken pride in his determination and ability to succeed, to strive forward, move on, but he was still there. Amelia had been right. He was still locked in the past, in his body, unable to escape—because *he* was the trap he had made for himself. *His* were the chains that roped his body and his mind and his heart.

It's you. You *are the one who betrayed me, this time, Alessandro.* You *are guilty of that.*

And in that moment, he realised how truly he had messed things up and finally he broke. The invincible shields he'd drawn around himself shattered all at once, falling to the floor, leaving him vulnerable and weak. And this time he allowed his mother to wrap her arms around him and protect him.

CHAPTER THIRTEEN

Three months later...

AMELIA FOLDED HER jumper and placed it in the suitcase beside the bed in the spare room of Gianni's penthouse apartment in London as her sister, Issy, hovered anxiously in the corner. She couldn't help but feel the pull of a smile tugging at her lips, knowing that her sister wouldn't stay silent for long.

'Don't go,' she begged.

'Issy.' Amelia turned and smiled. 'It's not far.'

'It's the other side of the river!' Issy cried.

'It's fifteen minutes away,' Amelia said, setting free the gentle thread of laughter beneath her words. Issy's eyes, though, were full of concern—a concern that Amelia understood. When Issy had first found her, she had been utterly devastated. Full of heartache, not only for the future she had lost with Alessandro, but the past she had lost because of her parents.

The first month she had spent with the new and delightfully happy couple had been hard in many ways. The conversations that she'd had with Issy about their parents had been honest, difficult, but ultimately deeply healing. And they were conversations she wouldn't have had, had

Alessandro not initially allowed her to come into those feelings in a safe space.

She resisted the urge to check her phone. Usually, he was quick with his one-word responses to her messages about her obstetrics appointments, but uncharacteristically he hadn't messaged in reply to her last one.

'Are you sure you're ready? I mean, you can always stay here a little longer?'

'Don't you want the place to yourself with your new husband?' Amelia asked.

'God, yes, but, oh—I'm sorry!' Issy had a hand pressed to her mouth, clearly worried about what Amelia would think, but she needn't have worried.

'Never be sorry, Is! Never. I'm thrilled for you,' Amelia said, wrapping her arms around her little sister and holding on tight. 'Really. But it's time that I got used to doing this on my own.'

Understanding shone in her sister's eyes, before she heard Gianni calling for her below. With a quick kiss to her cheek, Issy left Amelia alone in the lovely room that had been a haven for her when she most needed it. Her heart turned in her chest as she wondered about Alessandro, worried about what haven he had gone to after she had returned to England.

Over and over again she had replayed their conversation in her mind, seeing at almost every turn where she had gone wrong, but been unable to stop herself from doing so. She despised herself for not being able to give him what he'd needed when he—who had rarely ever asked anything for himself—had asked for it. She'd wanted to, but she'd been so battered and bruised, having only just accepted the damage from her parents, it had not been within her power.

Amelia had found a female counsellor in North London in the second month, knowing that she had many things to work on in order not to make the same mistakes as her parents when it came to raising her child. She would accept whatever help in whatever form to provide her child with the best that she could possibly give, and that had—she reluctantly realised—included dipping into the account that Alessandro had provided for her.

She needed her own space to think and to be. Looking back now, the unease she had felt, the desperation that had driven her to force Alessandro's hand, what had shaped so much of those last days with him, had been fear. Fear that had teeth and claws from the neglect of her parents who had left her alone carrying a burden that was too much for a young teenager. But she wasn't that scared young teenager any more. She was an adult now, who relished the chance to care for her child, to accept that responsibility not as a burden but as a gift.

Now she could see that she wanted to share her life with Alessandro because she loved him, because she admired him, because he was exactly the kind of man her father had never been to his family—but most importantly Amelia knew that she didn't *need* him to be the parent she wanted to be and the woman she knew she already was.

Her heart hurt to recognise it, but her soul knew it was right. As right as her need to find the right way to truly apologise to him. But for the first time, where Alessandro was concerned, she didn't have a plan. A fix. Something that she could prepare for. Only...she knew that she wanted to apologise. Because for all her accusations of betrayal, she *was* the one who had let him down when he had needed her understanding the most.

* * *

Alessandro knocked on the door, unease painting thick strokes of ice across his back. When Gianni opened the door, he caught surprise, shock, hurt all flit across his cousin's gaze, before it was replaced with indifference— a look Alessandro had never thought to see on Gianni's face. But he could concede that it was the least he deserved.

Ever since Amelia had left Villa Vittoria, he'd been acting like a stranger. After the painful confrontation with his mother, Alessandro had completely retreated. He'd handed over control of the project to the team with final oversight going to Gianni and Sofia. He'd left Italy and its memories so that he could have the time and space to think clearly about what he wanted for his child, what he wanted for himself, and what he wanted for Amelia.

Looking back on it, he could see how badly the lie about Firstview had sat with Amelia. The shadows beneath her eyes, her behaviour stilted and pained, until the truth had come out. And then her fierce love and protection for her sister, her determination to make it right, her adamant protection of their child and her desperate desire to give their child more than they had...it overwhelmed him.

He didn't just lust after her, that wasn't the connection that had formed between them—as he'd tried to convince himself early on. It was *her*. He loved her. He was inspired by her, awed by her. She was greater than him in every way and he missed her so much it was as if part of him had gone. A part he'd never known existed.

'Are you waiting for an invitation?' Gianni demanded as he beckoned him into the London apartment he was now sharing with his new wife. Isabelle Seymore had taken Gianni's surname and was now Isabelle Rossi and Alessandro was still wrapping his head around how the two cousins had fallen so deeply in love with the daughters of their one-time enemy.

'You!'

The hurled accusation from the living room where a woman who resembled Amelia was pointing at him as if she had accused him of being the murderer in a country house crime drama.

'You!' she repeated.

'Yes, me,' Alessandro replied in the hope that acknowledging it might make her stop—his hands might have also gestured surrender.

This, he knew, he also deserved.

She glared at him and he knew he'd made a mistake.

'You think this is funny?' she demanded.

'There is nothing funny about it,' he replied truthfully and something in his tone must have made her stop, as she glanced uncertainly at Gianni who, he saw, shrugged.

'What do you want?' Isabelle asked, eyeing him with a considerable amount of suspicion.

'I want to know where Amelia is.'

Isabelle snorted and he thought he'd heard her say, *yeah, not likely*, but he couldn't be sure. He looked at Gianni.

'I need to see her.'

Gianni shook his head. 'You are my cousin—my blood. But she is my wife. You'll understand one day.'

'Not if no one tells me where Amelia is,' he all but growled, his frustration getting the better of him.

'You broke her heart,' Isabelle accused.

'I know,' Alessandro admitted.

'No. You don't. She is my sister and I will fight to the

death for her and her child,' she said fiercely and suddenly he saw it—the similarity between the siblings, the passion, the fire, the determination. 'You—' she stabbed a finger at him '—broke—' another stab '—her.'

'And I promise you that—if I get the chance—I will spend every single day for the rest of my life ensuring that it never happens again. I know that nothing I say will fix the damage that has been done, but she needs to know that it was *me*, not her.' His words burned and cracked as they came from his soul, but he needed to say them. '*I* caused the cracks that broke a strong, powerful, beautiful woman,' he said, thumping his chest. 'I need her to know that,' he said to Isabelle, his tone all but begging.

Something flickered across Isabelle's gaze and he felt the hairs stand on the back of his neck. He felt the pull of that connection that he only ever felt when Amelia was nearby. He turned, slowly, vaguely registering Gianni pulling his wife from the room, because all he saw was Amelia. Amelia glowing, eyes bright, cheeks flushed healthily and skin still wearing the faint bronze of Italy. Amelia so round with their child that it took his breath away.

'You're here?' Alessandro couldn't believe his eyes.

'Yes, I… I wanted to be with family,' she said, unable to meet his gaze.

He took a step forward, but the way that Amelia held herself made him stop. She looked as if she were trying to hold the pieces of herself together and he hated that he'd done this to her. But he bore it, because that was his due.

'You heard what I said to your sister?' he asked, his words sounding as if they'd been dragged across gravel.

Amelia nodded, sending a wave of chestnut rippling

down her back. Her hair was longer, richer, more vibrant than he remembered.

'It was not... I wanted to...' Alessandro bit back a curse. He'd planned what he'd wanted to say to her, how he wanted to start, and this was going horribly wrong. He wasn't prepared, but that didn't, couldn't matter. She deserved to know and hear the truth of his feelings and he needed to tell them. He took a breath—a deep one.

'You make me flustered,' he admitted, helplessly. 'And I don't get flustered. At least not any more. My mother tells me that it used to happen to me as a child when I desperately wanted something,' he said, ruefully, rubbing the back of his neck.

'*Tells* you?' Amelia asked, picking up on the tense he had used.

He nodded. 'We've been spending some time together,' he replied, noticing the way her hand had begun to sweep slow, soothing circles over her round belly. He wondered if she'd felt their baby kick.

'I went to see her. You were right—about so many things. But the first and most important one was how trapped I was by the past. How it coloured everything and made it impossible for me to move on, move forward with any kind of life, let alone one that I want more than my next breath.' He hoped that she could read the truth in his gaze—that it was a life with her that he was speaking of.

Amelia was standing by the large window looking out onto the street as if only partially listening to him, but he knew—he knew that all of her considerable focus was on him. He felt it like a touch—warm, comforting, hopeful.

'I realised that it was not her I was angry with,' he said, willingly offering Amelia the deepest of his truths, baring his soul to her, hoping that somehow he might be worthy of her, 'it was me.' Some of the shame he had spent years wrapped in still lingered, but he was working through that knowing that neither he nor his mother deserved to feel shame or anger any more.

Amelia turned to him at his words. 'Alessandro—' She reached for him and he went to her, but he also needed to finish. As if she had read the thought in his mind, she held her words back.

'There is much more work I need to do, she and I need to do, but all this time I thought that I had left the past behind me and you were right. I was chained by it. And had it not been for you I would never have seen that, never have realised it. No matter what happens after today, or in any of the days that follow, I want you to know that you have changed my life for the better because of who you are. And I love you.'

Amelia's heart quivered, little gentle shakes rippling throughout her body.

'I love you,' Alessandro said again, as if he knew that she needed to hear it. 'And I will never stop loving you.'

She reached a hand to the chair to hold herself up. 'And I know that I offered you the security you wanted with one hand, and took it away with the other—the security to know that you were safe and loved and trusted—and I will never forgive myself for that.'

Amelia wondered if his words were magic, summoning all the broken shards of herself, raising them from the ground and bringing them back together. She wanted desperately to speak, to share of herself in the same way that he was, but she held herself back because she knew that he needed to say this. They had time, she began to realise with an expansion of her heart. They could take this time not to rush.

'I understand,' Alessandro continued, 'if you choose to move forward on your own with our child. I would...' His words stumbling once again, letting her know how hard this was for him, how much he struggled with what he wanted and letting her go to have what she wanted. 'I would like to be involved in my child's life,' he said, her heart cracking, but not breaking, reforming anew rather than what it had been like before, reforming to make room for him, right beside the love she felt for their child. 'But I trust that you know what is best for our child,' Alessandro said, and even the thought of him retreating, of him removing himself from their lives, cut her to the quick.

Finally, as if on the brink of his retreat, she found the courage to move towards what she wanted with her whole entire being.

'Alessandro,' she said, closing the distance between them and taking his face in her hands. 'I'm so sorry,' she said. The surprise in his gaze would have been near funny if it weren't so sad. 'I'm so sorry,' she repeated uselessly. Months of planning what she would say and her heart simply beat too loudly for her to hear what she had hoped to have the chance to say.

'I was so scared. I saw you retreating into work, shutting me out, which,' she said, holding up her hand to stop him from explaining, 'I understand, utterly and completely. It was what you needed to do in that moment. How *could* you have included me after I nearly destroyed your company? But I used that to feed fears I barely knew I had. I panicked and just couldn't see how you would want to stay with me when...when even my parents hadn't. But I'm working on that, and on much more,' she said, wanting to share the decisions she had made in the last few months, wanting to share so much of *her* life with him, not just their child's.

'I love you,' she said, her words overwhelmed by the depth of her emotions. 'I love you—powerful, proud, driven and occasionally flustered, you. The you who is loyal, caring, protective and who wears that love for his family on his sleeve.' His eyes exploded with hope, starbursts alight with love and want and the infinity that she had thought she had found with him once before.

He took a sharp breath, as if shocked by her declaration, and gently pressed his forehead against hers as if in reverence.

'If you take me back, I promise you'll not regret it. I'll spend every single day proving myself worthy of you.' He pulled back enough to look her in the eye.

'If you take me back, I promise to spend each and every day showing you the love and family that you are worthy of a hundred times over,' she said with a vehemence that matched the man she loved.

Her lips found his, and everything she'd ever wanted was in that kiss. Love, reverence, security, and everything she wanted to give him, she desperately hoped he felt. But when she wrapped her arms around him to pull him against her, something poked into her ribs. Angling back, and reluctantly breaking the kiss, she pressed her hands to his chest.

'What is...?'

Alessandro reached into his jacket inner pocket, a flush riding his cheeks.

'I've been carrying this with me for the last two months,' he said, and although there were nerves in his gaze, there was a dizzying anticipation. He pulled a small blue velvet box from his jacket. 'After all the mistakes I made, there will never be a right time. I know that. But I had hoped to at least do this properly,' he explained as he lowered himself to one knee.

Her hands flew to her mouth, stifling the gasp that caught on a smile. He opened the box to reveal a ring so perfect it could have been made for her. It had small green sapphire stones around a perfect red ruby, and it reminded her of the wildflower meadow at the heart of Alessandro's home.

'Amelia Seymore, you are the better part of my world, the whole of my life, and the only future I could ever have. I love you in a way that makes me better, that makes me want to be better and that brings me hope every single day. Will you do me the greatest honour, and be my lover, my partner, my companion so that I can love you, protect you and be with you for the rest of my days?'

Tears gathered in her eyes, and she happily shed them to see the shining love in his gaze for her.

'Yes,' she said, nodding. 'Oh, yes, please,' she added, pulling him from the floor so that she could embrace him. 'I love you, Alessandro Rossi,' she said, before placing her lips across his, and finally, after what felt like years of searching, Amelia Seymore came *home*.

EPILOGUE

'*CARA*, PLEASE, YOU'RE DOING it all wrong—*ouch*!' Alessandro exclaimed as his wife slapped his hand away from the meal she was trying to prepare. It wasn't the slapping hand that worried him, but the knife gripped in the other that he eyed warily.

'Mr Rossi. I have six years of experience when it comes to making our daughter's favourite meal. Would you care to argue the same?'

The look in his eyes plainly told her he could, but instead he said, 'I would care not to argue at all, Mrs Rossi, but if you insist, perhaps we can take this into the other room?' The innocent expression on his face was utterly obliterated by the heady desire pouring from his gaze.

His hand slipped around her back and pulled her as close to him as her eight-month baby bump would allow. As much as Amelia wanted to, and she really did, Issy and Gianni and their children were due over soon and so much still needed to be done.

It had been nearly six months since she'd last seen them, her current pregnancy had been a little difficult and had prevented her from flying over to the Caribbean Island Issy and Gianni spent half of the year on, and she was desperately looking forward to seeing her sister.

Amelia looked across the counter top to the large wooden table set for their entire family. She remembered once imagining Alessandro sitting at it all alone and it pleased her to know that she had never seen that come to reality. As her husband tried to distract her with kisses to her neck—his favourite place on her body, it seemed— she remembered with a full heart the Christmases, New Years, birthdays, and every celebration they could make, shared with family and laughter and love.

'They would understand,' he whispered seductively in her ear. 'They're worse than we are. At it like rabbits, as you English like to say.'

'Mamma, what are rabbits "at"?' their daughter, Hope, asked innocently from the other side of the kitchen counter appearing—as usual—from nowhere. Hope Rossi had inherited her parents' ferocious intelligence and her love of books from her paternal grandmother, if Aurora Vizzini's proclamation was anything to go by.

'Jumping. Running and jumping around the meadow,' Amelia replied without missing a beat while Alessandro choked on his shocked laugh.

'The one where we meet Uncle Gianni and Auntie Issy and Mia and Matteo for picnics when they're home?'

Amelia nodded. She wondered just how much her niece and nephew would have grown as Alessandro swept up their daughter in his arms and threw her into the air, catching her without even raising Amelia's blood pressure. He had kept true to the promise he had made, not only the day he proposed, but before then, in a café in Orvieto. He had kept them safe, he had given them everything they could have even wished for, let alone needed.

And she had never, in the days and years that followed,

questioned his love and unconditional support. She'd had it when she had chosen to work with Sofia Obeid, at first part time after her maternity leave and then full time as partner in Sofia's company. And she'd had it while she had explored her issues from her parents with the therapist. Sometimes she still felt the echoes of the past, as she knew Alessandro did, but the healing that had been done with Aurora, who was also set to arrive for his birthday meal shortly, was a beautiful thing to see.

'My love,' he said, gently moving her out of the way of the oven so he could check on the food. It turned out that Alessandro loved nothing more than providing for and feeding his family. A family that would grow again in just one month's time. 'Can you please sit down?' he asked, still concerned about how much she was doing at this stage of her pregnancy. She shot him a glare that had none of the anger of their early interactions and all the heat that had burned between them from the very beginning.

He could see that she was about to argue when Hope heard the chatter of her cousins and the laugh of her uncle and aunt coming from the garden and she was off like a shot, allowing Alessandro to steal a kiss from his beautiful wife. He remembered how he had once been shocked by the possessiveness that had made him fear he had lost his mind. Instead, he realised later, it had been his heart. And only once he'd accepted his love, and had that love returned, had he found a peace and sense of rightness that he had never imagined possible. That didn't mean that they hadn't argued or that there hadn't been hard times to overcome. But they had faced, and would continue to face, each and every challenge together, safe in the knowledge and assurance of their love.

No one looking at them from the outside would have ever believed that they had once been enemies. Enemies who had become lovers and then soulmates bound together for the rest of their days by a love that was true and everlasting.

* * * * *

HIRED FOR HIS ROYAL REVENGE

LORRAINE HALL

MILLS & BOON

For anyone who ever had a crush on Dimitri.

CHAPTER ONE

AL ASSUMED SHE'D once had a real name and a last name, but she didn't know it. And never would. She had vague memories as a small child of being called Alexandra and being taught how to survive by various people on the streets. Some were kind, some were cruel, some were indifferent, but she had survived.

That was all that mattered most days.

She did not remember anything before being on the streets, so like most of the others she'd met, she assumed her parents were dead or indifferent. Neither mattered. They were gone and she was here.

One of the best methods of survival on the dangerous streets of Athens was to pass herself off as a boy. Even now, at twenty-four, her short stature and small frame meant she could be believed as a teenage boy rather than a grown woman if she dressed and held herself accordingly.

As she did now. She wore tattered baggy pants that hid the shape of her hips. Over her shirts, she wore an oversized coat that gave bulk to her shoulders. Add thread-bare boots and shaggy hair pulled back with a small tie, and no one ever questioned her.

She leaned against the corner of a building on a tourist-laden street and surveyed the crowd.

She had a meeting, and she always preferred to meet in the bustling streets for a quick escape should things get *complicated*. Trading in information had a tendency to have tempers flaring, particularly in those men who fancied themselves powerful...then threw tantrums like children when they did not get their way...or could not hide their misdeeds.

Al usually didn't take jobs from people she hadn't been referred to and hadn't checked out carefully. She tended to be very careful about people who approached *her*. She made sure she knew everything about a *client* before she even spoke to them. But this particular afternoon, she didn't *truly* know who she was meeting. Only that the payout she had been promised was far too much to resist.

It was enough to possibly get her out of the spy game forever. In the beginning, it had been exciting. To realize that, since no one paid much attention to a little beggar on the street, she could hear things and see things that other people found useful.

And would pay for.

But as she'd gone from offering up information she *happened* to witness or overhear to people coming to her *for* information, spying had gotten more complicated, more dangerous. Like today.

It was possible this whole meeting was a trap. Things were getting a little...hot. She'd uncovered the misdeeds of a few too many powerful men who were now on the lookout for a boy spy roaming the streets of Athens. Who wanted Al dead.

She could shake that identity, of course. Live life as she truly was: a young woman. She could find a new city to live in as a boy. But those options seemed just as dangerous as the men after her.

At least they were the enemy she *knew*.

Her life had been the streets and survival for as long as she could remember, but she was tired of subterfuge and lies and mystery and danger. She wanted something… pleasant. Relaxing.

Safe, most of all.

This payout could buy her all of that. She only had to bend a few of her rules to get it and hope the mysterious man who'd sent his men to approach her was on the up-and-up.

So she waited for a man. That was all she knew about her client. His employee—a taciturn mountain of a man—had told her to stand exactly here and wait for his boss to approach.

She watched the crowd carefully. A few people looked her way, usually nervously. Women clutching their purses a little tighter, especially if Al arranged her face to look particularly surly. But most people just looked right past her short frame and out-of-the-way stance, more focused on their daily routines or the sights they wished to see.

Al did not see much point staring at ruins, vestiges of a life so long ago no one alive today would even recognize it. She much preferred watching the living people. How they reacted, what they did, the words they spoke in a variety of languages as they passed.

She was beginning to grow antsy as the agreed-upon time came and went. Frowning, she scanned the crowd around her one more time. That was when she caught the glimpse of a tall man in white. He seemed to cut through the crowd like some kind of archangel. Or apparition. Or just a deadly sweep of a sword.

People moved out of his way—some without seeming to realize it, some watching him move in awe. He did not ask anyone to. He did not excuse himself. It was just…done.

He was stunning—it was the only word she could think of. Like some gladiator brought to life, polished up perhaps for a portrait, because even though he looked like he could *handle* a fight, his expensive suit and bright white clothes didn't suggest he'd seen one recently. His dark hair was swept back, his face sculpted and bronzed as if perfectly created to draw attention to his eyes. Sharp, gold. *Obviously* dangerous.

And he was walking straight for her.

Al ordered herself to maintain her lazy posture, her combative expression, but it was more and more difficult to hold the closer he got. He walked right up to her, practically towering above her so that he blocked out the sun in the little alcove she'd agreed to meet him in.

Because this had to be the *him* who wanted to meet her—well, Al. She hadn't been given a name when his employee had talked to her, but she knew who he was now. It was nearly impossible to spend any time in Athens and not know *his* face.

Lysias Balaskas. *Billionaire*. Self-made, at that. One of those stories people trotted out to prove *anyone* could achieve *anything*, because Lysias himself had, allegedly, been a product of the streets. According to the people who spoke of it, Lysias had gotten himself a job above his station as a young man and then worked his way up until he'd owned…just about everything there was to own.

People said it was because he was brilliant and charming and determined and hardworking.

Al knew that success, especially success of Lysias's magnitude, required all those things but also a great deal of luck. Or *she* would be CEO of some conglomeration of companies that did something with...something. Because she could be all those things, if given the chance.

She had decidedly not been given the chance.

His gaze raked over her as he stood in front of her. He took her all in with a considering way that had her wanting to sink deeper into her baggy clothes and disappear into the shadows, because the hairs on the back of her neck stood on end. Something uncomfortable and unwelcome jittered in her chest as his dark golden gaze met hers.

She wanted to run, but the self-preservation instinct she had so much pride in was no match for the way his gaze pinned her to the spot.

"Al, I presume?" he said, his voice smooth and sounding vaguely...amused, when Al didn't have the first clue what would be amusing about the situation.

She felt a bit like she'd placed her life into his hands, and she hadn't even spoken.

She gave herself a second to get her bearings, to focus on the task at hand and not the gold of his eyes. The feeling of being *trapped* and wanting to lean into it. She tried to speak in her usual insouciant low tones but found her voice much higher than it should be. "Yes, I'm Al."

His beautiful mouth curved, likely at the shake in her tone. "Excellent."

Lysias Balaskas found himself wholly and uncharacteristically uncertain about this *Al*. Though he had heard nothing but positives about the boy and his ability to find even the most hidden information, something about the way he stared made Lysias feel even more aware than he usually was.

As a man bent on revenge, he was *always* aware. Of who looked at him. Of what people thought. Of where he was and how he moved. Because unlike most people who walked these streets, Lysias had only one goal in his life.

And he allowed *no* distractions.

"Why don't we take a bit of a walk, my boy," Lysias offered in an effort to perhaps jolt the boy into finding his wits about him.

Lysias tended to have this effect on people. He knew he was good-looking—add money and power, and people often found themselves at a loss for words. It was just an everyday occurrence for him. Though he'd expected perhaps *more* of the boy he'd heard had uncovered the secrets of some of the most powerful and dangerous men in Greece.

"You have a job for me," this Al said, taking a step next to him. Lysias noted the way the boy's eyes surveyed the crowd. Calm, cool, assessing. Looking for danger.

Well, that was more like it. Clearly he'd sussed out who Lysias was and, maybe after his initial surprise, would now behave the canny spy Lysias had been promised.

"There is a very old rumor I would like you to look into for me," he said, walking through the crowd as though he had not a care in the world. But his attention was on Al—the way the boy moved, what he looked at and how he reacted to everything Lysias had to say. "It involves the kingdom of Kalyva."

There was no flicker of surprise or reaction. Only a shrug. "I do not know this place."

"It is a small island. Tiny really. They are very independent, very private. And ruled by a king." And Lysias wanted to destroy said king, with his bare hands. But since that was not an option, he would settle for subterfuge to get his revenge. To enact all the destruction King Diamandis deserved.

"And what do you want with it?"

"That is not your concern. Your concern is to find out everything you can on the murder of Princess Zandra Agonas on Kalyva twenty years ago."

"You want me to get you information on some old murder that happened on an island I've never even heard of?" Al asked suspiciously. He looked up, but the minute their gazes met, the boy looked back down. "Seems a stretch."

"The entire royal family was murdered in a bloody coup. Except the current king. The rumor is Princess Zandra's body was the only one not recovered," Lysias said, unconcerned by Al's skepticism. "I need to know that this is true beyond a doubt. It will require you to find a way to get close enough to King Diamandis to discover the absolute truth, or what he believes to be the truth anyway. I will cover any costs on top of the already generous payout my man discussed with you."

The boy's mouth turned down, and there was just... something off about him. Lysias felt that old itch between his shoulder blades. A telltale sign that something was amiss.

But he had been assured of this boy's skill and, having once been a boy on these streets himself, knew what a smart one could do with an opportunity.

Besides, Lysias would make sure he had the upper hand. He always did.

So he would continue forward. His revenge on King Diamandis had been twenty years in the making, and no matter what Al found or didn't, Lysias would never give up.

The king was the reason his parents had been killed, the reason Lysias had scrabbled on the streets for the remainder of his childhood after being exiled from Kalyva.

The king would pay. For everything.

"You will travel to Kalyva with one of my men. Tonight. Then you will set about finding what the king knows. You will report to Michalis, who will, in turn, report to me. No one can know about our connection once you're on Kalyva. Trust me when I say that it would be as bad for you as it would for me."

The boy pursed his lips and kept walking. He glanced behind them once, so Lysias did the same, wondering what the boy was worried about. A tail? The police?

"Travel costs extra," he said at last.

"Was my initial offer not generous enough?"

Al stopped, stepping out of the way of teeming tourists with ease. He glowered up at Lysias, or tried to. "It's not generosity—it's compensation. Besides, I know how much you're worth."

"You know how much people *think* I'm worth." He grinned at the boy. "The truth is beyond most people's comprehension."

The boy's eyes widened, and his cheeks turned oddly pink before he looked away once more. He studied the world around them, clearly considering the deal. "I want some money up front."

"So you can run?"

He shrugged. "Call it insurance."

Al tried to keep walking, but Lysias reached out and took him by the arm. He pulled the boy close enough, all the way onto his toes, to get his point across. Not a violent threat. Lysias no longer *needed* violence. *He* was threat enough.

"Know this, boy. I *will* track you down if you take my money and run. To the ends of the earth. No one crosses me. I simply do not allow it."

Wide, dark eyes watched him. The boy was slight, with delicate features. Lysias couldn't fathom how he'd survived this long on the streets, let alone doing what he did. Part of Lysias's defense as an adolescent had been his size and strength. His ability to fight his way out of any predicament.

Al clearly would not be able to do that.

The boy jerked his arm away and Lysias let him, but something about the interaction left him…suspicious. He couldn't put his finger on what struck him as *off* about the boy, but he didn't trust him.

"I want an up-front payment," Al insisted. He nodded to the watch on Lysias's wrist. "That'll do."

Lysias raised an eyebrow. "Do you have any idea what this watch is worth?"

Al grinned, cocky and amused, the first glimpse at a boy who would make a very good spy. "Oh, I've got a pretty good idea, *ploúsios*."

Lysias was surprised to find himself enjoying the boy's cheek. Much better than the odd stares that left him feeling as if something were all wrong here.

Lysias slid the watch off his wrist and dropped it into Al's hand. "It would be easy to track that down if you defy me."

"Yes," Al agreed. Simply. Easily. He pocketed the watch, surveyed the crowds around him once more. "When and where?"

"Midnight. My private marina. I'm assuming you can find this on your own."

"Naturally."

"I'll be there with my man of affairs, so you can be assured you are meeting the correct person. I will ensure you are on the boat and on your way to Kalyva. Michalis will cover your costs while on the island and be your main point of contact. If you do not find me the information I require in a week, we'll reevaluate the deal."

Al didn't study him. He studied his own feet. Then he shrugged. "All right." And without a handshake or anything else, he took off on a run. Quickly disappearing into the crowd.

Lysias watched. He didn't think the boy was bolting from *him*. His impression of the boy was someone capable and likely to show up tonight and do the work on Kalyva, but *something* was off. Wrong.

Lysias knew this in his bones.

So, after the boy disappeared into the crowd, Lysias followed.

CHAPTER TWO

AL TOOK OFF for a few reasons. Number one, she knew she was being watched—and not by the magnetic Lysias— though him too. No, someone out in that crowd wanted to hurt her. She'd noticed the same man in too many places today, and while she'd never caught his eyes on *her*, it was too much of a coincidence.

She had to lose him. So she ran.

But it wasn't the *only* or most alarming reason she'd felt compelled to run. Lysias Balaskas was…problematic. She couldn't seem to hold his gaze without blushing. She was far too interested in the quirk of his beautiful mouth than what it said.

And those *eyes*. Nothing in her short but eventful life had prepared her for the effect this man had on her. She had dealt with the wealthy, the powerful, the good-looking, but he was in a category all his own. Deep within and elemental, Lysias was different. It terrified her.

Worse, it enticed her.

She had to get away from him. So she'd bolted. With his watch, sure, but that didn't mean she *had* to take his deal. If she decided not to meet him at his marina, she'd return it to him without him knowing it and stand him up tonight.

She pulled a face as she dove right into crowds, then

swiveled out again. The marina, a boat with a stranger. She didn't like the idea of traveling with anyone, let alone Lysias's employee. Just her and some *stranger* in the middle of the sea. Not even the unnerving man she'd met this afternoon—not that she trusted *him* either.

Al trusted no one.

She skittered down a tight alley, the hot sun beating down on her. She had a lead on her pursuer, but she could still *feel* that shadowy figure following her—she knew too well what pursuit felt like. She hadn't lost them yet.

Maybe a new location would be good. She had never heard of this island. Maybe it was because she was uneducated and unworldly, but maybe other people didn't know about it either. It might be the perfect opportunity to escape everything breathing down her neck here in Athens on someone else's dime.

She ducked down a wider alley, crossed a busy street, always keeping an eye behind her. She'd been the quarry in a few of these little chases, and she didn't revel in it, but she knew how to escape.

Had to escape.

An island would be an escape, wouldn't it? Strangers were dangerous, but the devil she knew was getting a little too close. A little too scary.

Maybe it was time for a new devil. Lysias definitely fit the bill.

Kings and murdered princesses worried her, but she'd been slipping in and out of the affairs of the rich and powerful for years now. Were royalty all that different? A change of scenery, a payout that would allow her to be herself, not Al...

It could all work out.

If she escaped her current mess. She climbed a ladder up onto someone's balcony, then took a hop over to the next and the next. Once she got to the other edge of the building, she jumped off, startling a young couple sharing a dessert on a bench. She flashed them a boyish grin, then darted across the street, holding her hat on her head as she did so.

And still someone chased her. Getting closer. Panic began to clog her lungs, but that was certain death. She had to think clearly, rationally. She was certain she was doing just that, but then she tripped over a man's foot, and though she narrowly missed a fall, a group of men angrily shouted at her.

It startled her, rattled her as much as the meeting with Lysias had, and so she ran without fully taking into account where she was.

A fatal mistake, as she ran right into an alley with no exit. She studied the wall in front of her, looking for any sort of foothold. Some way to climb it. Some way out.

There was nowhere to run. She blew out a breath as her world crashed around her.

She supposed she should take her fate philosophically. She would die at the hands of someone else. It had always been possible. And she'd done some good with her insignificant life. Uncovered many a man's misdeeds.

It was a shame she'd never truly gotten to live as herself. Have some sort of *life*. For some reason, that made her think of Lysias and his golden eyes and wicked smile. Which was foolish enough she turned to face her attacker.

He had a long knife. A scar that ran from his temple to where it disappeared under the collar of his shirt.

"That looks bad," she said, jutting her chin at the scar.

"I suppose you're going to do the same to me?" She eyed the knife and tried to breathe through the terror. Hold on to bravado. But she'd always had a fear of blades, more so than even a gun. A gun could take you out quick.

A knife took its time. A knife was torture.

Her legs shook, but she told herself to fight her way out. She'd get hurt. Stabbed, sure, and that was a nightmare of hers, but if she just *ran*, she could stay alive. Maybe. If she didn't bleed to death. If he didn't fully overpower her.

So she went with that. She just ran. Plowed right into the man, hoping to dislodge the knife. She didn't, but she *did* surprise him so that he fell back. Of course, that had her tripping over *his* body. But she got passed him.

She scrambled to get to her feet, could see the daylight and the alley opening and all the freedom it represented. But the moment she was *almost* there, the man's hand caught her around the ankle and jerked, sending her sprawling on the hot, hard ground. She fought desperately, but she was no match for the man who crawled on top of her.

She clawed, she kicked, but nothing dislodged him from his purpose. He used the knife to roughly cut away her shirt, and panic beat so hard in her chest she couldn't breathe. She saw the dawning realization on his face, even as she bucked and fought and kicked harder with panic, dread, the desperate desire to survive.

"You're a woman. A shame we couldn't have some fun, but my orders are clear. Consider this a gift from Mr. Pangali," he said, mentioning one of the powerful men she'd uncovered as a liar and a cheat *and* a murderer.

Slowly—as if he enjoyed causing pain—her attacker began to press the sharp edge of the knife through the bonds that held her breasts down and then upward—not just cutting away the fabric but slicing into her skin. Trying to create the long, jagged line from chest to temple that he had.

Pain had an unholy noise escaping her throat, and she bucked with all of her strength. Much to her surprise, the knifeman flew off her. He let out a yelp of pain as he crashed hard against the wall of the building.

Now able to see the entire alley, Al realized she had not magically overpowered her attacker.

Lysias was here.

For a moment, she was frozen. He'd *saved* her. She sucked in a breath, but everything hurt. Pain radiated from her chest, and the sticky warm feeling of blood seeping out of the knife wound made her dizzy.

She had to get up…she had to…

Lysias leaned over her, those golden eyes holding her still—but only for a moment. Because he reached out for the torn piece of shirt. "Where are you hurt?"

She pushed him away, tried to scoot out from his grasp, his gaze.

"Stop fighting, boy," he said impatiently. "I'm going to help you," he said so disgustedly, so authoritatively, she hesitated.

And in that hesitation, all was lost. Because his hands were on her where she bled, and all she tried to hide from the world was clear to him. She knew it when his hand rested over her breast—bound but not enough now that she'd been *stabbed* there.

He pulled back, looked at his bloody hand, then down at her. "You're not a boy."

She scurried out from under him, using his surprise as a means of escape. But there was nowhere to go. He blocked the only exit. So she stood, breathing ragged, the blood trailing down her chest and too much of her exposed. Who she truly was, *exposed.*

But she wouldn't cower. He'd saved her from one threat, but that didn't mean he wasn't one himself. She had to keep fighting.

"You're not even a girl," he said, studying her critically. "You're a woman."

Lysias did not often find himself shocked. In fact, he could not remember the last time someone had pulled such a con over on him.

Of course, he'd *known* something was off about the boy, but he had not considered Al might be a *woman.*

She tilted her chin upward, all challenge. She did not speak. Those dark eyes looked at him with pure hate. But pain also swirled in their dark depths.

He had already instructed his guard to take care of the assailant, so it was only he and Al—the *woman*—standing in this dingy alley in a poor, dangerous neighborhood of Athens.

He circled her, but she moved as well, never allowing him to be at her back. Smart woman.

She had survived on the streets for some time, he supposed, pretending to be a boy, though she'd narrowly escaped a gruesome end here. Intriguing.

But before he could work through all this and what it might mean, she needed medical attention. "Come," he said, holding a hand out to her to encourage her obedience.

She did not take it. She clutched her torn shirt together and studied his hand as suspiciously as if he were holding the knife. "Where?"

"Somewhere we can clean you up."

"I can take care of myself," she said.

"And yet, here you are. In an alley. Stabbed and bloody and saved. By me, I might add." The blood trailing down her golden skin and dirty shirt was concerning enough, but her face was also dangerously pale, and she reached out to stabilize herself against the wall.

Which made his decision for him. She had been manhandled enough, but she needed a doctor. He marched forward, did his best to avoid hurting her and carefully scooped her off her feet, despite her protests.

She fought initially, but the hiss of pain seemed to force her to realize her predicament. So she stilled here in his arms. Tiny thing that she was.

His thoughts were dark as he marched her to his car. That desperate men with knives and cruel men with power would try to harm someone in such a lower position than they.

"What happened to…him?" she asked, as they approached his waiting car. His driver stood expressionless, back door open and ready.

"My guard has taken care of it. Your attacker will be dispatched to the nearest police station."

"Without a victim, nothing will happen to him," she said, devoid of any emotion. "Even with a victim, really. It hardly matters anyway. He's just paid muscle."

He knew from experience living on the streets tended to beat the belief in justice out of a person. But he would ensure her attacker found justice—as well as the man who'd sent him.

He had built himself up out of the depths of poverty and abandonment to be the hand of justice himself.

"I'll make sure he pays."

She looked up at him. Her eyes were dark, that earnest gaze she hadn't been able to hold before. Maybe she could now because they were hazed with pain and worry. *Fear.* And because he knew her secret.

He did not relish frightening any woman, but it frustrated him that she would fear when he had just *saved* her. "A thank-you wouldn't go amiss."

She said nothing.

He found his mouth wanting to scowl, but he would not allow such feelings. He had saved her. She *would* thank him eventually. And he would get what he needed out of her.

This did not change their deal.

"Now, watch your head," he said, surprised at the softness in his tone. Uncomfortable with it. But she was injured. And a *woman.*

He crouched to carefully deposit her on the seat, then skirted the car to the other side. He slid into the seat next to her. He had already instructed his driver to take them to his private home outside the city center.

He had many residences in and around Athens, many closer, but this was the one he went to when he wanted privacy rather than attention. Though her wound needed a doctor, keeping her identity on the down-low was just as important. For her. And for him—as he had plans for this woman.

Old plans, and now new plans as well.

He reached forward and pulled open one of the many compartments in the back of his car. Though he tended to stay out of physical fights these days, he was a street urchin himself at heart. He had a first aid kit and, even more importantly, a nice bottle of brandy.

He handed her some gauze. "Hold that over where you're bleeding. Wouldn't want you soiling my seats." Then he poured her a small amount of brandy in a glass and handed it to her.

She took the gauze, but shook her head vehemently at the alcohol. He shrugged, took the drink himself, enjoying the slow burn of the expensive liquor. He wished it would settle the dark feeling coiled tight within him. Though he was familiar with such feeling, it rarely expanded any farther than the object of his revenge.

He made a few calls to prepare his residence. For a visitor. For someone who needed medical attention. She watched him the entire time, pushed up against the door as if she might try to escape the minute the car stopped. As if *he* were her attacker.

So he stayed on his side of the seat and watched her right back. Considering. Because this unexpected turn of events might actually be quite...good. For him, of course, but he was a fair man, mostly. He'd make it good for her as well.

She had her back straight, but she was clearly holding herself gingerly due to the pain. She clutched her torn shirt together, pressing the gauze to it. Without her hat, with her hair untied, she looked a bit more feminine, but really she could have kept the pretense if her attacker hadn't cut through the bonds that flattened her chest.

"What is your name?" he asked, finding himself unduly curious.

"Al."

"That is a boy's name."

She shrugged and offered nothing more.

"Do you dress as a boy because you wish to? Or as a

disguise?" She could be pretty, he supposed, given the right amenities and opportunities. Which suited the new plan he was formulating.

"Life on the streets is easier for a boy."

"Not easy." He had learned that at the age of twelve. When he had been tossed out of Kalyva with *nothing*. By the king, who'd barely been older than himself.

"No, but easier," she replied. She shifted in her seat, clearly trying to cover a wince. "Once you pay me, I will live as I please," she said haughtily. But he knew enough about desperation, about wishing for better, to hear the yearning in her tone.

And the fact her little dream was missing an important step in getting paid. "Once you complete your job, and *then* I pay you, will you live as a woman?"

She hesitated. "I don't see what it matters to *you*, but yes. As long as it's safe to."

"And what will you call yourself then?"

She hesitated, as if considering the ramifications of him having such a small piece of information. "Alexandra, I suppose. Though I've gone by Al so long I don't know why I'd change." She turned to look out the window, though it was tinted, so not much could be made out. "Where are you taking me?"

"My private residence. A medical professional will check you out—one I pay to be discreet. Once we know the extent of your injuries, we will determine the next course of action." But he already had the plan. A way to move up his timelines.

A way to taste revenge before the month was out.

Because revenge was his only goal. Not understanding this street urchin, no matter how interesting she might be. She was simply a tool to get what he wanted—a tool he would compensate generously for her work.

He studied the woman critically. She had the right coloring, more or less, when she wasn't pale from an attack. What didn't quite fit with her hair, with her nose and mouth, could easily be fixed in a salon or with the right clothes and makeup.

"I'm fine," Al said stupidly, in his opinion. "I just need a bandage or something. Take me back to *my* home. I'll find out about the princess. This won't stop me."

Lysias made no move to entertain her little attempt at orders. *He* did not get ordered around. "Do you *have* a home?" he asked instead.

"Perhaps not as fine as yours, but certainly a place to lay my head."

Yes, she was going to fit into his plan very, very nicely. The obstinate lift of her chin, the challenge in her eyes. With the right training, that could be seen as royal. "I'm afraid our plans have changed."

She got that wild look, panic, through and through. Like when she'd bolted from him in the crowd. "I don't want them to."

"Alas, I find that you now have two uses for me." He smiled at her, quite pleased with this turn of events. He understood that part of his success came from his tenacity, his spite that drove him in everything he'd done since the age of twelve, but there was also the element of luck to how far he'd been able to climb.

And luck was once again on his side.

"Asteri mou," he said, smiling at her. "It is your lucky day after all. You are to become my bride."

CHAPTER THREE

AL WAS CERTAIN she must have heard wrong. He must speak a different language—one where *bride* meant something else entirely.

"We will likely be able to avoid an *actual* union, of course," Lysias continued as if this were normal. As if…

Maybe she had a head injury. Surely she did since she was riding in this luxurious car, a stab wound on her chest, going to who knew where without having put up much of a fight. It was his eyes. His authoritative way of speaking that didn't feel like commands so much as the only reasonable course of action. It was the blood loss, the trauma. It was everything except *reasonable, rational* and *sane*.

"But, should push come to shove, you will be compensated for this as well. A large payout is your goal, is it not?"

"Money, not a husband." Bride. Husband. She pressed her free hand to her forehead. Was she in some sort of fevered delusion?

"Even a billionaire for a husband?" Lysias replied, though she didn't believe his feigned surprise for a second. Though he had stepped in to save her, though he was being hands off and allegedly going to get her medical attention, she saw that he was not really different from the man who'd sent her attacker.

Lysias had decided something—regardless of how strange—and thought he could sit there and smile charmingly and she would just go along. That she wouldn't poke or argue or *uncover* all that he was.

"*Especially* that," she said, giving an injured little sniff. "I have no interest in men of wealth and power who think of little else."

"It is not my wealth and power that consumes me, *Alexandra*. Though they are impressive."

He practically *purred* the name, which wasn't hers, but it seemed almost as if him speaking it into existence made it so. And every syllable felt like a caress down her spine. Not just a jitter in her chest but something dangerous and yearning blooming deep within her. Stuck again in the direct beam of his golden gaze.

Al tried to breathe normally, to let out all that had gotten clogged without giving away how affected she was by…him. But it was no use. His smile deepened.

She scowled at him. "Then what does *consume* you?" she asked, being sure to imbue the word "consume" with as much disdain as possible even though pain and fear coursed through her.

"Revenge," he said. Simply. Bland, almost, but she saw the fierceness in his gaze, in the way he held himself. "I was wronged many years ago. And I will not rest until that wrong has been righted."

Every word got more intense. Deeper and darker. She realized in the brief flash of it, there then gone, that he kept this fury banked or hidden away under some kind of mask. But it was there. Perhaps *always*.

And she did believe that it did in fact drive him. That he was a dangerous man, but she had never been afraid of dangerous men. Fear never accomplished anything good, so she had done all she could to eradicate it.

"Maybe I don't wish to help you enact revenge," she said.

He did not respond with surprise or fury as she had expected. Maybe even hoped. Both reactions she would understand.

The cold, cutting smile was not one she could make sense of.

"Let me tell you a little story about the kingdom of Kalyva." He leaned forward, those gold eyes seeming to gleam here in the dim back seat, where even the daylight couldn't make it through the tinted windows. And those eyes acted like some sort of hypnotist's tool to keep a woman still and rapt with whatever he said.

"It is small and independent, as I said. Some would call it backward, old-fashioned. They would not be wrong. The king and queen of my youth were good people, or so it seemed, but they were not *strong*. And so, as dissatisfaction with the old ways mounted, they buried their heads in the sand and ignored all the whispers, all the signs. And though the bloody coup ended their lives and the lives of all but their oldest child, the kingdom remained, because the eldest child survived."

Al didn't realize she'd leaned forward, that she held her breath, waiting for the rest of the story.

"The new king was not much older than a boy, but he was full of revenge. Understandably. But his revenge blinded him, and he had no interest in who was actually innocent or guilty. He was only interested in causing his own brand of bloodshed. He sentenced my *innocent* parents to death, labeled me a traitor, claiming I had not raised the necessary concerns against my parents' plot against the princess, and had me sent to Athens. With nothing. I was *twelve*."

Lysias was cold, angry, and even his hand had curled into a fist. Perhaps she should be afraid of him. He was a large man. A strong man—he'd thrown her attacker off as if it were nothing. He was full of fury and revenge.

But all she could think of was a boy of twelve tossed from everything he knew. Lost. She had always been lost, but she had no idea what had existed before. It would be much harder to adapt at twelve.

It was impossible to picture him as a youth, and yet she felt for the boy he must have been all the same.

"You are an avenger, Alexandra," he said, though she thought she preferred Al to the overly feminine name she'd considered going by someday and foolishly told him about. "You have sought, at your own peril, to un-mask the misdeeds of many a powerful man."

He was right, but it felt like losing whatever little power she had here to admit that. So she lifted a shoul-der, though it hurt—both her wound and her conscience. "For a price."

Lysias leaned back, some of that controlled anger banked in his eyes. He smiled at her. "Yes, a price. A smart person always takes payment for the work they do. But the payment doesn't matter if you're dead, and you have risked death. You've decided to take that risk, again and again, because you wished to see justice done, regardless of what you might lose."

She did not know how to argue with that. It was only

the facts. Though she took the money to survive and had gotten into the whole spying on people game as a means of survival, she had taken increasingly higher profile people down. At her own risk, because she'd wanted to see powerful men who did bad things *fall*. Because she had, too often on the streets, seen the victims of their abuses of power.

Lysias's smile widened when she said nothing. It was as if he could see through her, down to her very soul. Which had that same foreign warmth from earlier bloom deep within her. Her instinct was to look away, but his eyes compelled her.

"So now, Alexandra, you will help me enact my justice. Once and for all."

Lysias watched the emotions play out over Alexandra's face. He would turn her into Alexandra even though she tried very hard to keep her mask in place, a boyish kind of challenge she must have perfected over the years.

But she was hurt, and he knew his story compelled her. He could see it in the way she looked at him now: less hate, less suspicion, though some of both still. But it was all softer, there in her dark eyes.

"We are not that different, you and I," he told her. "We come from a similar place. Once my plan is a success, you can have much of this too." He gestured to the luxurious car they were in.

"Much, but not all?" she replied.

"No one can have it all. Except me."

She did not smile in return, but something lightened in her gaze that made him want to *genuinely* smile, instead of the media smile he trotted out to play the role of Lysias Balaskas. A man *not* bent on revenge.

The car slowed, no doubt pulling through the gates to his expansive estate. "Ah, we are home. We will get you patched up, then discuss the plan."

"And if I refuse to help you?" she asked.

He studied her. This woman, who'd posed as a boy for so long. Bloody in the back of his car. Alive because he'd saved her. And she dared suggest refusal? It should be an insult. An outrage.

He had no idea why he wanted to *laugh*. He did *not*, but he wanted to. He kept his gaze on her, his expression carefully bland. Because Lysias Balaskas had built himself into a man who got *whatever* he wanted.

And he would have his revenge.

"Your refusal is immaterial. You will do everything I say. For this, you will be rewarded. Beyond your imagination. This I promise you. But there will be no *refusal*. I have saved you. I know your secret. You are mine for the foreseeable future."

Her outrage was a thing of beauty. No matter how disheveled and bedraggled she was, her eyes flashed. Temper brought some much-needed color to her cheeks. She *could* be beautiful.

She *would* be once he was done with her.

"I have never cowed to a man before, *Lysias*," she said, drawing his name out like one might draw out a curse.

He found himself aroused by it. *Interesting*, but not something to think too much on in the current moment.

The car had stopped, and the woman needed medical attention for certain. The driver opened his door first. So Lysias got out without response. The doctor he kept on his payroll to ensure any and all necessary silence stood at the entrance.

Lysias waved him over, and the man was quick to approach the car. Lysias himself opened the door to Al's seat. She looked up at both of them with mulish distrust.

"Let me have a look now," the doctor said briskly.

She looked at the doctor, then at Lysias, then back. Then, as if sensing she couldn't really do *anything* until someone attended that wound, she dropped the gauze for the doctor.

Lysias left them to it. Seeing the wound on her created too many conflicting feelings. He only had room in his life for one revenge. Though he made a quick call to his guard to check on the fate of the attacker and then made a few more calls to ensure the man never saw light outside of a cell again.

He also set in motion a clandestine investigation that would put whoever was behind the attack behind bars. He considered Al—*Alexandra*—under his protection now, until his revenge was seen through. That protection included justice.

His staff would ensure she did not escape, and he had much work to do to move up the timeline of his plans. So he went to work.

A few hours later, he was summoned to dinner by his housekeeper. "And our houseguest?" he asked.

"She has been seen to by the doctor. Stitched up and cleaned up. We suggested she rest and eat in her room, but she insisted on seeing you, so we've seated her at the table should you wish to dine together."

"Excellent."

Lysias walked through his home, realizing with a start

the odd feeling in his chest was excitement. But of course he was excited. His plans for revenge were within his grasp, truly, for the first time.

He strode into his dining room, a finely appointed formal affair he usually entertained businessmen and diplomats and other influential people at.

Now there was a young woman with light brown hair at his table and he stopped short. She wore a shapeless but comfortable-looking cotton dress one of his staff must have obtained for her. Her face was fresh and she wore no makeup. Her hair was pulled back, much as it had been when she'd been posing as a boy, but it had been brushed rather than left shaggy and unwashed.

She looked like a stranger. A female stranger.

Until she met his gaze with that haughty disdain she'd tried so hard to maintain in the car. *That* he recognized.

"This is a lot of work just to eat," she said by way of greeting. "Is this what happens when you have so much money you don't know what to do with it? You have to make simple things into a wasteful production?"

"Perhaps I simply love a production, wasteful or otherwise." He studied her as he took the seat across from her. Her color was much better, and she didn't hold herself as though she were in pain. "How are you feeling?" he asked as the staff brought out dinner.

Al watched the food with avid interest. "That doctor, if he really is a doctor, stitched me up. Gave me something for the pain. I'm not supposed to lift anything heavy or go scaling buildings and facing off with men with knives for a few days, but somehow, I will survive."

Her bland description of events amused him. But not

enough to remember the one thing he hadn't gotten from her. "I'm still waiting for that thank-you."

She grabbed the fork and the knife on either side of her plate and merely scowled at him before attacking the food angrily. She did not thank him or say anything else.

But he was a patient man. When he wanted to be. He sipped his wine and watched her. She certainly still *moved* like a young, wild boy. "How many times did you try to escape?"

She hesitated before lifting the next bite to her mouth, decidedly not answering his question.

"My staff will inform me, so you might as well say."

"Twice." She stabbed a piece of meat with her fork. "You kidnapping me doesn't make me too keen on helping you with this whole revenge plot. Taking down a powerful king or no. Payout or no."

"I saved your life. Brought you to a doctor. I am feeding and clothing you. This is hardly a kidnapping."

"It's not *not* a kidnapping," she grumbled, gulping from her glass. Though he had spent years on the streets, he *had* been raised in a palace. As the help's child, yes, but he had learned how to handle himself at a dinner even before he'd become wealthy, thanks to a friendship with the young royals.

"Table manners," he muttered. "You have much to learn." Much work to do if he wanted to leave in a few days. Because for many years, he'd wished to return to Kalyva with a fake Princess Zandra on his arm, a twist of the dagger on top of his decade-long work to undermine King Diamandis on Kalyva.

He'd never been able to find the right woman though, and now that the plans were in place to take Diamandis down, it was the last little piece to the puzzle. A woman with no past, no history that could be unearthed. There was no way to prove, aside from actual DNA, that Al was *not* the princess.

Yes, luck was definitely on his side once again. Because he was close enough to all his plans that he could risk the bluff. A few days of media circuses and demands before any DNA test could be done.

As long as there was no body found—and Lysias was willing to risk the consequences as all his instincts told him there hadn't been—he would get *everything* he wanted. As long as Al cooperated.

So she would.

"I don't wish to learn *anything*," she said petulantly, wiping her mouth with the back of her hand.

So *much* work to do. "This isn't about your wishes, Alexandra."

She pointed the fork at him across the table. "Because you've kidnapped me."

"And what a terrible kidnapping it is. Eating a fine meal prepared by one of the best chefs in the country. A shower. A soft, warm place to sleep. The *horror*."

"Oh, I'm not sleeping here."

"That you are," he said, his amusement fading. This was too important and her resistance would ruin his timeline. "You wish this to be a kidnapping, I can make it so. You are an integral part of my plan. I will pay you handsomely, but I will not tolerate your defection. I have lived my life focused only on revenge against one man, but trust when I say this." He leaned forward, needing to make sure she understood the gravity of this situation. "No one crosses me, Alexandra. No one."

CHAPTER FOUR

FEAR FLUTTERED IN Al's chest. She did not think Lysias would *hurt* her. As he kept pointing out, he'd saved her, and he was feeding her. And the doctor who had stitched her up had actually been kind. All of Lysias's staff had been efficient and kind as well.

Not to mention, the food was some of the best she'd ever tasted, and she *was* hungry. The dress she was wearing wasn't anything beautiful, but it was more comfortable than anything she'd ever worn. And the bath she'd taken—at the insistence of his staff—had been like nothing she'd ever experienced—warm and inviting and relaxing, even with the stab wound on her chest they'd had to work around.

She did not think Lysias was an *evil* man per se.

But she understood he only *cared* about his revenge. That she was only a tool in it, not something he was tending to because she mattered. He was making it very clear that if she got in the way of his revenge, she might be the next target of it.

And that *did* scare her a bit.

Al had enough self-preservation instinct to acknowledge, in her head, that going along with his plan, and taking her money and running when all was said and done, was likely better than escaping or trying to thwart him.

At least for now.

But she also didn't know how to simply sit back and accept that her circumstances had changed at the whim of a *billionaire*. That she was suddenly being bossed around by someone else.

Even if she went along with all this—enjoyed the food, a nice place to sleep, et cetera—that didn't mean she had to cede *all* control. He *needed* her after all. He'd said so himself.

"So, tell me about your plan," she said as irreverently as she could manage, with the delicious food and likely the painkillers twisting together to make her sleepy. But she was determined to stay awake. "So I can decide what parts I agree with. And what parts will need to be altered. Or require more compensation."

He raised an elegant eyebrow. She figured she was meant to wilt at that. But she held her head high. She was hardly intimidated by silence from an impressively gorgeous face.

Of course, when his surprise and condescension morphed into that slow, dangerous smile that caused dark, twisting sensations low in her stomach, she had to curl her hand into a fist underneath the table to remind herself not to let her unease…or interest show.

"First, we will attend a gala here in Athens," he said, turning his attention to his crystal wine glass. Al figured she could get a decent sum if she pawned just *one*. "I will introduce you as my fiancée to the eager media and crowd."

That got her attention. "You expect *me* to attend a gala as your *fiancée*?"

"You will have a considerable makeover." He met her gaze with all that amused gold. "Of course."

She tried not to scowl at him. Obviously, she would not fit into some billionaire *gala*. She wasn't sure even a "considerable" makeover would ever make it seem like she belonged. That didn't mean she *liked* it being pointed out to her with such obvious derision.

"Are you my fairy godmother, then?" she said sweetly.

"If you wish to see me as such, feel free." He waved a hand as unconcernedly as she was acting. Too bad she believed it on him.

"All right. So gala, introduce me—what does this have to do with the king of…wherever?"

"Kalyva. You will need to study up, as well as learn those table manners. After the gala, we will embark on a trip to my homeland. With the media in tow. I will claim that I have finally found the long-lost Princess Zandra so many thought—feared—dead. There will be a media circus. Lots of attention and distraction. The timing is perfect, as the king's spring ball will be held the weekend after we arrive, so there will already be much attention on the palace. The next morning is the annual council meeting, an integral part of my plan."

"I thought you needed to know about the body."

"It's true. My intel has not given me this information, but this is where Al comes in. You will find out while we tell all and sundry that Zandra is alive. My appearance and yours will be enough of a distraction to the kingdom that it will take some time to sort through. Even if there was a body, we'll be able to insist, for a few days, that it was an imposter's."

"Won't they be able to do tests to figure that out?"

"Yes, but such tests take time. If we are found out to be liars before I get what I want, I will say I was conned by a stunningly beautiful seductress." He flashed that alarmingly potent grin at her. "You will become Al, and no one will know what happened of said con artist pretending to be Zandra. However, if there is no body and never was, my plan will move forward. Regardless of the outcome, you shall receive your payment."

It was a ridiculous plan, made all the more ridiculous by her involvement. "Do you really think you can pass *me* off as a princess?"

"This is why the plan is perfect. You don't need to look the part of princess or act the part. You have enough a passing resemblance to be Zandra, who no one has seen for the past twenty years. And in my story, you have been suffering amnesia all these years. Secreted out of the palace to Greece, then raised by some poor farm family somewhere in a remote area of the country, with no education or training in royalty or wealth. Then, when your elderly parents passed, your grief led you to remember who you really are."

"That is some story," Al replied. "Who would buy it?"

"Everyone. Because I will ensure they do. You see, a fake princess has always been my plan, but I was never able to find someone who was quite right. You have no past to be uncovered. You can disappear into another identity should the need arise. You're well adept at all the sneaky things a job like this entails."

She did not know how this plan could possibly work. It was far-fetched at best. But she supposed if she held up her end of the bargain, it didn't matter if it was believed. She'd get paid either way. "What of those who are after me—after Al?"

"I will protect you, regardless of your identity, for as long as you are in my employ."

The word "protect" sent such an odd warmth cascading through her. She had never been protected. No one had ever cared...

But this was not about care. It was about revenge.

"So, when is this gala? How much time do I have to prepare?" She figured she'd need weeks, at the very least, to turn herself into someone who knew even how to *pretend* to be the fiancée of a billionaire. Particularly *this* billionaire.

"The gala is Friday. You have three days."

She laughed, though it was clear he wasn't joking. Just... "You're insane."

"No," he replied, sharp and foreboding. "I am determined."

Lysias answered the rest of Al's skeptical questions. And he had an answer for all of them. This had been his plan for so long, and it was finally coming together. Better than even he'd imagined.

Because she *was* perfect. No past for anyone to unearth. A passing resemblance to the Kalyvan royals. A willingness to pretend to be someone else for money, and the backbone to deceive whomever she wished.

Lysias was *mostly* certain the body of Princess Zandra had never been found, because the reports had always been that she'd been found with her brothers—which Lysias knew firsthand couldn't be true. He'd been in the palace that night, though he tried not to think too deeply on this. His theory was that the palace had planted that story so that the rumors and conspiracy theorists did not run amuck.

The rumors and whispers had anyway. Though, admittedly, not with the same fervor they might have otherwise. But enough, paired with the truth Lysias himself had witnessed, gave him this opportunity.

And he had his contingency plans in place on the off chance he was wrong. So, yes, the plan was perfect. So perfect he didn't even mind her questions.

But her eyelids began to droop, and before she'd even finished dessert, she'd fallen asleep. Right there at the table. Her head resting on her arm.

He wasn't sure how long he watched her careful, easy breathing. Wasn't sure *why* he watched it. Only that in sleep, she was just as compelling as awake. She did not look like a boy, or even the prickly young woman she'd been at dinner.

She reminded him of an old fairy-tale book his mother had read to him. A cast-off from the nursery of the royal children. Filled with old and faded illustrations of fairy sprites and brownies. Sweet and innocent-looking but full of mischief. Ready to lead you to danger if you were not careful.

Lysias was always careful.

Still, though he could have called his staff to take care of her, he did it himself. Moved over to her side of the table, lifted her from her chair. She barely made a sound, clearly exhausted by the day's events.

He carried her through the house, his footfall soft. She was so slight it was no hardship. He had set her up in the rooms just outside his private quarters—to keep his little flight risk close.

He nudged open the door and stepped inside. There was a light on, but only one, and it cast a soft glow. He made it to her bed and set her down on the mattress, then paused, glancing down at her. In the dim light, he had the flash of someone, something familiar. It stabbed through him like pain, so he shoved it away. He did not go back to those dark recesses of his mind, and whatever resemblance she had to anything back then was mere coincidence.

And would serve him well.

She didn't so much as whimper. She lay exactly where he put her, limp and helpless, the dress nothing but a baggy sack. And yet, something speared through him. A dark, possessive *want*.

She seemed unable to believe herself capable of becoming a princess, but Lysias knew everyone would believe it. She had the confidence, a kind of quiet beauty that could be teased out by all the tools women used. But even without her hair cut and fancily done makeup and a pretty gown, cleaned and fed, she had her own, unique beauty.

Her eyes fluttered opened, met his. But there was something far away about them, like she was still sleeping. Perhaps a waking dream?

"Am I safe here?" she murmured.

He heard someone else ask him that long ago. An old failure. An echo of an old loss amongst so many.

He said nothing to her. Made no assurances. He simply turned and strode out of the room, leaving all those distracting feelings, those old swirling memories behind.

And if he kept his distance the next three days, it was only because *he* had no experience turning a woman into a princess. He hired people who could do that. Who would polish her up to a pretty shine.

He had his staff pass along anything he thought she needed to know about Kalyva, hired an etiquette tutor for her so she might feel comfortable attending the ritzy charity gala. And he did not see her for three days.

The night of the gala, he readied himself in his rooms, ensuring with his man of affairs that all the details for their travel tomorrow was settled.

Tomorrow, he would be in Kalyva. Tomorrow, he would tell King Diamandis that the princess was alive.

And engaged to him.

Just the very thought of it all made Lysias smile as he straightened his tie. Tomorrow would be the beginning of all his revenge.

But first he needed to get through tonight. He strode through his house and down to the entryway. "Is she ready?" he asked the housekeeper.

"They are bringing her down."

"Excellent." Lysias didn't often have to wait on others, but he enjoyed the drama of an entrance. Why shouldn't she? His pretend bride. The perfect little tool of revenge.

It wasn't too much longer before he heard murmurs from the top of the grand marble staircase. She appeared, sandwiched by two members of his staff who seemed to be offering her last-minute advice as they moved forward.

She walked down the staircase at a careful glide. She was watching her feet, which gave the whole production a kind of authenticity. That of born princess raised farm girl plucked out of obscurity by a smitten billionaire.

In this moment, he didn't care for the idea he would need to pretend to be *smitten*, because the gown she wore outlined the body beneath all the baggy layers he'd seen her in. Her shoulders were bare, though the dress somehow came up high enough to cover her stitches so that no one would suspect she was the kind of woman who'd nearly been stabbed to death in a dangerous alley in Athens a few days prior.

The deep purple fabric of the gown swept around the slight curves of her body, the color of the dress making her skin warm, like she glowed from within. They'd trimmed and cleaned up her hair so that it curled gently under her chin and showed off the graceful, enticing curve of her neck.

Her face was made-up, though there was still something natural about it. Except the deep color of her painted lips.

Heat fisted into him, a blow he had not expected under any circumstances. As she reached the end of the staircase, her dark eyes lifted to meet his, and he found himself utterly speechless.

Lysias often accepted mistakes and failures as learning opportunities. A man did not get to his position without accepting that life would humble you, if you let it.

But he did not know what to do with *this* mistake. Because Al had already drawn too many reactions out of him, but this one was worst of all.

For blinding seconds, he did not think of Kalyva, King Diamandis or everything he'd spent the last twenty years planning.

He only thought of what he might find if he peeled that dress away from her.

CHAPTER FIVE

AL STOOD AT the foot of the stairs. She stared at Lysias because he was looking at her with...hunger in his eyes.

She tried to tell herself she was imagining things. After all, she'd never been the object of anyone's desire. But she had also seen enough on the streets to recognize desire if she saw it.

And it was there in that golden gleam. Creating a matching claw of need within herself. She had wondered about sex before, but she had also known it was not in the cards for someone trying to disguise their gender.

Which she wasn't doing any longer. That thought spiraled through her like a strange, new, foreign kind of freedom. She could be a woman now—in whatever ways she wanted to be.

Then Lysias blinked, and everything in his eyes was gone. He moved forward, holding out his arm. She knew from her many meetings with the etiquette teacher that she was meant to lightly place her fingers on the crook of his arm.

She felt even more unsteady than she had trying to walk down the stairs in heels, though she had practiced that as much as she could. But something had shifted within her. A realization. An understanding.

Her life was different now. Not just because a payday that would change her life was within her reach, but also because she had this new identity. Alexandra. Woman. Fiancée. Princess.

She sucked in a breath and put her hand on his arm. Stepped forward in time with him as the possibilities swirled in her mind.

"You look perfect, Alexandra," he said, and though his eyes were cool and assessing now, there was a grit to his voice she had not heard from him before.

It was such a strange thing to find herself wanting to preen at the compliment. When she'd spent her entire life trying to keep her looks *under* the radar, so no one discovered her true sex. So no one paid too much attention to her while she spied.

But she liked it. She liked thinking that he might be right and that she was *perfect*.

She had to focus on the job, though. On the task. The payout. Which was no different than spying, except this was the endgame. She wanted to make Alexandra and safety *permanent*. And it was now within her grasp.

Unlike Lysias, who felt like a potential earthquake, which could happen out of nowhere and ruin *everything*. "Shouldn't you be calling me Zandra?" she asked, trying to speak the way she imagined her character would speak. Softly. With a kind of deference that was *definitely* not natural to her.

Lysias led her out the door and toward a sleek limousine waiting for them. "I think it'll be easier if we use Alexandra. We'll say that this is the name your adopted parents gave you and that you are currently most comfortable using it."

She nodded. Sensible. Smart. Why did he smell so good? How could a smell be so distracting?

She tried to get into the car elegantly, as many people had instructed her over the past few days, but she was sure she failed. She watched Lysias get in after her, all graceful and fluid movements.

"How did you learn?" she asked him. "All this..." She waved, frustrated that her vocabulary could not encompass that which she wished to ask. Frustrated he claimed to be *like* her but somehow fit into this world of wealth with such ease. "If you began life on the streets—"

"That is not where I *began* life. That is where I was *exiled*. I grew up in the palace of Kalyva."

She stared at him. Shocked by this simple admission. "But..."

"I told you, my parents worked for the king and queen. The *real* king and queen, not their disgusting excuse for a son. We lived in the palace. I was a servant's child and treated like one, of course, but I was always a curious boy. So I watched. I learned."

Every time he spoke of his childhood, she tried to picture him as a boy. And came up empty. She could only imagine the impossibly large man sitting next to her. Existing always as this beautiful example of what the human form could be.

They fell into silence as the limousine pulled away from the house and began the journey toward Athens. Al tried to keep her gaze on the window, but it kept finding its way back to Lysias.

"Where have you been?" She hadn't meant to ask him that. She hadn't meant to acknowledge she even noticed she hadn't seen him since that dinner three nights ago.

Still, she couldn't take back the words, so she watched him and waited for an answer.

His face was blank—which was different than his revenge anger. Different even from the billionaire mask. This was something else. Something…dark. It had an uncomfortable mix of fear and sympathy entwined in her heart.

"Did my staff not take good care of you?" he asked offhandedly. Almost.

"You can't answer a question with a question."

"Ah, but I can. And do. And will."

Al frowned at him, but he didn't look her way. He settled himself into his seat and made a big production, *she thought*, of looking the handsome, relaxed billionaire on his way to any of his many important events.

She tried not to sigh, because nothing about Lysias mattered. The job, the payout mattered. She smoothed her hands down over her skirt. Everything was tight, which was a strange sensation. Showing off what she'd spent a lifetime hiding. But she'd seen herself in the mirror. She knew she looked pretty and sophisticated. It had been a shock to see her reflection in the mirror, and yet she liked it.

But it was still *strange*.

She was doing all right with the heels, though why any woman chose such torture devices was beyond her. She was more bothered by the fact she wanted to itch her hands through her hair as she had been expressly told not to so as not to ruin the sleek hairdo the stylist had spent nearly an hour creating.

Without warning, Lysias took her hand in his, and she

jolted. At the way his touch sizzled through her. At how much effect he could have simply by taking her *hand*.

It was dangerous. But she'd spent too long dealing with danger not to revel in it a *little*.

"You are my fiancée. You must have a ring." And with that, he slid a cool piece of jewelry onto her finger.

She looked down at the sparkling stone. It looked like the kind of ring a billionaire would give his fiancée. Big and gaudy. She loved it. The way it sparkled. The way it felt. Which she knew wasn't the point. It wasn't *really* hers.

So she ripped her gaze from it and tried to focus on the reality of the situation. "Maybe we should go over everything again," Al said, worrying her bottom lip between her teeth before she remembered her lipstick and stopped herself. She *liked* looking pretty, but it was an awful lot of work to remember how to maintain it all.

"There is nothing more to go over," Lysias said with a wave of his hand. "Tonight you need only to smile prettily for the cameras, stick close to me, and I will handle the rest. In fact, the less talking you do, the better. You are to be nothing but arm candy tonight."

Arm candy. She didn't like that term at all, but she supposed that is what *Alexandra* should strive to be. The quiet, happy billionaire's fiancée. "Do I know how to smile prettily?" Al wondered. "I have been given quite a few lessons over the past few days, but smiling was not one of them."

He finally turned his attention to her, and it was like a spotlight. She felt warmed, lit up. Like someone else.

"Well then, let us see a smile."

She tried to smile at him. It felt ridiculous, because she

was attempting to look how an *Alexandra* might look. Or a princess. *Her* smile was that of a roguish street urchin. Not a sweet or even sophisticated woman. So she wasn't quite sure how to rearrange her features.

Lysias tutted and shook his head. "*That* is a grimace," he said, then reached out and touched her. His long fingers stroked up her cheek. "Relax, *asteri mou*," he murmured. "Do not *try* so hard."

But she had to try hard. To breathe normally. To stay in this moment rather than be transported somewhere else by the heady drug that was his eyes on hers. Still, her body relaxed as if she had no choice. He was *willing* her through his touch, his gaze. The warmth that surrounded them convinced her to lean closer.

His smile in return felt genuine, soft almost, but the idea that Lysias Balaskas might be *soft* in any way was, of course, a fantasy.

"Better," he said, then dropped his hand.

She felt like drooping at the loss, but the car was pulling to a stop, and now she had to…pretend. Because that may have been pretend for him, but her reactions were not in any way an act.

They were real, and they were such a novelty, no matter how her brain warned her to be careful. Her brain insisted this might lead down a dangerous path, but the heady freedom of stepping out of the limo as a *woman*, as Lysias Balaskas's *fiancée*, seemed to eradicate the sensible voice in her head that had kept her alive for so long.

Inside the glittering soiree, Al did as she was told. Spoke little, kept to his side. It was easy to feign obedience because she was so far out of her depth in the glitz and glamour. Clutching to his side like a child to a mother felt safer than brazening it out alone.

She saw men she'd uncovered terrible things about. She saw their wives still at their sides. It took some of the buzz of Lysias's closeness off.

How did these men still have their wealth, their power, their lives even after everything she'd brought to light about them?

She watched some of these men. Wondering if they'd look in her eyes and know who she was. When she saw no flickers of recognition, even as their gazes raked hungrily over her body, she wondered if it was the conceit that someone like her would never be in their hallowed halls of wealth and opulence. Or was it that she looked *that* different?

"Where are you, Alexandra?" Lysias murmured in her ear, that dangerous purr like a live wire through her system.

"Some of these men," she said, being careful not to point, to hold any of their lascivious glances. "I've exposed terrible things about them, but they are still…here. Not locked up. Not ostracized."

"Yes, power and influence can often make even your misdeeds someone else's problem," he said, as if it didn't bother him at all. But when she looked up at him, his gaze was fierce. "If you give me a list of names, I will ruin them all. Without a thought."

"Why?"

Lysias lifted a shoulder. "Why not?"

She supposed many of them were his adversaries in business. But… "What if you are friends with some of them?"

Lysias laughed. "Friends? None of these men are my friends. I do not have friends."

"Why not?" She could not have friends because she could not risk her secret, but it baffled her that a man of his power and influence would be similarly alone.

"Friends only ever end in betrayal, Alexandra. Best you know that now. Come, there's someone photographing the crowd of dancers. Let's join them so we will be splashed across websites and papers come morning."

He had that look on his face, much like when he spoke of his all-important revenge. Determination and the excitement of the hunt. He had a fierce one-track mind.

He'd experienced betrayal. Now wanted revenge *this* badly all these years later. He had been hurt as a young boy, no doubt, but Al wondered why twenty years hadn't dulled any of those old feelings.

Of course, she'd never had anyone to be betrayed by. These feelings were as foreign to her as protection or care.

Lysias pulled her into the soft, slow dance. She was dazzled by all the fabrics, the way they swished together. The way every woman glittered beautifully. It was such a strange world, and she was intrigued.

Lysias held her close, the hot, hard wall of him expertly moving her to the beat of the song. She'd had a few lessons, but not enough to do anything other than follow his lead.

He leaned his head down, his mouth grazing her ear. She knew this was all an act. He was hoping to be photographed. And yet, her body did not care *why*. Only that he was close. Only that one large hand was on the small of her back, that she could feel his breath on her skin.

"I will let it slip to someone at the very end of the

night that your real name is Zandra Agonas," he whispered. "Someone who will immediately tell the press. Then they'll work themselves into a frenzy trying to get to the bottom of it. Some of them will likely arrive in Kalyva before even we do."

He smiled down at her—though it seemed wrong to call that curve of his mouth a smile. It was self-satisfied from a revenge well plotted. Hardly joy.

But it had that warm lick of desire twisting itself deep inside of her. So many women's eyes had followed him around the room tonight. She'd seen hands trail down his arms, lips lean in close to whisper.

Lysias had smiled at all these women, flirted with many, but he had always made it quite clear *she* was the object of his fascination this evening.

An act. Put upon. And yet, it was like becoming drunk, but it wasn't liquor. It was his attention, no matter how fake. She craved more and more. She wasn't sure she cared how authentic it was, as long as it spiraled inside of her like joy.

She wanted... In ways she'd never allowed herself to want. It hadn't been safe on the streets.

But she wasn't on the streets any longer. She let her hand slide up his arm, curl around his neck. She let her fingers drag across the skin, soft here, like the ends of his hair. She trailed one finger along the line of his hair, then down his jaw.

He stiffened. Looked down at her—not in the disdain she feared, but in a kind of alarmed warning.

She didn't mind that at all. She was enjoying this too much. The harsh cheekbones, the sensuous mouth. She outlined it all with her finger, letting her body press more and more against him as he moved her. She felt the large, hard length of him pressed to her and shuddered out a sigh.

She wanted him. Because this seemed so fleeting. She wouldn't be a princess forever, and even if she escaped with her money at the end of this and built a new, quiet, safe life somewhere, it was hard to believe a desire like this would ever follow.

The hand on her back seemed to tighten. "You are playing a dangerous game, *asteri mou*." It was an order, a warning. Sharp. Dismissive...almost.

But when she looked from his mouth to his eyes, all that gold told a different story. So she smiled at him, with all she felt swirling inside of her shining through.

"Life is a dangerous game, Lysias. Why not play?"

CHAPTER SIX

THE BOLT OF need that slammed through Lysias was alarming. His little Al was dangerous, that was for certain. Who would have guessed that might extend past her abilities as a spy?

A hundred thoughts seemed to fight for purchase in his mind. Over the alarming fog of lust, of want. There *was* rational, sensible thought buried underneath those layers. But he struggled to bring them to the surface.

When he *never* struggled. Not anymore.

The music ended. He knew that much from the brush of bodies around them. So he used the hand on the small of her back to lead her away from the dance floor.

He had a plan, and he had to enact it. He could not be distracted by what she was offering. He knew exactly who he wished to slip the name *Princess Zandra Agonas* to, but he would have to tear his gaze from Al to find the other woman and that seemed impossible.

No. Nothing was impossible. Not for Lysias Balaskas. He searched the crowd, looking for his quarry. But Al and her wandering hands were a distraction. Enough of one that he led her out of the main room and into the hall. He moved her swiftly, taking her hand in his so it stopped its distracting trip down his shoulder blades.

He cornered her in a little alcove, where he was all in shadow, and a small shaft of light crossed over her face. He meant to lecture her. Tell her that some things were more important than a little flutter of lust, and she would need to learn this lesson.

But looking down at her, he couldn't seem to find any of those important words. There was only the knowing curve of her smile, the way her breath caught when he moved closer. That impossible burst of heat and need, unfamiliar in its intensity.

Where had this come from?

He meant to ask her—she must know. The words were on the tip of his tongue, he was sure of it. But her mouth was a dangerous, dark red. It glistened, beckoned to him, like a drug. She was a drug.

And he gave in.

He covered her mouth with his. It wasn't just heat here, but power. He smoothed his hands over the fabric of her dress, tight enough that it allowed him the delicious tour of her body as he used his to press her against the wall behind her.

He did not think of where he was, what his plan had been. His only thought was that she felt like velvet, smelled like something dark, spicy, exotic.

She pressed against him, moaning into his mouth. Her hands clasped in his hair. It was wild. Reckless. And Lysias did not *mind* these things, usually quite enjoyed indulging in them, in the right setting.

But this was more… Just more. And it had to be stopped before he forgot his purpose. He pulled away from her, kept her pressed to that wall and held her at arm's length.

She looked up at him, those dark depths were hazy with lust. With need. And the need echoed so deep within, he nearly forgot himself and everything he was here for. Her breathing came in little pants, and...this was not the place, but that did not mean there was *no* place.

"Go wait for me in the car," he said, or growled, the fight for control taking over everything.

"But..."

"You want to play dangerous games...you will win dangerous prizes. I will have you in private, Alexandra."

She let out a sound. Maybe an *oh*. Her tongue darted out, pink against her now smudged lipstick. Then she nodded and turned away from him, walking toward the exit.

And he could only watch her. The confident swing of her hips, the beautiful, alluring slope of her shoulders. Then she looked over her shoulder at him, and when she caught him watching her...she smiled.

Another punch.

But he could not be laid flat by that blow, by all that crackled between them. He was too strong. Too determined. And while he was not against enjoying himself in the midst of his many plans, revenge would always come first.

Focus. The plan. Revenge. Bringing King Diamandis to his knees.

These reminders helped steady him. He found the hostess of the gala, offered thank-yous and goodbyes, and pretended to accidentally drop the name Zandra Agonas. Over-explained his error, until the woman's eyes were narrowed with suspicion.

And curiosity. He watched as her gaze moved across

the crowd, land on a prominent journalist. Lysias kept the smile to himself as he said his final goodbye knowing that by morning wild stories about the maybe-not-dead Princess, and her connection to Lysias Balaskas, would be splashed everywhere.

Then he strode for the exit. For his car. For Alexandra.

His driver stood by the door, opened it for him with a nod. Lysias stood there on the curb, looking into the dim back seat where she sat. Looking right back at him. His driver stood by the door, waiting for Lysias to get in. "I can take it from here, Giorgio."

"As you wish, sir." The driver went back to the driver's side and Lysias stood where he was. Surveying the woman in his back seat.

This was not part of the plan. This woman. This need. The danger he could feel encroaching around. He never let his focus waver. Never took on something that might risk what he needed to do.

But plans sometimes needed to be altered. They needed to accommodate changes in the landscape, and Alexandra was indeed a change.

It would not matter, he decided then and there. He took lovers as a matter of course. Enjoyed women, and sex. Surely this woman who'd grown up on the streets knew better than to look for something more than he would ever give.

He would have her. And his revenge. And when they were both over, settled and satisfied, they would part.

"Just so we are clear, I am not looking for any *real* wife."

She laughed, low and husky, arrowing right to his sex.

"I think I can see that about you, Lysias. I only want…"

She trailed off, then shrugged those slim shoulders. "For so long, I have denied my wants, or had them denied for me, because I did not have the means to get them or because I had to hide who I was. Now I have the means, and I no longer need to hide. And I want. That is enough." She sat there for a moment, then raised an eyebrow. "Are you coming in?"

It felt like walking over a threshold that would change things, when he wished nothing to change now that he was here. Successful and poised on the cusp of his revenge, everything and all he'd wanted for twenty years.

But it was in the struggle of those twenty years—of his loss, of his exile, of his rise—he knew he could conquer whatever this was. Whatever threat she posed, he would simply not allow it to win.

Lysias Balaskas came out on top. Always. Forever.

He slid into the car, this back seat their own private oasis with the raised partition between driver and passengers. "You speak of these nebulous wants, Alexandra. Perhaps you should name a few, so as I am not confused."

She laughed again, and the enjoyment he got from this simple sound, the light in her eyes, might have startled him. If he could think beyond the need to taste such a laugh, such a woman.

"You are *never* confused, Lysias. But if you want to hear it, I don't mind. I want you to kiss me again."

He leaned forward but kept his mouth just out of reach even as she tilted her lips to his. He held this distance, a beat, and then another. She watched him, her breathing coming quicker, the pulse in her neck scrambling. He wanted to taste that spot of her neck, but he would be patient.

When he finally spoke, his words whispered over her lips, though he kept his hands to himself. So it was only heat that drew around her, their breaths comingling and nothing else.

"Is that all you want?" he asked, his voice a silken whisper in the dark as the vehicle moved forward and they began to leave the lights of the city behind.

She sucked in an unsteady breath. If he was addled by the chemistry blooming between them, at least he was not alone.

"Touch me," she said. Demanded, actually.

Which would not do. "Ah, but I do not take orders from anyone, *asteri mou.*"

"And I do not *ask* for anything, *leventi mou.* I simply take it." She fisted her hand in his tie and pulled his mouth to hers. Fire. Need.

He could have avoided it, of course. She *was* strong, but no match for him. But he enjoyed her strength, her demands. That she would grab onto whatever power she could scrabble together.

It didn't matter. Because she would be begging him for more before all was said and done.

So he kissed her. Tasted her deep and allowed himself, in the world of this car, to forget everything else. For these brief moments, she was all that existed. And he lost himself in her.

She was dark and sweet, wild and fearless. An earthquake. A challenge to all his previously held beliefs, and yet he welcomed it. Weathered it. Absorbed it all. And created his own response. So that she was quaking in his arms.

He slid his hands up her legs. Slight, but strong. He

pushed the fabric of her skirt up and away. In the dark of the back seat, she was but a shadow. A rustle. A whisper. She could have been a phantom.

Except she was warm and real, and he wanted more. All. He slid his hands beneath her underwear, found the center of her. Where she was wet and ready for him. He teased her with his fingers, the drugging scent of her arousal filling the car.

He wanted her more than he could remember wanting anything. Which was dangerous, because he'd only wanted revenge before. Too dangerous to feel this...under her spell. So he took what power he could. He stopped his ministrations.

"Thank me." When she stilled and her eyes flew to his in the dim light, he smiled. "For saving your life."

Her mouth opened, but it seemed to take her quite a bit of time to find her voice. Still, he held himself exactly where he was, his fingers within the tight heat of her, still.

He could see the war play out over her face. Which did she want more? Her pride? Or him. Eventually, lust won. "Th-thank you," she whispered. And he didn't know if she meant it.

He wasn't sure he cared. He touched her, over and over again, until she was writhing once more. He watched what little of her face he could see change from wonder to desperation. Shock to ecstasy. He took his time, enjoying the swell of her climax, the sounds of her desire throbbing through him—pleasure and the torturous pain of holding himself back.

She came apart so beautifully, his name on her lips, there in the dim light of the limousine. What a surprise she was. What a glorious, delicious surprise.

"Lysias," she said, ragged and weak. For him. Because of him.

He removed his hand from underneath her dress, kissed down the elegant curve of her neck. He tasted her there, just where he'd wanted to. Where she smelled of something secretive and uniquely her. "Yes?"

He drew back, studied her shadowed face. She seemed to be struggling with something.

He smiled at her. "If you want more, you will have to ask nicely." But he pulled her dress back down over her legs because he realized the car had come to a stop.

"Ask..." She straightened herself as Giorgio opened the back door. Lysias slid out, quite pleased with himself, no matter how hard he was for her. How his body was tormented by all this unspent desire.

He held out his arm, watched expressions chase over her face before she finally placed her hand on it. She allowed him to lead her inside and she said nothing.

Darkly amused with her, and himself, Lysias walked her all the way upstairs. Up to her bedroom door. He even offered her a little bow, as if she really was a princess.

"Good evening, Alexandra."

She blinked. Once. Then her eyes narrowed. "You're really going to make me beg you?"

"Who said anything about begging? I only said you had to ask nicely. Though, I also appreciate begging. And reward it handsomely."

"And what happened in the car wasn't nice enough?"

"Nice for *you*." He shrugged lazily, then turned away from her. He walked down the hall toward his own bedroom door. Because surely, she would give in. Surely...

"Please," she said, on a quiet mutter. Perhaps even through gritted teeth.

He turned to her, raised an eyebrow, with far too much distance between them. But she would always be the one to give in. Never him. "Please what?"

She hesitated, which surprised him. But it was only a moment's worth, and then she was crossing the hall to him. All determination and fire.

"I want you. All of you." She slid her arms around his neck, pressing that delicate body to his much larger one. Her dark eyes an enchantment all their own. "Show everything to me, Lysias. *Please.*"

CHAPTER SEVEN

AL DID NOT believe in retreat. She also knew that good never lasted, so she had to grab what opportunities were within her reach without hesitation.

She didn't *relish* asking, let alone nicely, when she was so used to taking. But something about the way Lysias looked at her when she said please—that golden gleam in his eyes leapt like a flame. And something hot and dangerous grew inside of her.

Who knew when she might be able to have this? She had almost died earlier this week. She had struggled for so long up to this moment. Why not finally live in all the ways she hadn't been able to?

Enjoy the gowns, the excess and this man. This desire. Take it all, experience it all, while she could.

She lifted to her toes, pressed her mouth to his. His hands, which had remained frustratingly at his sides, now moved up to cup her face, angle her head differently. He took the kiss deeper, wilder, like he had in the car. She wanted everything she'd felt then, but more.

She wanted her hands on *his* body. She wanted to feel what she could do to *him*.

He pulled her down the hall, and she was so unused to the heels that she nearly tripped. But he held her upright, leading her into his bedroom with a single-minded purpose. She stepped inside, taking it all in. The wealth, the beauty, this shocking and wondrous feeling inside of her. The way the sound of the door closing behind her filled her with anticipation and want.

The room she'd stayed in was beautiful, more luxurious than anything she'd ever seen, but his was remarkable. Not just the space but how comfortable everything looked. How warm and soft.

But when he pressed his mouth to the back of her neck, she could not have cared less about the big windows with their view of the night sky or the soft give of the plush carpet underneath her heels.

She only cared about the sensations his mouth, his hands could create in her. No wonder people did stupid things for this. *This* was a drug worth risking for. She wanted to turn, but his fingers brushed the top of her dress, and she heard and felt him pull the zipper down. Until the dress slithered down and pooled at her feet.

The dress had not allowed her to wear anything underneath it up top, and though her breasts were small, it was strange not to have them bound. She brought her arms up to cover herself reflexively, even as she stepped out of the dress, back still toward him.

"Face me, Alexandra."

Yes, she was Alexandra now. A woman. A powerful woman. With money and position and whatever she wanted. Including a lover. *This* lover. So she turned, though an old ingrained habit or shame or *something* had her keeping her arms over her bare chest.

He shook his head and reached forward, taking her by the wrists, but the touch was so gentle it was like he barely held her at all. And when he pulled her hands away from her breasts, she didn't even think to fight him. Not with the way his gaze raked over her. Hungry.

"How you have hidden such beauty is beyond me," he murmured. His thumb brushed over one darkened peak, and pleasure shot through her from that point to the aching center of her.

"Lysias." She didn't know what to say. What to ask for. She understood sex as a kind of impartial bystander—she had lived on the streets too long not to hear how people spoke of it, witness what people would do for it. She understood, too, that there were many different uses. That it could be unwanted, transactional, but also she knew that some people sought it out. The pleasure, the release. The wild rush of it all.

She wanted that. With him. Here and now and for as long as they could, because it would not last, this wild, desperate feeling. Nothing this wonderful ever did.

"What is it you want from me, *asteri mou*? Do you wish me to touch you again, to watch you fall apart here in the light?"

"Yes. No. I…" She wanted everything and had no vocabulary for all her wants.

"Or perhaps I should taste you," he continued, maneuvering her deeper into the room until the back of her knees hit the bed, and she found herself seated.

Lysias kneeling before her, as he spread her legs apart.

She opened her mouth with a thought to say something. Anything. But she could only stare, magnetized as he pulled her panties from her, leaned forward and, with no preamble, licked deep within her.

She might have bolted off the bed, if he'd not hooked

his arms around her legs. Holding her in place. His strength felt like a safe haven, even as new needs clawed at her, and pleasure climbed and climbed into its explosive peak.

When she managed to open her eyes, she was sprawled out on his bed, completely naked. And he stood at the foot of the bed, completely clothed. The only sign he'd done anything untoward was his slightly disheveled hair and the smudge of lipstick—*her* lipstick—on his jaw.

She had the strangest desire to put her mark all over him.

She pointed at him. "Now you. Take off your clothes." Because this wasn't fair, and she wanted to see him. Needed to see under all that polish.

He raised a dark brow. "I thought we had established that I do not like to be demanded about." But he loosened his tie, his golden gaze holding hers as he slowly pulled it from his shirt.

Her heart thundered in her chest, and everywhere he'd touched—with his hands, with his mouth—throbbed with the desire to feel him. Naked against her.

So she moved to the end of the bed and onto her knees on the mattress. She did not ask or plead. She reached out and began to unbutton his shirt. She pressed a kiss on his chest for each undone button, the faint smudges of whatever lipstick she had left giving her a darkly sensual satisfaction.

When she reached the end, the buckle of his belt, she looked up at him through her eyelashes and slowly unhooked then pulled it out of the belt loops. And though she fumbled as she undid his button of his pants, faltered for a moment with the zipper, she could not seem to tear her gaze from him.

Until she spread apart the fabric of his pants and was met with the large evidence of his arousal. She sucked in a breath, feelings and sensations such a powerful cyclone in her mind she had no fully formed thoughts at all.

Only need. She tugged his boxers down so that he was free. She smoothed her hand down the silky, hard length of him. Need and satisfaction shot through her at the noise he made, a harsh sucked-in breath.

She managed to look up at him again. So handsome, like a statue. But he was made of muscle and skin. Blood pumped through his veins, and his heart beat fast. She was sure she could reach out and feel it do so through his chest.

Because it felt as if hers was doing exactly that. And she found herself stuck, because she did not know what to do. She did not wish to let on that she was inexperienced. She wanted only to be the Alexandra he'd turned her into.

He fitted his hand over her cheek, then led her head forward. She knew what he wanted, and it became what she wanted. To take him deep within her mouth. The slick friction, the salty taste of him. She absorbed the sound of his groan, his shattered breathing, and she wanted to be the reason he fell apart.

But he pulled her back, his golden eyes so fierce she was nearly afraid she'd done something wrong.

"Lay down," he ordered.

She no longer cared who ordered who. If she had to beg or plead. Something clawed at her from inside and the only escape was him. Inside of her.

He rolled a condom on, and Al refused to be afraid.

That was how a woman such as her got through any un-known situation. Believing you belonged in it. Believing you could handle anything.

And then he was on top of her, careful around her wound. Heavy and strong. Her protector. The man who had saved her. Who had given her pleasure, and now this.

Poised at her entrance, and she had no fear. Not here. Not with him. Not as he slid inside of her, with inexo-rable pressure and determination.

She had heard stories of varying experiences. That there was pain or discomfort or only glory. That it depended on the man, his size or that foolish thing called love.

She found her experience somewhere in the middle of all that noise. He was so large, and it felt as though she would never accommodate him. And yet there was pleasure everywhere else. And as he moved within her, as she moved against him not knowing what else to do with the pressure and the need, any mild pain, any dis-comfort melted away.

And then there was only this, where they joined, the little world of ecstasy, of rising tides of pleasure, one after the next. His hands were everywhere, his mouth devoured her, and deep within, he moved. Closer and closer to an edge she now recognized, now knew, now craved.

She sobbed his name, needing something from him she did not know how to express. Except his name. Over and over again. Until the world upended in a magical crash of ecstasy.

On one last thrust, he crushed her to him, power and passion in one explosion before they both fell limp to-gether on the bed. For stunning moments, they breathed in time, slowly coming back to themselves.

This real world where she would now have to deal with the consequences of her wants. Except, what was so bad about this? It was an enjoyment for both of them. He'd made it clear there would be no union, and she knew that she had some new life far away from this one in her future once she helped him with his revenge and was paid.

Besides, finding enjoyment in each other would suit the role they had to play of an engaged couple. Why would there be an ounce of regret?

He moved off her, saying nothing. He disappeared into the bathroom, and when he returned, he stood in the doorway between bedroom and bathroom. He looked angry, which she could not understand.

"You should have told me," he said, his voice tight, that golden gaze of his hard.

She didn't see the point in doing anything other than lay in the middle of his bed, enjoying the soft linens and mattress beneath her as the remnants of her pleasure petered out pleasantly. "Told you what?"

"That you have had no lovers before me."

She wrinkled her nose at him, trying to make sense of him. "Why?"

"So I could have been more…careful."

She stretched out her arms, letting out a contented, satisfied sigh. "No worries. I quite enjoyed myself." Which was an understatement, but maybe understatements were safer when he looked so stormy, standing so very far away.

When he said nothing and stayed exactly where he was for long, tense moments, she finally rolled over onto her stomach so she could stare at him. "Lysias, I don't understand why this bothers you. I knew what I was doing. I asked for it. I even said please, if you recall."

Something ticked in his jaw. But even better, she saw the flare of desire at the recollection in his eyes.

"Would you like me to leave?" she asked, smiling cheerfully at him. "I'm afraid you'll have to say please."

He made a noise, maybe a growl, then stalked over to the bed. But he did not join her on it, did not gather her into his arms with a punishing kiss as she'd half hoped. He stood there looking like some kind of ancient warlord she'd wronged.

Which she did not hate as much as she probably should.

"Do not forget, Alexandra. I am in charge. No matter what happens in the bedroom, my revenge is all I care about."

"And I do not care about your revenge at all," she said, enjoying her flippancy in response to his intensity. "But I would very much like to do that again. Shall I beg?"

Lysias could not say what bothered him about the realization she'd been an innocent. Perhaps that it had never occurred to him she might be. That she likely *had* to be, as she'd been hiding who she truly was for most of her life.

He did not, as a rule, dally with virgins who were likely to get…ideas about such things. Mountains out of molehills and such. No matter how mountainous this had felt.

And she had the audacity to lay there on his bed, naked and sheer perfection, smiling at him as if she were the queen of his world.

Perhaps what bothered him was that she surprised him. That he could not predict her. Read her or understand her.

Except in the fact that she wanted him as much as he wanted her. Even now, when they should be sated and exhausted.

So he did not send her away. He kept her in his bed. Another rule broken, but they *were* pretending to be engaged. They would share a bed in Kalyva, and Kalyva had to be what he focused on. They would leave in the morning. To begin all the plans for his revenge.

But the strangest thing happened in the middle of the night. He woke, as he often did, torn from a nightmare that was mostly memory, though sometimes twisted with monsters and figments of his childhood imagination.

He expected that he might have wakened her, cursing himself for the weakness of allowing her to share his bed.

When he looked over at her, ready to lecture or tell her to leave, she was indeed awake. But she was sitting up in almost a mirror of the same position he found himself in. Hands pressed to the mattress, sheet twisted about her body, her hair plastered in sweat and sharp breaths coming in terrified pants.

Their gazes met and held as their breathing evened out. He realized, somewhere in his sleep addled mind, that she had been having her own nightmare.

It speared through him, this realization. That they might have things in common. That they might understand each other, when he did not wish to be understood. He only wished to find vindication.

He should pay her for her services at the gala and then tell her to go. He would find a different Princess Zandra. One who did not threaten *everything*.

But they were too far gone in the plan. She was his Alexandra, the tool he would use for his revenge.

And revenge was the only thing that mattered. Perhaps she might come to understand pieces of him because she knew the hard truths of life. But this would not become *more*, even if he was her first. She had said it herself, she only wanted to enjoy her wants.

She would not weave fairy tales.

He was determined, even as they headed for the island kingdom of Kalyva the next morning.

Where kings and dead princesses and the haunted history of his past waited for them.

CHAPTER EIGHT

THE BOAT RIDE was uneventful. The boat, of course, a luxurious vessel that sped through the beautiful Aegean Sea with ease and grace.

That did nothing to ease Al's queasy stomach. She was coming to find she much preferred land.

"Don't tell me you're seasick, Alexandra," Lysias said, taking a seat next to her on the deck—the only place she could seem to handle the movement, with the cool air slapping against her face.

"I am definitely not sea *well*," she replied, pressing her cheek to the cool railing. "Mark me down as not a fan of boats."

"It is a *yacht*."

She shrugged. "It is all the same to me."

"Well, never fear. Land is near." He pointed out across the blinding blue. She saw it then. The island in the distance. The gray craggy offering of stone, the colorful parade of boxes that must be buildings, against the contrasting white of the beach and what could only be the palace at the very top of the slope of land in the middle of the sea.

Al watched it as it got closer and closer, but it did nothing to soothe the unease in her stomach. So she looked at Lysias.

They had said nothing to each other last night when she'd woken to find him also awake. She was certain he must have had a nightmare just like she had. Instead, once their breathing had evened, they'd found a silent solace in each other's bodies. And then gone back to sleep.

She hadn't wanted to face the darkness of her dreams in that bed, where she'd felt safer than she'd ever felt. But here on this boat… "What do you dream of, Lysias?" she asked him. Already knowing he would turn the question around on her.

"Many things, naturally. What do you dream of, Alexandra?"

She sighed. "I don't know. It is always in shadow. Screams and pain and confusion. A hand reaching out to save me, and then variations of a theme of losing that savior from there." She shrugged. She'd often been embarrassed by having nightmares at her age, and it was hard to shake that feeling, but Lysias had them too. Maybe that meant she was not so very different.

And she just needed to know that she was not alone. That he might understand. She reached across to him, curled her fingers around his arm. "Tell me. Please."

He did not look at her, but he also did not dislodge her hand. He simply squinted behind his sunglasses at the approaching island, the sun painting him a stunning, golden figure in the midst of all this blue and white.

"Memories mixed with monsters. But once my revenge is complete, I will conquer them the same as I will conquer my old friend."

"This king was your *friend*?"

"I thought he was, anyway. But it is of no matter. We

are enemies now. And once I have vanquished my enemy, all will be put behind me."

"You're sure of this?"

He glanced at her, though the glasses hid any hint at what expression might be in his eyes. "Absolutely."

She wondered if she would ever have the confidence to believe she could vanquish her subconscious coming out in dreams. When, if she had that power, she would have conquered it already. Really, men were such ridiculous creatures.

The boat pulled up to a dock, and Lysias threaded his fingers with hers as they waited for his staff to secure the boat and ramp that would allow them to disembark.

Al studied his hand in hers. It felt oddly familiar, here in this place.

She shook that strange thought away and surveyed the island before her. It looked cheerful on the sunny, warm morning, and yet she did not find herself *cheered*. She felt cold.

It was nerves, she supposed. Lysias said he had no doubts the king would be there to greet them, and their act must begin at once.

She had to pretend to be the man's sister. *Dead* sister. It seemed a bit cruel, but she knew life was cruel. It had been to her *and* Lysias. Perhaps it had been to the king as well, but he was a *king*. He could no doubt weather it.

She had been forced to scramble, to fend for herself at too young an age—and so had Lysias. Perhaps it was dangerous to view herself on the same team as Lysias, but it was temporary. And if they could trust one another, it would serve their purposes at deceiving the king—which would lead to her payment.

Lysias drew her down the ramp to land, and Al worked very hard to look her part. The wide-eyed princess who'd only just remembered who she was. The, if not sophisticated, graceful and *feminine* fiancée to Lysias Balaskas.

"Ah, home," he said, but with a sharp edge. Certainly not a warm homecoming, what with revenge clearly holding his whole mind in its grip.

It *was* a beautiful little jewel of an island. Al had never been out of Athens, not that she could recall, but she'd seen the pictures and paintings of all the beautiful Greek islands and knew people sought them out.

The air was warm and smelled of the sea. And just beyond the docks, there was a small crowd. Everyone was dressed in black except one man, who wore black and red and stood on a kind of platform that led to a large official-looking car on the road beyond the beach.

He was also the only one without a gun.

Beyond him were buildings—homes and shops, she supposed—but then, high on the hill, a bright white building—devoid of any and all color against the dark blue of the sky. Stone turrets, stout and tall, reached up into all that blue just as domed spires did. It was beautiful, clearly old and important.

Something like pain sliced through her. She had a sudden bolt of panic. She stepped backward, thinking only she needed to run, but she was met by the hard wall of Lysias himself.

"What is it?" he asked. She supposed she was imagining any true concern in his tone. This was an act, after all.

"I…" She didn't know how to explain it. This feeling of dread that seemed to coil around her heart and squeeze. "I don't like the look of this place."

"Kalyva is beautiful, Alexandra."

"Yes." It was. Objectively. This wasn't about beauty though. It was about a feeling. Deep in her gut. The feeling she had always listened to on the street. The one that had kept her alive. She didn't feel safe here. She didn't feel right.

But Lysias was behind her, moving her forward. He was her protector. Maybe that was temporary, but for now, she would take it. She would relax within that knowledge. Or try.

They moved toward the man who stood on the road that was lifted above the beach and docks. He looked down at them as if they were bugs. Yet there was something about him... Al tried to breathe through the scrambled racing of her heart. Panic twined around her lungs. Squeezing.

She wanted to run. *Had* to. But Lysias held her there.

"You are either very brave or very foolish," the man said in clipped tones once Lysias came to a stop not far from him. The man was clearly ignoring her and talking specifically to Lysias.

Who flashed his fake billionaire smile. "Both, likely. And I know you will not fall to your knees and thank me just yet, though you should, but I have brought your sister back to you, Your Majesty. You are most welcome."

Lysias stared at King Diamandis, and yet his attention was fractured because Alexandra was acting so strangely next to him. Skittish and tense. Perhaps he should have let her arrive as Al, an identity she was more comfortable with.

But that was ridiculous. How she felt, how comfortable

she was, it was all immaterial to his goals. She would be paid handsomely for her subterfuge, and so there was no need to *protect* her.

"The rumors are swirling, as you have no doubt ensured," the king said. "But, as my people have told everyone who has come sniffing thus far, the princess died when the rest of my siblings did."

It was strange to stand here in what he still considered his homeland, though he'd lived in Athens now longer than he'd been a boy here. Because nothing had changed except the man before him. Who was no longer a boy of fourteen, but now a man. A king.

Twenty years between then and now. Between friends and enemies.

Because Diamandis *had* been his friend. Lysias had considered this man a brother, though he'd known Diamandis's standing much more important than his own. But Diamandis had never made him feel it.

Until that night.

And Lysias could have forgiven Diamandis much. His own exile, certainly. But he would never forgive the man responsible for his parents' deaths, without even their dignity in that death. Buried as traitors, accomplices to murder. With nothing.

So Lysias smiled wider. "Ah, yes, and it's a neat little lie, but it *is* a lie." Lysias widened his smile that he did not feel. "I should know. I was there."

There was a beat where Diamandis looked at him with such cold hatred, Lysias felt the strange need to pull Al behind him. Protect her from the destruction he wanted to enact here.

"You will come to the palace," the king ordered, with

the flick of a wrist. His armed men began to move forward. Toward Lysias. Toward Al. Lysias held on to her.

"We have secured our own accommodations, of course," Lysias replied with the kind of fake deference that had Diamandis scowling down at him. "Our own transportation as well... But if you'd like to show your sister around the palace, we would be happy to meet you there this evening. Perhaps a nice din—"

"Enough." Temper flashed on Diamandis's face, but the man *had* changed in twenty years. Not just moving into adulthood, into being king. It seemed he'd finally learned to control his disastrous temper. "You will come to the palace. We will discuss all of this there. You can come of your own free will, or you can be dragged." He nodded toward the little army of guards that were even now surrounding them.

Lysias was not surprised. He knew what a threat he was to his old *friend*. Still, he didn't relish Alexandra being part of this. But she had a role to play. So Lysias's smile did not change.

Nor did he act *threatened*.

"So, you would make us prisoners?" Lysias replied, feigning surprise. "This seems extreme, Diamandis."

"The appropriate term is *Your Majesty*, as you well know, Mr. Balaskas."

"Come, Diamandis. Let us not pretend we don't know one another. Think of all we have shared." Lysias thought of it. Too often. And how all his youthful innocence had been betrayed.

"I wish I'd *never* known you," Diamandis spat. "You may use your own transportation, but have no fear. My guards will accompany you to the palace. Immediately."

Lysias lifted a negligent shoulder. "If it's so important to you, *Your Majesty*, we are happy to oblige." He even gave a little bow, because he knew Diamandis would see the gesture as flaunting, not deferential.

The king whirled away, muttering something to his guards before he was led back to his vehicle. The guards that remained for him did not bother Lysias in the least, as it all went to plan. He smiled winsomely at the guards, leading Alexandra to where one of his own employees waited next to the car he would use on Kalyva.

She looked perfect here. The dress she wore was elegant but suited for the warm temperatures—the top hooked to the skirt with little ties—offering tempting little glimpses of her golden skin. The hairdresser had done something with her hair so that it curled, looking a bit wild and yet beautifully suited to the smoky makeup on her face.

And he wished he could take her somewhere else. Somewhere decadent and safe where she could...

He blinked at the odd course of his thoughts. There was nowhere else. There was only revenge.

He opened the passenger side door for Alexandra himself, then got into the driver's side. A heavy-duty car pulled out in front of him, and another waited behind. The king's little cavalcade.

He flicked a glance at Alexandra as he drove toward the palace. She was staring up the hill at the estate with a furrow across her brow and a frown on her face. He could not say he fully understood her reaction to this place. Was she nervous? Afraid? Having second thoughts?

It did not matter, as he would not tolerate a deviation to his plan. And still the words tumbled out.

"You have been quiet."

"I don't like this place," she said plainly. "Everything gives me a bad feeling, and I have always relied on those feelings to keep me safe. It's very…unsettling to not be able to listen to them now."

"Well, there is certainly danger to be found here. And this island—the palace specifically—was the site of many an atrocity. So, perhaps your feelings are valid, but they do not change what we must do."

"No, I know." She frowned deeper. "It isn't that I'm regretting anything or thinking of backing out. It's just, as I said, unsettling." She straightened her shoulders and seemed to stare down the palace like she could scowl it into obedience. "I'm sure I will get over it."

Something strange moved through him as he drove over the bridge that led up to the palace, following the guard's car ahead of him. It was like a warmth. He supposed, if pressed to define it, he might have called it *pride*, that she would be so determined to overcome her discomfort.

The car in front of him rolled to a stop at one of the back entrances. Lysias had to laugh, if darkly. The servant's entrance. He was very familiar with *this* part of the castle. It was meant to be an insult, no doubt, but if Diamandis was bothering with insult, he knew Lysias was a threat.

The guards in both cars began to get out, so Lysias leaned over to Alexandra and spoke quietly.

"I believe the king will want us to stay in the palace. He'll want to keep us close and under careful guard. I will put up a *small* fight, but in the end, I'll let him have his way. This will allow you to prowl the palace as Al, if necessary."

Alexandra studied him with wide eyes he couldn't read, but she eventually gave him a nod. Then the vehicle doors were opened for them. And Lysias had to put on the role of careless billionaire, who truly believed Alexandra a princess.

He stepped out, made a few irreverent quips, then offered his hand to Alexandra when they met in front of the car. The guards marched them up to and then inside the doors.

So many painful memories. Most he'd worked very hard to forget. But they crowded in the shadows, slithered around him. And the worst part, they weren't all of *that* night. There were warmer ones. Of his parents. Of his friendship with Diamandis. Of the kindness of the king and queen. Those were worse than the nightmare reality of bloody coups.

He looked over at Alexandra as they were lead away from the servant's area and more toward the royal wing. Something darker, more hidden tried to claw forward as he caught a glimpse of her profile against the background of the ancient marbled palace. Time wanted to warp, send him back into old terror.

But he wouldn't go there. He never went there. Except in dreams.

And this was no dream. Only his long-awaited revenge finally within his grasp.

CHAPTER NINE

AL TRIED VERY hard to shake off the feelings of unease. But every step they took deeper into the palace, flanked by intimidating men in military-looking gear, the anxiety coiled so tight she worried she wouldn't be able to pretend anything at all.

She looked over at Lysias. His gaze was forward as they walked, his expression a kind of blankness that reminded her of last night. When she'd woken terrified and breathless and turned to see him the same.

"You may wait here," one of the guards said outside giant ornate doors. They depicted some kind of ancient scene in golds and bronze and bright blue paint. Alexandra studied the images, tried to make sense of them.

"The first battle of Kalyva," Lysias said loudly. "Perhaps it will bring back some more of your memory if I explain it to you."

"It seems familiar," Al said, reaching out to touch a golden horse with its legs reared. And that wasn't a lie. But she was an adept enough liar to find as much truth in her falsities as she could. "But so many of my memories are a jumble."

Lysias put his hands over hers, drew her index finger forward to trace the horse. "Then allow me to help."

He told her a story about two warring groups of ancient warriors—one made for battle and one that found battle by necessity. He weaved it so it sounded more fairy tale, more myth, than actual historic episode.

And she was rapt, not sure which side she rooted for or which side would come out on top. He told the story with such relish she turned her gaze from the door's art to him. The harsh profile, the slight curve of his lips, the deep tenor of his voice.

She felt all that heat from last night and something else. More tender. Like when she'd looked over to find him awake from a nightmare as well and wanted to soothe him in some way.

He glanced at her in the midst of a sentence, and either he trailed off, or she stopped listening. Amidst all her fear and anxiety and discomfort here, one thing was very clear in this moment.

Lysias had not changed. She wanted his mouth on hers again, to feel him inside her. No matter how she felt about Kalyva or the palace, she wanted him all the same.

The doors opened abruptly, and Al assumed she must have been so startled by her own reactions to him that she was only imagining Lysias looked as startled by the interruption as she felt. Because, in a blink, he was facing down the king with that laissez-faire smile. And golden daggers in his eyes.

"Sit," the king ordered, pointing to some delicate-looking chairs in front of a large intimidating desk. The room was some kind of office, likely the king's office. Alexandra took in the plush rugs, the elaborate window treatments. Every wall had panels of art much like the door, depicting different scenes—she assumed of the history of the royals.

Lysias drew her forward and took a seat on a small settee, pulling her down to sit next to him. She was glad for his proximity, for his lead. It felt a bit like an anchor in the midst of all this unfamiliar discomfort.

The king did not sit behind his desk. He came to stand in front of it, glaring down at them impressively. He was severe, his features dark. His clothes matched his face, all perfect crisp lines and shiny buttons, as though nothing would dare wrinkle or tarnish under his watch. He *looked* like a king, if a little on the young side to preside over an entire country.

Lysias had said she had enough resemblance to the royal family they might believe a connection were true. She stared at the king, but she saw very little, aside from coloring, that might connect them. Of course, she'd never spent much time studying her own face.

"If you wish to push this farce," the king said. "We only have to do a DNA test to prove you wrong."

"Naturally," Lysias replied, resting his ankle on his knee, and flicking imaginary lint from his pants. "Do you think I would really bring you a fake, knowing how easy it would be to prove me wrong?" He turned to exchange an amused look with Al. "I told you he would be suspicious, but we will get through to him."

She forced her mouth to curve and nod at Lysias. She was afraid she wouldn't be able to sound just right yet. She didn't have the reserves she needed to be Alexandra, lost princess.

"I hope you both understand that I don't have to entertain this. You are not welcome here, Lysias. You were exiled. I can have you tossed right back out or in a cell or even killed."

"You can do all those things, certainly. But can you look at this woman here and tell me you do not see the resemblance? The evidence of your own blood in her veins?"

The king did not look at her. She realized it was purposeful. He *would* not look at her. He focused on Lysias and tossed some more threats around, while Lysias had an answer for everything. Their voices felt like thunder rumbles, distant and incomprehensible, so she got up without fully thinking the movement through.

They argued and she went to stand at the window to get away from the anger in the room—no matter how calm they tried to sound. She looked out at the blue of the sea, the white of the sand, the people walking down there, small and disconnected from the storm raging inside here.

Why did it all feel so familiar?

She reached out, touched the wall next to the window. Her fingers traced the wallpaper design, and she studied the art panel next to the window. This did not appear to be a depiction of battle but of a coronation.

She studied it—not just the art but the frame of the panel around it. She knew it wasn't familiar, as she'd never been here. But she'd seen something like it…somewhere. It must have been in her early spying days. Some of those jobs ran together on the heady mix of fear and the thrill of success.

That had to be it.

She reached out, felt around the little framed edge, found the button...and pressed. A door popped open with a loud *snick*.

She stood there looking at the dark interior behind the door for she didn't know how long. She didn't know what was happening to her, what strange sensations were coursing through her. So she turned to Lysias, her protector. Her anchor.

He stood now, next to the king, and both men stared at her as if she'd sprouted wings and flown. She felt a bit detached, as if she *had* flown away. It didn't fully make sense, even to her. But she supposed she was used to such things. Finding hideaways and secrets in rich men's houses. That must have been how she'd discovered this little secret passageway.

"How did you know about that?" the king demanded, and he was angry, clearly, but he'd also gone a little pale. So that she almost felt sorry for him.

"She remembered, obviously," Lysias replied for her, but he was also looking at her in a strange way. After a moment, he seemed to find himself and crossed to her. "You are overwhelmed," he said, and he sounded so kind and worried about her that she suddenly *was* overwhelmed.

"She remembers certain things, but others come back only in snatches," Lysias said to Diamandis, curling his arm around her waist in what felt like a protective gesture. "She needs some rest. Some quiet. I will take her back to—"

"You will take her upstairs. My staff has readied a room for her."

"Where she goes, I go. She is my fiancée, and I will not leave her alone to be tormented by the likes of you."

"If she really is my sister, an impossibility of course, I'd be saving her from the likes of *you*."

"Please," Al said, irritated with the both of them. "All this bitter fighting will get you nowhere. You both believe you are right and above reproach, and you'll never convince the other differently. So instead of bothering with all this male posturing, let us get to the heart of the matter."

Lysias smiled, but it was as fake as this little act. Still, he lifted her hand and brushed a kiss over the top of it, and no matter how off-kilter she felt, that was still a jolt of lust.

"Of course, *asteri mou*." He turned that sharp gaze to Diamandis. "Your Majesty, I did not expect you to believe me as a matter of course, but let us pursue civility." Lysias even smiled at his enemy. "We will get to the truth. *After* she has gotten some rest."

A muscle in Diamandis's jaw twitched, but he nodded. "We will indeed. Allow my staff to escort you to your rooms."

It was the king's turn to smile.

Lysias was not surprised exactly when it came to Alexandra's behavior in the king's study, though he didn't know how she'd figured out how to open the secret door. But she was the kind of woman who strode in and solved problems.

It was just so strange. This place. The cascade of emotions. *Her.* He had not prepared for this level of…upheaval.

This did not mean he was unequal to it, simply that he needed to center himself. Revenge required calculation and planning, and he was getting lost in pettiness that didn't matter. Not to his true goal.

But the hits kept coming. In the form of the cruel king. Because he recognized this back hallway. The more casual decor. No murals or gilded art. This was softer than the austere royal areas of the palace.

Because this was where the servants lived. Where *he* had lived. And when the guard, as if they really were prisoners, stopped in front of a door, Lysias's entire body went cold. The guard opened it and Alexandra stepped inside, but Lysias...

He should step inside. Freeze it out. Ignore this attempt at pain and suffering. He would prove to Diamandis that he could not be hurt. He *would*.

When he didn't follow, Alexandra looked back at him. Confusion and then concern clouding her features. "What's wrong?" she asked.

He should lie to her. Laugh it off. Something. But he could only find the means to tell her the truth. "These were my parents' quarters."

She blinked once, looked around the room. "That is cruel. That is..." She whirled, her expression an alluring mix of fire and her own revenge. She pushed passed him and the guard, striding down the hall back the way they'd come.

Both he and the guard were so surprised by her reaction, for a few moments they simply stood and stared after her.

But it was clear she wasn't going to come to her senses. Lysias strode after her before the guard could—making sure to block the guard's way so Lysias would be the first one to get to her.

"Alexandra."

She didn't so much as pause. She just kept walking quickly and certainly, retracing the exact path they'd just taken.

"*Al.*"

But she did not stop, and he found himself so compelled by her anger, by *her* that he did not reach out and stop her, even though it would have been easy to do so.

The force of her. The way her skirts flowed behind her, like she was some sort of avenging Medusa. He wanted to see how this all went down.

She reached the office they'd just been in and threw the doors open with all the drama of a stage actress performing for a large crowd. The guard and Lysias followed her inside, where the king stood slowly from behind his desk, his expression a mix of such surprise and horror that Lysias had to bite back a laugh. Well, this was unexpected but rather enjoyable thus far.

Alexandra glowered up at Diamandis, hands fisted on her slim waist. "If you expect us to stay here, you will change our accommodations at once."

The king was silent for ticking seconds, but Alexandra did not back down. She held the king's gaze, her chest heaving in fury.

She truly was a beautiful little thing.

"If you were truly the lost princess of Kalyva, you would know better than to speak to your king in such a way," Diamandis said in a low, threatening tone.

Alexandra was clearly not intimidated. "I don't care if you are the king of the entire world." She flung her arms in the air, then pointed back to Lysias. "To put him in his parents' room, after the way he lost them, was a move of disgusting cruelty."

The king's face hardened more, if that were possible, and still Lysias could only watch in awe.

"But the two of you conspiring, lying, and you pretending to be my late sister is an act of charity?"

"So, an eye for an eye." She made a scoffing noise. "A king should be better, and I think we both know it's as possible that I am Zandra as anyone else. Whether you want to believe that or not, I do not care. What you have tried to do here is despicable. Perhaps I do not *wish* to be part of any royal family who would behave in such a way."

"The royal family, as you may have noticed, is dead."

"You are not."

Diamandis moved his gaze from Alexandra to Lysias. "You should control your fiancée," he said, drawing out the last word with disgust.

Lysias only smiled wider. "Oh, I much prefer her out of control. She is a thing of beauty, is she not?"

Diamandis looked Alexandra up and down. "I will enjoy proving you both to be the scheming, lying, charlatans that you are." He lifted his gaze to Lysias, who lounged quite comfortably against the wall. "So that there will be no question, Lysias, once and for all, that you are the same kind of traitor your parents were."

The words hit like the blow they were meant to be and reminded Lysias he was not here to watch Alexandra take Diamandis down a peg, no matter how much he enjoyed it. He could not be distracted in this way.

But when the guard showed them to a *new* room,

Lysias could not seem to find his old self. His singular focus on revenge.

For here was Alexandra, still angry and beautiful. And she'd faced down a king. His oldest enemy.

For him.

CHAPTER TEN

"I HATE HIM." Al seethed, pacing the new room. Oh, she'd
gotten her way, but the anger hadn't receded. What a disgusting thing to do. Unforgivable. Lysias had looked so...

For the first time in that room in the servant's wing,
she'd been able to picture the boy he might have been—
the boy who'd allegedly been *friends* with the man who
would torture him like this. The look on Lysias's face
as he'd stood outside that room had cut her in two. And
she'd felt honor bound to protect that hurt, abandoned,
betrayed *boy.*

Lysias had said nothing as they'd been taken to their
new quarters in a more elaborate part of the palace. Even
she could tell the differences between the two areas, and
that only made her angrier.

"I hate this *place*," Al said. Because she had so much
anger twining with so much of that unsettled feeling, she
simply needed to rage.

"I suppose both these things will only aid in my goal
of revenge."

She turned to face Lysias, the odd note to his tone
causing her some confusion. She thought perhaps he was
trying to sound bored, but it did not come out with quite
the same sarcasm he usually managed.

For the first time she considered that perhaps she should not have poked at the king like that. "Did I mess up your plans?" she asked. It struck her suddenly that she was not worried about upsetting his plans for the right reasons.

She didn't want him angry with her. She wanted him pleased. Approving. When she shouldn't care about *that*. She should care about enacting his revenge so she could get paid.

"No," Lysias replied, still hovering near the door, though he studied her with an intensity she could not fully understand, even if it made her heart begin to beat double time, and something improbably bloomed deep within.

"If anything," he continued. "I believe that little performance only adds credence to the belief we are devoted to one another. Which is good, as once it is proven you are the princess, a marriage to me will be his second-worst nightmare."

"But how can you prove…"

"I have worked for many years to get the people in the king's employ on my side. Some were glad to be the minute I approached…some took more time. Just this morning, I received confirmation that the palace doctor will falsify the DNA results for us."

Alexandra nodded, but his words did not bring her comfort. He was staring at her a bit like they had never met, like he knew nothing about her and was surprised to find her here at all.

She didn't know what to say to him with that expression on his face. She did not know what the next step of any of this was. They were in the palace. They'd met with the king—who was as determined to prove them liars as Lysias had promised he would be.

He crossed to her then, and the look on his face sharpened, turning into something she might have called *feral*. There was something in his gaze—like last night, but not. He reached out and cupped her face with his large hands. He studied her for a moment more as her heart clattered about and her breath backed up in her lungs. As her body seemed to simply *come alight*.

And when he kissed her, it was not like yesterday. There was heat, yes. Passion. But something softer. Deeper. Whatever sharp-edged anger over Diamandis that had still been swirling inside of her settled, melted.

She leaned into him, into the kiss. She did not feel comfortable in this palace, and the only thing that seemed able to penetrate her unease was her anger.

And now this.

His hands smoothing over her back, large and possessive, drawing her closer against the hard evidence of his arousal. His mouth a dangerous demand of heat and something *more*.

When she managed to flutter her eyes open, his golden gaze was on her. Even as he kissed her rough and deep, he watched her. Lust bloomed suddenly, a bolt so hot and sharp it was nearly painful.

"Touch me," she managed, though her voice was ragged with that drugging need. She pressed herself against him, desperate for the way he could make her feel.

"You have forgotten the magic word, Alexandra," he said, his voice a deep purr. He'd stopped kissing her, and now he held her hips, his fingers curling in the fabric of her skirt that was held to the top with little fanciful ties of fabric.

She tried to move against him, find some satisfaction for herself, but he managed to hold her just out of reach. "Perhaps you should be the one saying please to me," she replied, looking for that balance they'd found last night. None of the disquiet she'd felt today.

He laughed darkly. "That will never happen." Then he ripped her skirt from the little ties in one hard jerk. She gasped at the arrow of pleasure that shot through her at such a reckless act. The skirt fluttered to the floor, but before she could even step out of it, he swept her into his arms and strode across the room to the bed—even larger than the one in his home.

He laid her down, straddling her body as he removed the top from her. She reached out and fumbled with the buttons of his shirt. She wanted to feel him. The heat of his skin, the power in his muscles.

He shrugged out of his shirt, then pulled her up by the shoulders to kiss her again, hard and deep. The tenor had changed from that first kiss, or so she thought. This one so fierce and wild and much more like last night.

Then he kissed down her neck, her chest, in between her breasts to where she still had a bandage. He brushed a light kiss over it. "Ah, *asteri mou*, no one will hurt you again. I will not allow it."

A warmth spread inside of her, along with all this passionate want. A strange moisture collected behind her eyes. It was a promise that he would not be able to keep, even if he meant to, because he would not be there once their little mission was finished. They would part. He had made that clear and she expected nothing more.

But he made her yearn for a more she had not imagined when she'd been Al and alone. She had never known anything of passion, but he had shown her last night. She had never known anything of whatever this was. She did not understand *this*. A tenderness that she had never seen in her life. A connection that felt beyond what physical sensations they could draw out in each other.

Like they were two sides of the same coin, melded together at last. *Belonging*. When she knew better than to belong to anyone or anything. The only permanence in life was oneself.

But his hand smoothed down her body, then cupped her and the pleasure arrowed so deep, she was flying through her climax in mere moments. "Lysias…"

"More," he growled, and sheathed himself in protection before he thrust inside of her in one delicious slide. She moaned out his name, met each thrust with her own. She clung to him and chased every sensation wildly and wantonly, as he told her how beautiful she was, how *good*.

It never seemed to end, and she did not think her body could stand such pleasure, over and over, and yet the wave built. Larger and larger.

His hands tangled in her hair as he chased his release and she relished in the wild, uncontrolled beauty in it. In him. Her Lysias.

Finally. Finally. This was all she wanted. To be one with him. To ride this wave together. To forget all the world except him.

Except them.

And when he roared out his release, she didn't weep no matter how the tears built. She simply held on to him and did not let go.

* * *

She slept with her hand fisted at his heart, the ring on her finger sometimes catching the moonlight that slithered in through the curtains.

Lysias didn't sleep because a dark pain gripped him in its iron clutches. He knew if he slept, he would dream.

And he would dream of the monsters that even now he was trying to slay.

So he did not sleep. He lay in this foreign bed and felt the easy rise and fall of Alexandra's breathing.

Alexandra, *Al*, was a problem. She was perfection. The way she matched his passion for her. The way she had stood up *for* him. The whole of who she was…

She was a distraction he couldn't afford, and yet neither could he afford to set her aside. Her acting as his fiancée was an integral part of Lysias getting everything he wanted, of causing Diamandis the most amount of pain. He needed the princess she would play in order to take Diamandis out at the knees.

So something had to be done. He would need to be more careful. More guarded. He did not think resisting her was necessary per se. After all, that was simply… physical. Chemistry. A natural consequence to sharing so much time and space, and the beauty that she was.

He had simply not factored in that there would be an emotional response to returning to Kalyva. That seeing Diamandis would remind him of the time *before*. And while he had predicted many of Diamandis's moves, the king trying to put Lysias in his parents' old living quarters had been a cruelty he had not seen coming.

So he had learned his lesson. Expect pain and suffering and cruelty. Really, it was his life motto. It was ridiculous he'd been caught so off guard.

No matter. Diamandis would pay for it all.

Lysias couldn't forget himself just because his fake princess was...whatever she was. In the end, it did not matter. All that mattered was maintaining a certain wall of distance, of control.

It would be simple enough. There was much to do.

The king would demand a DNA test, and Lysias had to ensure all his men were in place to falsify the results. Something he had been working on for years, but even he could not have predicted the perfection that was Al. Without a past, there would be nothing to cast doubts on the falsified results.

But this was only a part of his plan. This was only a distraction. Perhaps it was even petty—much like Diamandis's attempt to put him in his parents' quarters. The main part of his plan was taking Diamandis's kingdom away from him.

For ten years, he had been finding not just people in the palace to betray Diamandis but people in the council, in Kalyva. It had taken time, subtlety, patience.

He finally had enough support to get a no-confidence vote. And Al—*Alexandra*—was the twist of the knife. While Diamandis was reeling over finding out his sister was alive, Lysias would tip the domino to ruin Diamandis's life.

He had *much* to do, and none of it included watching his fake fiancée begin to thrash in her sleep.

"The door," she muttered. "The door, the door." Then she began to cry quietly, and Lysias could feel her hot tears on his chest. "Am I safe here?"

Pain ripped through him, shadows creeping through the corners of his mind. *The door.* Someone else's voice. The cries and echoes of death. Of murder.

He squeezed his eyes shut, but that was worse. Images he'd long banished assaulted him. He opened his eyes again even as she thrashed more, cried harder.

He simply could not *bear* it. He gathered her close. Kissed her forehead. "Shh, *asteri mou.* You are always safe with me."

She let out a ragged breath, and the crying stopped. Slowly, she began to still. To breathe evenly once more. Without ever waking up.

Once she was calm, Lysias slid out of bed, surprised to find his hands were shaking. He curled them into fists and crossed to the window. He looked out into the night, where the stars and moon shone and rippled on the sea below. He took a deep breath, forced himself to settle.

All the ghosts and pain of his past existed on this little island, but once he took Diamandis's kingdom away from him, all would be well. All would be *soothed.*

He watched the sea as morning began its slow stretch toward dawn. Before the sun was fully up, he was dressed. He gave Alexandra one look. She was curled into a tight little ball, even as the sun made her skin glow gold.

No doubt she'd slept like that on the streets, and somehow she had survived. She was a marvel.

He dressed silently, then strode out of the bedroom and to the door that would lead him into the hall. He jerked the door open, something like panic trying to find some purchase inside of him. But he would not let it. He was in charge. He was Lysias Balaskas.

The guard stood there and Lysias scowled at him. "I wish to see the king."

The guard nodded, pointed down the hall. "He is waiting for you."

Of course he is. Lysias was led through the maze of the palace to Diamandis's office once more, though he knew the way himself. It was early, so the palace was even quieter than it had been yesterday. But there were guards stationed here and there in a way there had not been when the king and queen had been alive.

Lysias hoped it was because of him. He strode into the king's office and forced a smile. "Good morning, Your Majesty." Lysias greeted him with as much put-on cheer as he could muster—if only because it would serve to irritate the king. "My fiancée and I have much to accomplish today. I wish to show her the island, her birthright. Can I expect an armed guard tail as we do?"

Diamandis reacted to none of this. He simply sat at his desk and glowered. "I will see her alone."

Lysias had expected this, and still it was hard to keep his easy smile in place. "She will not want to see you without me. You may be surprised to find your welcoming demeanor yesterday did not win her over, and she is quite concerned about being here at all."

Diamandis looked at him with a raised brow. "Then leave."

Lysias tutted. "Now, no need to get all aflutter. Whatever you have to say to her, surely you can say in front of me. Her one true love."

"I don't know what you have done to this poor girl to make her believe there is an ounce of goodness in you,

Lysias, or that she could possibly be a *princess*, but if you wish to remain, I will see her alone."

Lysias already knew he'd give in to Diamandis's wish. It was the only way, and he trusted Al to handle it beautifully. But he had to put up a fight for the show. "It is a blow, I know, to have your sister sullied by a *servant* such as me." He wasn't sure why *that* sentence felt so true when he was only playing a part. Only poking at Diamandis's weaknesses.

"A *traitor* such as you as long as you wear the last name Balaskas."

"You enjoy that word too much. Perhaps you need a lesson on its definition."

"You forget, Lysias, we had all the same lessons." Then Diamandis turned away, a cold dismissal. He began to walk out of the office, but he spoke as he did. "If she is not alone, I will not speak with her. And that will be that. I'll wait in the dining room."

Lysias said nothing, but he smiled at the king's retreating back. Because, yes, this was the plan.

When he returned to his rooms, Alexandra was still in bed, though she was pushing herself into a sitting position as he entered the bedroom. Blinking at the light, holding the sheet lightly to her chest.

He wanted her with a powerful bolt of need, so much so he took a step forward. Ready to take and take and take until it was sated.

Then he remembered himself. He could enjoy her when the matters of the day were done, and they'd only just begun. "Ah, good morning, Alexandra. Best to be up and dressed." He strode through the room, keeping his gaze on anything but the tantalizing view of her beautiful frame.

He stopped at the window, looked out at the pretty, sunny beach below. He spoke to her without looking at her. "The king wishes to see you alone. I have, of course, put up a grand tantrum about the whole thing but eventually pretended to agree. You know your role, and while the king is busy with you, I will be able to ensure all the other puzzle pieces are in place."

"Lysias."

She said nothing else, and the silence stretched out until he forced himself to look at her with a self-satisfied expression. With the knowledge that revenge was within his grasp and nothing—*nothing*—else mattered.

There was some question in her dark gaze, some uncertainty in her expression. He did not know what she questioned, what worried her.

I do not want to know. Cannot know.

"Do you object to this plan?" he asked genially.

When she spoke, it was carefully, as if considering the question very seriously. "No, but—"

"Then dress, Alexandra. You have much to prove."

CHAPTER ELEVEN

ALEXANDRA GOT DRESSED. She supposed if she was breakfasting with a king, she should choose something elegant—not that any of the wardrobe Lysias, or rather his *team*, had supplied for her was anything other than elegant—but she didn't want to wear a gown or heels. She knew she *should* dress the part of the princess, but she just felt...exhausted. Oddly wrung out.

And yes, some of that was the way she felt in this place, but most of it was Lysias. The feelings he was pulling out of her. She didn't understand them—so new, so foreign, but she knew they were dangerous, and if anyone suffered from them, it would be herself.

She sighed and found some trousers, though they were flowy and silk and not like the kind she'd worn when she'd pretended to be a boy. She paired these with a matching shirt and then studied herself in the mirror. Even without doing her hair or makeup, she looked like a woman. It was quite a marvel what the right cut of clothes could accomplish.

But because she enjoyed it, and it added a regal air to the whole facade, she sat down and did her hair and makeup just as Lysias's staff had taught her. A few days' practice was hardly enough to make her an expert, but she managed well enough.

Then she studied her face, her profile, then straight on. *Did* she look like Diamandis? Maybe something in the way their eyes were situated on their face. And the color, sure, but many people had dark brown eyes. *Obviously*, they weren't actually related, but clearly, Diamandis had not fully refused the possibility out of hand.

When she returned to the main room of their quarters, she found them empty. And simply stood for odd moments of... What was this feeling? It camped out in her chest and moved into her throat. As if she might cry.

Which she would *not* do.

She sucked in a breath and focused. She was to face King Diamandis alone. She had thought Lysias would be with her at least until they got to the dining room, but no matter. She often worked alone. She *always* worked alone. It would be better. She could handle this how she saw fit.

Without worrying so much for Lysias's approval.

She frowned at the voice in her head speaking truths she did not wish to acknowledge. Poking at feelings so deep and foreign and new, the thought of parsing through them was...terrifying.

So she straightened her shoulders and marched out into the hall. A guard stood there and bowed when she emerged.

"Miss. The king wishes for you to join him for breakfast. I will accompany you to the dining room."

Alexandra smiled *prettily* at him, just as Lysias had taught her to. "That would be wonderful. Thank you."

The guard led her through the palace. It was a long walk to the dining room. "Why are there so many armed men within the palace?" Al asked, as much out of curiosity as anything. No doubt Lysias already knew the answer, but she hadn't thought to ask him yet.

"We protect the king."

"Yes, but couldn't you protect him outside? Isn't it usually some kind of…butler or some such that leads prisoners—oh, *dear*, I mean guests—about the palace?" She smiled at the guard and watched the expression on his face, but it did not change at the word "prisoner." Either he thought she was being foolish enough to ignore, or he was just comfortable with her actually being a prisoner. Al supposed it didn't matter which one.

"We protect the king," he repeated, rather robotically. He led her to yet another huge pair of double doors and opened them before pointing her inside.

It was a huge room, with a long, long table at the center. At the very end sat the king. Al knew she should forget about being put in Lysias's parents' quarters yesterday, but she found she could not. Nor could she ignore the fact this man had exiled Lysias at the age of *twelve*. Even if he'd been only a few years older himself.

Clearly, King Diamandis *was* the villain Lysias made him out to be, and so she would win this little round of make believe. For Lysias.

Because he had called her an avenger, and she would avenge the little boy he'd been. Treated so cruelly by this *king*.

Do you really think that will make him love you?

Love. What had she ever known of love? Nothing. So it was foolish to think on it at all. She was savvy enough to know that sex did not equal love, even if she'd never engaged in the act before.

Men were pigs, after all. The one sitting at the table inspecting her like a bug was chief among them.

"Shall I sit down here so we can shout across the room to each other?" Al called out, smiling a bit at the way her voice echoed in the large room.

Though it was quite a way down the line, she saw the king startle a bit. Clearly not expecting her voice to boom across the tall, grand arched ceilings.

"There is a seat for you down here," Diamandis replied, and while his voice was commanding, it didn't seem to echo quite the way hers had.

So, Al made her way down the long table, taking in everything. The richness of the wood, the way the art in here depicted feasts of days gone by. The soaring windows with their beautiful views out to the sea.

When Al finally found the place that had clearly been laid out for her, she made sure to lower herself as gracefully as possible into the plush seat. She fixed the sweetest smile on her face. "Good morning, Your Majesty."

The king's eyes narrowed. "What is he promising you?"

"No pleasantries, then? Ah, very well. I believe he's promising me a lifetime of commitment," Al replied blandly. She lifted her engagement ring and allowed it to sparkle in the light streaming in through the window before she studied the spread before her. Platters of food—pastries, breakfast meats, yogurts and such were laid out with little tongs. There were also pitchers of juice, a pot of coffee. Such choices. She supposed it paid to be the king.

"May I?" she asked.

The king's expression became more and more thunderous, which Al could admit brought her some petty joy. She didn't wait for his permission. She poured herself some coffee from the ornate pot. She helped herself to a little of everything laid before her and vowed then and there that no matter how much money she had after her payout, she would always be grateful for food without worry.

"You will be found out. I am a *king*. I realize our country is small and not well known. That many in the outside world consider us so old-fashioned that we have no power, but I have the power to find the truth about you. And destroy you."

Al did not laugh, though a strange bubble of it rose inside her chest. "I suppose it's handy then that there's nothing to destroy."

"You sound like him," Diamandis muttered disgustedly.

"We are quite alike, my beloved and I." *Beloved* landed a bit clunkily, but Al did not look at Diamandis when she said it. She pretended to be so engaged in her eating she couldn't possibly look up.

"I will destroy you both."

Al sighed heavily and leaned her chin on her hand before studying the man who was king of this pretty little island. There was no doubt in her mind he didn't deserve the power, the position. "Do you men ever get tired of wanting to destroy things?"

Diamandis pushed back from the table, tossing his napkin down on his plate. "I have work to do. To find the truth. Feel free to pass that along to Lysias."

"Oh, I don't need to. I think you must underestimate him. Do you really believe he'd bring me here without having thought of everything?" She looked up at the King, wholly unbothered by his bluster.

Because underneath, she saw something that reminded her of fear. Not of Lysias or his revenge, she didn't think. But fear that it could be true. That she might actually be Princess Zandra.

Which meant they'd never found a body, if he could worry about *truths*.

He leaned in close, all thunderstorms and rage. "Tell me one thing," he demanded, eyes blazing. Eyes like her own. "One thing only Zandra Agonas would know."

If he was questioning her, it meant he thought it was possible she was Zandra. She didn't let her triumph at that show, because his face was too close. She could *feel* the hot anger radiating off him. And she had the strangest impulse to reach out and...poke him right in the middle of his Adam's apple.

She didn't even stop herself. She just did it. *Poke.*

He stumbled back, his hand flying to his throat. She frowned a little, because while it had no doubt felt uncomfortable, she'd hardly *punched* him there. It shouldn't have hurt *that* much.

But he'd paled, his hand on his throat like she'd stabbed him clean through. "That proves nothing," he said raggedly, stepping away from her as if she were suddenly venomous.

Which was an odd thing to say since she didn't know what poking him was meant to prove. She'd only done it out of impulse, out of frustration. Perhaps he just wasn't used to people not being afraid of him. He seemed the kind of king who dealt in fear.

Then he strode out of the dining room, and since Alexandra had nothing else to do, she gorged herself on breakfast.

* * *

Lysias returned to the palace in a good mood. Though he'd known the guards had followed him, he'd also lost them here and there to do what needed to be done before allowing them to catch up to him once more.

They would report to Diamandis that they had lost him for pieces of time, and Diamandis would, of course, find this suspicious, but even if he found out what Lysias was doing, he wouldn't be able to stop it.

It was a decade in the making. At first, Lysias had bribed people because he'd been new to money and power. But as the decade had gone on, as he'd grown in that money and power, he'd begun to understand people better. Kalyva better. And the way Diamandis ruled more clearly.

So over the years, he'd learned to prey on people's sense of injustices done against them. Though Diamandis treated most of his staff well, according to what Lysias heard, the man was hard on people who disagreed with him or who failed.

So, Lysias had begun to target those men. Sway them to his side. And let the spiderwebs of discontent spread out until the perfect moment.

That was the beauty of public opinion. Because everything was set up perfectly. When Diamandis presided over the council meeting next week, there would be a vote of no confidence. It paid to know the laws of Kalyva, and that while the monarchy ruled exclusively, the council had the right to run checks and balances.

One of the rarely used balances was a vote of no confidence against the king, and if popular vote of the council resulted in no confidence, it could choose a new king.

Lysias had considered himself for the position but wasn't sure he wanted to deal in the politics of it all.

Then there was Al, but she would need to make herself scarce in case the truth every came out.

So, some stranger would take over Kalyva, and for Diamandis, that would be failure enough.

Lysias smiled. Much could still go wrong, but he simply wouldn't allow it. He was too close and had come too far.

So he strode through the palace, knowing he was being watched but was thrilled with the successes he'd made today. He also told himself over and over again as the anticipation rose within him that this feeling was all about the future success of his plan.

Not returning to his Alexandra.

He opened the door to the main room and ignored the jolt of worry and frustration that twined within him when she clearly wasn't there. He moved through the bedroom, the dressing rooms, then back out to the bedroom with increasing frustration.

When he finally caught a glimpse of her, it was through the large-windowed door that led out to a little balcony. She stood out on it, leaned over the rail, her hair blowing gently in the slight breeze. She wore pants today, but the material looked like silk and billowed in the breeze like her hair.

He simply stopped and watched. Her eyes were on the blazing sunset meeting the darkening sea. It was hard to believe he'd ever taken her for a boy. She was so beautiful. Alluring and self-possessed with a curiosity for life that he'd never seen matched. She'd attempted to protect him, *avenge* him, when no one had since he'd been a boy.

And when she touched him, kissed him, came apart around him, he was transported to another world entirely. One where revenge didn't matter at all.

He was desperate for her, and he didn't understand. Had she cast a spell on him? Poisoned him? Because he wanted her naked and beneath him, but he also wanted to stand here and watch her for eternity.

It was the thought of *eternity* that had him moving forward, breaking this little moment of insanity, because he needed to know how her breakfast had gone, and keep her abreast of her next steps.

Because revenge was all that truly mattered here in Kalyva.

She looked over her shoulder at him, and everything in her expression lightened. She smiled as if she were happy to see him. As if she'd been waiting for him.

An echoing warmth bloomed within him, and it reminded him of his childhood here. Of that feeling of belonging, being so sure of his place. It had not mattered that he was a servant. There'd been little struggle. So much freedom.

And love.

And then everyone he loved had been murdered. Had betrayed him. How dare she bring that out in him again. Muddle all his revenge with this…this…*feeling*.

But she seemed clueless to the storm within him. "Were you successful?" she asked pleasantly.

He worked very hard to chain down his volatile emotions. To speak as pleasantly in return as she spoke to him. "Very. Everything is in place. We will agree to the DNA test the next time Diamandis presses the issue, and my men will ensure the results show a match with Dia-mandis. Did you do any work as Al today?"

Some of her smile dimmed at this, and she began to worry her bottom lip between her teeth. She looked back at the sea. "No. My meeting with the king was very short, but I think… There is no body," she said, almost thoughtfully. "The king asked me to prove I was Zandra. I guess it could all be his own game, but he seemed…" She paused as if searching for the right word. "I think he's afraid I *could* be her, which means he knows that no body was ever found, doesn't it? He seemed so genu-inely angry, demanding I prove myself. I just don't see how there is a body anyone knows of."

Lysias wasn't sure why he was surprised. He'd sus-pected this ever since Diamandis brought them to the palace. There was simply no reason if he was *certain* Zandra was dead. And still, it shocked him a bit to hear Alexandra confirm it because he'd still been suspicious of Diamandis playing a game.

"What did you mean at the beach yesterday?" she asked, turning her attention back to him. "When you said you knew she wasn't with her siblings because you were there?"

He was already feeling volatile, nearly unhinged with a million battering emotions. Remembering that night would break the chain of his control. So he tried not to *remember*, only to repeat basic facts.

"I was in the palace that night," he responded, as if by rote. "I knew Zandra was not with her siblings. She was in her own nursery. She might have been killed, but not with them." It was not the full truth, but it was the only truth he wanted to live in.

Alexandra nodded thoughtfully. "Do you think I could be from here?" she asked, pointing down at the village below.

"What do you mean?"

"I don't really remember my life before Athens. Maybe I didn't have one. But something about this place is so familiar and uncomfortable. If there was the upheaval of a coup or what have you, maybe I was here. Maybe that's the source of my nightmares." Her gaze moved from the sea to him. "Do you think it possible?"

With her, anything seemed possible. And since he knew firsthand the pain and suffering of that night, he would not put it past anyone to have nightmares and to have forgotten. Especially since she wouldn't have been more than four herself.

He reached out, though he knew he shouldn't, ran his hand over the silk of her hair. The way it burned with hints of red as the sun disappeared behind him. "I am falsifying the DNA results for the king, of course, but if you wish, I could run a real test. Anonymously. See if you match anyone. It is not a surety, as any relative would have to be in a system we run it through. But…it would be a chance."

She stood very still, staring at him with wide eyes. "Really?"

"Of course," he said roughly.

She leaned forward, reaching out to put her hands on his chest. Over his heart. She was searching his face. "Lysias…"

He saw something in her eyes, something soft. Dangerous. And he shook his head. He would not allow it. He would cut this off at the pass. "I have been clear, Alexandra," he said stiffly.

"Yes. You've been clear," she agreed. Easily and with no hint of hurt, but that only made him unreasonably angry. That she'd leave her hands over his heart. That she'd look up at him as if she understood him when he hadn't even explained.

When no one could understand.

But she thought she did. He saw it there in the way she looked at him. She thought she saw *him*, and he had to prove to her that she was wrong. It was a raging anger inside of him.

He curled his hand in her hair, used it as leverage to tip her head back, so she met his gaze head on. And she didn't look away, didn't struggle. She simply looked up at him. So calm. So sure.

"Everyone I have ever loved has died brutally or betrayed me," he told her. Because she *would* understand. If he had to bellow it from the mountaintops. "I will never shackle myself to another. I will never let anyone have power over me again. I am the only power."

"Yes," she agreed, so readily. So *calmly*, not even trying to pull her hair from his grasp. "Except you want me," she said, reaching out to trace the evidence of this fact, without ever taking her gaze from his eyes.

"This is *all* I want from you," he growled.

"Then take it, Lysias."

Was it challenge? Was it surrender? He didn't know. He didn't care. He took her mouth with his in angry demand. Fisted his hands in her hair to hold her still while he took what *he* wanted. What *he* desired.

But she met him there, in this fiery insanity between them. Where all rational thought burned away into only their bodies. He ripped her trousers away from her, even as she worked his belt free.

He didn't bother with her shirt, didn't want to see the evidence of where she'd been injured. Didn't want to believe her capable of being hurt. He backed her against the wall, so that she stepped out of her pants and underwear.

The breeze rippled through his hair, and he didn't care they were outside. All he cared about was possession. The deep, dark thing that beat within him, twining with the anger and the other emotion he refused to acknowledge. But it gave everything claws. Teeth.

He pulled her leg up to wrap around his waist but held her there so he could look at her. Where she was wet for him. His gaze raked up to meet hers.

She breathed heavily, but she only looked at him. With softness in her gaze, even as he was rough with her.

"You want me like this?" He could see that she did, *feel* that she did. And yet he wanted to hear her say it. As if that would give him permission to take whatever he wanted, however he wanted.

"Yes. There isn't a way I don't want you," she said, and it didn't sound soft, it sounded strong. Like she was the one in control.

Never. How dare she sound so calm. So perfectly *rational* when he wanted to rage against everything that swirled inside of him. Everything she brought out in him. Everything he'd buried so deep it lived with the shadows and monsters of his nightmares.

So he took her. Her back against the wall, her legs wrapped around him as he plunged. He gave her no quarter, no rest. And she didn't ask for any. Simply begged for more, shattering over and over again. Her nails dug into his back. She set her teeth to his neck. She said his name, sobbed it. As night fell over them.

But it did not matter how rough he was with her, how much he'd hoped to drive some wedge between what they were and the feelings she'd unwisely left clear in her eyes.

Even as he carried her inside, bent her over the bed and slid into her from behind. Even as he made her say *please* over and over again, until he finally roared out his release, his fingers digging into her slim hips.

Even with all that, when all was said and done, she still curled up next to him and fell into a quiet sleep.

With her hand fisted over his heart as if she held it there.

CHAPTER TWELVE

ALEXANDRA WASN'T SURPRISED to wake up alone. Even though she knew Lysias had stayed with her for a portion of the evening, it seemed impossible to think he'd actually face the aftermath in the waking hours if he'd only faced them with sex the night before.

She sighed and looked up at the ceiling. She didn't know what he thought he'd been doing last night. Driving her away from him? Proving some point about emotions? All he'd managed to do was strip away everything until she couldn't deny one simple truth.

She loved him.

What a strange series of events. She knew that it was foolish for a girl such as her to think she knew anything of love, that love could bloom in a matter of days, but... She just did. She wished to help him, to avenge him. She wanted to spend time with him—inside and outside of their bed.

The Lysias who forgot about his revenge was a caretaker, as if he couldn't help himself. An avenger too. She'd seen an Athenian paper yesterday in the sitting room with a pile of newspapers from all over. On the front page had been a picture of Vasilis Pangali in handcuffs.

The man who'd sent her attacker. She *knew* Lysias was behind it—because no one else could possibly be.

And yet she knew Lysias did not fancy his moral code above anyone else's. She loved him because she understood him. Everything he must have endured to rise to the top and still remain cognizant of the lows he'd come from. He was wholly himself and not afraid to enact what he believed in.

Except when it came to love.

She thought, perhaps foolishly, that he might love her too if he could get past the fear that held him in its grips—that he hid with fake masks and revenge plots.

It seemed a rather big if, considering that fear had clearly driven his need for revenge across two decades. That his fear lived deep within an old trauma he could not seem to face.

She rolled onto her stomach, surveyed the world outside the large windows and doors that led to the balcony. The sun had begun its rise, but it was still early yet, so the world glowed a dim gold as the sea moved in the distance.

She had no doubt Lysias was out enacting plots and plans. She likely wouldn't see him again until evening. Like last night.

She thought of last night. Of the rough way he'd taken her, out on the balcony and then on this bed. She was getting warm and excited just thinking about it.

She had reveled in the wildness because she understood it. She understood *him*. Something as soft and dangerous as love felt like a loss of control. Like a threat. He'd needed to fight that threat.

And the fight had been glorious. They had left marks on each other, yes, but they had climbed to new heights of pleasure. And maybe he had not come to the same conclusion she had—that loving him was simply an inescapable fact of life, no matter how vulnerable it made her—but it had burned away some of the fear. For her.

Growing up as she had, accepting things became necessary, whether they were comfortable or not. If she denied simple truths, she would end up in danger or worse. So she simply had to accept that she'd fallen in love with him.

If it hurt, if it ended, that would be terrible, yes, but life was oftentimes terrible, and she would simply move through the terrible as she'd done so many times before.

For whatever reason, Lysias did not have that skill. He was stuck in the tragedy of his past. Maybe... She hoped so much that dealing with all of this revenge would make him more open to the idea, the possibility.

But if it didn't, she would survive. She was certain she would be able to survive. Had to be.

Lysias would as well, survivor that he was, but she wanted to give him more than survival. Which would require being careful with him, with her feelings.

How would he behave this evening?

Would he pretend nothing had happened? Try to be cruel to her now? Maybe they would repeat the intensity of last night. Or maybe...maybe he would send her away.

The first trickle of fear slithered around her heart. She could handle it all—she could pretend with the best of them, and she could weather his cruelty. She reveled in his demands, but she could not be sent away. She *needed* to be by his side. Especially as he took on the king.

The king who clearly thought Alexandra *could* be his long-lost sister. She didn't know how she felt about that. In preparation for this time on Kalyva, it had only been about *her*. That she could play the role that had been designed for *her*. She hadn't thought about *him*. About Diamandis.

Now she'd come face-to-face with him, so she had no choice but to regard him as a human being. Even though she rather detested that person, it was cruel what they were doing. To make him believe his sister was alive and here.

She blew out a frustrated breath and crawled out of bed. Naked, she padded over to her wardrobe. She considered dressing as Al, sneaking about the palace as a boy, but when faced with her closet, she reached for a colorful sun dress instead.

She might be forced to return to Al yet. Why not enjoy Alexandra while she could?

So she dressed, she curled her hair and took time on her makeup. She studied herself, as it seemed she was incapable of passing a mirror without looking for the similarities between her and the king that would make anyone consider the possibility they were related.

Did they have similar ears? Was their chin pointed in the same way?

She shook her head and looked away. She never found answers, and it was a pointless endeavor anyway, as she was not his sister.

When she stepped out of the rooms, the guard was waiting for her in the hall as always. She smiled pleasantly at him, even though she was tired of being followed and led about. "Oh, would the king like me to breakfast with him again?" she asked, making sure to sound sugary sweet. "Or are you just today's chosen jailor?"

"I will take you to the dining room, miss," he said. Not answering her questions at all.

She let the guard guide her to breakfast, but she'd been watching them. And taking note of the different areas in the palace that were guarded and not. The dining room was empty, save a place set for her, so she sat down and ate another delicious, filling breakfast.

All the while, she watched the guard by the door out of the corner of her eye. When he was busy flirting with one of the kitchen staff, Alexandra slid silently out of the room through the hallway that led around the kitchen and into another wing of the palace.

She stood in the hallway listening for guards or people but heard nothing except an oppressive kind of silence. A velvet rope hung at the end of the staircase at the end of the hall. Like they were in some sort of museum, and this section was not allowed visitors.

Naturally, she couldn't resist. She stepped over the rope, then took the stairs. The carpet was so plush she didn't even need to try to soften her footfalls.

Something whispered through her, over her skin as she took each stair. A kind of foreboding, and yet a curiosity so deep she couldn't resist.

She let those odd whispers guide her up the ornate staircase, pausing to gaze out the large windows that lined the walls along the way. She took in all that sea that surrounded so much of the palace. No matter how it made her feel, it was a truly beautiful place.

The staircase spiraled up and around until she was at the top and greeted with another long, grand hallway. There was a huge painting at the end of it. Alexandra moved for it. A cover hung from the bottom edge, like someone had recently pulled it off.

When she approached, she stared up at the portrait of a

couple in grand royal garb, down to crowns and scepters. They were both smiling. The man looked so much like Diamandis she almost thought it *was* him, but the woman…

In the woman's face, she found a startling resemblance. Not identical. In fact, she might not have noticed at all if she hadn't spent the past few days studying her own face, comparing it to Diamandis's. But this woman's cheeks moved into her nose in the same delicate fashion Al had always tried to hide when living as a boy. The sweep of this woman's hair revealed ears and a dainty jawline that just…felt familiar.

And her eyes, even just in the painting, radiated a warmth that made Alexandra struggle to breathe.

A dark, cold fear took hold of her, and she had to look away, or she might burst into tears she did not understand.

She was faced with a row of doors as she fought the emotional outpouring. All were closed. Except one, which was opened a crack.

Compelled, Alexandra moved forward. With all the stealth of her spy days, she eased the door open a little bit at a time. It was a room. Maybe a bedroom? But it was hard to tell as most of the furniture and belongings were covered. Except a few things had clearly been disturbed recently.

And someone was in here. She could hear their audible breaths, though she would need to open the door wider to see who it was.

It didn't matter who it might be. She should leave. She had no business being here.

But she didn't leave. She pushed the door open wider until she could see a man. Gazing out a high window— the only source of light in the entire dark room. The shafts of light danced with dust motes and haloed him standing there.

"Lysias," she breathed.

He stilled—the only sign she might have startled him. Then slowly he turned to face her, his expression utterly blank.

"Were you followed?" he asked.

"Of course not," she replied. Luckily, the question offended her enough that she wasn't shaky when she spoke. "No one can guard me for long. What about you?"

He turned to look back out the window. Unlike most of the other windows in the house that she'd seen, it did not go to the floor. It started above Lysias's tall frame and reached to the high ceiling. "I know the palace too well not to be able to slip away as it suits me."

"No doubt they'll find us soon enough with the way guards roam this place," Al said, carefully taking steps to come closer to him. But not too close. Part of her was afraid if she got too close, he'd be cold or cruel or make them both leave.

"He is paranoid of his own bloody coup." Lysias shrugged. "Which is fair."

So they were to ignore last night. Ignore their feelings. Alexandra found she was okay with that for the time being because this room gave her a disquieted feeling in the pit of her stomach, and yet she could not find the sense to want to leave.

"What room is this?" she asked, studying what she could make out of it in the dim light. Though many things were covered, the walls were visible and beautiful. Painted with bright, vibrant scenes that looked like something out of a fairy tale. Princesses in the forests and fairies flitting about trees.

"A nursery," Lysias said after a beat of hesitation.

"Who's nursery?" Alexandra replied, smiling as she reached out to touch the outline of a glistening dragon painted gliding above the trees.

He sighed. Heavily. "The princess."

Alexandra jerked her hand back as if she'd been burned. It felt wrong, she did not know why. She turned to Lysias, though he still simply stood there, hands clasped behind his back, staring out the window. "Why are you in here?" she asked, desperate for him to give her an honest answer.

Because *this* didn't seem to be about revenge. There was something…sadder at play here.

He didn't answer or react right away. Almost as if she weren't here at all. "I did not mean to be," he said after a while. Which broke her heart.

She crossed to him, needing to comfort him whether he would accept that comfort or not. He sounded so pained. Looked so lost. She slid her hand up his back. She opened her mouth to speak, but the scene below the high window caught her eye. It depicted a very thick tree trunk, little, colorful birds dancing around it.

But it wasn't a tree, she knew. Much like the art panel in Diamandis's office. This was something else.

Another door. She could see the outline of it in the dark paint of the tree trunk.

"Lysias," she whispered, because she felt a very real fear even though she was in no danger.

"What?"

She pointed at the tree. "This is the door. The door in my dream."

* * *

Lysias didn't speak. He could not find the words. He wanted to call her a liar, but he saw the way she looked at the tree, where there was indeed a door.

He'd *heard her* mutter about the door in her sleep. Say something he'd once heard someone else say. When he'd set her inside that door.

Am I safe here?

The clawing at his chest he couldn't eradicate squeezed at his lungs. Memories, yes, but something more. Something to do with Alexandra.

Who crouched down, reached out, and touched the exact spot on the tree that popped the door open.

He saw her in profile, and it melded with a flash of the queen. A kind woman. Whose profile looked so like Alexandra's. He'd pushed those memories out of his mind. Blackened them in shadow. Until he'd found himself compelled to walk up here and come face-to-face with the dusty portraits of the king and queen he remembered.

But it couldn't *be*.

Alexandra looked up at him, tears in her eyes. "What happened here?" she asked.

And he knew he shouldn't tell her. That whatever this was, it wasn't about the events in this room. It wasn't about… Alexandra. No matter what strange parts of the palace she knew.

But the images were there, dancing around, and it seemed he had to speak them into existence or be haunted forever. How would he enact his revenge if he could not deal in hard truths?

"This was Princess Zandra's nursery, as I said. Diamandis's room was at the beginning of the hall, as he was a teenager and the heir. The two middle boys, they had their own rooms on the opposite side of the hall, but they were twins. So similar, they were an inseparable duo. No matter how their nannies or parents tried, they always ended up together in one room. Wreaking havoc. Zandra was the only girl and much younger, so this was hers."

Alexandra stayed crouched there, but then she opened the door wider. Without thinking it through, an impulse born of sheer terror, his hand reached out and grabbed her roughly away.

But she looked up at him, even as he held her elbow. "Lysias, what *happened*?"

"On that night… I was with my parents, in our quarters, when we first heard the screams. Gunfire. People fled, crying that the king and queen had been murdered. My parents… They put me in the tunnel to keep me safe. The tunnels, they are old. From early denizens of the palace. By the time I was a child, they were simply used as a playhouse for the children. Including me. So my parents thought I would be safe there."

"Were you?" she asked, breathlessly. As if he wasn't standing before her, alive and well.

"I was, but I knew… I knew the men who'd killed the king and queen would go after the children."

It all came flooding back. Everything he'd blocked out for so long. The gunfire, the screams, his parents' wild eyes as they'd huddled in their rooms, praying the rebellious group would not come for the servants.

Their desperation to save him when it seemed they would.

He'd known the memories would attack him if he came up here, but he hadn't been able to resist. Maybe he'd had some foolish belief he could stare it down and forget it forever. Instead he was reliving it, holding Alexandra there at arm's length.

And it poured out of him. How he had paused there in the tunnels, wondering what he should do. That it had been the thought of his best friend being killed that he could not stand. So he'd made his way through the maze that would lead him to Diamandis's room. But he searched the room, and Diamandis wasn't there.

"I thought perhaps he'd gone to save the others, so I looked out of his door. There were men breaking into the room across the hall, where I knew the twins were. Shooting. The screams…"

Maybe she said something, but he didn't hear it. He was too lost in that old nightmare.

"But I thought if the gunmen were there, they hadn't gotten to the princess yet. And maybe Diamandis was with Zandra. I could not save the boys, but maybe I could save them. So I went back to the tunnels, came out here." He pointed to the door she'd opened.

"Diamandis was not here, but Zandra was. She was sitting in her bed. I told her she had to come to the tunnels, to be safe. She didn't respond. I don't know what she'd seen or hadn't, but when I finally went over to her bed, she got out and took my hand. I took Zandra through the door. I told her we would go to my parents. My parents never would have harmed a child. *Never.*"

"You saved her," Alexandra whispered, and there was awe in her tone. Misplaced awe though it was.

"I tried. I do not know what became of her." *Will I be safe here?* But he had never had time to answer. "I could hear them coming, so I shoved her into the wall

and closed the door before the men burst into the room.
They said something to each other about me being a servant, not what they were after. I do not know what they
did to me, only that it rendered me unconscious. When
I woke up, bloody and hurting, I was in a prison. Alone.
I was never allowed to speak to my parents again. They
were taken away and executed the following day."

"Lysias…"

"I don't know what saved me from the same fate. My
age. My friendship with Diamandis. They said the princess was dead, and I believed them, but I knew my parents had nothing to do with it. Maybe she took the wrong
tunnel. Maybe the men found her. I will never know, but
I know my parents did not kill her, and they did not deserve to be executed."

She nodded, swallowing convulsively. "I believe you,"
she said.

All the old monsters roared in some kind of pained relief. For no one, not one person since that night ever had.
He felt torn apart, flayed open. A wounded animal with
no recourse but to lash out.

Except his Alexandra was all color and light, standing there with teardrops on her cheeks. Brown eyes wide
and sympathetic.

"If you do not know what became of her…" Alexandra looked down at the door, and he knew she was considering the impossible idea that had been trying to take
root in his mind since she had opened the door in Diamandis's office.

"It couldn't be true, Alexandra," he said harshly. Because maybe some strange part of him *wanted* it to be.
"It couldn't be possibly true."

"No, of course not." She looked up at him and smiled, but there was a sadness in her eyes that carved him up inside. "Perhaps I was like you. A servant here. That would explain things, would it not?"

He doubted it very much, as he couldn't think of any servant children young enough to be her, but still he nodded, because it was better than the alternative.

The impossible.

"Perhaps."

"I doubt very much we will ever know, as it seems unlikely my true family would be in some DNA database, and it truly is of no matter. Your parents were wronged, and we will find a way to right that wrong. Together."

There had not been anyone on his side since he was twelve. But he did not want her here. He wanted to do this alone. To prove to Diamandis that nothing, *nothing* could touch the man he'd made himself into.

He meant to tell her that. To chastise her for butting her nose into his business when she was a tool. Nothing more. But the words did not come out, and he heard the squeak of the door, the sound of new footsteps.

He turned, reflexively keeping Alexandra behind him in a move of protection. He scowled at Diamandis, who stood just outside the door with his own deep scowl.

"What are you two plotting?" he asked darkly. "*My* death this time around?"

CHAPTER THIRTEEN

ALEXANDRA WAS MORE shaken than she could remember being. Except maybe when her attacker had caught up to her back in Athens.

But this was not an attack. It was just…sad.

And strange. She glanced back at the tree door. How had she known? Why did this palace awaken such strange things inside of her?

But she could not worry over it now. They needed to face down Diamandis. As a united front.

Alexandra hooked her arm through Lysias's. She smiled sadly at Diamandis and used all the truths that made even her wonder why she felt connected to this place. "I suffer nightmares. Of a door. When I explained the door in my dreams to Lysias, he brought me up here."

Diamandis sighed disgustedly. "You mean he brought you up here to fill your head with lies?"

"No, I do not mean that," she replied, firmly, as if she were speaking to a child.

"I know your game, Lysias. You've told her your own memories so she can pretend they are her own." Then, surprisingly, his gaze turned toward her. "You think you can poke me in the throat and convince me of this ridiculous charade? I am not so easily swayed. My private doctor is here ready to administer the DNA swab. Let's get this over with."

Lysias did not move forward. He looked down at her like Diamandis had accused her of speaking in tongues. "You...poked him?" Lysias said, sounding oddly ragged. "In the *throat*?"

"I realize he's a king and all, but he was in my face. I don't understand the big deal." But clearly it was some kind of...deal.

"Where will she be given the swab?" Lysias asked, returning his gaze to Diamandis, his tone back to being detached and firm.

"In my office."

"We will meet you there in a moment."

"You think I'd leave you here alone? That I'd let you continue to desecrate my sister's memory?"

Lysias laughed darkly. "You care for her memory? As I recall, you were nowhere to be found that night." They moved toward each other, two angry men seething with all their old hurts and tragedies dressed up like fury.

But they were both just...injured, traumatized boys, Alexandra realized.

She stepped in between them before they could land the blows they both clearly wanted to. Their anger tied her stomach in knots, though she couldn't quite work out why. They were enemies, but it felt wrong that they should fight. Here of all places.

"Come, Diamandis. I'll let you take your little swab," she said, with a wave toward the door.

He sneered at her. "You'll not order me around, imposter."

"I suppose I understand why you feel the need to rage

and threaten us, but the fact of the matter is you haven't tossed us out yet. So you know it's possible I might be your sister. If you feel better to treat me so shabbily because you think there's a chance I'm *not*, very well. But I find it tiring."

She surveyed them both, decided to take the role of cool, regal *princess*. She wasn't, of course she wasn't. No matter what strange snatches of memory seemed to exist here. But that was the role she'd been brought here to play.

"If you must have a bit of manly fistfighting to make yourselves feel better, you should take it outside. And leave me out of it." And with that, Alexandra left the room with its echoes of pain and violence. The strange tree door from her dreams.

She wanted this over now more than ever. But then, she would not have Lysias, and that was a new pain. To think of life without him.

She had to push away that thought. She couldn't *make* him love her. Or be brave enough to love her. Maybe she didn't need to. Maybe she could simply convince him that since they got along so well, they should continue to enjoy each other...until they didn't.

Somewhat relieved by this plan, she walked back down the staircase. The men followed, though a few paces back.

Alexandra didn't look around this time. She ignored the whispers and shadows. She wanted no memories. No snatches of this possibility that *she* was the princess. It was entirely *im*possible.

If Lysias put the young princess in the tunnel, and his parents did not get to her, then likely someone awful had. If she had not died, she'd likely met terrible things and *then* died. It was far more plausible that Alexandra was simply from the island, that she'd been caught up in the violence of the coup—perhaps even her parents had been perpetrators in the whole thing. They or she had escaped or been exiled to Athens, and then she'd either been abandoned or orphaned.

A much more plausible story than being a *princess*.

She swept into Diamandis's office without waiting for him. There was an older gentleman standing next to a little table where a variety of small tools where arranged. She smiled at him, putting everything of the past hour behind her. "Good morning."

He was clearly flustered that she'd approached him without the king, but Diamandis soon showed up, Lysias behind him, both looking thunderous. It didn't appear as though they'd physically fought each other though.

So there was that.

"Dr. Nikolaou," Diamandis greeted brusquely. "This is the woman I'd like you to test."

The doctor nodded at her. "Simply have a seat, miss."

So she did. Let the doctor swab her mouth with his little cotton swab and pack it away carefully like it might be gold. "That should be what we need," the doctor said as he began to pack up his materials.

"When will we have the results?" Lysias demanded.

The doctor didn't even look up. "A few days. Friday at the latest."

"I don't need to remind you of how important privacy is in this endeavor, Doctor," Diamandis said coldly.

The doctor looked up at him, and maybe Alexandra was seeing things, or maybe she was overly suspicious. But there was something like hatred in the doctor's eyes. "Of course."

The doctor left without looking at her or Lysias. Lysias had said he was falsifying the results. Did that mean the doctor was under Lysias's influence?

And would Lysias do as he'd promised and search for her real genetic family?

Diamandis turned his attention to Lysias. "You are both dismissed, and you will stay out of the family wing, or I will throw you in a cell. Again." Diamandis did not look at *her*, she noted, so she moved before him.

She studied the angry man and decided to fight all that anger and rage with something else entirely. Because he'd become king at the age of fourteen after his family had been brutally murdered. Maybe like Lysias, maybe like herself, he had not seen gentleness since.

She approached him, took his hands in hers. "I look forward to the answers, Diamandis. It will never be able to answer all our questions, but I hope it will bring us both some clarity. So that you may set some of this anger aside."

He jerked his hands away from her, but she did not let him respond in any other way. She simply turned on a heel and followed the doctor's exit out of the large doors.

Lysias found himself standing shoulder to shoulder with Diamandis, watching Alexandra's graceful exit. Much like upstairs.

She could be the princess.

But it was impossible. It had to be impossible. She found secret doors because she'd been a spy. She had nightmares because, much like him, something terrible had happened to her in her childhood.

But it didn't mean it was the *same* terrible somethings.

The odds were impossible, or so he told himself over and over again. But as the memories forced themselves on him, clearer than they'd been in years, he just kept seeing the princess in Alexandra's brown eyes.

"She's a liar," Diamandis growled. "As are you."

"And yet you keep us here," Lysias replied, trying to find his lazy veneer. Trying to remember what was important. His plans. Falsifying the DNA results.

Are you sure you need to?

"I will prove to my people, and all their whispers, that you are the scheming traitor, just as your parents were. And you will face the wrath not just of me but all of Kalyva."

"Such a shame I am a grown man these days, not so easily conquered instead of an orphaned boy—due to you, I might add. I will not be so easy to sweep aside this time."

"I did not…" But whatever Diamandis had meant to deny, he stopped himself as a young woman appeared at the open office doors. She held a clipboard and curtsied prettily to the king. "Your Majesty, Mr. Kronos is here."

Diamandis nodded at her, then turned his attention to Lysias. "You will not win." He pointed at the door: a clear sign he would not leave until Lysias left first.

Lysias considered a standoff. Simply waiting for Diamandis to bodily remove him, but they'd already tempted their tempers and nearly come to blows.

Only Alexandra's clear lack of interest in their fighting seemed to cure them of their bloodlust.

She really was a wonder. And if he was honest with himself, he did not want to have to go back to their quarters and face her.

Her questions. Her memories. The feelings that lurked in her eyes.

But he would not be a coward. So he bowed at the king with a sardonic lift of his brow, flashed the assistant a charming smile, then walked back to his and Alexandra's quarters.

He found her standing on the balcony, much as she had been last night. His body hardened at the thought, the desire as intense as it had been, but there was something else. A vulnerability from being in Zandra's room, from the things Alexandra seemed to know...

He would find a way to keep his hands off her. He would keep his physical distance. He could not risk a repeat performance. He had always prized his control, but nothing had ever tested it as Alexandra did.

So he would simply not let himself be tested.

She turned as if she sensed him.

They studied each other across the way for quite some time. Eventually, she came back inside, but she still stood by the balcony door. "Does the doctor work for you?" she asked.

"No, but he was willing to help set the wheels of justice in motion."

Her curiosity morphed into a frown. "What does that mean?"

"People are tired of Diamandis's iron reign. The king has made many errors in seeking to make up for his parents'. He is too hard, too controlling. The people do not love him. He has lost the trust of many."

Her brow furrowed. "You're not planning..."

He might have been offended at what she insinuated, but bloody coups *had* crossed his mind. If he hadn't known so many vulnerable innocent bystanders in the coup he'd survived, he might have used it.

But he only wished to harm Diamandis. Not innocents. "I am not a murderer, Alexandra," he chastised. "Not like Diamandis. I will not have him executed. I will simply have him lose his throne and give Kalyva to the people. His place as king is all that matters to him. Living without it will harm him more than ending his pitiful life."

She began to cross to him, but he could not allow her to get close. It was too much to risk. "I have much to do," he said abruptly. "I will sneak away from the palace to do it. I may not be back until morning this time."

She stared at him for a long moment, almost as if she understood exactly what he was doing. "All right."

"We will attend the ball Friday night, and then Saturday will be the council meeting. Diamandis will be deemed unfit. You will be gone by evening, with your earnings."

"And what will happen to Kalyva?"

Lysias shrugged. "Whatever the people wish."

She showed no response. Just kept looking up at him so that he had to look away or remember shadows. The questions.

"I could go with you tonight," she offered. Not timidly. Not as if she were afraid he would say no. In the same way she'd always spoken to him. Because there was no timidness in his Al.

"Unnecessary," he said, likely too harshly for the situation.

"I didn't say it had to be necessary." She stood in front of him now. Put her hand on his chest.

He ignored the fire within. Focused on the cold glint of revenge.

"I'm offering my company, Lysias. Not my services."

"No."

She sighed. "Very well. But you could kiss me good-bye." She tilted her face to his, a dangerous knowing in the brown depths of her eyes.

She was smiling, tempting him. Poking at him. But he would not give in. "I will be back in the morning," he said, and turned for the door.

"I know you're afraid, Lysias," she said quietly but firmly. "But I also know you are brave. You tried to save the princess at your own peril. You survived losing everything as a *boy*. Because you survive. Because you are you. You needn't be afraid of me."

He turned back to face her down, because in this he was certain. "But I am not, *asteri mou*. Fear has nothing to do with it."

She said nothing, at first. He made it out the door, but before it closed behind him, he heard her say one thing.

"Yes, it does."

CHAPTER FOURTEEN

LYSIAS WAS TRUE to his word. He did not reappear until morning. Alexandra could admit it was a disappointment. She did not wish for distance, and she thought she'd been very considerate of his feelings by not telling him she loved him.

Of course, she had told him he was afraid. No doubt that was a deep affront to Lysias.

But he acted unchanged in the morning. Perhaps stiffer, more like the man she'd first met, whose only focus was revenge. And he maintained that as he spent the days leading up to the ball, keeping her busy during the day—and staying far away from her at night.

He showed her around the island—or pretended to, as there was always media in tow, snapping their pictures, shouting questions, usually to Lysias, as if she didn't know how to speak at all.

It shouldn't frustrate her. It shouldn't matter, but every day she felt more an imposter and less an avenging angel.

She went to meet with the woman Lysias had hired to make her a dress for the ball and had measurements taken, alterations done. It was a beautiful gown. Ornate and fit for a princess, with golds and blues threaded through that reminded Alexandra of much of the art in the palace. The dramatic cape attached the gown made it stand out—different and fussier than what most other women would be wearing, she had been told.

After her final alteration meeting, Lysias picked her up, and they went to lunch with a young journalist who seemed in awe of them both. Asking Lysias about his meteoric rise and Alexandra about her memory.

Alexandra smiled and played the part, even as a headache drummed behind her eyes. She was growing tired of performing. Of plastering fake smiles on her face while Lysias sat beside her but was clearly a million miles away.

He never looked her in the eye, and it was a loss that made Alexandra question too much. She'd been so sure she could handle this, but the more he withdrew from her, the more she felt the loss like a grief she had never fully known before.

But she smiled at the journalist, didn't need to feign any loving looks at Lysias for the cameras.

Because she did love him, even when that love hurt.

"We used a computer program to age Princess Zandra's royal portrait to how old she would be now," the journalist said, pushing a piece of paper toward them. "Can you believe the results?"

Alexandra looked down at the picture. It looked so much like her reflection, she could only stare, her heart beginning to thunder in her ears. An uneasy jangle of nerves and the hot liquid behind her eyes she'd yet to let spill.

She was very afraid they would. Here and now for all and sundry to see. "You used my picture though?" She looked up at the journalist, desperate for an answer to this that would set her at ease. "I mean, my picture now? That's why it looks so similar?"

The woman shook her head, her eyes alive with excitement. "No, seriously, the computer did all that with just the old portrait. Isn't it amazing what the program can do? It's right on. We're going to run it with the profile on your engagement to Mr. Balaskas." The journalist smiled at Lysias. "I think you'll be very pleased with the results."

Lysias smiled back. "*Efcharistó*, Ms. Karras. I cannot wait to read it. But I must take Alexandra back to the palace. We have many meetings yet today."

Lysias stood, so Alexandra did too, her fake smile plastered as the journalist went on and on and even followed them out to their car. Chattering. Chattering. So that Alexandra's head pounded as her stomach churned.

Because all Alexandra could think about was that picture. It looked *just* like her. Surely, the girl was lying. They'd used her new pictures. It was a fake. A fraud. Maybe Lysias had even paid her to do that. He seemed to be paying everyone to do *something*.

Panic was sitting on her chest, and she did not for the life of her understand why. When Lysias drove by the beach on the way to the palace, she ordered him to stop.

He looked at her skeptically but slowed. "Is something amiss?"

Everything. Everything.

"I need air," she managed to say, throwing herself from the car. She strode down to the water, the flowing skirts tangling around her legs as the tang of sea met her nostrils. She slipped out of her shoes and left them where they laid as she continued toward the water.

She had the strangest impulse to run right into the sea.

To swim far away, as far as she could go, and just see what happened. A wave splashed against her toes, cool against the heat of the afternoon, and it reminded her there was nowhere to go.

She wanted to fall to her knees and cry, but she did not. She simply stopped her forward movement and found some comfort in the maternal rocking of the waves. She sucked in a deep breath and calmed herself.

Like she'd done so many times before when she'd narrowly escaped danger in her old life. Her old life that seemed so far away. So behind her, even though it was all she'd known a week ago.

She felt Lysias come stand beside her, but she could not look at him. Not while such emotions warred within her. Her complicated identity, the holes in her memory, her connection to the palace. To *him*.

His hand curled over hers, but she knew this was not for *her*. She could tell in the stiff way he held himself. In the fact he did not murmur her name or call her his star as he so often did.

No, this was for the cameras. She stepped away from his grasp.

"Mind the cameras, Alexandra," he warned coolly.

She wanted to throw a grand tantrum *for the cameras*, but she didn't. It wouldn't get her anything she wanted anyway. But when she spoke, she spoke with clear honesty even if she didn't throw him angry looks. "I don't care about the stupid cameras. I need a moment to breathe. To…be myself. To not have to be someone *else*." She felt as if her lungs had been tied in knots. Why couldn't she breathe?

"You lived as a boy for decades, and suddenly you

need to be yourself?" he replied with his usual distant sarcasm.

"Yes. A boy. A nameless, unimportant boy. Not a real-life person." She turned to face him then because she could not argue with the implacable sea. Might as well argue with the implacable man standing next to her. "Not a *princess* who people actually knew. Who's probably dead, and if she is not..."

She might be me.

That picture... It *had* been her. Real or fake, she didn't know, but it rattled her to the bone.

It terrified her to believe it possible, but the signs kept piling up, and she could only deny so much for so long. What if she *was* Zandra? What then?

She was almost too embarrassed to voice that to Lysias. He thought it was impossible, and it should be. It *should* be.

But what if...

She should not ask. She knew, deep in her bones, his response would only hurt her. It wouldn't be what she wanted. And yet there was some tiny sliver of hope that what had come to pass between them might change *something*. "Lysias," she said, taking the hand she'd stepped away from only seconds earlier. She gripped it in some kind of desperation as she looked up at him, tears sliding over her cheeks. "Lysias...what if I am her?"

His expression and voiced hardened. "You're not."

"I didn't ask if I was," she replied, still clutching his hand, though he held himself stiff and closed off. Even as he looked away. Out to sea. "I said *what if?*"

"It would be of no matter," he said, clearly not knowing or caring the words shattered her heart to pieces. He kept his gaze on the waves. "Nothing would change. My plan, my revenge, it remains the same regardless of who you are or ever were."

"Because I am unimportant?" she asked, ragged. A glutton for punishment, apparently.

He looked at her now, and there was *nothing* in his golden gaze. No heat, no hurt, none of the fear or confusion she'd seen flash there. "You're an important tool, but you are only a tool."

She knew this. Or had known it. She had been naive, apparently. She would forgive herself for that at some point, but for now, she had to set it aside. Survive this. Survive him. "Then I could stay. After your revenge is enacted, I could stay, because I belong here. If I am her."

"It would not be safe for you to stay."

"You mean it would not be safe for *you*. Because I might tell the truth. Because someone might find out *you* were behind the vote of no confidence. But if I'm not here, you can blame it on me."

He did not flinch. No guilt lurked in his eyes. He was blank. Perhaps down to his soul. Perhaps he had no soul left. "There will be no need for anyone to blame. And trust me, Diamandis will know it was me. I will make sure of it. This was never about you, Alexandra."

A stab through the heart, but only fair. Of course it wasn't. Nothing ever had been.

She suddenly felt exhausted. So tired she couldn't hold herself up. "I want to go…" She'd almost said *home*. But she had no home. Not a hovel in Athens, not Lysias's house outside the city, not the palace here.

Lysias felt like home, but he would be gone. He did not view her the same at all. And she had to find some peace there. Because she would not back out now. She'd come this far. She wanted her money.

You want him to change his mind.

Maybe she did. Maybe that made her weak. She would work it out…at some point. But not now. They walked back to the car, and Lysias drove them to the palace. They walked to their rooms, guards trailing after them, everyone silent.

They stepped inside their quarters, and Alexandra did not look at him. She strode for the bedroom and, once inside, turned to face him. He was moving as if he would follow her in, but for the first time, she didn't want to be near him.

"I think I would like to be alone," she said, and closed the door on his face.

Lysias stared at the door, beyond shocked. He did not understand for the life of him what had changed in her. What had altered.

Surely she didn't think she was the princess. It was a ridiculous avenue to go down. He'd been telling himself that for days. On a loop. Because it was, quite simply, *unfathomable.*

And, as he'd told her. That impossibility would change nothing. Nothing could change. His plans were set in stone.

He turned away from the door. No matter what she was thinking or feeling. No matter that she'd cried and that he'd wanted to gather her close and promise her whatever she wished.

No *matter.* Because revenge was in the cards. So he left her. For the rest of the day. Yet again, he did not return to their quarters to sleep. The past few nights, he'd prowled about the island, meeting with whom he needed to meet, catching snatches of sleep in corners and alleys much like he had as an adolescent in Athens.

Tonight, however, he snuck down to the servants' quarters. It was late and mostly quiet, so it was easy to slip into his old rooms. Diamandis had wanted him to stay here, and for some reason that he did not wish to examine, Lysias wanted to prove he could. Even if only to himself.

It was not exactly the same as when he'd been a child, and it was clear no one lived in these rooms. Whether they had stayed unoccupied for years, or Diamandis had some poor family moved out to hurt Lysias, it did not matter.

It was empty and Lysias was here. This room did not scare him. The ghosts of his parents... Now that he was actually in the rooms, he did not feel them here. It was a room like any other.

Perhaps, because no matter how unfairly, they had been in his life less than he had been without them. His memories here were only fond ones. Of good people, good parents, a good childhood before the night that changed everything.

He could picture his mother in the rocking chair doing her mending while his father read on the sofa, his glasses always sliding down his nose. He could picture them working in tandem as they always did.

They had been devoted to one another and, in turn, to him. Something about that realization, that memory, turned uncomfortably over in his chest. Made his heart ache.

So he left the family room and went to the small little

room that had been his. No more than a closet, but he'd been happy here. He lay down, right there on the floor, and—thanks to a few days of little rest—fell asleep.

When he woke with a cramp in his neck and his muscles screaming from an uncomfortable night on the floor, he realized that he had not dreamt. Good or bad.

A rarity.

He had no time to consider what that meant because it could mean nothing. Tonight would be the ball.

Tomorrow would be revenge.

Lysias got up. He would need to go back to his quarters and shower and change. And get up there without the guards following him about. But before he could do so, the phone in his pocket buzzed.

"Balaskas," he muttered.

"Mr. Balaskas. I'm sorry to call you directly, but there's a bit of a problem with the DNA test," said the doctor, his voice nervous in Lysias's ear.

"You did not follow my instructions to the letter?" Lysias demanded.

"No, I mean, I followed them exactly, sir," the doctor said, stumbling over his words. "It's just, I cannot do exactly what you want because—"

"I will *destroy* you," Lysias growled, but the doctor was stumbling on, not having the intelligence to shut his traitorous mouth.

"Mr. Balaskas. You don't understand. I created the false test, but then I ran the second test you requested. To discover any genetic matches for the woman. The king *is* a genetic match. Your woman is no imposter. There's an irrefutable sibling percentage match. She *is* the princess. No tampering needed."

Lysias stood with the phone to his ear, but whatever else the doctor said was lost to the buzzing that invaded his mind.

She is the princess.

It could not be. He didn't just pluck a random woman pretending to be a boy out of obscurity only for her to be everything he needed.

Everything indeed.

He managed to thank the doctor, but he hung up on him before he could listen to more of the man's babbling.

He looked around the world of his childhood. Alexandra, his Alexandra, was the princess. Was the little girl he'd saved. She *was* Zandra. All the memories, the resemblances—it was all true.

She would... Would she be happy? Would she revel in the information? He moved forward. She had to know. Immediately. Maybe it would be a difficult discovery for her. It would certainly change...

He stopped halfway to the door. It would change everything.

And it could change nothing.

What had he been thinking? He'd told her just yesterday, even if the impossible were true, it changed nothing.

Now it was so. It was *so*, but it could not alter his plans. The forces were already at work. So she didn't need to know.

He curled his hands into fists.

No one ever need know.

CHAPTER FIFTEEN

ALEXANDRA STUDIED HERSELF in the mirror. She looked every inch the princess as the woman Lysias had hired to prepare her for the ball fluffed her skirts and made last-minute touches to her hair. She tried not to look at the clock again, but it was impossible.

They were meant to make their entrance in less than fifteen minutes. Would Lysias expect her to enter the ball alone? What was he off doing?

Her helper stepped back, examined Alexandra. "Is there anything else you'll be needing, Miss Alexandra?"

"No, thank you." She opened her mouth to ask the woman about Lysias but then decided not to as the woman exited quietly.

Alexandra stood alone in the room dressed up like a princess and felt as alone as she ever had.

Quite the irony for a girl who'd always been alone on the streets. To protect herself and her identity. She had been lonely then, but this was new. Worse. Because it wasn't a generic loneliness. It was loneliness from yearning for a very specific person who'd pulled away from her.

And you let him pull away. You have not told him how you feel. You have only closed doors in his face.

She frowned at the voice in her head, the *truths* if

she was only brave enough to look at them. Because she thought Lysias understood the depths of her feelings, but she had not said the words.

Maybe…maybe she could get through to him if she did not allow herself to be distracted or overwhelmed by the situation at hand. If she walked in with her eyes wide open, planning to tell him. *Determined* to tell him, no matter what it cost her.

Except no amount of preparation or clear thinking could have prepared her for Lysias. For what she felt for him. What had grown between them so quickly. She had been prepared to do a job, collect a paycheck.

Not fall in love with a man so afraid of it, he'd avoid her. When she was quite sure he avoided very little.

She needed to decide what to do about it, but maybe it was best to see through Lysias's revenge, *then* worry about what came after.

Like finding out if you're really the princess.

She laughed to herself in the quiet of her room. It was impossible, and she needed to put it out of her head.

A knock sounded at the door. For a moment, her heart tripped over itself, thinking it was Lysias.

But Lysias wouldn't knock. She rolled her eyes at herself and walked over to the door, the heavy cape and dress trailing behind her. She opened it and stepped back at the unexpected arrival. "Um, hello."

King Diamandis moved into the room carefully around her large skirt. A young woman hovered behind him. She was often hovering somewhere around him with a clipboard and a word about his next meeting. Yet Alexandra had never been introduced to the assistant. Apparently he did not plan to introduce them now.

"I thought we should speak before the ball begins. I do not have much time." He looked at the woman with the slim folder. "Knock when it is time," he said to her.

She nodded, then pulled the door closed, leaving Alexandra alone with Diamandis. Nerves and concern fluttered in her chest. But she kept her face carefully arranged in an expression of condescending distrust.

"Whatever we have to discuss should likely wait for Lysias."

"He is not here?"

"He will be," she said with more certainty than she felt.

"Well, I will need to speak to him as well, but perhaps this is better first between the two of us. About the test."

There was something different about the man. There was still that icy control, a tightly wound posture that spoke of wrought iron determination.

Yet the usual anger did not seem to flame in his eyes, and he stepped forward and gently took her hands in his. Much as she had to him the other day.

"I have heard from the doctor. The DNA match is inarguable. You are indeed Zandra. It's hard for me to fathom how that came to be, but I want to assure you that I am grateful it is. Even if you don't remember me."

She stood, frozen by the words. Words she knew were false. The results were a fake. She wasn't *truly* the princess.

Except you don't know for sure, because Lysias had the results doctored without even finding the truth.

"I suppose it doesn't make much sense to you that I didn't believe. Who else would go around poking throats?" he chuckled, but there was a thickness to his voice that spoke of pure devotion. "My baby sister was the only one I've ever encountered who has done so."

That was why he'd reacted so strangely. The princess had done so to him before. But…

Before she could make sense of it or find words, the door flew open, and Lysias strode in looking furious.

"What are you doing in here?" he demanded of Diamandis.

Diamandis's calm demeanor changed, that flash of temper back in his eyes. But he didn't tense or drop her hands. "Lysias. The test results have come back."

Lysias eyed Diamandis's hands, then Alexandra's face. She wondered what he saw—what was real reaction and what was an act. She thought she could see through him, but he was nothing but a mask today.

"So, you finally believe me, then?" Lysias said.

The king dropped her hands gently, then fully turned to face Lysias, shoulders back, chin up. He was stiff, formal, but not antagonistic. "I owe you an apology."

Lysias raised an eyebrow. "Naturally."

"Not for disbelieving," the king said, though he was clearly irritated with Lysias's flippancy. "I think I had every right to be suspicious," Diamandis said between gritted teeth. "But I was harder than I needed to be. And more… I don't expect it to matter, to change your opinion of what happened." Diamandis looked back at Alexandra, and she wanted to not believe the kindness she saw lurking in his expression, but surely there was *some* good in this man.

He turned his attention back to Lysias. "I was not the one who gave the order to have your parents executed with the traitors. I was…not myself in the days after the attack. I wrongly relied on my advisors to make the decisions of how to deal with the coup. They have since been dealt with, but it remains a mistake I have regretted for quite some time."

"Perhaps you would have ordered the same if you *had* made the decisions," Lysias replied with absolutely no softening. Even as Alexandra felt herself warm to the man who thought himself her brother.

"Perhaps I would have, you are right," Diamandis agreed. "And I realize this is unforgivable. I do not seek your forgiveness. But I have seen the way you care for her and she for you. So I will grant you my permission for your marriage."

Alexandra's heart twisted. With pain at Diamandis being kind. With guilt over it not being true. And worst of all, longing. That this was all real and true. That she would have a chance to marry Lysias. Maybe even have a family in Diamandis.

But she saw the look on Lysias's face and knew this was not to be.

"I don't recall asking you for permission, Diamandis," Lysias said, wondering if he sounded as casual as he attempted to, or if everything swirling inside of him leaked out through the mask. There was a fury inside of him, and he knew he could not unleash it. His revenge would give him everything he wanted.

But seeing them stand so close... The man who'd once been his best friend, who was *apologizing* and trying to excuse away his parents' murder. The woman...

He'd saved her as a girl. Somehow, some way. He had put her in that tunnel and started some unknown domino of events that had led her here.

Here.

Alive and beautiful. A fierce woman. A fighter, an avenger, and yet there was a softness in her. A great capacity for feeling and passion. There was no one like Alexandra, and on top of all that, she was royalty. The long-lost princess.

"Lysias," Alexandra admonished gently, reaching out to rest her hand over his arm. "Let's try to move forward with some civility."

"It's all right... Zandra," Diamandis said, as if testing out the name.

Because it was *her* name. And Diamandis was *her* brother, and Lysias knew what this would mean to the man he'd once called a friend. So much warred within him, he had to drown it in more of that anger.

Anger that Diamandis would call her that, as if he could sweep away twenty years of pain and suffering. Anger that it was all true, and he did not know how to grapple with it, no matter how many hours he'd tried.

"Her name is Alexandra," he snapped, wishing it were true. "That is the name she goes by. Because, by some miracle, she was spared your inaction, your failures. She might be biologically your sister, but she is *not* Princess Zandra back from the dead simply because you want her to be."

The room plunged into silence, except for the sound of his own ragged breathing. Why couldn't he get control of this? It had to be her fault. She'd done something to him. Unleashed something in him.

He needed to find the tools to put it back. And get the hell out of Kalyva.

"Obviously this is...emotional," Alexandra said softly, her hand still on his arm. "Perhaps we could take some

time to individually calm down before we discuss it."
Alexandra said. And he *hated* the way she smiled sadly
at Diamandis. Who would see it as someone happy but
overwhelmed.

But Lysias saw the guilt lurking there. The questions.
He could practically see all those wheels turning in her
head as she gazed at her brother, not that she knew it.
And still...

Still, she wanted to ruin his revenge. He could *see* it.

Diamandis bowed to Alexandra. "I will see you both
at the ball, and after tomorrow's council meeting, we
will have much time to work through this... Everything.
Together."

Alexandra nodded. Lysias did not move. Diamandis
exited the room and they both stood as if rooted to the
spot.

"We should talk," she said eventually, breaking the
spell.

But he could not be alone with her. The truth wanted
to escape. And all these damn *feelings*.

"I do not wish to talk," he replied, striding for the door
so that her hand fell off his arm. "I wish to make our necessary appearance at the ball. Have you announced princess. I wish to enact the plan in which I am paying you
to accomplish. There will be no talking." He opened the
door, pointed outside. "Come."

She crossed to him, but she did not walk out the door.
She smiled at the guard, then wrenched the door out of
Lysias's hands and closed it. "No, Lysias. I'm not going."

CHAPTER SIXTEEN

ALEXANDRA STRUGGLED TO breathe evenly. She felt too much. Hurt too much. She could not go on.

She could not…be part of Diamandis's downfall. Not when he'd seemed truly…humbled. Eager to have some kind of relationship with her. He'd looked at her and called her Zandra, not as if she were a princess.

But as if she were his *sister*.

Her. Who'd never had a family she could remember. Maybe she had memories tied to this place, but…

But you are not the princess.

Maybe, that was the true source of all this pain.

She wanted to be.

She closed her eyes and rested her forehead against the door. She fought against the tears that wanted to fall because she needed to get through to Lysias, and emotional outbursts would not do it.

"You must go to the ball," he said from behind her, his voice like a razor, so sharp, so cutting. "It is what I'm paying you for."

She turned to face him, back against the door, large skirt and cape twisted around her. She curled her fingers into the decadent fabric as if it might grant her some strength.

She couldn't go to the ball now. Now when Diamandis thought…

She'd never expected this to be so hard. What a fool she'd been to think revenge could be simple. Someone always got hurt in the game of payback. She had been okay with that when they had been the distant wealthy figureheads dealing in terrible atrocities.

It was harder to feel righteous when the person was clearly dealing with their own trauma, their own betrayals, their own guilt.

Still, she could not go back in time and undo what had already been done. She could only deal with the events before her.

"Lysias. This no longer feels right."

"It isn't about *right* or how anyone *feels*. It is what's to be done."

She stared at him, wondering if she could get through to him. The pieces of him she'd fallen in love with. Was it love if you couldn't agree with the destruction a person was choosing? Knowing that the destruction wasn't even what he had planned for Diamandis.

It was what enacting his revenge would do to Lysias. He thought his problems, his nightmares, his *pain* would be cured once he hurt Diamandis. He truly believed that.

And she did not know how to combat that belief. She had no great understanding or experience that could prove to him he was wrong. She only had what he was so desperately afraid of. She only had the one thing that would *actually* see him through.

"Lysias, I love you."

There was a beat. A flare in his eyes. But he did not move. He tensed until he seemed to be nothing but a statue. But the statue spoke. So cold. So *lost*. "Love me?" He laughed bitterly. "You know nothing about me. Or love."

"I know you have saved me when you didn't have to. You have protected me. You don't think I've seen the Athenian papers? I know that Vasilis Pangali was finally jailed after ordering that attack on me. And I know you were involved, as I have found so much evidence on that man, and he had never faced any permanent consequence until you saw to it."

"This is irrelevant."

"It isn't. It speaks to who you are and how you care. Underneath the revenge you've sought for so long, you've forgotten why you started on this cursed road to begin with. You are a man who seeks to right wrongs. And that is one of the reasons I love you."

"Alexandra. You will be quiet. You will open that door and we will attend this ball. Tomorrow, I will have my revenge. You will be paid. And then we will part ways. Love has nothing to do with this, and we needn't speak on it any longer."

She wanted to laugh that he thought he could simply order love away or that not speaking on it would change anything. "*I* need to speak on it. I also love you because I understand—along with the luck of the draw—how hard you have worked to become who you are. I know because I did it too. I understand you, Lysias, as few ever will."

"You are full of fairy tales, Al."

And she didn't misunderstand that he'd called her Al for the first time in days on purpose. To create distance. To make her feel like she was only that tool he'd originally sought. But she wasn't Al any longer. *She* had been changed. By what he'd done. By who he was.

"I love you, *Lysias*, because I *know* that beneath the pain you have turned into your armor, there is a man who only wants to belong again. Love again."

"Enough!" he shouted. Loud enough and angrily enough that she did indeed stop.

He stepped forward her, jabbing his finger out as though he meant to poke her in the chest—though he never got close enough to do so.

"You know all these things, but do you know that I had those tests run?" he demanded, a whirlwind of fury and wildness. "The ones you wanted. To try to match you with a family? Did you know that it's true?"

True. The word echoed inside her, a bomb detonating, because he could only mean...

Lysias took her by the shoulders because he needed to touch her. Needed to find his anchor so that he could *fight* her. So he could make her understand that there was nothing about him she could ever love. There was no good in him. Everything in him had died that day twenty years ago, except revenge.

He was made of revenge and revenge only.

"Do you know that it's *all* true?" he said, giving her a small, gentle shake as if it would make the words penetrate. As if he could shake *sense* into her. "You are Princess Zandra, and I have been keeping it from you. And planned to. Forever."

Her eyes were big as she stared up at him. He wanted to see them morph. From all that damn love to confusion, to understanding. To hate.

She should hate him. He wanted her to hate him.

"You...ran the test," she said, but only sounded awed. Only looked up at him as if she'd never doubted him when he was giving her every reason to doubt. To understand. "And you don't see that this was a kindness? Taking care of me. Caring *for* me."

"Are you hearing me? You *are* Zandra. *I knew* and did not tell you."

"When did you find out the results, Lysias?"

He wanted to lie and tell her ages ago, because he knew somehow that she would turn this on him. But he didn't know how to make the lie come out, when he'd never once struggled to lie to get what he wanted. He dropped her shoulders, stepped back. His hands were shaking and this was inexcusable. She was inexcusable.

"When, Lysias?" she demanded.

"This morning," he said. Though it did nothing. Changed nothing. *She* changed nothing. Certainly not twenty years of pain and rage that had driven him. To survive on the streets. To build his empire. To return here triumphant. With the true princess at that.

He refused to acknowledge the little voice in his head that told him she was no different. She too had survived. Had succeeded in her own way. Had somehow found herself back where she belonged.

She could belong to Kalyva. He didn't care. If she wanted to stay, so be it. It mattered not to him. Nothing about her could matter to him.

She could not belong to him.

Alexandra let out a long breath, like a sigh of relief. "Ah, so that's why you stayed away." And she had the gall to *smile*.

"I have been busy."

"Oh, yes, fomenting your peaceful rebellions and what not." She even waved her hand as if this were nothing. As if his whole life's work was *nothing*.

"But really you were avoiding me because you knew you would tell me the truth," she continued. When she didn't know a damned thing. "You have always told me the truth. Except in one thing. Love."

"I do not love, Alexandra. Not anyone." Love was pain. Someone else's power to destroy you. Love was a lie.

"Perhaps this is true. You certainly do not love yourself. Maybe it means you do not have the capacity to love anyone in this moment. But I don't believe that you're incapable or unlovable. I believe all this hate you carry around is just an expression of your love, your grief that was once love."

"That is ludicrous. And it makes no sense." He was desperate for it not to make sense. "If you will not attend the ball with me, then I will attend it without you. You are no longer a necessary pawn, Al. You are simply window dressing now."

There was a flash of hurt in her eyes that landed like a knife to the gut. But he did not go down in pain. He accepted it. Knew it was nothing more than his due.

"How can you hurt him this way?" Alexandra asked, her voice soft. As if she pitied him, and that was the greatest insult in a pile of them.

"He had my parents *killed*."

"You heard him. That wasn't *him*."

"It was him enough. Because I risked my life to save his family, and whether he ordered it or allowed it, he did *nothing* for my parents."

Her shoulders slumped a little, and she did not speak. "No impassioned rejoinders for that one then?"

"No." She looked at him with that pity—not love, *pity.* "I can only beg of you, Lysias. I *beg* of you," she repeated, as if to underscore how important this was. "Do not do this. You don't have to. It doesn't need to be revenge. It could be a life. You could repair your relationship with Diamandis. You could marry me. We could live here on Kalyva, where we belong. We cannot erase twenty years of suffering and survival, but we can *change* that. It can be a happy ending. If you let it."

"There are no happy endings, Alexandra. Because the only endings are bloody coups and death. So I will have my revenge, because anything else would be temporary."

"My love is not temporary," she replied fiercely, with all that warrior's fire. As if it could be true, as if she would *make it so.* As if…

But it was no matter. He did not believe in her love. He would not. "How would you know? You say you know me, but I know *you*, Al. You don't remember your family. You'd never been with a man before me. You have been nothing but alone for all the life you remember. Why would *you* know anything about love?"

If it hurt her, she did not show it. Except perhaps in the way she stood exceptionally still. And had no words to say back to him. But she also did not move—to go to the ball, to get out of his way.

It didn't matter. He could go to the ball without her. He could do *everything* without her.

"If you do not move out of the doorway, I will move you myself."

"You'll regret this course of action, Lysias," she said,

her voice vibrating with emotion as she fisted her hand at her own heart, reminding him of all the times she'd done that to him as they'd slept in the same bed. As she'd slept, as she'd dreamt, as she'd cried. "I know you will regret it."

But he regretted this horrible, destructive pain more than he could regret anything else. Why not pile on? Then at least he'd know how to move forward. Pain he could survive. Suffering he could weather. He did not know how to handle any of what she wanted from him. "So be it."

She moved out of the doorway, but as he strode past her, she uttered one last word in a pained whisper. *"Please."*

He stilled, but he could not give in to the way that word cracked through him like shrapnel. "I have given you much, Alexandra. A new life. A reunion with your precious brother. I have restored your crown to you. But you ask too much of me now."

"Perhaps I do," she agreed, surprising him enough so that he turned to look at her over his shoulder.

She looked so beautiful there in that dress. So strong, like the warrior she was. Like the royal she was.

"No matter what you do, Lysias. I will love you. That does not change. I will *mourn* for what you do, but I will still love you."

"Then you're a fool."

She lifted her chin, his Alexandra. "As you said. So be it."

And with that, he strode from the room. He would go to the ball. He would enact his revenge. He would have everything because it was *within his grasp.*

And he no longer needed her to accomplish any of it.

CHAPTER SEVENTEEN

LYSIAS WENT TO the ball. He strode through the palace on the force of his anger, his rage.

His pain.

But he did not go in the main entrance to the ballroom. The guards were busy with the ball itself, so he ducked into the servants' wing and took the narrow hallways toward the ballroom. Everyone was too busy bustling around, getting things accomplished for the ball, to care that he did not belong here. He took a twisting empty hall that would lead him to a little platform above the ballroom. Sometimes performers sang up here to the crowd below. Or had back when he'd been a boy.

Tonight, it gave him a familiar vantage point of the ball. He'd done this as a boy as well. Always hoping to watch Diamandis do something embarrassing so he could make fun of him afterwards.

And perhaps because he'd enjoyed the glitter, the opulence, the spectacle of it all. His parents had been happy in their comfortable, plain lives, but Lysias had always been drawn to the royal production of it all.

He looked down at the sea of flowers and sparkling lights and expensive gowns. The hum of conversation, the plaintive vibration of string instruments.

For twenty years, Lysias had banished every pleasant thought of this place, and he assumed this ball would only bring back bad memories. He'd been a servant. Foolishly friends with a prince. Naively happy in his servitude.

And he had been naive, to a great many things, but underneath all the real-world implications of his position, at twelve, he had been loved. By his parents. People had always been kind to him. He had felt safe here.

And then a group of people—whether they'd had reasons or not—had violently ripped that safety from him. But not just him.

Diamandis and Alexandra as well.

Lysias found the king on the front stage. Diamandis stood as his father once had many years ago. He looked so much like his father, but there was a coldness to him that King Youkilis had never had. Not *ever*.

Diamandis had not had this inside of him back then either. Oh, the Diamandis who Lysias had known had always had a nasty temper. Though they were friends, they'd often gotten into little tussles—often egged on by the boys...the dead boys.

Diamandis had lost much, as Lysias had. As Alexandra had, whether she remembered or not.

Still, he could not let her ridiculous speech soften him to his cause. So Diamandis had lost? This was of no fault of Lysias or his parents. Why shouldn't Diamandis lose *more* for the way he had handled that loss.

At fourteen.

Damn Alexandra. Damn her to hell. He could not alter his plan. He could not give her what she wanted.

If he did...

She would think there was a chance for them when

there could never be. She would believe in love. She would think herself safe, and then something would happen to rip it away from both of them.

It was the way of the world. Even his billions could not protect him from tragedy, from loss.

But he could protect her from it. He could protect *her*. It would mean giving up everything...

Lysias looked down at the glittering life he'd once envied and was now a part of, if he wanted to be. He could be in the midst of it. He could be swirling Alexandra around the dance floor if he wanted to.

Except she was a princess. And he was the child of servants.

She did not understand this yet, but it would be made plain to her. And all her grand talk of *love* would evaporate. Once she understood the difference in their stations, she would do just as Diamandis had.

Turn her back on him.

He would not allow it.

And still...the thought of enacting his twenty-year revenge left him feeling sick.

It would be better to wash his hands of this place. Forever. Once and for all. Leave Zandra here so that Diamandis had to always live with the fact that Lysias was the one who'd returned her to him. Lysias would return to his life in Athens. Throw himself into his work once more. Erase all mention and existence of Kalyva, Diamandis and Alexandra from his mind.

Yes, *that* was the answer. Get as far away from this as he could. Forever.

He climbed down from the platform, cut back through

the way he'd come, once again fueled by something. Not anger this time.

Fear, Alexandra's voice whispered inside of him.

But she was wrong. *Wrong*. He entered the ballroom and ignored anyone who spoke his name. He did not smile. He made a beeline for the king.

He went right up to Diamandis, didn't bother to acknowledge that the king was speaking with people.

"I need to talk to you. Privately," Lysias said.

Diamandis's eyebrows raised. "Can it *wait*?" the king said through gritted teeth, keeping his smile on the couple he'd been talking to.

"It cannot."

Diamandis sighed, motioned for his assistant. "You'll have to excuse me. Perhaps you can give your information to Miss Floros, and I can be in contact with you soon regarding the matter."

The assistant moved forward with her ever-present clipboard, and Diamandis led Lysias out of the ballroom.

"We need privacy," Lysias said.

"Very well, we may use my office. Is Zandra all right?" he said as they strode through the halls. "She has not arrived yet."

"She is, but you are not."

Diamandis frowned at this but led Lysias into his office, closing the doors behind them. Diamandis stared at him suspiciously but crossed to his desk and leaned a hip on the corner.

"Go on," Diamandis said.

All that ferocious anger and hatred the king had first held toward Lysias was…missing. As if finding out Alexandra was Zandra cured everything.

Could it be that simple? That Zandra was alive, so all the pain and suffering of the past twenty years could be swept away? Forgiven?

But why would life be that simple? That was a childish way of viewing things. That was the way he'd viewed things at twelve. He had survived too long to believe in something as simple as forgiveness. How could he forgive a man who'd been instrumental in his parents' death? How would Diamandis forgive a man who'd stripped him of his crown?

Forgiveness was a childish pipe dream. Nearly as bad as love.

"There will be a vote of no confidence at your council meeting tomorrow," Lysias said, and it was almost as if he floated outside his body. Watching himself ruin everything he'd worked twenty years for. "Everything is in motion, but I can stop it."

"Is that so?" Diamandis replied. He was calm, but Lysias recognized the seething temper underneath.

"It is. And I will stop it. If you meet three demands."

"Demands. So, you've come all this way to blackmail me? Well, that makes more sense than you having heart enough to return Zandra to me."

She is not yours. She is mine.

But that wasn't true, and not only because Alexandra was her own person. "It was meant to be revenge. You can thank your sister for the downgrade to blackmail."

"I hope these asks will be reasonable," Diamandis replied, sounding bored. But his gaze was direct, explorative.

"It won't matter if they are. You will meet them, or you will lose. First, you will have my parents' graves marked.

You will absolve them of all wrongdoing in every law, every history book. *Everywhere.*"

"This is not an ask, Lysias. Zandra being alive is proof enough that they were not part of the plot to murder her. I had already begun to set this into motion the moment the doctor called me."

A band around Lysias's heart loosened, and he did not understand this. That a weight he'd carried since then and assumed would always be there would simply...lift. All because he'd asked, and Diamandis had agreed.

And not even because of the blackmail. He'd already started to right the wrongs. Diamandis had been clearing his parents' names as if the truth mattered, as if he could admit a mistake, as if he could make what few amends there were to make.

Impossible.

"Second," Lysias continued, needing to hurry, to finish. So he could leave Kalyva once and for all. Before he had to *feel* anything. "You will take care of and protect Alexandra at all costs."

"She is my sister."

"I want it written into law."

"It already is. She *is* alive, so she *is* the princess. All laws protect her. Ensure her place."

Why was this so easy? Why wasn't Diamandis arguing with him? Why...

It did not matter. It only mattered he finish. He escape.

"And what is your third condition?" Diamandis asked.

"That when she asks where I've gone, you tell her that you uncovered my potential revenge, and you paid me a significant amount of money to undo it all and disappear from Kalyva forever."

Diamandis's brow furrowed. "Why would you wish her to believe such a thing?"

"It is of no matter. These are my requirements. Either they are done, or you lose your crown tomorrow. And if you go back on any of these promises, I will ensure you lose it in the future. You will never be able to hunt down all who helped me. Revenge is *always* an option."

"But you choose not to use it tomorrow. Because of Zandra," Diamandis said slowly, as if he did not understand what Lysias was doing.

Do you *understand what you're doing?*

What did it matter if he understood, as long as he did it? As long as he escaped.

"Very well," Diamandis said as if he sensed Lysias's urgency at being gone. He reached out a hand. "Consider it done."

Lysias did not shake the king's hand. He turned and left. The palace. Kalyva. And vowed he would never ever return.

Lysias never came back. For a while, Alexandra had considered going to the ball after all. It seemed a shame to waste her fancy dress.

But she was a princess now. Truly the princess. So she would likely have more opportunities to wear it, and she did not feel like smiling at anyone tonight. So she got undressed and allowed herself the luxury of crying herself to sleep.

Because she was safe. Found. Maybe she was heartbroken, but this was... It was not the catastrophe Lysias seemed to think it was. To Alexandra, it was something of a novelty. To care so much for someone they could hurt you… She could only see it as a blessing after twenty years with no one.

So she wept and grieved, and then she slept. In the early hours of morning, she dressed and prepared to find Diamandis so she could warn him of Lysias's revenge. She was still conflicted about the decision since she knew Lysias would see it as yet another betrayal, but she was saving him from himself. And if he gave her the opportunity to explain herself—

No. She wouldn't wait for him to *give* her the opportunity, she would *take* it. Maybe Alexandra, Zandra, whoever she was from this point on, was someone new. But she was also still Al. Still strong and fierce and determined.

Maybe Lysias would be a brick wall *forever.* Then she would spend forever taking it apart brick by brick.

Alexandra opened the door to the hall and was shocked to discover there was no guard. Alexandra could not decide if this was a good development or a terrible one. She crept down the hall, feeling a bit like a burglar.

But when she stepped out of it into the large foyer that offered her different hallways and staircases to different parts of the palace, she saw Diamandis. Sitting on a bench as he looked through his phone, his assistant standing next to him.

When she stepped forward, he looked up, then stood. "Good morning, Zandra," he said, greeting her.

She looked from him to his assistant, looking for some kind of hint at what this was. "Have you been…waiting for me?"

"I wished to speak with you before my council meeting but did not wish to disturb you."

She took a deep breath to steady herself. "Yes, about the meeting, Diamandis."

He cocked his head, furrowed his brow. "You knew of his plans?" he asked.

"I… *You* know of his plans?"

"Yes, Lysias came to me in a fury last night. Went on about revenge and votes of no confidence, then demanded a large payout to avoid such eventualities. All in the middle of the ball, I might add."

"A payout. I…" Alexandra tried to make sense of this, but she could not. Lysias didn't need money. No doubt Diamandis was not hurt by offering money. "I do not understand."

"I don't either." Diamandis shrugged. As if it didn't matter. As if it was nothing.

It couldn't be nothing. Had she gotten through to him? And if she had, if he'd listened to her about revenge, why would he take money? Why would he not *be* here?

"Zandra," Diamandis said gently, moving forward and after a brief hesitation setting his hands on her shoulders. "I do not believe he intends to return to Kalyva. I think he simply wanted his petty revenge and then to be gone."

"He isn't petty, Diamandis. He is hurting."

Diamandis looked at her with abject pity, but she was still reeling too much to fully absorb any offense.

"I know he has made a big deal in the press about your engagement, but I can do everything in my power to ensure that he is the one held responsible for the breaking of it. You have the full force of the royal—"

"We are still engaged, Diamandis," she said, even knowing it hadn't ever been real in the first place. Even knowing Lysias had no plans to marry her. And still, she could not accept the idea that it was simply...over.

If that made her an object of pity, so be it.

"Zandra—"

"That is *not* my name," she snapped. Then squeezed her eyes shut in regret. "I'm sorry." She reached up and patted his hand on her shoulder. "I do wish... I am so happy to know I am the princess, that I am your sister." She looked up at him. "I want to be Zandra, but... I cannot just ignore the past twenty years. They are a part of me."

And maybe that was what Lysias needed to face. That he could not demarcate time. That his revenge—enacted or not—was never going to erase his twenty years of exile. He could not win and forget.

He had to accept. And heal.

"I will try to be more cognizant of that," Diamandis said, a little stiffly but clearly still trying to be kind. Warm.

She smiled at him. She knew he'd been a strange kind of victim here. The weight of remembering could not be easy. "Do you think we'll ever know how I escaped?"

"I have spent twenty years trying to find an answer that wasn't your death, but I've found nothing. We will keep looking though."

"No. No, I think maybe it is best not to know. Best to just be grateful for what we have. What we *can* have." In a future, without Lysias. "Though to be honest, I haven't the first clue what the next step in my life is."

"You needn't worry about it. You're home."

But that didn't feel right. Of course, without Lysias, very little *felt* right. She still could not understand why he would have taken *money* and not his revenge. Why he'd listened to her, but then not returned to her.

"He made Diamandis promise not to tell you the truth," the assistant blurted from where she hovered just out of sight.

The king whirled on the woman even as Alexandra tried to make sense of her words.

"What are you saying?" Diamandis hissed.

"He made *you* promise not to tell," the assistant said, lifting her chin at the king. "Not me."

"He didn't know you were listening and neither did I."

She shrugged, her gaze settling on Alexandra. "I was right outside the door. He left so quickly and angrily he nearly crushed me with it, so he didn't see me. Zandra, Your Highness, Alexandra, he was *not* paid. He did not want a payment. He wanted—"

"Miss Floros," Diamandis snapped, taking her by the arm and beginning to pull her toward the exit. "You will cease—"

"First, clearing his parents' name," she continued, even as Diamandis pulled her away. She simply turned her head to keep facing Alexandra and spoke louder. "Protecting you—"

"Katerina!" The king almost had her to a door that led somewhere Alexandra had never been.

Still, the brave woman shouted over Diamandis's attempts to silence her. "And not telling you."

He slammed the door on her. Then stood, back to Alexandra, as the words landed. Nonsensical words, of course.

"Diamandis, I don't understand. Is it true?"

Diamandis sighed heavily as he turned to face her. "I had to meet all three demands to keep him from enacting his little revenge, Zandra. If you know, then I have not kept up my end of the bargain."

She shook her head. There would be no revenge. Not now. Not ever. "I shall keep it for you." Because Lysias had changed course, yes, but more than that, he'd ensured her protection and wanted that kept from her?

Perhaps it was warped, but she knew him. She understood him. It meant he loved her. If he didn't, he wouldn't be afraid. If he didn't, he wouldn't have changed his twenty-year revenge plot. Only love could have done that.

Only love. The thing he was so afraid of. Afraid enough that the powerful, determined, proud Lysias had run away. Like the hurting boy he was on the inside.

She supposed she could sit around and wait for him to realize it. He would eventually. He was too...enduring not to.

But she didn't want to wait around. She too had endured, and she wanted more. And to not waste a moment of that more.

"I must go to Athens, Diamandis. But I will be back. Mark my words, we'll both be back."

"You will be welcome. Him?"

"He will also be welcome," she replied firmly. "Because I love him, and I am the princess." Still such an odd thing to say, to be real. But she wanted to hold on to it for dear life. It and Lysias. "For all his faults, he is a good man at heart. I think you must be able to understand where his struggles come from. How hard it is to believe in good when it was so cruelly stripped from you so young."

Diamandis grunted. "You need only ask Michelis. His office is in the front hall. He has been instructed to take you wherever you want," he grumbled.

Alexandra turned to move, but Diamandis stood in her way. "I know we do not truly know each other, but I am your brother. And the king of Kalyva. No matter what happens, know you always have a place here. And I will always be a safe place to land." He looked so kind in the moment, so vulnerable, Alexandra followed her impulse.

She wrapped her arms around him and held on to him tightly, blinking back the tears. "Thank you. I may never remember those first four years…" She pulled back and looked up at him. "But we have whatever years ahead of us to make up for the ones we lost."

Because she believed in possibilities. In joys and futures and in love.

Now she had to track down her fearsome fiancé and convince him that he could too.

CHAPTER EIGHTEEN

LYSIAS STARED DOWN at Athens from his office window. He was in a foul temper and had instructed his staff that no one bother him. They had listened.

He couldn't seem to concentrate on work. His mind was still back in Kalyva. In the palace. With Alexandra. *Princess* Zandra.

Surrounded by all he'd amassed—his position, his money—it was hard to hold on to the idea he was somehow not worthy of someone with her title. It was hard not to acknowledge that the way he felt inferior was born of a system he'd understood only from the eyes of a boy.

Now he was a man. And what he was not worthy of was *her*. Her determination. Her love. Her courage.

He scowled. How had she come to mean so much? How had she crawled into his life and turned it inside out? It had only been a day since the ball, and still he *grieved* that she was not here. That he could not walk down the hall and see her. Not catch a glimpse of her or sleep next to her in his bed.

His life had always felt busy before. Work had filled his days, and revenge had filled everything else. He'd thought that was something.

But Alexandra had shown him it was nothing. She

had even ruined his revenge for him. He had not taken Diamandis down a peg, but clearing his parents' name had eased some of the dark guilt that had twisted him up. Some of the injured rage that had kept him going for so long.

He still missed them. Still loved them. Still grieved everything that happened to them and him in the tragedy. But the blinding anger had ceded. All from one simple action by a man he'd been hating as a symbol for twenty years.

Alexandra had been right. His revenge would not have given him that satisfaction. It would only have driven the hate deeper.

So, he had absolutely nothing now. Except his wealth. And his desperate need for a woman he'd left behind.

But he was Lysias Balaskas. He did not *do without* when he could accomplish and obtain everything he wanted. Unfortunately, she was no simple want.

How could he go back to her, knowing what he stood to lose? How could he risk every wall that he'd built, that had allowed him to become Lysias Balaskas, billionaire, success? She threatened everything.

Everything...that she had turned into nothing. How could he live without her?

There was some commotion behind his door, then it swung open, and he heard someone arguing.

"Never mind," a female voice said quite firmly. "I'm sure he will see his fiancée regardless."

That voice. And then she glided into his office as if she belonged there, followed by his stuttering assistant.

"I'm sorry, sir," Marcus said, stumbling.

"Never mind," Lysias muttered, never taking his eyes from Alexandra. "You may leave us."

She was here. He nearly went to her. Without thought. Without hesitation. He wanted her in his arms. He wanted his mouth on hers. He wanted to hear her voice. He'd thought the payoff, the disappearance would insult her enough that she would realize she did not love him, need him.

But here she was.

"Well, what do you have to say for yourself?" she demanded. She was wearing all black, like some kind of avenging ninja. Her eyes were fierce, her voice fiercer.

And he had no words.

"Diamandis's assistant heard your little…whatever you thought you were doing," she continued, prowling over to the wall of windows and peering down at Athens below. Then she turned to him, cut him in half with that dark brown gaze. "You didn't enact your revenge. You asked for very little in return."

"I asked for everything I required, and even that he could not give me if you know about it," he said, but his voice was rough, and his hands itched to grab her. Hold on to her. Bury himself in the scent of her.

"What about what *I* could give you, Lysias?"

"Your love?" he said, trying to sound disgusted, uninterested. Even as it thundered within him. The only answer to all this nothing was her *love*.

"Yes. My love. My forever. Belonging. A home. A family." Her mouth began to curve, which made no earthly sense. "I know you love me."

He wondered when he'd fully accepted the simple truth of that. It had been gradual, not sudden. In retrospect,

the more he'd felt out of control in Kalyva, the more focused on revenge, the more he'd been trying to avoid the
simple fact.

The unavoidable fact. A truth of life even he could
not bend.

Yes, he loved her.

She closed the distance between them, put her small
hand over his heart, where the ring he'd given her glittered in the light. "You think love is pain, and you are
not wrong, but this is why you surround yourself with
it. So when loss inevitably strikes, you lean into the love
you still have. The love that can grow. I know you did
not mean to, but you have opened a new world for me.
You have given me my family back. More love than I
dreamed—and I want more of it, Lysias. Not less."

More not less.

"You can run away from me like a boy, but you are
not one anymore. You are a grown man, so this is only
cowardice. And I will not be afraid. I will chase you
down. I will follow you to the ends of the earth to prove
my love to you."

"That sounds like stalking, Alexandra."

But her smile only widened. "Then convince me,
Lysias, somehow, someway. That you do not love me. I
will leave you alone forever if you do."

He lifted his hand to cover hers and he watched her
stiffen. As if she were bracing herself for him removing
it. As if she weren't as sure as she acted.

It struck him then, that this truly was an act of courage. She had doubts, but she loved him enough, believed
in him enough, to set them aside. To put her heart on

the line. To chase him down and insist he face the worst parts of himself.

She had asked him to spare Diamandis, and he had. Now she only asked for his heart, and was that really such a terrible thing to give?

So he curled his hand around hers. "Anything could take you from me. I thought it would best to be the one who did it. So I could control it. I can control everything, except the whims of fate."

"Lysias—"

"Allow me to finish, Alexandra. Zandra. So much was taken from me, I decided to take from everyone else. But I wish not to take from you. Only give. For twenty years, I locked old, violent memories away. But also the good ones. Being back at the palace reminded me. Of warmth. Of love. The deep and true kind my parents had for one another and me. And the kind I have for you."

Her expression remained calm, but she sucked in a sharp breath.

"I love you, Al, Alexandra, Zandra, Princess. Whatever name you choose. If you take my last name, I will call you whatever you wish."

She swallowed before she spoke, tears glistening in his eyes. "We haven't even discussed that you saved my life not once but twice."

"Ah, *asteri mou*, but you have saved my heart." He pressed a kiss to her forehead. "So I must thank you."

"You should probably also ask me nicely to be your wife. And smile prettily while you do it."

"No, I will not ask nicely." At her scowl, he bent down onto his knees. "I will beg you, my love."

Her smile bloomed.

"Be my wife. Through all the wonderful things I will ensure life gives us, and through all that life will no doubt take from us. I promise, I will not run away from you ever again. You are my star, my heart, my princess."

The tears that shone in her eyes fell to her cheeks, and she knelt too—so they were knee to knee, hands clutching each other. "I will be all those things, Lysias. And more we cannot imagine yet. But what the future holds does not matter. As long as we are together."

"Forever, *asteri mou*. Forever." And he sealed this promise with a kiss.

EPILOGUE

Three months later

"WE CANNOT SIMPLY move up a royal wedding, Lysias," Diamandis said from behind his desk.

Alexandra sat with Lysias on the settee across from the desk. Lysias held her hand in his. He looked over at her, gave her his mischievous smile. Before straightening and saying to Diamandis very seriously, "The original date poses a problem."

"Do you know everything that would have to be changed? Altered?" Diamandis asked. They'd had a few rows over the past few months. Neither Alexandra nor Lysias were very good at following royal decrees blindly.

But they always found a compromise. They always made up. They were a family. A growing family.

"I realize this is unfortunate and annoying," Alexandra said, matching his officious tone. "But as I might be in labor, it seems irresponsible to go on as planned." She smoothed her hand over her still mostly flat belly. It amazed her that a child grew inside there. They'd kept it to themselves at first, wanting to bask in the glow of it all. But as royal wedding plans ramped up, it seemed imperative to bring Diamandis in on the news.

"You might be…" Diamandis stopped, blanched. "Zandra."

"The doctor confirmed a due date of the same day as the current wedding. Now, of course, we can roll the dice. I have heard babies don't really care about your plans, but she could—"

"She…?" Diamandis said, almost on a whisper. As if he'd never heard of such a thing before.

"Yes, you will have a niece in about six months' time. Which is why I'd like to move the wedding. Now, Lysias and I are already married—"

"Do not remind me of your unsanctioned, irresponsible *Greek* wedding. It does not signify here in Kalyva," Diamandis grumbled.

"Be that as it may, you may choose how you wish to reschedule. Before or after the baby. But it will need to be rescheduled."

Diamandis closed his eyes, breathed in and out slowly. "You couldn't have done this when I had an assistant worth a damn?"

"I do miss Katerina. You never did tell me what you did to run her off."

Diamandis scowled darkly. "We will move the date up if it can be managed. I will let you know. Now, I have much work to do. Thanks to you two." He waved a hand at them, his attempt at dismissal.

But Alexandra was not so easily dislodged. "We've chosen a name."

"The royal tradition is—"

"Yes, Diamandis. I know. Lysias told me. But it doesn't feel right for me to use our mother's name when I don't remember her, and you may have a daughter someday to use the name on."

"I do not plan to marry. Or have children. This is happy news indeed, as your child will now be considered the heir, and I will be under no pressure to provide one." He said it darkly, and Alexandra felt sympathy for him.

She also looked up at the portrait that hung in his office. Of their parents. She did not remember them, not really, and still she said a little prayer to them.

Give him love, as I have been given.

"We will be happy to use it as a middle name," Lysias said, playing peacemaker, as he sometimes did. Which was rare, but it always amused Alexandra. "But we have decided. We will name our daughter after *my* mother."

Diamandis sighed, clearly incapable of arguing with *that*. "Very well." He pressed a finger to his temple. "You two might be more trouble than you're worth. I hope you know this."

Lysias looked over at her and grinned. "Ah, Diamandis, have you not learned? Love is always worth all the trouble."

Princess Zandra Balaskas grinned right back. "Always," she agreed.

* * * * *

COMING SOON!

We really hope you enjoyed reading this book. If you're looking for more romance be sure to head to the shops when new books are available on

Thursday 25th May

To see which titles are coming soon, please visit

millsandboon.co.uk/nextmonth

MILLS & BOON®

Coming next month

WHAT HER SICILIAN HUSBAND DESIRES
Caitlin Crews

"Truly," he said, in that low voice of his that wound around and around inside her, "you are a thing of beauty, Chloe."

"So are you, Lao," she said softly, then found herself smiling when he looked surprised she should compliment him in return.

It made her wonder if he was so overwhelming, so wildly intense, and so astronomically remote in every way that mattered, that no one bothered to offer him compliments. But any such thoughts splintered, because he carried her hand to his lips and pressed a courtly sort of kiss to her knuckles.

It should have felt silly and old-fashioned, but it didn't. Not in an ancient castle, perched here above an island so steeped in history.

And not when the faint brush of his lips across the back of her hand made everything inside her seem to curl up tight, then begin to boil.

"Welcome, little one," he murmured, the heat in his gaze making everything inside her take notice, especially the tender flesh between her legs. And that heart of hers that would not stop its wild thundering. "To our wedding night. At last."

Continue reading
WHAT HER SICILIAN HUSBAND DESIRES
Caitlin Crews

Available next month
www.millsandboon.co.uk

LET'S TALK

Romance

For exclusive extracts, competitions
and special offers, find us online:

 facebook.com/millsandboon

 @MillsandBoon

@MillsandBoonUK

@MillsandBoonUK

Get in touch on 01413 063 232

For all the latest titles coming soon, visit
millsandboon.co.uk/nextmonth

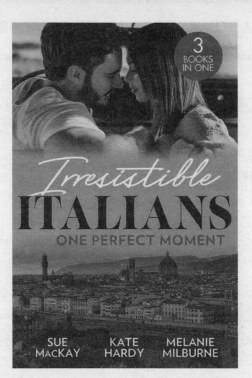

MILLS & BOON

THE HEART OF ROMANCE

A ROMANCE FOR EVERY READER

MODERN — Prepare to be swept off your feet by sophisticated, sexy and seductive heroes, in some of the world's most glamourous and romantic locations, where power and passion collide.

HISTORICAL — Escape with historical heroes from time gone by. Whether your passion is for wicked Regency Rakes, muscled Vikings or rugged Highlanders, awaken the romance of the past.

MEDICAL — Set your pulse racing with dedicated, delectable doctors in the high-pressure world of medicine, where emotions run high and passion, comfort and love are the best medicine.

True Love — Celebrate true love with tender stories of heartfelt romance, from the rush of falling in love to the joy a new baby can bring, and a focus on the emotional heart of a relationship.

Desire — Indulge in secrets and scandal, intense drama and sizzling hot action with heroes who have it all: wealth, status, good looks…everything but the right woman.

HEROES — The excitement of a gripping thriller, with intense romance at its heart. Resourceful, true-to-life women and strong, fearless men face danger and desire - a killer combination!

To see which titles are coming soon, please visit

millsandboon.co.uk/nextmonth